NEW WRI
UNIVERSITY

paper scissors stone

CCPA PUBLICATIONS

Acknowledgements

Paper Scissors Stone was made possible by the support, advice and enthusiasm of: Jon Cook, Val Striker, Andrew Motion, Paul Magrs, Denise Riley, and Aileen Davies. Special thanks to Andy and Vanessa Vargo, Phoebe Phillips, Vicki Winteringham, Mike Oakes, Anastacia Tohill, Tanya McQueen, and Lucy Brownlow at the Norwich School of Art and Design. We would also like to acknowledge Random House Ltd's continued support for new writing, without which this volume would not have been possible.

A CCPA Paperback

Paper Scissors Stone

First published in Great Britain 2002.

ISBN 0-9536072-3-2

Typeset in Plantin Light

Printed and bound in Great Britain by Biddles Ltd, Guildford, Surrey paper scissors stone

is dedicated to

W. G. (Max) Sebald.

The loss feels unbearable. Premature death has brutally imposed a retroactive shape on Max Sebald's life and work, turning early or middle things into last things. Perhaps in the future it may come to seem inevitable that the elegiac intensities inscribed by Sebald in literature did not result in a large body of work. That, instead, we have the imperishable gift of a few books written once he found the voice in which to deliver his commanding, exquisite prose arias. But, for the moment the loss simply feels . . . devastating. Unacceptable. Difficult to take in. He had an exemplary sense of vocation, full of scruples and self–doubts. The work is restlessly literary and inspired by a thrilling variety of models. These writers—from Adelbert Stifter and Jean Henri Fabre to Virginia Woolf and Thomas Bernhard—illustrate Sebald's connection to several kinds of moral seriousness, luminousness of description, and purity of motive. He was one who demonstrates that literature can be, literally, indispensable. He was one by whom literature continues to live.

Susan Sontag

After Nature and so on
In Memory of W.G. Sebald

Dear Max,
it would be so like you still to be here

twinkling behind your sad specs,
smoothing your sleek walrus down

to bring *a diminution of disorder*
after a whole morning of listening

to questions no–one on earth can answer.
But then you were always a past—

master at taking the weight,
and later, knowing the best response

must be *to arm ourselves with patience*,
sliding away to worry it through and over.

I see you now just as you are for ever—
out of the wreckage and off once more,

footing the stop–start quick white line
which holds two halves of the road apart

and joins them together, until such time
as you turn again and abide my questions.

Andrew Motion

Introduction

In the twelve months since I last wrote an introduction for the annual UEA Creative Writing anthology, the course has suffered three grievous blows: Malcolm Bradbury, who, with Angus Wilson, founded the MA in 1975, Lorna Sage, who helped to establish its 'Life Writing' component, and W.G. (Max) Sebald, who co-taught the prose stream for the past three years, have all died. The loss of one of them would have been dire; the fact that all their deaths fell so close together has been a tragedy. They are very painfully missed, and always will be for the inspirational brilliances of their own writing, and for their exemplary kindness to others.

Inevitably, the mood of the past year on the Creative Writing course has been darkened—and some of that sombreness shows in the work gathered here. But what also shows is a courageous refusal to be put down or deflected. As in previous years, this anthology, which students themselves compile, edit and design, serves as a treasure–house and shop window. Treasure–house in as much as it gathers together shining examples of the work produced by writers presently on the course; shop window in that it allows the wide world to examine their qualities.

And also, as before this quality is exceptionally high, as well as impressively diverse—not just in terms of genre (there are stories, excerpts from novels, poems and scripts included here), but in terms of idiom and reference. The UEA Creative Writing course has long had a name for nurturing exceptional talent. This year's anthology will only add to that reputation.

Andrew Motion *Spring 2002*

CONTENTS

MARY ALLEN *SHAPE OF MEMORY* 1

MATTHEW BELLWOOD *STORIES FROM THE SICKBED* 11

ELEANOR BIRNE *EFFIE AND NAN* 25

ROBIN BOOTH *DIMINISHING RETURNS* 33

SARAH BOWER *ODO'S WOMEN* 47

ALIX BUNYAN *AS FOR ME* 53

FRANCA DAVENPORT *TIME'S EYES* 61

JAKE ELLIOT *TRAVEL SICKNESS* 73

OLIVER EMANUEL *THE LOST* 81

GUY ESSEX *SPOONS* 91

PATRICK EVANS *EQUALIZER* 101

SUSAN FLETCHER *EVE GREEN* 109

YONA F. FRIEDMAN *WINGED* 117

MATT FULLERTY *FOR KICKS* 127

JO GALLAGHER *THE BOOKHOLDER* 137

RYAN GATTIS *IN HELIOS* 145

STUART GLASS *MINCEMAN* 151

GEMMA GREEN *SIX POEMS* 157

KATE GRUNSTEIN *LEAD AND SUNLIGHT* 163

LUCY HANNAH *HOOVERING UP THE SAND* 171

NICHOLAS HARROP *THE BOMB* 179

Sara Heitlinger *Goodbye!* 187

Andrew Knight *Something Shorter* 195

David Lambert *Providence* 207

Zoe Lambert *Carol's Cross* 217

Andrew Loudon *Road Rage* 227

James Manlow *Six Poems* 241

Robert McGill *The Treaty of Ursa Major* 247

Sarah Emily Miano *Don't Take the One I Want* 255

JoAnna Minshew *Boundless Boobs* 267

Dave Paul *King* 275

A. Pearmain *Picture Me (in Ten Years' Time Watching)* 283

Siobhan Peiffer *Five Poems* 293

Eleanor Rees *Eight Poems* 299

Chris Regan *Jenny Ringo* 309

Sarah Ridgard *Suffolk Lace* 321

Kathryn Simmonds *Six Poems* 329

Natasha Soobramanien *The Gift* 335

Kim Upton *Shopping for England* 343

Luke Williams *Questions, 1* 355

Anna Ziegler *Six Poems* 363

Mary Allen

Mary Allen was born in London. She has spent most of her career in arts administration, and now lives in London and Suffolk.

Shape of Memory

(extract from a novel)

Sara is returning from a business trip, during which she met an ex-lover. She and her husband, Christopher, share their house with his half-sister, Claire, who lives in the basement flat with her daughter, Ellie. Immediately prior to Sara's departure, she and Christopher had had their first session with a marriage guidance counsellor.

It's too cold for the middle of September. Goose pimples brush the insides of my sleeves, as the taxi thrums along the road from the airport. Leaves shudder on the trees, a dull and bitter green, and branches scrape their bark in front of grey buildings. Advertising hoardings clamour in English. As we near the city centre and the road narrows to four lanes, houses give way to department stores and museums, and groups of tourists in jeans, trainers, and transparent plastic macs, gather on the pavements in front of them. I cross my legs, winding the toe of one foot round the ankle of the other.

'Been somewhere nice, love?' The taxi driver has studs all the way up his ears; his hair is mousy stubble at the back of his neck, and a microphone distorts his voice.

'Lovely, thanks, much hotter than this though.'

Each year I'm surprised by the weather, I don't seem able to keep a calendar in my head of what to expect, but it's only a couple of weeks after summer, I shouldn't need a coat. If I had one, and my body was warmer, maybe my wrists and ankles wouldn't feel so cold, skin rippling as though ice were forming beneath.

'Would you mind turning on the heater?'

'You *are* cold. Where've you been?'

'I'm sure it's not normally like this in September.'

'Bit chilly, nothing special.'

Perhaps it's not the wind and rain making me feel I'm freezing from the inside: Diana once told me icy skin was a symptom of shock, but I haven't had a shock, at least not a sudden one. Heat blows from a grille near the floor, making me sweat without warming me. I hunch in the corner, as London's landmarks skid past the window. The Thames is swollen, thick with mud, whirlpools breaking the surface as though the river is choking on itself. I wish Diana had come back with me.

The taxi drives away quickly. Four storeys of blackened brick stand to attention, taller than I remember, Claire's basement burrowing beside the front garden. I walk up the steps and feel around in the bottom of my bag for keys. When I push the door open it thumps against the inside wall: for the first time I notice the dent in the plaster and the white ring hammered into the crimson wallpaper. I close it behind me and there is silence. The smell of furniture polish fights with pine disinfectant; a woman's scent smothers the decaying stems of flowers. The carpet is thick under my feet, the Persian runner rucked at the corner; the tapestry on the wall is crooked. Crusted smears run across the grain of the wallpaper beside the kitchen door.

'Sara. You're back.'

Christopher is standing at the other end of the corridor, immediately outside the door to the basement. He looks like a plant grown in too little light, dark hair straggling round his face.

'Hi. Good to see you.'

'You're early.'

'It's really nice to be home. I've missed you.'

'I thought your flight got in late tonight.' It's too dim in the passage to see the expression on his face.

I walk towards him, leaving my bag at the foot of the stairs. 'I left a message with Claire, saying I'd managed to get on the one before. Didn't she tell you I'd rung? Diana's had to go on to Paris.' I reach forward to put my arms around him.

'What's that smell? Is it you?' Even if I'm anxious about seeing him again, I'd expected a warmer welcome than this. 'Have you been smoking?'

I want one now: the taxi had notices thanking me for not smoking, and I didn't think to have one in the street outside the house. 'Just a few, in the last couple of days.'

'Why? You don't smoke.'

'I used to. Before we met.' I lean towards his face but he turns his head to one side and my lips brush his earlobe, soft and downy, skin smelling fresh and baby-like.

'Why have you started again?'

We walk into the kitchen, and the windows are mirrored in curves of copper pans, glass bowls, enamelled plates, and polished casseroles; queuing in rows on shelves, hanging from hooks in the ceiling, stacked in the corners of work surfaces. Basil droops on the windowsill and a rose in an empty tumbler withers in the middle of the kitchen table. I open a cupboard to find something I can use as an ashtray. 'Don't know really. All that sun and sand, I suppose, I used to love smoking on beaches.'

'You're not going to have one in here, are you?'

'Why not?'

'You know I can't bear the smell, not since mother died. Can't you smoke outside?'

'It's cold outside.' I take the last cigarette from the packet, which I leave on the kitchen table, foreign words flaunting themselves against brightly coloured paper. 'Do you really want me to stand in the garden to have a cigarette?'

'It's not good for Ellie.'

'Ellie doesn't live here.' I open the kitchen door and stand in the doorway, lighting the cigarette and inhaling deeply. The smoke burns into my lungs.

'Coffee?'

'Thanks. Cappuccino.' No reminder of him in the frothy milk and powdered chocolate. The machine hawks and spits into a painted mug, which Christopher leaves on the kitchen table before taking some homemade pâté from the fridge.

'Do you want any supper?'

'I'm not hungry.'

Ciabatta and unsalted butter join the pâté on the corner of the table furthest from the door. I look out into the garden: hydrangeas are darkening into heads of viridian and burnt sienna; drops of water cling to the tips of drooping leaves, and mist dampens the paving stones.

'How did it go?'

'What, the conference?'

'No, Diana's told me about that. Afterwards, did you enjoy yourself?'

'Diana won a good contract.' A plane flies overhead and fades in the distance; birds are silent. A hammer hits wood. Secateurs click against dead branches next door. The sounds are muffled and without echoes.

'And you?'

'As I said on the phone, I talked to some people, tested a few restaurants, you know the kind of thing.'

'You and Diana split up, didn't you?'

'She was talking to a consortium, I'd have been in the way.'

Christopher has been eating the pâté, his face turned away from where a slight breeze is carrying my smoke back indoors. I stand on the cigarette, pick up the stub and put it in the waste bin, and drink my coffee.

'Why didn't you tell me you'd been there before?'

I feel naked without the smoke. 'It was a long time ago.'

'Diana told me you were looking up friends. Who were they?'

'When did you speak to Diana?'

'She rang from Paris this evening, just before you got in, told me you'd seemed upset when she met you again. She's worried about you.'

I walk over to the sink, and begin stacking dirty crockery. Diana doesn't speak the language; there'd be no reason for anyone to tell her. 'I'd eaten something that disagreed with me. I'm fine now.'

'So, was it good seeing your friends again?' Christopher saws at the ciabatta. There's a smell of garlic, grease and old meat.

'I didn't know whether they'd still be there.'

'Tell me about them.'

I turn on the hot tap and squirt green liquid soap under the jet. 'Well, there's this lovely woman who I met when I was there before—'

'Which was?'

'Before I knew you, a long time ago, a year or so before we met.' The rubber gloves are new and too small for my hands. 'Anyway, she was a great friend. She introduced me to all her family, taught me how to cook some of the local dishes.' Soap bubbles burst, sounding like tiny rounds of applause. 'It was really good to see her again, it had been much too long.'

'What's she called?'

The water is scalding and I hold a plate by one edge. 'Marina.' I hate naming.

'Marina what?'

'I can't remember.' Egg yolk has hardened on the white china and I scratch it away with my fingernail. 'I think she told me once but I've forgotten now.'

'Does she ever come to London? She could stay with us.'

Marina away from her family, in London. From nowhere comes the image of refugees on the underground, hunched around their babies, signs in front of them whispering their homeless state while they stare at the ground. I turn round and lean against the edge of the sink. 'She's got children to look after, she wouldn't be able to get away.'

Christopher takes off his glasses and rubs his eyes; he looks tired, with lines of anxiety around his mouth. I take half a step towards him but he stands up and switches on the kettle, taking a peppermint teabag from a packet in the cupboard. I turn back to the washing up. Coffee stains the soapsuds. Someone's been eating something red and sticky.

'What's that?'

'Ellie's, from last night.'

Filling the dish with water brings fragments of red floating to the surface; I leave it on the windowsill, before pulling the plug. I can't be bothered with the drying up.

'You haven't asked how things have been here.'

'You told me about Ellie being ill, is she better now?'

'Why are you suddenly so interested? It didn't seem to matter when we talked on the phone.'

'Of course I'm interested in Ellie. Is she okay?'

'She was in hospital for three days.'

'Is she okay now?'

'They came back the day before yesterday.'

'And what about Claire?' I dry my hands on a clean tea towel. At least my fingers haven't started going yellow yet.

'She stayed with Ellie in hospital, she's very tired.'

I open a fresh packet of cigarettes. These are the last I have that will remind me of him.

'You're not having another cigarette already?'

'What else has been happening? Did you go to many concerts?' This time I stand just inside the door, blowing smoke over my shoulder into the garden.

Christopher sips his tea. 'I had to miss a few when Ellie was in hospital, but otherwise I've been out most nights. Claire came with me.'

'What did you do about a babysitter?'

'We found an agency, we were lucky, had the same girl each night.'

'Good. That'll mean Claire can go out when she wants, without having to wait and see whether we're going to be in.'

'How do you mean?'

'If she has a professional babysitter.'

'Oh, that was only while you were away.'

I blow smoke across the table, but it's too wide for me to be able to reach his face.

'Don't do that.'

Christopher finishes his tea, washes his plate and mug, and dries up everything I've left on the draining board, polishing each piece of crockery with the tea towel before stacking it in the cupboard. It's only when he starts putting things away I realise how messy the kitchen is. 'Have you had problems with the cleaner?'

'Sara. You have just been away for three weeks. It's the busiest time of the year for me, as you knew perfectly well when you decided to go. Claire has had a bad fright with Ellie. Funnily enough, cleaning the kitchen has not been our number one priority.' He wipes the table with a damp cloth, even though I can't see any crumbs on it.

'How much was Claire around while I was away?'

'No more than usual, apart from when Ellie was ill.'

'I thought she was staying with Ellie in hospital?'

'She moved into the spare room for a couple of nights when they came back.'

Something's undoing, I can feel a knot slipping and I'm not ready for it. 'I'm going to have a bath.'

'I've got to go out.'

'This evening?'

'I'm meeting a producer about a new programme. I'll be back in a couple of hours.'

There's a soft hiss as I stub my cigarette out in the sink. 'Did you see Brian while I was away?'

'A couple of times. He's good. I think you should go and see him by yourself as well.'

I've swung my bag on my shoulder and started up the stairs, when Christopher shouts after me, 'Don't forget, we've got an appointment together, tomorrow evening.'

Four flights to the bathroom; why do I live in such a tall house? Two people don't need so much space, there should be a family here. Something's different in the bathroom, I'm not sure what, but I lock the door and start unpacking my bag, putting my clothes in the linen box. Everything goes in, even things that are unworn; I'd wash my bag if I could.

Now for me: I can feel him in my pores, my hair, my saliva, even my breath; I can't talk to Christopher again until I've got rid of him from my body. I don't want to think about the possibility I mightn't be able to, at least not with hot water, but I fill the bath deep, adding cold gradually until the temperature is just bearable, stinging my skin and turning it pink as I lower myself below the surface. Two white stripes cut my body into sections. I lower my head and hair floats out around me. The bath's not quite long enough for me to stretch out fully, but if I lie sideways my knees don't break the surface. I don't understand how people can commit suicide by drowning in a bath: surely the moment you breathe in, the coughing forces your head out of the water?

I wash my hair, three times, rubbing in handfuls of conditioner. My body reddens more as I scrub it with the pumice I've taken from beside Christopher's sink. When I get out of the bath I massage myself with thick cream, kneading it in with long strokes; then I clean my teeth, rasping the brush across my tongue, toothpaste stinging the smoke-tender skin inside my mouth.

The mirror clears for a few seconds when I wipe a towel over it, before starting to fog again. My face looks mostly as it was, hair sticking up in blond spikes, skin a slightly darker olive. Only my eyes seem changed, paler and larger, a watery grey.

That's what's wrong with the bathroom: someone's removed all my plants.

The bedroom feels much the same, except that a fuggy, fusty smell I haven't noticed before drives me to open the window. Rain drizzles out of the dark so I loop the curtains back behind the radiators. The quilted bedspread is placed perfectly on the bed, each corner the same distance from the floor, five lace cushions lines up symmetrically along the bed head. China figures beckon to each other along the mantelpiece, and the candles in the candleholders on either side of the gilt mirror have been replaced. Everything is tidy; it's obvious I've been away for a while.

Winter clothes are soft, wool rather than cotton; rust-coloured trousers and an orange cardigan. Ginger lipstick and brick-red glass earrings.

On the landing, Christopher has tried to mend the rip from three weeks ago, a thin, jagged, white line showing where the torn paper hasn't stretched quite enough to cover the plaster. He's also nailed down the carpet. Something sticky, like jam, stops my hand sliding down the banister.

The door to the basement is behind the stairs on the ground floor, at the end of a short passage towards the back of the house. The upper panels are made of smoked glass, a pattern etched into them like a pub window, semi-transparent, but not so it's possible to see anyone standing on the other side. I had always thought the pattern was of flowers, but the right-hand panel has a face in the middle of the large, central blossom. I reach my finger towards the glass, which abruptly swings away.

Claire is standing on the step immediately below. Her face reaches my breastbone, skin even paler than Christopher's.

'Hi.'

She says nothing for a couple of seconds. 'Why are you standing there?'

'I was looking at the engraving on the door. It's interesting, I'd never noticed the face before. Look.' The glass panel is now behind

Claire, and she could see it quite clearly if she turned to look.

'Can I come past?'

'Why?'

'What do you mean: why?'

'I mean: why do you want to come into my house?'

Claire takes a step back down the stairs and leans against the wall of the stairwell. 'I want to fetch some stuff.'

'What stuff?'

'Stuff I left last night.'

'I'll get it for you. Where is it?'

'I want to get it myself.'

I'm giving way, I don't have enough anger to continue standing here, barring her way into my house, already nervous about my aggression and what Christopher will say when she tells him.

Her feet are bare, white and doll-like, and she makes no noise as I follow her up the stairs to the sitting room. Inside, several empty wine bottles have collected on the mantelpiece. A dozen or so fat candles, white with cream centres, sit on plates.

'Did Christopher have a party?'

'We had a few friends round last night. He played the piano.'

'Why the candles?'

'Atmosphere.'

'So what do you want to take?'

'The candles. They're mine, from downstairs.' She picks up a couple of plates; I do likewise. 'I'll do it. I don't need any help.'

I go into the kitchen and listen to her climbing up and down the stairs.

Matthew Bellwood

Matthew Bellwood is twenty-two and thin. He has just completed a drama degree at the University of Kent.

Stories from the Sickbed.

(extract from a play for radio)

Interior. A small room in a busy hospital. From somewhere nearby, we hear the constant steady 'beep' of an E.C.G. machine.

COMA-BOY

The hospital is quiet.
I am Coma-boy.
Endlessly waiting.
Waiting to be allowed back in to my
body.
Coma-boy.
Twenty-two and aching, watching,
sleepless, dispossessed.
Coma-boy.
My body lies like roadkill on the
bed.
Battered, bruised,
An empty shell,
A mannequin,
Unliving and undead.
I watch it from across the room.
I long to return.
I long to feel its sinews and its

warmth.
I long to touch and taste once more.
Now all that I can do is listen.
Listen and observe.
I am Coma-boy.
Separated from my body.
Smashed in two
By a pair of Mercedes headlights.

A nurse enters.
Twenty-five,
Slim hips,
Here to change my drips.
A new day is dawning.
I cannot bear this beeping, bleeping,
beating any more.
God!
And I am desperate for the living;
For those whose lives still skitter
swiftly onwards.
Desperate for the life beyond this
room . . .
Listen!

Faintly, as though in the distance, we hear the quiet babble of voices.

There are stories calling.
Stories full of sticky life and joy.
Stories moving forwards, full of
purpose,
Sticky stories calling Coma-boy.

Stories.
My only lifeline.
My only way of living,
Since the car crash,
Since the fateful smash.
My only link with life,

Since I left my body.
Since I was drunk-driven into
oblivion . . .

And so I follow.
Slip through the bricks of the red
brick wall
And out into the morning air.

Cross-fade to exterior of hospital. Early morning. birds and distant traffic.

And now I'm there, I look around.
There is Donald on the gate—
Never late—
Chatting to the chaplain from the
chapel.

DONALD

I'm a big believer in God as you know, Reverend. Now my first wife. She was from Bohemia and she was very interested in the spiritual side of things. Always kept her mind open to extreme possibilities. Tarot and suchlike. She was the one who taught me to open my eyes to the strange beauty that lurks in the apparently banal.

CHAPLAIN

Oh. Er. . . . Really?

DONALD

Oh yes. Now a lot of people said she was daft. Called her a witch some of them. Just because she had the sight. But I tell you. When she died, she died a happy woman. She always knew when God was talking to her, you see.

CHAPLAIN

She sounds like a very wise lady.

DONALD

She was. And that's the thing. She always said that God was talking. All the time. Chatting away like—well. You know the type I mean, Reverend. But the thing was, she said, that people had stopped listening.
Forgotten how to, she said.
And that's the problem with people today.
They're expecting miracles but they don't know what they're looking for. Wouldn't know a miracle if it bit them on the bum, a good half of them. There's no such thing as God, they say. If there is then why does he never get in touch? Why is my life still the way it is? Why do I never have enough love stroke money stroke electrical appliances?
And I say to them. If you but raise your head, there's miracles to be seen all around you. I mean. Just think of the amazing feats performed every day in that building there.
Everyday life, if you look at it hard enough, is just brimming over with the extra- hordinary.

COMA-BOY

Feeling he's on safer ground,
The chaplain nods his head in agreement.

DONALD

Now just you take a look at this.

COMA-BOY

He grabs the chaplain by an arm
And leads him to a dark, black oil stain on the road.

DONALD

Look at that. Look at the way that that stain's been formed. Now if that's not the face of our Lord Jesus Christ, then I don't know what is.

COMA-BOY

I leave them.
There are other stories here.
This world is buzzing with them.

Once again we hear the distant babble of voices. It continues until. . . .

I follow them once more—
Up the road and onto a concrete
patio.
Past the smokers and the mobile
phones,
Through the sliding doors and
Underneath a banner
Saying 'Welcome to Sir Jimmy.'

. . . we enter a bustling soundscape of people talking and laughing. We hear the tinging of lifts and the clatter of a trolley. As the narrator continues, the sounds die down so that they are a background hum.

This is the 'Commercial Zone.'

Get Well
A balloon shaped 'thing'
And a too-big houseplant.
The smiley face grins as it bobbles
up and down,
Attached by a string to a sad woman,
Her dark, dyed hair a shade too
brown.
Just visiting.
Here to see her mother,
She is in from out of town.
She sits on a black, plastic bench
with a sigh.
Sits with her back to the café and
watches
As the bustle of the world goes by.

Just visiting.

A black man, a white woman
And their coffee-coloured child,
Share a happy flapjack and a smile
As they line their jelly babies up
Along the table.
Across the hall, by the wall
Stand the ranks of the disabled.
Just visiting.
Newly arrived.
Here on the community ambulance.
On a day out.
On a day trip.
On a ragga tip.
Anna dances alone
Strutting her funky stuff—
The Gloria Gaynor of Down's Syndrome.
Her audience marvels.

In the café at a grey plastic table,
Sit Ron and Joe.
They have been together for nearly
 forty years.
Partners in crime.
(Their mothers would have called them
 queers.)
Joe speaks.

JOE

Of course, our Vera's lad was one of those.

RON

What's that?

JOE

You know. A cripple.

COMA-BOY

He mouths the words in a confidential hiss.

RON

I'm going for a piss,

COMA-BOY

Says Ron.
He winces as he stands.
He is here for a check-up on an
inflamed nipple.
Just visiting—you understand.
Just visiting.

The door slides open and in walks
Thora Shaw,
The last wisps of smoke
Still streaming from her mouth and
nose.
She pats the sleeve of her black
leather jacket,
Reassuring herself of the nicotine
patches
Concealed beneath her clothes.
She watches
As an old man
Causes a traffic jam—
Arms flapping wildly,
As he decides which way he needs to
go.

A wheelchair swerves to avoid
A pantomime dame,
A frail old frame,
With a stick and a leopard-print
coat.
She doesn't even notice.
The man in the chair

Carries his prosthetic leg on his
knee.
He clutches hold of his wife's hand
As she wheels him past an ancient
couple,
Eighty-three
If they are a day,
Sitting in high-backed chairs
Like thrones,
Waiting to be seen.
They could be King and Queen
Of this frantic realm.
They sit and watch the people
Scything by them.
But they too, are only travellers.
Travellers passing through
This restless world
Of dark grey plastic
And plastic wood.
This land of missing limbs,
And gammy eyes,
And problems of the blood.

Just travellers
Wanting causes,
Seeking answers,
Visiting the inhabitants.
Here to tap the knowledge of the
local seers.

Just visiting.
Here for reassurance,
Checking out a lump she's found.
Just visiting.
Here with his prickly daughter.
Unmarried and in for an ultrasound.
Just visiting.
Here to see her husband,

Who works for the water
And nearly drowned.
Just visiting,
Here with his greedy son,
Hungry after coughing up a missing
pound.
The air is filled with constant
conversation.
The chatter of the sick and the
babble of the healthy,
Loads the room with a heavy hum.
Today perhaps, they are just
visiting.
Just visiting.
But their time will come.

The background babble builds to a crescendo as a hundred different voices fill the air. It fades as THORA *starts to speak.*

THORA

I've had this, I've had that. I'm supposed to be going to Tenerife on Tuesday. This has put a spanner in it. They think it's my lungs this time.
Oh. It's Thora. Pleased to meet you.
Lot of rubbish if you ask me.

COMA-BOY

She sighs a sigh that sounds like running water.

THORA

Ooh, I'm gasping for a fag.
What are you in for?
I remember when I was in for my hysterectomy. Two days I went without. I felt terrible. I said, 'I'm in here to get better, you know. To recuperate. Relax. I don't bloody feel relaxed.'
Mind you, once I was on my feet, I was able to go down and stand outside the lobby. Took me a day

and a half though. Mind you, when you think about what I'd had done, it's not bad.
When I came out of theatre, I woke up in the middle of the night, and I remember them saying, they said, 'Your operation's been very successful. We've taken out your womb and your ovaries and a fibroid the size of a grapefruit.'
Which was good.
I've never liked grapefruits.
And after that, I can just about remember them sticking a bedpan under me—'cos they like you to wee. And that was it. Out cold.
Mind you, I *was* on morphine.
And that's the other thing. They put you on bloody morphine, which is a whatever you call it—class A drug, our Byron says—and then they have a go at you about the odd bit of tobacco.

COMA-BOY

She fiddles with a nicotine patch.

THORA

Doctor came to see me—the one who
whipped 'em out. Young fella.
Right cheeky. Sat down on me bed.
Told me, smoking was a filthy habit
and I was, 'seriously jeopardising my
health.' Filthy habit. I saw him
picking his nose. That's worse. For a
doctor. Unhygienic that is.

Mind you. My daughter's as bad. She's just finished over at Park Lane, doing the nursery nursing course. She thinks she knows best. Just 'cos she's educated.
She said to me the other day. 'What would you do if they told you it was too late? What if the damage is done?'
I just looked at her.

'I tell you what I'd do,' I said.
'I'd go down the Nag's and get
fucking slaughtered.'
'Mother,' she said, 'language at
your age.' (*Cough*)
Mind you. Perhaps she's right.
(*Pause*)
Oh God. Have you got to drink this, as well? Five
pints I've got to get through. And then they're
gonna
Irradiate me.
Honestly.
It can't be healthy.

COMA-BOY

Stories. . . .
I move onwards.
Leave Thora to her pints of sweetened
    water.
I float down the corridor,
To a deeper floor.
Slip down the lift shaft—
Down,
Down,
Down,
To the kitchens,

Fade-in background of kitchen. The sounds of vegetables being chopped, water gushing into sinks, clatter of pans, etc. It plays quietly as a backdrop throughout the next section.

Where a band of women,
Overalled,
Are working,
And a thousand non-existent lunches,
Still to be prepared,
Are lurking

Gretchen, tall and clad in latex
gloves,
Rips the belly from a box of frozen
fish cakes,
And spills its intestines on to a
gleaming, steel tray.
Slides out its guts and throws its
carcass,
Squeamishly away.

At her side
Stands Carol,
Who is big boned
And bulges
Barrel-like
Around the thighs.
Her face,
Round,
Like a belisha beacon with the light
gone out,
Surveys a pile of vegetables with a
fishfinger pout.
Her features are coarse
But against the cheap, red, plastic
net
Which keeps her curls
Well furled,
Her ears nestle like radar—
Listening out for secret messages
from another world.

GRETCHEN

You still seeing that Keith?

CAROL

What Keith?

GRETCHEN

You know. The one up in X-ray. He was well up for you, he was.

COMA-BOY

A dark look, and Carol chops her carrots with an increased fury.

GRETCHEN

Oh.

COMA-BOY

A pause.

GRETCHEN

You don't want to talk about him, do you?

CAROL

No.

COMA-BOY

Carol cocks an eyebrow and stares at
the kitchen clock,
Measuring out the hours in cold
contempt.
She was not meant to languish here,
Amongst the pots and pans.
The trappings of the kitchen
Do not befit her.
Her scalpel slices slowly
Through the outer layers
Of a leek.

She watches as her hands move,
Her face a rigid mask of
concentration.
But she is isn't scared.
This is perhaps the thousandth time

She has performed this simple
operation.
The final cut.
Spontaneous applause.

MOTHER

You saved his life!

COMA-BOY

A grey haired mother weeps.
And then, oh joy,
Strong hands clasp her round her
ample waist.

GYNAECOLOGIST

I knew you could do it, Carol.

COMA-BOY

Cool teeth flash under a blonde
quiff.
Oh God,
Her handsome Gynaecologist.
There for no other reason than to
watch her
And to stand and marvel
At the skill
Of her thick and heavy wrist.

GRETCHEN

Eh, Carol. I'm gonna put some tunes on, okay?

Music blares, then fades out.

Eleanor Birne

Eleanor Birne was born in Cambridge in 1977 and lives in London. Effie and Nan *is an extract from a novel in progress.*

Effie and Nan

I'm not sure about cutting Effie's hair but she wants me to and she's found the kitchen scissors and explained to me in front of the mirror how she wants it to look.

'Your dad will kill us,' I say as I twirl the scissors in my hand.

She's holding a length of hair between her fingers. She's stopped them at the point she wants it to be cut, just below her chin. Effie has long brown hair that nearly reaches her waist. She says she's always had it long because her dad won't let her cut it. He won't let her shave her legs either: he says she'll regret it for the rest of her life because they'll go all bristly like a scouring cloth, which might be true but I think is better than being all hairy.

Effie looks at me in the mirror.

'I'll worry about him,' she says. 'You worry about making a decent job of it.'

The gold mirror makes a frame round Effie's face. One corner of the glass has a crack in, I guess it's because it's old. I take a towel off the rail and put it round Effie's shoulders. The rail is gold like the mirror and the towel is thick and springy. It's the kind of towel I'd like to wrap myself up in because it's nothing like the ones at home. Ours are thin so when you get out of the bath you're freezing.

'Where do you normally have it cut?' I say in my hairdresser voice.

I start combing out the length of her hair which is smooth and doesn't need much brushing. The comb moves through it easily as if it's cream and not hair at all.

'My dad does it,' she says. 'With the nail scissors.'

I laugh because it's a strange thought, all that hair and just a tiny pair of nail scissors.

'It must take him ages.'

'He only cuts off a little bit.'

'These are what you need,' I say, snapping the scissors in front of the mirror.

The blades are long and shiny and cut quickly through the air and they have orange plastic handles.

'Get on with it then,' she says.

'Alright.'

Under the plastic shower cap, my scalp is starting to itch and I have to stop myself from scratching it. The itching means the dye is working. It's called Deep Red and it says on the box you should leave it half an hour before rinsing but I want to wait an hour to be sure.

'How long have I had?' I ask.

She looks down at her watch.

'You've half an hour to go.'

There are blobs of purple dye on the towel round Effie's shoulders. I look down and see there's dye on the bathmat too. It's not an ordinary bathmat but an antique one, so it's tatty round the edges. Effie calls it a rug not a bathmat and it's made with different red and green and blue threads.

'Oh God, Effie,' I say to her. 'There's dye everywhere.'

I show her the messed-up towel. I point out the stains on the bathmat.

'We'll have to clear it up,' she says, one hand clutching her mouth.

'We'll have to clear it up properly.'

She springs up from her stool and it's like her dad's already in the room because she's so jerky and panicked. She takes a face cloth and runs it under the tap and starts scrubbing at one of the purple stains on the mat. It makes a scraping, scratching sound. She scrubs the mat with one hand and keeps the other over her mouth, like she's in shock. I stand over her and I'm not sure what to do. All the while I'm thinking how I hope my hair doesn't turn out the colour of the blobs. That kind of stuff has happened before. Last time I had it done at the hairdresser's and got the trainee to do it because it only cost five pounds. When she'd finished, it was the colour of a fire engine and I couldn't help crying. The manager mixed up another colour and put that on top so in the end it didn't look too bad but it was dark outside by the time I left.

'It comes off!'

Effie sits back and holds up the face cloth. It's purple now and there's a big patch of wet on the mat where the dye used to be. She throws the cloth into the sink.

'Thank God for that,' she says. 'Thank God it comes off.'

She sits back down on the stool. I make my fingers into scissors and slice them into her hair at the point she showed me before.

'You want it just here?'

She nods at me in the mirror and I take a breath and try to relax my shoulders.

'How long before he gets back?'

'Ages,' she says.

I take a section of hair between my index and middle fingers. It feels cold and smooth and I slide my fingers down towards the ends, which are neat and squared and not split like mine used to be when I had long hair. I raise the scissors and push them in and make the first cut halfway up the length, just below her jaw. The bottom half crumbles away and lands on my right foot. I kick it onto the floor and it lies there looking like something that just died.

Effie smiles at her reflection in the mirror. I take another section of hair, a bigger bit now, and make another slicing cut with the scissors because this is what she wants. My scalp is still prickling but I know I need to finish the haircut before I can wash the dye off so I make another cut and then another, so that one side of Effie's hair is almost level with her chin, though the other side still hangs down low.

'Shall we leave it like this?' I ask.

She laughs and flips the long side with her hand. There's a pile of brown hair at my feet now and it looks like one of those photos of the camps in World War Two. It gives me the creeps.

Effie fidgets on her stool.

'Hold still,' I tell her. 'Unless you want me to cut your ear off.'

'It tickles,' she says, laughing and rocking on the stool.

I bend down and pull back the towel from her shoulders. Then I blow the cut hairs off her neck and from behind her ears. The skin there is white like a baby's and soft as butter. Effie stops laughing. I put the towel back in its place and raise the scissors again.

'You have to keep still,' I tell her. 'Or I'll mess it up.'

She's serious and I watch her face in the glass. She's beautiful and is the kind of girl other girls are jealous of. She has a face like you might get on a china doll, but not so spooky because some china dolls have faces like corpses. I used to collect china dolls and they're different from normal dolls because you can't play with them, in case they break. Sometimes I think Effie might break too. She has these pale thin arms and legs and her face is white like a doll's face. She has long eyelashes and dark brown eyes like chocolate mousse.

I cut into the longer side and it starts to fall away. Soon Effie's hair is a ragged bob shape that runs out just under her chin. I take the comb and run it through what's left.

'I need to shape it now,' I say to her in my hairdresser voice. I'm starting to panic a bit because the only other person's hair I've ever cut is the dog's, which was when I was about ten, and I don't think that counts. But Effie doesn't look worried: in fact she's grinning at her new reflection.

I take small snips with the scissors, trying to make the ends straight. I keep cutting away more than I mean to because one side is always longer than the other and when I shorten the long side, that ends up being too short.

I think the reason I can't get it right is because of Effie's dad. He'll go crazy when he sees the bathmat and he'll be twice as crazy when he sees her hair. The day she told me about her dad was the day we became friends. It was soon after Kara left. Effie came up to me on the field where I was standing with Anne-Marie and the others. Effie didn't know any of them because she was new to our school. She didn't know me either but that didn't stop her talking to me. Anne-Marie was my best friend then but I was getting sick of her. None of the others liked Effie. They still don't like her and I think it's got something to do with how beautiful she is. Anne-Marie called her a freak once so I slapped her. It left a red handprint on the side of her face and it looked like someone had painted it on because the hand shape was so perfect. Now Effie and I have a rule where we don't talk to the girls at school. Sometimes I forget and end up saying something rude to Anne-Marie when I mean to keep quiet, but Effie never makes that mistake.

That first day I met her, Effie told me about the time her dad threw her mum down the stairs. Her mum crawled out into the road with blood everywhere and her front teeth chipped. Her mum left because of it. Soon after we got to be friends, Effie and her dad went away to Turkey. She sent me a postcard and wrote they'd had a fight and that he'd hit her and she had bruises all over her bum. By the time she got back the bruises were gone, but it took two weeks.

'How long has it been?' I ask.

Effie looks at her watch. 'You've another five minutes.'

Her hair is almost diagonal, sloping down to her chin on the right side, and up to her earlobe on the left. I know I should stop because the cutting is out of control, but at the same time I want to make things right.

'I've made a mess of it,' I say.

Effie turns her head from side to side in the mirror. She looks like she's in one of those shampoo adverts, except her hair is all over the place.

'I like it. It's unusual.'

I take the towel away from her shoulders and give her hair one final run over with the comb. The floor is covered with strands of long brown hair that's the colour of the floorboards and just as shiny.

Effie tilts her head up and gives me a kiss on the cheek.

'Thanks,' she says.

I bend down and pick up one of the strands and lay it in the palm of my hand and along my forearm so that it looks like a brown ribbon. I stretch my arm towards her.

'You should keep this,' I say. 'As a memory.'

She shakes her head. 'I don't want it.'

'Really?' I say.

'I don't want it.'

I let it drop back onto the floor.

The front door slams and I look over at Effie. She's ruffling her new hairstyle in the mirror.

'Oh God,' I hear myself say, and before I know it I've moved over to the bathroom door and shut it and pushed the bolt across.

I lean against the door and my heart is panicking inside my chest. Effie's face has gone the colour of milk. She's so white she looks like she might go see-through. All of a sudden she starts moving.

'We've got to be calm,' she says, pulling me over to the bath. 'Let's get this stuff off your head.'

I yank the shower cap off and lean over the bathtub. Effie takes hold of the showerhead and tests the water before turning it on my hair. When the water comes it's warm and even in the middle of all this I realise how sweet it is to have Effie wash my hair for me. I watch as the purple dye slides off in the water. Then I close my eyes. Kara used to do this for me too. She'd wash it when she had nothing else to do and put on two rounds of shampoo, lathering it up to make crazy, punk spikes out of my hair. She put conditioner on as well and combed it through. The only time my hair looked good was after Kara washed it. I've never been bothered with messing around with stuff like conditioner or two rounds of shampoo.

I'm bent over the tub so all the blood rushes to my head and it feels heavy. When I open my eyes I see the water is starting to run clear, which means the dye is coming out. There's water as well as dye all over the bathmat now and the sides of the bath are stained purple too. It's one of those bathtubs which has feet underneath and it's big and deep and they've had a Jacuzzi machine fitted. If you use bubble bath as well as the machine the bubbles get enormous.

There's a loud knock on the bathroom door that I can hear even over the water noise and with water in my ears.

'What are you up to in there?'

Effie doesn't say anything but she seems to have forgotten she's holding the showerhead because she's pointing it out of the tub and water is spraying all over the walls. I quickly grab it and point it back into the bath.

He knocks again.

'I said, what are you up to?'

I nudge Effie with my elbow.

'I'm washing Nan's hair,' she shouts back. It's like she's trying to hold on to her voice and make that calm, straight-line sound. It seems to work because the banging stops. I wrap my hair up in a towel and Effie uses the showerhead to clean the dye off the sides of the bath. I collect up the other towels, which are mostly stained with hair dye, and roll them into a ball. We work quickly but there's not much I can do about the hair on the floor. Effie picks up a clean towel and uses it to dry the sides of the bath and then the walls.

I rub my hair, trying to make it dry.

'What colour is it?' I ask.

'It's too wet to see yet.'

I gather up the towels in my arms. I move over to the door and press my ear up against it trying to hear him out there but there's nothing.

I'm about to pull back the bolt when Effie puts her hand on my arm. She's pointing at the bathroom window. She slides up the sash. I look out and there's an extension roof below which slopes down and has a fence running next to it.

'If we get onto the roof we can climb down the drainpipe,' she says.

'Okay.'

Effie climbs out through the bottom part of the window. Then she's on the roof and level with me outside.

'Come on out, it's lovely,' she says. 'You can see the stars.'

I drop my towel and climb out of the window. The night is warm and the roof is slippery because the tiles are new and shiny. The tiles are warm under my socks from baking in the sun all day. Effie takes my hand and when I look up, the sky is like a cinema screen with silver holes in. I have to look down quickly because the roof slopes and Effie is taking me to the edge.

She pulls me into a squatting position beside her on the edge of the roof. Below us I can see a big green water butt and beneath that the garden stretching out of sight. It's a long garden with a pond with giant fish in and wooden benches and a willow tree.

'I'll go first,' says Effie.

'Are you sure?'

'He'll go mad when he sees the bathroom,' she says. 'This is the only way.'

I realise we're talking in whispers and it's like we're burglars but in reverse. I wonder what the police would do if they saw us and try to imagine what we'd say. 'We got locked in the bathroom and this was the only way out, Officer.' I think about telling Effie but she looks too serious.

All at once Effie disappears. I look over the edge of the roof and see her shimmying down the drainpipe and I watch as she jumps from the water butt and lands in the grass. She looks up at me and her face is like a little moon.

'Your turn,' she hisses.

Robin Booth

Robin Booth was a scriptwriter for museum exhibitions before coming to UEA. He lives in Norwich.

Diminishing Returns

Three men, dimly lit, in isolated areas of the stage. KRIK *in an overcoat, squat and comically bulky.* KRAK *with a large tea urn under his arm.* KROK*, a huge man sitting on the ground with a small, painted Russian doll.*

KRIK: Overcoat.

KRAK: Samovar.

KROK: Doll.

Spotlight on KRIK*, admiring himself in his overcoat.*

KRIK: Very nice. Fine piece of, brrrup, 'scuse me, the pork chops—fine piece of work. Hmm? Yes. And the stitching? (*Puffs out his belly*) Can't fault the stitching. Won't fall apart on the first, brrrup, wearing. Good. And the cut? Hmm? Generous. And—what? Under the arms? (*Flaps his arms*) Plenty. And the style? Simple. Very good. Won't go out with the season. Hmm? Yes. And the collar? Ah. Sable. Excellent. Won't let the, brrup, blizzard in. Very good. And the what? Hmm? The reckoning? Eleven roubles? (*Swallows his dismay*) It's a fair price.

As he reaches into his trouser pocket for the money . . . the spotlight snaps to KRAK *holding the samovar.*

KRAK: Have a seat, please, please. Wherever you—or nearer the fire? That's it, good, now . . . So thank you for coming, and indeed what a blizzard, yes, good. And how about a cup of—sorry, yes, Maria, would you take the doctor's coat?

Pause. Meanwhile, KRIK, *in a separate part of the stage, takes off his coat and discards it. Underneath he is wearing another one, almost identical to the first but shabbier.*

KRAK: Good. Good. Thank you. Now. Now. Now you'll want to see her for yourself, I am sure. And of course. Good. So in a minute, yes, up the stairs, and you shall, for yourself, in a minute. Good. But I must, just a word, if you will. Yes. Now. . . For a month, well, not a thing passed her lips, no, not a word, not a thing, only tea. Yes. Only tea. And we don't know what to think . . .But you're here, doctor, now. Good. So. If you're warm, if you will, will you go for yourself up the stairs? But wait, sorry, yes—will you have some tea?

He opens the tap on the samovar and pours a thick stream of tea into a cup. He closes the tap and offers the cup.

Spotlight snaps to KROK, *dabbing at his doll with a tiny paintbrush.*

Long silence. Intense concentration.

The spotlight fades.

KRIK: Overcoat.

KRAK: Samovar.

KROK: Doll.

Spotlight on KRIK. *He takes off the second coat and discards it.*

Underneath, another one, the same but with brand new patches.

KRIK: Very nice. Fine piece of work. Done a good, brrrup, 'scuse me, the dumplings—good job on this. Hmm? Yes. And you've taken in the waist? (*Sticks out his backside*) Just a touch. Yes. Much improved. And the elbows? (*Lifts his elbows to reveal large patches on them*) Very good. Won't give out at the first, brrup, hot dinner. (*Mimes eating with elbows on the table, shovelling it in*) Hmm? Yes. And the what? Missing button? Present and correct. Excellent. And a good match. Won't give itself away in a, brrup, identity parade. (*Laughs*) Hmm? Yes. Very good. Good as new. And the what? Hmm? The reckoning? (*Barely concealing his shock*) Eleven roubles! . . . That's er, that's hmm, that's . . .

He digs in his trouser pocket for the money. His spotlight fades as . . . spotlight up on KRAK, *holding the samovar.*

KRAK: Hello doctor, come on in, come on in, good, now. And aren't we lucky with the, yes, not so cold, not at all, there, good. So. Now will you—ah, yes, there we go. Maria?

Pause. Meanwhile KRIK *removes his coat. Underneath, another one, the same but ragged and stained, the collar hanging off.*

KRAK: Good. So. Now. Now I understand you're taking her away. Or no, not away, just, yes, 'in', for a month. Just a month. I understand . . . And I'm sure it's best for her. Yes . . . And so we thought, now, will she need, while she's there, we don't know? . . . Will she want, while she's there, if you will, a little bag? Maybe just a little bag? So, all she needs, while she's there, in the little bag, yes, tea. Only tea . . . And will you please, if you can, when you go, will you take the little bag? It's all she needs. Now. Will you sit, will you stay, for a minute, for a month, will you take a cup of tea?

He opens the tap on the samovar and this time only a drizzle comes out. His spotlight fades as . . . spotlight up on KROK. *He is buffing his doll with an old rag.*

After a while he puts the rag away and sets the doll down in front of him. He lifts the top half of it and takes out a second one, identical but half the size of the first. He replaces the top half of the original one. He looks at his two dolls.

Silence.

The spotlight slowly fades.

KRIK: Overcoat.

KRAK: Samovar.

KROK: Doll.

Spotlight slowly up on KRIK. *He takes off the fourth coat and discards it. Underneath, another one, the same but with new patches, new buttons, a new collar and belt loops. Everything cheap and flimsy. In fact, nothing survives of the first coat.*

KRIK: Very hmm, very yes. Good. Given the, brrrup, 'scuse me, the broth—the circumstances. Hmm? Yes. Given the circumstances. Good. And the what—loops? (*Sticks his thumbs through the belt loops*) For the belt. Commendable. Won't sag around the belly. Good. Very prudent. And the collar? Cat? Well. Looks like sable, from a distance. In a blizzard. Hmm? Yes. And the lining? What? Gone? Well. Can't be helped. Won't be missed. In the, brrup, summer. And the, what, hem? Gone? And the, what, pocket? Gone? Well. Done your best. Good. Fine old coat. Served me well. Hmm? Yes. (*Pause*) Very good. Yes. Now what's hmm, what's er, what's the reckoning? (*Putting a brave face on it*) Eleven. Well that's . . .

He pats his trouser pockets apprehensively. The spotlight remains on him as . . . spotlight slowly up on KRAK, *hugging the samovar tightly to his chest.*

KRAK: Hello doctor, well I never, unexpected. What a blizzard, yes indeed, so unexpected . . . By the fire, very welcome, will you please . . . And here's Maria.

Pause. Meanwhile KRIK *removes his coat. Underneath he is shirtless and very skinny.*

KRAK: It's been months now, and our daughter, is there any news? We understand, it's not that simple, is there any change? Can we visit, can we see her, is there anything that's needed, any sign? We understand, we're not expecting, all we want is any hope . . . Well. It's a long way through the blizzard and you must be very weary, is there anything you need, or any hope?

KRAK *opens the tap on the samovar. Nothing comes out. The spotlight remains on him as . . . spotlight slowly up on* KROK *and his two dolls.*

Pause.

KROK *takes a third doll from inside the second. Again, it is half the size of its parent doll.* KRIK *is watching.*

KRIK: (*to* KROK) Hey. Hey you.

KRAK, *hugging his samovar, looks at* KRIK. KROK *looks only at his dolls.*

KRIK *approaches* KROK.

KRIK: You, my friend.

KROK *looks up at him.*

KRIK: *Your* dolls? Hmm? (*No reply*) You made them? Yes? . . . One, two, three, hmm? Pretty ones. Fine bits of work. How much?

KROK: Not cheap.

KRIK: Ah, well. Good. Hmm? Yes. Do I look like a, brrup, beggar? Hmm? Asking for credit? (*Laughs*) No, my friend. (*Reaching into his pocket for money)* What's the reckoning?

KROK: A fair price.

KRIK: Fifty kopeks?

KROK: (*Picking up the largest doll*) This, one kopek.

KRIK: A fair price! But now. And her sisters. I want them all. How much? Three kopeks? A fair price.

KROK: All of them?

KRIK: My friend. I am but a, brrup, man. Hmm? (*Laughs*) Mortal man, yes? (*Laughs*)

KROK: First, one kopeck for this doll.

KRIK: (*Pause*) Ah. Good. We'll have some fun, hmm? Yes. (*Giving* KROK *a coin*) There. One kopek.

KROK *sets the largest doll aside and picks up the second.*

KROK: Two kopeks.

KRIK: What? Half the size, double the price? Hmm? This how you sell your girls, my friend? The smaller, the fresher? (*Laughs*) No, that's er, that's hmm, there, two kopeks.

He gives KROK *two coins.* KROK *sets the second doll aside and picks up the third.*

KRIK: So. Third doll, three kopeks.

KROK *shakes his head.*

KRIK: What, double again? Four kopeks? (*Pause. He smiles*) Very good. Clever man. Won't go hungry at the end of the day, hmm?

No. Four kopeks.

KRIK *offers him four coins.* KROK *shakes his head and takes a fourth doll from inside the third. As he does this,* KRAK *approaches holding his samovar, fascinated by the dolls.*

KRIK: Ah! Another. Hidden inside. Well. I like her. Hmm? Yes. Unexpected. I'll have her. What's she come to? Four kopeks for the, brrup, third, yes? And, what, eight kopeks for the last? (*Digs in his pocket*) Come. It's settled.

He offers KROK *the money but* KROK *ignores him. He is taking out a fifth doll, very small.*

KRIK: And what? Another? Ingenious. A rarity. Even better. She's mine. Where are we? Twice eight is sixteen, sixteen kopeks. She's worth it.

As KRIK *digs for more money,* KROK *gives the fifth doll to* KRAK, *who looks at it in wonder.*

KRAK: It's my—

KRIK: Hmm?

KRAK: It's my daugh—

KRIK: No, it's *my* doll. Hmm? Mine.

He rattles the coins in his hand at KROK, *who ignores him.* KRAK, *with his samovar under one arm, takes the top off the fifth doll to reveal a sixth inside, about the size of a fingernail. He nervously hands it back to* KROK.

KRIK: What is that, what is that, another? Is it? Or just a piece of cork, hmm? Dipped in tar? Let me see. (*Takes the sixth doll from* KROK. *Pause while he scrutinises it.*) Well. Brrup, 'scuse me, the rotten turnips. Very good. Lifelike. And the colouring? Ruddy. Fresh. Outdoor girl. And the shape? Buxom. Can't fault the chiselling. And the lips? Glistening. Perfect. Just like the first. Precisely. A carbon copy. Only—small. Hmm? Yes. Too small. Thirty kopeks.

KROK: Thirty-two.

KRIK: What? And the shirt from my back?

KROK *offers the sixth doll to* KRAK.

KRIK: (*Digging in his pocket*) No, no! I'm made of money. Thirty-two for the last. I get the whole lot. Four, five, six dolls. Done. Thirty-two.

KROK *gets out a pair of tweezers and improbably takes a seventh doll out of the sixth.*

KRIK: (*Pause, amazed*) So you throw in one for free! (*Laughs*) Very good, my friend. Thirty-two, as we agreed. Thirty-two, that doll, and everything in it.

KROK: (*Holding it up for* KRAK *to see*) Sixty-four.

KRIK: Kcha! Preposterous! Sixty-four kopeks? For a speck of sawdust? Not much to, brrup, look at, is she?

KROK *is already taking out an eighth doll. Despite himself,* KRIK *is enthralled by the intricate operation.*

KROK: One rouble twenty-eight.

KROK *places the eighth doll on the end of* KRAK*'s finger. It is little bigger than a flea.* KRAK *holds it up to the light to examine it.*

KRAK: Her eyes. Her hair. The hair is just like hers.

He carefully passes it back to KROK, *who takes it in his tweezers.*

KRIK: Give me my dolls and off I go. Yes?

KROK *takes his tweezers to the eighth.*

KRIK: Enough!

But KROK *goes on working in silence. And soon he places a ninth doll, too small to see with the naked eye, on* KRAK*'s finger.*

KROK: Two roubles fifty-six.

KRIK: No. Too far. Pay for something I cannot see?

KRAK: It's my daughter.

KRIK: (*Pause*) What? Hmm? Your daughter?

KRAK: It's her.

KRIK: (*Pause*) Let me see. (*Squints at* KRAK*'s finger*) Pfff—brrup—no. Nothing there.

KROK: Two roubles fifty-six. Too small to see.

KRAK: My daughter.

KRIK: No. Choose another, old man. (*Indicates larger dolls*) Hmm? Won't get a dowry for that.

KROK: The eye cannot see two roubles fifty-six.

KRIK: And my two roubles fifty-six stays in my, brrup, pocket. Won't make a, brrup, profit out of me.

KROK: (*to* KRIK) It passes your understanding. (*to* KRAK) To paint it I use an eyelash. Split in half.

KRAK: She has returned to me.

KROK: (*to* KRAK) Forty days it took.

KRIK: Watch. It takes this long. (*Mimes grasping something tiny out of the air. To* KRAK.) Look, old man, your wife. Fifty roubles a night.

KROK: (*to* KRAK) I was tempted to give up. But I needed a place to put five roubles twelve.

KRIK: Pfff! Insanity.

KROK: (*turning to* KRIK) Five roubles twelve. It's half the size. And do you know what I can fit in five roubles twelve? The sum of your soul. And I close the lid. (*He makes a gesture of snapping his fingers shut.*)

KRIK: Nyah! Charlatan! Give me the dolls I paid for.

KRIK *brushes* KRAK *aside dismissively to get at the other dolls.* KRAK, *with the samovar under one arm and the invisible doll on the end of his finger, loses his balance and topples onto* KROK. *In the tumble the doll is lost and the samovar goes rolling across the stage.*

All come to rest, appalled.

KROK *gets to his feet. He really is a big man.*

KRIK: (*cowering towards the wings*) That's er, that's um . . . (*Turns to run*)

KROK: (*with spellbinding menace*) My friend. (KRIK *stops in his tracks*) Five roubles twelve.

KRIK: Me? (*Pause*) I don't have it.

KROK *advances on* KRIK *and grabs him by the neck.* KRAK *begins searching the ground for the lost doll.*

KRIK: Wait. Here. (*Clutching at his pockets*) Take everything. Keep your dolls.

KRIK *takes out a handful of coins and drops them to the ground.*

KROK: Five roubles twelve.

KRIK: Look. I'm broke. Not even a shirt. Where will I find five roubles twelve?

KROK: Inside two roubles fifty-six.

KRIK: The doll? Find the *doll*? A joke!

KROK: Look for it. (*He throws* KRIK *to the floor*) Sixty seconds. Then I will break your neck. Sixty.

KRIK: Sixty seconds? No.

KROK: Fifty-seven.

KRIK: What doll? Invisible one?

KROK: Fifty-three.

KRIK: Don't ask *me*. Never set eyes on it.

KROK: Forty-nine.

KRIK: Not my fault. Ask him. Ask his daughter!

KROK: Forty-four.

KRIK: What about him?

He points at KRAK, *who is on hands and knees searching the ground, crying silently.*

KROK: (*Pause*) Thirty-three.

KRIK *makes a pretence of looking for the doll.*

KRIK: So. I'm looking. I'm looking. (*to* KRAK) Keep looking! . . . No . . . no . . . (*Looking up at* KROK) Not here. (*No reply*) How long? (*No reply. Continues searching.*) I'm looking. Not here. No. (*Stops*) DOESN'T EXIST!

KROK: Seven seconds.

KRIK: CHARLATAN!

KROK: Three.

KRIK: Wait. (*Searches again*)

KROK: Two.

KRIK: Ha! (*Makes a conspicuous 'discovery'*)

KROK: One.

KRIK: Stop! There. See? Yes. Just in time.

He holds 'it' out on the end of his finger. KROK *comes over and looks at it. Delight spreads across his face. He carefully takes 'it' from* KRIK.

KRIK: What's the reckoning? Hmm? Lucky. I am always lucky. There you go.

KROK *sits down by his dolls.* KRAK *kneels, bewildered.* KRIK *brushes dust from his knees and elbows. He picks up his coins. He weighs up his chances, then:*

KRIK: Thirty-two kopeks? For the set?

KROK *looks up angrily.* KRIK *backs off.*

KRIK: There we are. Luck always turns.

KRIK *exits.*

Pause.

KRAK *picks up his samovar.* KROK *packs away his dolls, fitting each in turn into the next size up until only the one-kopek doll remains apart. He picks it up.*

KROK: This was the first one I made. My apprenticeship. The rest of my life fits in here. Everyone will buy this one. But no-one has the soul to buy five roubles twelve.

He opens the one-kopek doll and puts the rest inside.

KROK: See that man? He sees nothing. His soul rattles inside him. He thinks if he picks up some dust on his finger . . . he thinks I'll never know.

He gets out the old rag and wraps it around the doll.

KROK: Blind luck. He thought it was only dust on his finger. No. Five roubles twelve. Inside two roubles fifty-six.

He stands up and starts to leave.

KRAK: I'll buy it.

KROK: Five roubles twelve?

KRAK: Two roubles fifty-six.

KROK: Why? (*No reply*) Why not five roubles twelve? (*No reply*) What will you buy it with?

Pause. KRAK *offers his samovar.*

KROK: It's an old one. Does it work?

KRAK: No.

KROK: All the better. I don't drink tea.

KROK *takes the samovar and gives* KRAK *the bundle of dolls.* KROK *exits.*

KRAK: All of them?

He sees that KROK *has gone. He looks at his bundle of dolls.*

Lights slowly fade.

Sarah Bower

Sarah Bower has worked in the steel industry, drawn dole in the benefits office made famous by The Full Monty, *been a charity administrator and a freelance journalist. She has had poetry and short stories published in* QWF, Buzzwords *and* Spiked. *She lives in rural Suffolk with her family and two dogs.*

Odo's Women

This is an extract from a novel whose themes are organised around the history of the Bayeux Tapestry. It takes place in a house inside the stockade of the Norman castle at Canterbury, in which the women manufacturing the Tapestry are working. They work under the supervision of Agatha de Conteville, its designer, the sister of both Odo of Bayeux, who commissioned the work, and William the Conqueror. Agatha is a nun and her religious name is Soeur Jean Baptiste. The year is 1070. In this scene, Odo is checking up on the women in secret.

Odo is proud of what he has done in building this singular house; of the great stone chimney rising through both storeys, so that fires can be lit without sparks catching on the embroidery or smoke lingering in the room and discolouring the linen; of the glazed windows that run almost without interruption along the south-east wall. Odo brought the glaziers from Constantinople where, he has heard tell, the Emperor's palace has glass so fine and clear you would not know it was there unless you touched it. He still keeps the glaziers, stiff with cold, sick of salt fish and pasty light, in case the precious panes should crack in frosts or be broken in some other way. It is only two summers since the Kentish rebellion and for all his thoroughness in dealing with the rebels, Odo is not fool enough to imagine that none are still living who would destroy him.

The surfaces of the great trestle tables standing beneath the windows have been polished by craftsmen to the smoothness of marble so that there can be no danger of twine catching on wood splinters. He wants the record of what they have achieved, the two sons of Huerlain de Conteville and their brother the Bastard, to be perfect, pristine, in no way obfuscated by dust or singeing or snagged threads. Safe from revolt.

The women work in the long upper room every day as long as the light lasts, save for Christmas, Easter, Whitsun and Ascension Day. They leave it only to hear Mass and take their meals. The room is orderly, but not tidy. It smells of ash and candle wax, blood, lavender, cat's piss, stale bread. Despite Odo's fear of fire, several braziers stand about. He will have to speak to Agatha about this. The embers whisper as they settle, sifting ghost grey ash onto the dark wooden floor. Skeins of coloured wools hang from eight frames, one for each colour, ranged around the tables like servants offering dishes at dinner.

The cat is currently curled up on Agatha's lectern. Agatha reads to the women from the Bible, of course, but also from various dog-eared parchments on which she has noted down from memory tales of King Arthur and favourite verses from Ovid and Catullus. Catullus? Why was she so desperate to become a nun?

'The nun, the priest'

'And Nick, the Beast . . .' sings Gytha, leaning back on the bench, stretching her arms in the air then folding them behind her head.

'That's a wicked song,' says Margaret.

'I wonder you should know such a thing,' says Judith sternly.

'I wonder Margaret should,' Gytha retorts. 'I thought you came from a good family, Margaret.'

'Not that good. I had four brothers.'

There is a short silence. Emma begins to sniffle nervously.

'I'm sorry for your loss, Meg. I didn't think,' says Gytha. She picks up her needle and resumes her work. From time to time she glances along the line of women, looking for sympathy, but finds none. The twins glare at her.

'Big mouth,' says one, and her sister nods vigorously.

'I'll have you know, Berthild.' (Of course, Odo remembers, Berthild and Balthild.) 'That King Harold used to say my greatest charm lay in the size of my mouth. Generous mouth, generous cunt, he used to say.'

Emma shrieks.

'Gytha, really,' says Judith.

'What? In front of Lady Edith?' asks Margaret, aghast.

Odo rams his fist into his mouth to stop himself laughing aloud.

'No, dear. Usually when we were preparing her for bed, when he had that sort of thing on his mind. There was a little ante-room outside her bed chamber where he used to wait. I'd be topping up his nightcap or doing some other little job about the place and he'd tease me. It meant nothing. He was devoted to Lady Edith, she was so beautiful, and wise with it.'

'Poor lady,' sighs Judith, and all the women cross themselves.

'God and her children forgive me for saying so, but I hope she's dead,' says Gytha.

Odo is not certain of Edith Swan Neck's fate, though he is sure William knows what became of her. She visits Odo sometimes in dreams. In his dream, she is kneeling among the corpses, the dark red blood seeping into the white stuff of her gown, veins of crimson unfurling, creeping upwards like the wild rose in the tale of the Sleeping Beauty. She holds a chunk of flesh out to him. The skin is bruised, marrow oozes like pus from the yellow bone, blood drips from hanging sinews. He tries to recoil but cannot. It is as though his eyeballs have been speared to the vision.

'Look,' Edith says to him, 'You see? This is Harold. Here is a mole in the small of his back known only to me.' Then she starts to howl, her body clenched like a fist around the bleeding chunk as though she is trying to protect it, to absorb it into herself. Her howls wake him, sweating and shivering as though he has a fever, and he wishes he were as hard of purpose as William or as unquestioning as his younger brother, Robert.

'Now, Gytha,' says Margaret in a strong voice designed to mask emotion, 'come and tell me if I've got King Harold's cloak right this time.'

Gytha rubs her sleeve across her eyes, then climbs over the bench and walks, swaggers almost with her hip-swaying gait, to where Margaret sits, flexing her shoulders to loosen them. Gytha leans over Margaret, resting one hand familiarly in the small of the girl's back where her curls begin to thin out into loosely coiled gold springs.

'Ah yes, that's much more like it. And you have his face to perfection. That's exactly how he wore his moustache. He was very particular about shaving . . .'

'I saw him once, you know, on the march from York,' says Margaret as Gytha returns to her place. 'He came with Tom to collect our youngest brother, Eric. He came in person and spoke to my father, to tell him how bravely Edward and Alfred had fought before they were killed. I think he was afraid we wouldn't let Eric go. It was awful, Mother wailing and tearing at her hair like a madwoman, Eric red in the face, checking his weapons, Tom's wife, Enid, snivelling and begging him to stay at home for the sake of the baby. Father burst into tears right there, in front of the King. The King was kind; he even put his arm around Father. I couldn't think about Edward and Alfred then. All I thought was, when Eric goes it'll be just Mother and Father, and snivelling Enid, and me. There was a devil in me. Perhaps King Harold would have left Eric behind but Eric wouldn't have stayed, not with the others gone.'

Odo relives similar scenes in towns and villages all over Normandy, when he has been the commander with the firm jaw, the manly squeeze of the shoulder, the cold comfort of immortality. Your sons are with the saints, he has assured the grieving mothers, the silent fathers who know as he knows, and Godwinson knew, that the saints are no consolation for the agony of spilt guts or bowels gripped by fever, and the loneliness of dying.

'When King Harold came through our village,' begins Emma in her meek, wavering voice, 'I made my Gird hide in one of his beer barrels.'

'Shame on you, Emma,' says Judith, though without vehemence.

'I'd five children, my lady, one still at the breast. What was I to do? I thought we had more need of Gird than the King did.'

'Didn't Gird protest?' asks Margaret.

'He wouldn't dare, would he, Emma?' mocks Gytha. Emma blushes and lowers her eyes. 'It's the quiet ones you have to beware of, girls,' continues Gytha. A muffled snort escapes Emma. It is difficult to tell whether it is a laugh or a sob.

'Stop teasing,' admonishes Margaret.

'I suppose if that was the Bishop arriving we shall have to wait for our midday meal. My stomach's growling like a mad dog. Listen. It must be close to Sext.'

This takes Odo by surprise. The time has passed more quickly than he thinks.

'Always thinking of your stomach, Gytha.'

'Well what else is there to think about, shut up here? No plays, no music, no fairs. No men, if that's what you fancy.' She leers at Margaret, who drops her head back over her work. Odo tries to see her face but from where he is standing, it is covered by her hair, which she wears loose.

'Actually,' says one of the twins, 'I think the Bishop's not bad looking.'

'For a Norman,' adds her sister.

'You can't say that about a bishop,' says Judith, but her tone says something else entirely.

'He's not a bloody bishop here, though, is he? He's the bloody Earl of Kent. I'll bet there's only one bishop in his bed at night, and it's not the Bishop of Bayeux.'

'Gytha!' Margaret shakes with laughter, her curls shimmering over her breasts and shoulders. Gytha is warming to her theme.

'Mind you, he's a holy one, that bishop. Takes a discipline every night, I'll be bound.'

By now the women are overcome with laughter. Even Judith is smiling and her long face has turned pink to the tip of her beaked nose. Odo boils with shame. He knows he can stop this at any time, yet feels that he cannot, that he has been crushed into immobility by the weight of his humiliation.

'A hair shirt?' suggests Emma in her meek voice.

'To tickle his fancy?' Margaret elaborates.

'Margaret, that sort of remark is hardly fitting in a maid.'

'Maid my arse, madam.' Gytha turns towards Judith so that Odo can no longer see her face. She has her hair bundled into some sort of cap, and he stares at her bare neck, notes the way the tiny hairs, too short to be caught up, form dark scribbles on the pale skin. 'You don't really think Soeur Jean's teaching her Latin, do you? I reckon she's more of a man than the Bishop, that one. She's got less tits anyway.' No one laughs.

'I can't think what you mean, Gytha.' Judith lays down her needle. She leans forward, folding her arms on the table, and stares at

Gytha. Odo detects a squaring of Gytha's shoulders, a shiver of muscle beneath the grimy fabric of her bodice. Margaret bends over her work and says nothing. The twin who started the conversation vents a high pitched whinny.

'I'll weave the Bishop a hair shirt if he pleases.' No one takes any notice.

'Be careful, Gytha. How long do you think you could last without Soeur Jean's protection?'

'Judith, do you carry your head so high you can't see what's going on under your very nose? Soeur Jean isn't our protector, she's our gaoler. The only reason we're given light and air and enough to eat is because the Bishop needs our skills. Don't you ever wonder what will happen to us when we finish this . . . *mistress*piece? I don't blame Margaret for buttering her bread. I'd do likewise given half the chance. As it is I try to work as slow as I can. I wonder the rest of you don't do likewise.'

'Some of us still have self respect.' Judith leans closer over her work and makes a careful stitch, drawing her needle through the linen in a neat arc. Odo thinks, with a mean blossoming of revenge in his heart, that he can identify King Edward's funeral scene. She was probably there. Did she feel the draught from William's foot in the door?

He lets his revenge take root, breathes deeply, gives it room to grow, then steps out from behind the pillar into the middle of the arched entrance to the gallery. He does not speak but continues to breathe, calmly, rhythmically, pulling in lungs full of air. In the full force of his presence, he waits.

Hearing the clank of spurs, the women look up. They suck in their breath sharply, as one. Nine pairs of stricken eyes fix on him, staring somewhere in the direction of his chest. He wills them to catch his eye. His fists are clenched tight, nails gouging the soft flesh of his palms. It is a good thing he is not wearing a sword.

Alix Bunyan

Alix Bunyan grew up in Canada. Her major youthful work was entitled, The Lousy Pilot. *She is currently attempting to improve on it with a novel.*

As For Me

I

You know I don't write much or anything and I am sorry about that. But I thought today I would. You remember when we moved in here and there was all that trash in the attic and I threw most of it out. Well I guess it belonged to those people who lived here before. Those baby clothes and everything and the dirty magazines in that box up there. We took it to the dump remember. Strange people I guess. Today some mail came for them and I started thinking. Did you see them because I never did. I think they moved to Florida. Anyway they got a catalogue from a kind of dirty movie mail-order place. It said Barely Legal on the front and I thought that was probably true. Ha ha ha. I can hardly believe the things they can show in pictures now and what those girls will do. Also they got a super shopper card from Safeway with some coupons. For Chicken Tonight and things. Do you like it I wonder. It was all kind of funny I thought. Maybe I will use them. Well I hope you're okay.

II

Isn't it funny but those people got a bunch more mail this week. Nothing for months since they left and now all kinds of it. Their last name was Crisp remember. The husband's name must start with R and the wife's name is Crystal if her mail is right. That sounds funny don't you think Crystal Crisp. I would have changed it if I was her.

Wasn't there somebody on Dynasty named that though. Not Dallas I don't think. Crystal something or other. I wonder if his name was something funny too. I can't think of anything though. Anyway Mrs. Crystal Crisp got some more coupons for different places and some advertising. She must have done an awful lot of shopping. And Mr. R. Crisp got some different junk and also something more interesting which was from the National Institute for the Deaf. So I wonder if he was deaf or maybe he just helped them out or something. I put the envelope back in the mailbox for the postman so he can send it on. He must know where they went I guess. Oh yes I took those coupons down to Safeway but they were sold out of Chicken Tonight and there was nothing else I wanted so there you go.

III

I thought I would write again and fill you in about the continuing story. Just like one of those soaps or something isn't it. Well you see I talked to the postman and he said there was no forwarding address for those people so that was too bad. Then this morning there was some more mail. None for me today but Mr. R. Crisp got something else. I opened up the envelope because there was no return address and well I thought it might be important you never know. I read the letter inside and it was from the bank saying that they wanted to see him about his account problems. What was interesting was that they said they had not been able to reach him by phone because it seemed to have been cut off. They wanted him to come in as soon as possible. The letter was dated July which is a long time ago now around when they moved so it must have been lost in the mail I guess. It was from somebody called Senior Accounts Manager so it must be important and I can't think what to do with it now. So this has all been a bit of a bother but interesting at least you know. As for me I'm just fine.

IV

I hope you like this postcard. I thought it would be a change. No I am not in Falaraki in case that's what you thought. I don't know for sure where that is but I think it's one of those Greek islands. There are so many aren't there. The picture looks really nice anyway with the nice white sand! It came for those people the Crisps the other day but it didn't have anything written on it except for The Crisps and then the address. I put white-out over it to write yours over the top so I hope it doesn't look too bad. I thought you would like to see the picture since it's so nice. I do wonder who sent it though. Somebody must be having a good holiday over there I guess. Wouldn't it be great to go somewhere like that. You would think they would want to tell all about it. Well if I went somewhere like that I would. You would too I bet. I know you'll like this picture anyway. I know you.

V

Well hello there today I thought I would write you a longer letter since I have the time. I already put the birds' food out and the home help came to clean yesterday so there isn't much to keep me busy today and that's nice. By the way did you know that birds like chicken. I put my leftovers out for them and they picked the bones clean! It seems pretty strange but there you go. That's nature I guess. I watched those birds all morning eating that chicken leg. The starlings scared the sparrows away poor things. Remember how one time that starling flew into the window poor thing. Well then I heard the postman coming so I went out to the mailbox and got the mail. I got something from a travel company and would you believe it it was all about that place Falaraki. They do all kinds of tours and some are not too expensive so maybe I'll think about going. It looks like a nice place all right but maybe too young for me. But then you're only as old as you feel isn't that right. The brochure shows a picture of a fellow pulling down his swim trunks in the middle of the beach so everyone could see what he had but at least the picture only shows his behind and not his doings. He has one of those tattoos on his behind and it says Romeo. So then I started to wonder whether it was a picture of Mr. Crisp since his name starts with R and maybe it's Romeo. But I can't believe many people are named that nowadays can you. There is another picture of a woman swimming in a bikini and underneath the picture it says Crystal Enjoying The Crystal Waters. That seems odd doesn't it because of Crystal Crisp and all. Well maybe that's where they moved to but I thought it was Florida. If you ever think of it will you let me know. Oh those birds are back now but there is only the bone left.

VI

I thought I would tell you about this because it is strange. When the mail came today I went out and got it and I had a letter with no return address on it. I opened it up when I was having my coffee and do you know I nearly spilled the coffee all down my front when I read it. I'll tell you what it says it's from the bank well in fact from the Senior Accounts Manager and he says he wants to see me about my account problems. It says they've been trying and trying to phone me for weeks and that the phone seems to have been disconnected so I need to come in right away. Well I tell you. I know exactly what my bank balance is because I always always write it down and the last time I was at Safeway my cheque was just fine. So I thought this was very strange not to mention rude and I checked my phone which is working just fine too. Then I started to think about it all and I remembered that letter for Mr. R. Crisp. Remember I told you about that one. Well I went and got it because I had kept it on top of the fridge since it was important and it was just exactly the same letter as the one I got only with his name on it instead of mine. So I don't know. The bank must be having some kind of problems I guess. Maybe the computers. Still it just burns me up that they can treat you this way and I am still a little upset. I will go and see that Senior Accounts Manager whoever he is and tell him. Mrs. Crisp got some more coupons today but not for anything anybody would want.

VII

I know I just wrote to you yesterday but just wait until you hear what happened now. I got the mail today and I wasn't thinking much about it but then I saw I had an envelope from the National Institute for the Deaf. Of course I opened that right up because I wondered what on earth they wanted and if it was money they weren't going to get any. Well do you know it was a letter addressed to me personally welcoming me to their help society for Deaf People and saying they could offer all kinds of resources to a deaf person like myself. I wonder how in the world they got my name and why they would think I was deaf because I certainly am not! My hearing is still just fine. I can hear those birds outside at the feeder right now I'm telling you. I guess I should write and tell them that I'm not deaf and to leave me off their list but it isn't very funny I think. I wonder if that Mr. Crisp was deaf and they have got us mixed up somehow. It's strange all right. Well I am still too upset to go to the bank today to talk to that Manager man. I'll make a cup of coffee I guess and take it easy. I really think I might go on a holiday maybe to that place I told you about. I need to get away from home I think and it's supposed to be good for you. That brochure did look nice. Did you like that postcard I sent you I wonder. Nice wasn't it.

VIII

Now I have seen it all. It was all just funny stuff before but now it is not funny. I wondered if the mail would be strange today like yesterday and I was still a little upset about being called deaf which I am not! Well I went out to the mailbox and brought the things inside to read with my coffee. There were some more coupons for Mrs. Crisp some from Safeway which could be useful and some other ones for places I never shop at. And there was another letter for me from the bank that is exactly the same as the last one which is a big nuisance. I suppose I will have to sort that out. But then I got to the bottom of the pile and there was another one of those catalogues from the dirty movie place. Of course it was for those Crisps but I looked at it I don't know why. Now I wish I hadn't done it because it was just disgusting and just filthy filthy stuff that you would not believe. I was wondering how people think up the kind of things they were doing in the pictures because they would never occur to me or anyone else with normal sense. Well there is one picture in there for a movie called Male Order Babes. I am not making that up that is the real title in there and anyway the picture they showed was of two people doing something I won't bother to tell you but the caption said Crystal Receives Her Romeo's Package Special Delivery. I am sorry to have to write that down because it is really not nice but I had to tell you because I am sure the people in the picture were the same ones in that travel brochure I told you about. I can tell you that this fellow has the same Romeo tattoo on his behind since he is showing it off to the whole world like it's something to be proud of. And Crystal is the same name again isn't it. So I wondered if it's the Crisps again which is just so strange let alone disgusting. But just you wait that's not even the worst of it. I turned the page and then there was an advertisement for another movie which is called Antiques Peepshow and it has a picture of someone with only their underpants on and it's a picture of me. I know it's me but I don't know how anyone got that kind of picture. It makes me feel sick really sick. Why would someone do something like this I just don't know. It certainly is not one bit funny if that's what they think. What kind of people are living in the world now.

IX

I'm home again now so I thought I'd tell you what has been going on today. First thing this morning I went down to try to talk to the police but nobody understood what I meant and they didn't seem to believe what I said anyway even though I showed them the disgusting picture in that catalogue which was truly embarrassing. Well then I went on to Safeway to get my groceries but even though I had all those coupons I would never use them since they came for those filthy Crisp people. When I went to pay for my chicken and gravy mix and things the checkout girl said she couldn't accept my cheque since my name is on her list of people who write bad cheques! She got very snippy and said I would have to put back the things myself if I couldn't pay cash! Well would I do that! I walked right out and said very loudly that I will never shop here again but I don't think anybody listened to me. You can imagine I felt just ashamed although I don't know why since there is nothing wrong with my cheques and if anybody should be ashamed it is Safeway. I went to the bank and tried to check my balance but would that machine work. Of course not and by then I felt a bit teary so I didn't want to wait in line to see that Manager or anybody. I went straight home and I saw the mailman had come so I got the mail even though I was wondering what on earth would be there today. Well there was a huge pile of it stuffed in the box. Coupons everywhere again but hundreds of them. And ten copies of that very same letter from the bank if you can believe it and then about thirty copies of a magazine for the deaf called The Quiet Times. And then a letter from that holiday company saying that I had not yet paid for the Falaraki trip I had taken this year and if I did not do so immediately then a collection agency would be informed. You know I have not been anywhere farther than Safeway this year. Now what if they come to start bothering me. I just do not know what to do and I am getting to the end of my rope with this. Those Crisp people are awful I am sure. I am going to go and sit down now and think about everything. I hope you write back soon and tell me your thoughts on all of these goings on. You know I would like to hear from you don't you.

X

I will just write quickly to say that it has all gotten worse. This morning my mailbox was filled with more of those dirty catalogues only a different one this time. My picture is on the front of this one as an advertisement for some kind of filthy movie called Pictures From An Exhibitionist. I guess they think that's funny but it is not. I just do not know how anybody got this kind of picture of me without my clothes on. And I am certainly not an exhibitionist of any kind. The catalogues are all over the front walk but I don't want to go out and pick them up. I don't want to go anywhere. So I'll just sit right here I guess.

XI

I guess I'll write to you again since I've got the time. I feel bad about a lot of things right now like not being able to feed the birds because there's no chicken or anything in the house. But what I feel worst about is that I feel like I can't hear. Maybe the birds are just quiet. The house is awfully quiet I must say but I'm not going out. I will tell you what I did today. I didn't want to see the mailman coming so I left the blinds down which I have been doing because I don't want anyone getting pictures of me. Then I went up into the attic. I haven't been in there for ages you know since we cleared it out when we moved in. Well this is hard to believe but the attic was just absolutely full of mail. There were stacks of coupons and piles and piles of envelopes from all kinds of places including the bank and they were all for the Crisps. Crisp Crisp Crisp all over the place. Postcards and those bad catalogues and all. Everything is just piled up to the rafters. I'm not sure what to do with it so I just left it up there. I should try to phone somebody I guess only who would believe all this. I am astonished myself. I never did anything bad to you or anyone did I. I wish you would phone or write back. It seems you have been gone for such a long time now.

Franca Davenport

Since graduating in Psychology, Franca Davenport has done many jobs. She has mainly worked as an assistant psychologist and a psychology researcher, but has also been a youth worker in Bosnia, an intern in the European Commission and worked in a Swiss watch factory. She currently pulls pints.

Time's Eyes

(extract from a novel)

This part of the novel is set in the north island of New Zealand, in a place called Petri Bay.

He knew there had to be a reason for it, or he knew he had to find a reason, and he knew he had to convince Jack of it. It was Jack that had shown him the place. The tiny sheltered beach where the sea pushed a thin needle of water into the land and where the objects arrived week after week. And it was Jack who told him to just watch and that would be enough.

That was why he kept going there. To observe and to prove to Jack there was a scientific reason for it happening. Nothing else.

★

'I know why she does it.'

Jack lay on his back and kept his eyes shut to the words. He breathed in and out, feeling the rise of his chest and the drop of it.

'Jack. I know why she does it.'

Jack's mind surfaced. It had been working, surfing in the wash between dream and being awake. It was the best place for visions, when the images came weird and clear. Before Keith had spoken, there had been a big glass door opening in his head and a wedge of white light splaying from it.

Jack opened his eyes. Keith was standing over him, his long hair making a tunnel to his face. Above him, the branches of the big pohitikara tree weaved through the sky.

'Your hair's grown,' said Jack.

'What?'

'I said your hair's grown.'

Keith took hold of a piece of it and held it in front of his eyes, then pushed it behind his ears, removing its distraction from Jack.

'I know why she does it.'

Jack breathed out heavily and sighed the word 'why?' from his lips.

The ocean is made up of strands,' said Keith. 'Big long strands that flow through it. Not strings of water molecules, but strands of glucose whose properties are specific to the water that they are in, and when they catch things in them, like plankton and stuff, they make this jelly.'

Jack looked out towards the sea. Her waves were gentle, beating a small froth into themselves as they washed the beach.

'And I was watching Eriko make this soup today,' said Keith. 'She cracked this egg and put in the white and whisked it and it made these long bobbled white strings in the soup.'

Jack looked at the tree. He was sure he could see a face nested in its branches. Calm and smiling. Then the wind blew and it went.

'The thick cold egg white hitting the hot soup,' continued Keith, then he stopped and looked down at Jack expectantly.

'But eggs always go white when you cook them.'

'That's not the point, Jack. The point is, near to the cove there could be a place where the water is colder and denser, say in a large underwater cave. And nearby to this could be a place where the water is hotter and thinner, maybe because of an outcropping of rocks.'

Jack closed his eyes. He knew it was all part of the process. He knew he just had to keep waiting.

'And when the cold viscous water meets the hot water, the strands, the sucrose strands, thicken and roll, like the egg white, whisked up by the currents, and making these invisible rope things which trail through the sea and trap the objects. Except unlike the egg they stay transparent, so we can't see them.'

Keith smiled and looked at the sea again. Further out, the early morning sun was frosting the tips of water. A gust of wind scooped over so the waves rose and hackled then simmered down again.

'OK. So what happened to the co-thingummy lines?' said Jack, raising his eyes to Keith.

Keith looked back down. 'The co-tidal lines?'

'Yes.'

'They're still involved. I'm sure they still converge here making an amphidromic point at the cove.'

Jack dropped his eyes along the length of his lying-down body. His legs were rolling outwards so that his feet were stuck out to the side and he could see his toenails thick and yellow poking into the air. He remembered the co-tidal lines. Keith had come and told him about them with the same eager look on his face, his hair a bit shorter, Jack's toenails not so long. Eriko, Keith's Japanese ex-girlfriend had been eating noodle soup, and as she chopsticked the noodles out of the bowl a big knot of them had appeared caught up with all the mushrooms and vegetables. That was when Keith had the idea about the co-tidal lines converging at Petri Bay and all the objects moving along them.

'You see,' said Keith, 'even though it's not marked on the oceanographic maps, I still think there is a small amphidromic point here where the co-tidal lines meet. Or maybe one that is not stable, but that fluctuates with the weather. And this combined with the strands causes the objects to come here.'

Jack rolled his legs together. His big toe nails met, but he couldn't feel them touching. He clacked them together. It seemed strange that parts of his body could touch without a sensation. As Keith's voice floated above him on the branches, Jack wondered how on earth he would manage to cut them.

'So the co-tidal lines link all the points where the tide is at the same stage of its cycle, so where they converge would be like an attractor. And that would mean all these strands through the water, these rope-like strands I've been talking about, would be pulled together at that point.'

Jack curled his toes so the nails disappeared and all he could see was the curves of the rounded stumps. He put them together, hinging his knees outwards, and looked at the two toeless feet together. They reminded him of toothless gums. He thought of them sucking up noodles and remembered sitting in Eriko's house, struggling with noodles, feeling like a big heap of mud in the middle of her tidy ornamented house. And he remembered the look on her face when she saw his feet as he first walked into her house with no shoes. He had thought the Japanese liked people to take their shoes off when they came into their house. He hadn't thought about the fact that he hadn't been wearing his shoes all day; that his feet were his shoes, and he couldn't take his feet off.

It hadn't surprised him when Keith and Eriko split up. Jack had liked Eriko but he had known she wasn't right for Keith. But it was all part of the process.

He hated noodles. The way they straggled in his beard. And those watery soups with nothing in them but the odd piece of green.

'I thought you weren't seeing Eriko anymore,' he said, lying his legs straight again. 'I thought she chucked you out because of the mess you made with all your stuff.'

'She did,' said Keith. 'But we still meet up. We're still friends.'

'And she still cooks for you?'

'Yes.'

'Soup?'

'Yes.'

'And noodles?'

'Yes,' said Keith, an irritation biting his reply. 'You know I think this could explain why she does it, Jack.'

Jack closed his eyes again. The pohitikara tree and Keith, gone behind a drop of skin.

It was all part of the process; Keith's theories on why the sea brought him so many things. His search for a 'real' explanation for why she did it. Jack would just have to listen. But he was heartened by the fact that the theories were becoming more ridiculous. At some point they would become too scrambled for even Keith to hold onto and then he would have to realise the truth of the matter. Not the reality but the truth. That it was him making the sea bring him things. Nothing else but Keith watching and waiting.

'So?' said Keith.

'So? What?'

'What do you think? It could explain it, couldn't it?'

Jack raised himself on his elbows. He didn't look Keith in the eye but turned and looked out to the sea. It was the colour of Keith's eyes. Pale pale blue.

'Did you go there today?'

'Yes,' said Keith.

'How long were you there for?'

'I don't know. Three, four hours.'

'Longer than before then?'

'Yeah, I suppose so.'

'And you still stay there?'

'Yeah.'

'Watching the sea?'

'Yeah.'

'So if it's these strands and these co-thingummy lines making the stuff come, why do you stay?'

'You wouldn't understand, Jack. The science of it. You wouldn't understand.'

'Right,' said Jack, 'I wouldn't understand.'

'No.'

'So why do you keep trying to make me then?'

'I don't. I just want you to see.' Keith was becoming more cross. His fingers were moving on the pad of his thumb, over and over. 'To see why it happens.'

Jack slumped down again, laid his head back and meshed his fingers over his chest.

'So what did you find there today?'

'A pack of cards,' Keith said. Jack lifted his head from his chest.

'A pack of cards with glasses and moustaches drawn on the royalty and a tiny nick in all the aces.'

'I wonder who could have owned that?'

'I don't know,' said Keith. 'Probably a communist poker player.'

'Yeah,' said Jack, grinning at the thought of it. 'And one who cheats.'

A slight smile tugged at the corner of Keith's mouth. His fingers had stopped tapping now.

Jack watched the wind making the ends of the branches draw circles in the air and then looked at Keith looking out at the sea, watching the wind rough it up and then drop again.

He reckoned it wouldn't be too long until Keith's mind softened and accepted the truth.

He looked at his toenails and wondered who he could get to cut them for him.

'I'm going to grab some breakfast,' said Keith. 'Do you want some?'

'No,' said Jack, 'I need to do some more work.'

'Alright then.'

Jack watched Keith loping towards the town. Then he closed his eyes and let his mind sink back to the semi-conscious wash where it had been before, trying to get back to that bright white door in his head. Trying to get back to work.

It was that morning that Keith met Maria.

As he walked to the Green Man Café, Keith looked up the hill at the road towards Eriko's bungalow. His ex-girlfriend. He remembered the sound of her voice when she spoke Japanese with her friend. Burbling along like a stream, suddenly grabbing the words in little mouthfuls then softening around them, making the consonants hush out. And he remembered Eriko's laugh, staccato and tiny, pecking at the sound.

The curtains were drawn, gathered at the middle by loops of material. He had always forgotten to put the loops on, leaving the curtains hanging or sometimes just completely forgetting to draw them.

Keith wasn't surprised when she threw him out. He had slowly squalored her bungalow with his stuff from the sea and she had learnt too much English. But he didn't mind, and Eriko didn't seem to mind either. She already had a new boyfriend. Keith suspected she had been seeing him while they were still going out, but it didn't bother Keith.

As he walked into the Green Man Café, the familiar smell of grease and stewed tea cosied him. Vassilos, the owner, nodded at him, acknowledging Keith's 'usual', and went into the kitchen. Keith sat down and listened to the sound of plates clattering, fried food spitting and the sound of Greek voices chatting in the kitchen, letting the words drift through his head.

But as he listened to voices, Keith could hear a new one. A girl's. He listened to it. A funny mixture of hard and soft, rattling along with the words. And she was making Vassilos laugh. Keith could hear him gruffing in the background.

Keith stared into the kitchen. A thick curtain of steam had risen from the tea urn. Then the girl walked through the steam. Carrying his breakfast, her head turned to the side, still talking to Vassilos. Keith held his breath, held it.

As she set down the mug and plate, Keith scanned her face, skimming her features then resting his eyes on her mouth. Her lips were full and a browny-red like the skin of a plum. A small dent in the middle of the lower one, with the half-cello of the top one resting on it. As she bent down they seemed to swell, blood pushing at them like a beautiful bruise. He could see the breath moving over them as she concentrated on setting down his food. He thought of them moving over those Greek words. Clacking and lilting them. She stood up, wiping her hands on her apron, and smiled. Her lips pulling tight and spreading their swell.

Keith let out his breath and stared at her, holding her in his blue eyes then smiling too. Letting the smile travel his face: lifting his cheeks and creasing his eyes. Keith had learnt about his blue eyes. The power of them. Keith sat. She stood. They smiled at each other.

'Maria!' Vassilos shouted from the kitchen.

*

'I know why she does it.'

Jack sighed and opened his eyes straightaway. There was no point in trying to be asleep. He saw his moustache flutter on his breath. He raised his eyes and looked at Keith. His hair wasn't hanging straight. He had it tied back in a ponytail.

'It's the buoyancy of the things,' Keith said.

'The buoyancy?' said Jack.

'Yeah. All the objects have, like, the same buoyancy. Their

density and surface area is such that they have a similar buoyancy so they float in the same way. You see Maria had these olives and they were mixed up with all these other things like bits of pepper, bits of celery, garlic. All swimming about in this oil. But some of the olives sunk and some of them floated. And some of the peppers sunk and some floated.'

Jack dropped his eyes and grunted. He still hadn't cut his toenails. They were beginning to curl, yellow and ridged as if he had been smoking with them, and bending up from the nail-bed. He wished he could smoke with them, but his bones were too cranky for that now.

'It didn't matter if they were different,' continued Keith. 'There was some other quality that made them all float and move in the same way.'

'So you're still seeing Maria then?'

'If you mean going out,' said Keith, 'no.'

'Oh,' said Jack.

'She finished it. Said I wasn't seeing her enough and that we never talked.'

'But you still see her?'

'Yeah. I still see her.'

Keith looked up at the sea. It was almost flat. He remembered sitting in Maria's kitchen listening to her and her flatmates talk. Their words bouncing in the air. Maria holding her palm out flat like she was holding a plate, her rich mouth pursing and unpursing above it. He had liked listening to the rhythm of their talk. Enjoying the way the conversation could whip itself up into a frenzy and then quieten down again, without him ever knowing why. Behind it, the sound of the sea constantly strumming the beach.

Maria's house had been right on the beach.

A small wind picked up and started pinching the water's surface. The sun making silver specks on the waves. Keith looked back down to Jack.

'But I reckon it's to do with the texture of the objects as well. That the frictional force the objects provide against the orbit of the water molecules on the waves combines with the buoyancy so they all get carried in the same way, moved in the identical way with the currents. And come here.'

'Does she still live in that house with those two other Greek girls?'

'No,' said Keith. 'She's moved in with her new boyfriend.'

'Oh,' said Jack.

'He's a nice guy,' said Keith. 'Talks a bit much, but nice. I'm going round there for a meal next week. She wanted to know if you could come.'

Jack remembered Maria's house, sitting with Keith amongst the chatter and the smell of good oily food. Watching Maria sit herself next to Keith, look at him and ask him if he was bored and then watching Keith shake his head and smile and sit back so the conversation fell around him.

Jack had felt comfortable in that house. More comfortable than in Eriko's. And he had enjoyed teaching English to Maria, hearing his own words and his own pronunciation repeated back to him tinged with her accent. He had wondered if Maria would cut his toenails for him, but her nails were manicured and polished. She hadn't been quite right for Keith either.

'Yeah. I'd like that,' said Jack. 'It's nice you two still see each other.'

Jack looked back up to Keith. 'Do you still see Eriko?'

'Yeah, sometimes,' said Keith. 'She's going back to Japan.'

Jack nodded, remembering Eriko's noodles. He had liked Maria's food. The cheese blistered slabs of moussaka ruffled with pasta. Battered rings of chewy squid. But he hated olives. Stupid slippery things with stones in. He thought about olives and longed for a nice chunked stew.

'I'm going to do some research,' said Keith. 'Work out the buoyancies and the frictions the objects might have. See if they are the same or similar. And then look into the patterns of the surface currents.'

'So you reckon it's the weight of these things that brings them here?'

'The buoyancy, Jack. It's the buoyancy combined with the texture.'

Jack knocked his feet together. 'And what about the co-thingummy lines?'

'Yeah, well. I still reckon the tides have something to do with it.

They've got to.'

'And the strands?'

'Them too. I think they could link in with the viscosity of the water.'

Keith could feel the band from around his hair slipping. He reached behind him and pulled it out, gathering his hair together and lifting his thumbs underneath it and passing it from hand to hand, thinking about the objects that had arrived that month. An old sheepskin rug, bobbing like a sea-kill run over by a ferry, dashed with wine stains and flecked with dog hairs. A glove with the tops of one of the fingers chewed off. A deflated inflatable doll, her face surprised and watery as she lapped up onto shore. They had to be connected somehow.

'And how long do you stay there now?' said Jack.

'I don't know, five or six hours.'

'And you watch all the time?'

'Yeah.'

'The sea?'

'Yeah.'

Jack stroked the end of his beard, and saw Keith pulling out a piece of hair from his ponytail and rubbing it between his fingers. 'And what do you think about when you watch?'

'I don't know. Stuff. I can't really remember.'

'Anything?'

'Yeah. Something.'

'What does it feel like?'

Keith looked out onto the sea. 'What do you mean?' he said.

Keith knew what Jack meant. The way his mind felt as if it had been in another place. The way it seemed as if a system was forming in his head. The sense of a structure lowering itself, formalising the method by which he was doing things, by how he watched the sea.

'When you watch? What does it feel like?'

'I don't know,' said Keith, 'I can't explain it.'

'Good,' said Jack.

'What do you mean good?' said Keith.

'Just good,' said Jack. 'I can't explain it, but good.'

Keith looked up and grabbed one of the pohitikara branches, pulling it down then letting go of it so it whipped into the air. 'I'm going for some breakfast. Do you want some?'

Jack shook his head. 'I've got work to do.'

Jack watched Keith walk into town and looked back to his toenails. He really needed to cut them. He was going to trip over them soon.

It was that morning he met Diedre.

Jack met her first.

Jake Elliot

Jake was born in Cornwall in 1974. He studied for his first degree at Manchester Metropolitan University. He currently lives in Norwich.

Travel Sickness

When he woke up she was still asleep. He watched her as she lay curled in dreams that caused her back to twitch and shift, then he turned and slipped quietly out of the bed. As he did so his hand caught the ashtray on the bedside table and it upended; grey waste began a fluttering descent to the floor. He swore silently, smeared the side of his hand against the duvet, and padded softly out of the room.

Having showered, he sat in the kitchen with a cup of coffee and a cigarette, reading through the mail that had been delivered. He dropped two dull-coloured bills to one side, unopened, and scowled slightly at the mis-spelling on the next envelope: 'Mr. P. de Frieze.'

He tapped the end of his cigarette neatly into an ashtray and slit the letter open with the bread knife, then sat staring at the letter for a while after he had finished reading it until his cigarette demanded attention. As he was stabbing it into the ashtray, Gabrielle walked into the room. She crossed over to him, bent to kiss his cheek, and then carried on towards the draining board to excavate a mug. A droplet of water from her freshly washed hair sat on his temple. He drew his thumbnail down through it.

'I have to go away.'

Gabrielle clicked the kettle on then turned to rest against the work surface.

'What is it?'

He held the letter up.

'Some of the research results aren't right—we'll have to rearrange some parts of the sequence. I'll have to be there.'

Gabrielle returned to the table with her coffee and sat down.

'When are you going?'

'Tomorrow, I guess. I'll ring later to sort it out.'

She sipped at her coffee and reached for the packet of cigarettes which lay on the table with her other hand.

They sat in silence for a moment, watching their cigarette trails make a lovers' dance.

'What were you dreaming about?' he asked eventually, flicking at the ashtray and disengaging the trails of smoke.

As he spoke he remembered a fragment of his own dream, a beautiful girl with a damaged face.

She exhaled a tight tumble of smoke. 'I don't think I was,' she said, sounding unsure.

De Friese sat in the study, staring impassively out of the window at the empty green fields stretching into the distance. A few bars of pale sunlight cut across the dark wood of the desk. He interrupted the pattern to flick at an ashtray and watched as part of his smoke-trail was turned opaque by the light.

Gabrielle appeared in the doorway. 'Do you want me to drive you to the station?' she asked.

'Thanks,' he nodded. He swivelled his chair around to face her fully. 'I'll be gone longer than I thought,' he said, his voice deepening into a resigned sigh. 'Some of this stuff's invalid so we'll have to rerun it.'

Gabrielle walked slowly across to the desk and looked down at the sheaf of papers headed 'Viral Statistics.' Beside them was the letter—a confused jumble of acronyms and percentage values covered most of the page.

'How long?' she asked.

'Three, four days. Something like that.'

She didn't respond, except to raise a hand to his head and twitch her fingers through his hair.

'At least it gets me away from here,' he said suddenly.

The fingers stilled instantly.

'Sorry, I didn't . . .' he inclined his head to look up at her, '. . . that came out wrong.'

'It's okay,' she murmured. 'I know what you meant.'

She dropped her hand and when he turned she had left the room. He stared at the doorway, as if confirming an absence, then turned back to the desk.

They lay together in a twist of sheets, engaged in disconnected sex. He was vaguely aware that she had retreated deep beneath the surface that he was in contact with, leaving a mannequin presence. She acknowledged only a scend of energy above her, diverted from somewhere else and inchoate in its new form. They climaxed simultaneously and perfunctorily; as they rolled apart he seemed to fade from her, dissipating into the gloom. She turned her head away and the image of a flower appeared in her thoughts like a slide deposited into a projector. It opened in fast-motion, the straining and swelling accompanied by a crescendo of screaming that jarred her with the recognition of it as her morning dream. The flower opened to reveal a scarious darkness.

It was early morning when they drove from the cottage. The clear sky cast a warm, lacy sunlight over them and he watched insects scutter around the car as it bounced down the rudimentary lane towards the village. They turned a corner and passed by a row of trees heavy with blossom. A slight breeze sent a scattering of pale confetti over the car. Despite the brightness he felt cold. He clicked open the briefcase on his lap and began rooting through the documents inside.

'Everything there?' asked Gabrielle.

'I guess so.'

'If you've forgotten anything I'm sure you'll be alright—you must have memorised it all thoroughly by now.'

He started to smile but realised she was speaking without a trace of humour, her gaze directed on the track in front of them. In the brightness, Gabrielle was contained in a little cocoon of shadow that conspired with her dark clothes and black hair to highlight her pale face to a translucent marble. Mask-like, he thought involuntarily.

As they sat in silence they both heard a shout and then a squeal of merriment. De Friese turned in his seat, hooking the belt forward to free him, and Gabrielle glanced in the mirror. Behind them a child on a bicycle shot across the road and disappeared into a narrow footpath concealed by the hedge. The child was quickly followed by another, younger, child who was pedalling in furious pursuit.

'Are they still on holiday?' wondered De Friese out loud.

Gabrielle remained silent and he thought he momentarily saw her knuckles whiten slightly against the wheel.

When they reached the station the day was warm as well as sunny. He shifted a travel bag onto his shoulder and stooped to pick up his briefcase. Gabrielle closed the boot of the car and brushed her hair back with her hand.

'Goodbye then.'

'Goodbye.'

They kissed stiffly like marionettes mindful of getting their strings entangled, and she clasped the car keys to her stomach as she backed around to the driver's side.

'Call when you get there,' she said.

He nodded and then headed towards the station entrance as the car pulled away. An oblong of light that clung to its roof hovered in the corner of his vision until he disappeared through the doorway.

As he walked across the foyer to the platform a child in a pushchair broke off its smeared assault on a chocolate egg to stare at him. He gazed back at the child and then looked up at the mother who was collecting her tickets from the booth—she registered him only briefly, in between counting change and tucking the tickets into a purse, and when he looked back down to the pushchair, the child was preoccupied with drilling his tongue into the side of the egg. De Friese realised he hadn't seen any person other than Gabrielle for eight days.

Overhead, the arrivals and departures screen flickered and a new line appeared, announcing his platform number.

The cottage sat ticking to itself quietly. Gabrielle stood in the hallway, listening to the silence and reminding herself that it was emptier than usual. She hung her jacket on a hook, paused, transferred it to the adjacent hook, then walked through to the kitchen. Two mugs rested on the table next to a loaded ashtray. She stared contemplatively at their breakfast and then slumped onto one of the seats. The screech of the chair legs over the floor sounded enormous. She lowered her head to the table top, enjoying the coolness of the wood against her skin, and began dancing her fingers over the surface, creating thin streamers of shadow that flowed to the edge and spilled over. Once again the building emitted a few short clicks—the thermostat sounding, pipes responding—and Gabrielle thought of an animal nestling itself in the sun. Then she realised the thought was caused by her own quickened heartbeat.

By midday the morning chill had dissipated and light as thick as cream filled the cottage. Gabrielle sat at the desk in the study. In front of her was a folder filled with papers and she idly flipped through a thin bound volume—pausing to look at a set of fuzzily printed images that resembled constellations but were labelled as a rare bacterium—before returning it to the folder and pushing it to one side. When she pulled open one of the drawers a photograph of a diseased mouth yawned at her. She closed the drawer with a bang, then rested her head in her hand and stared out of the window: a vista of green tilted into the horizon under a pure-blue sky. All still, all silent. The vacancy left her uncomfortable in a way that she couldn't articulate. The whole countryside developed a tensile quality. When the tiny insect of a plane flowed into her view, leaving a furrow in the emptiness, she felt the sensation of wrongness weaken. Scar-tissue, she thought suddenly, and then realised this was not the sort of connection she would make. She frowned in irritation at the alien idea. In front of her the words 'Virus: Notes,' scrawled on the cover of the folder, caught her eye.

The telephone burst into life, filling the kitchen and echoing along the hallway. It shrilled eight times before the answerphone clicked on.

De Friese listened to his voice say sorry we're not here to take your call please try later or leave a message after the tone. He pressed the receiver closer to his ear and put his other hand to the opposite side of his head, blocking out the babel of the station.

'Gabrielle? Are you there?' he said. His voice was echoey and nestled within the sounds of bustling crowds. Nearby, somebody laughed. 'I'm just calling to let you know I've got here. I'm on my way to the hotel now so I'll call you a bit later. Oh, and my phone's packed up. Bye. Love you.'

He said the last words with the phone closer to his mouth, both instinctively and because a tannoy announcement was booming across the concourse. He hung up and quickly turned to pick up his baggage as a sullen teenager, chattering bubblegum between his teeth, edged forward to take his place. As he hurried away into the crowd, De Friese's eyes flicked across the 'Terminal 99' slogan on the youth's T-shirt.

In the kitchen, the green light on the answerphone blinked insistently. Gabrielle stood resting in the doorway, watching it impassively, pulling gently on a fingernail with her teeth.

The phone rang again. The answerphone clicked on. 'Hi, Gabrielle, it's me. It's just gone six o'clock. Can you call me? I'm in room 201. Okay. Bye. Speak to you soon.'

Gabrielle woke suddenly, rolled over and looked at her watch. She slid to the side of the bed and sat up. Sleep still clung to her thoughts and muscles. She yawned and stretched—as she tilted her head upwards and arched her back, she placed her hand behind her and felt the residue of warmth her body had left impressed on the bed. The light was thinner now, heralding a mellow spring evening. As she reached for a cigarette her gaze was caught by a tiny dappling across the carpet. She turned to see a brightly-patterned moth flitting across the inside of the window. It suddenly stopped, resting on the pane and twitching its wings slowly. Gabrielle lit her cigarette and shifted gently onto her knees to look at it. The light silhouetted the body under the wings and she noticed the patterning wasn't symmetrical. She trickled a line of smoke from one side of her mouth and lent closer to the window. The moth took off, hurling itself in random paths against the glass as if trying to escape the half-life of beauty. She drew on her cigarette again and then reached around to locate an ashtray.

As the evening closed, Gabrielle sat in the kitchen, a plate containing a half-eaten sandwich forgotten beside her elbow and a sheet of paper in front of her. She gnawed absent-mindedly on a pen as she stared at the words 'Dear Pete' at the top of the page. After a few minutes of indecision she began to write more, gaining speed as she progressed until she had covered most of the page. Finally she stabbed a full stop into the paper, feeling it jolt against the table. She put the pen down and stretched her hand towards her cigarettes. As she lit it she noticed her hand was shaking. She stared at the paper for a long time as if reading something new to her: eventually a finger of ash collapsed from her cigarette over the table. She inhaled, then picked up the paper and snapped open her lighter, touching the flame to the corner. She moved the paper in an arc, describing a slow fan, as it curled, blackened and broke up.

'Gabrielle, it's me again. Where are you? I'm calling at half past seven. I need you to get me the account number for my phone. Call me? Love you.'

The sound of the boot closing elicited a flurry of birdcall from a nearby hedgerow. Small things rustled and darted out in random trajectories across the ground. Gabrielle walked to the front of the car and climbed in. She turned to look at the cottage through the back window. The sun was slowly dipping into the horizon far behind and a ghost moon was just beginning to appear. As she edged the vehicle into the lane she realised the moon was moving with her, hovering just in the edge of her field of sight through the window. She smiled slightly and clicked on the radio. A bell rang nearby. She stopped at the mouth of the driveway as a kid raced along the lane on his bicycle—he slowed as he rounded the corner to look at her but then lowered his head and accelerated to regain his lead in some nominal contest.

Gabrielle turned into the lane and breathed heavily—feeling herself somewhere between calmness and enervation. She pressed in the cigarette lighter and the car dipped through a pothole. The jolting set off spores of energy within her. She began to rummage under the map spread out on the seat beside her for her cigarettes as the car swung into the avenue of blossom and the kid pedalled along his return journey.

'How long?'

'It'll be at least an hour, sir.'

'An *hour*?'

'All our cars are busy.'

De Friese put down the payphone without bothering to respond, exhaled a steady breath before picking up his bag and walking out of the station. A few cars were in the small car park in front of the entrance and he scanned them vainly, squinting against the sun which dazzled over windscreens and bonnets. He paused to search through his coat pockets until he found a few coins. He looked at a twenty pence piece for a few moments then closed his fist over it and returned it to his pocket. Sighing, he picked up his travel bag, slung it over his shoulder and crossed the street to a bus stop.

Inside it was cooler and offered some shade. He rested his bag against the side and started to decipher the timetable, although he had to squint and blink furiously as his eyes were sensitive from the sunlight. Once he had cross-referenced the relevant lines of minuscule print, he looked at his watch, tracked his finger again along an axis obscured by a crack in the plastic covering, and scowled. He swore silently. Picking up his travel bag he left the shelter and walked away along the deserted street, his feet kicking through the mulch edging the road.

In the lane the trees rustled delicately in a dry chorus. More blossom fell, obscuring the tyre marks, before it tumbled along, coming to rest against the small huddled shape on the ground and tangling in the bent spokes of the bicycle wheel.

Oliver Emanuel

Oliver Emanuel was born in 1980 in Kent. He has studied at the University of Leeds and at the University of East Anglia. His short story Let's Skip *was published by Piccadilly Press (1999) and his play* Gemini *was nominated for a Scotsman's Fringe First Award (2001) at the Edinburgh Fringe Festival.*

The Lost

(extract from a novel)

3rd SEPTEMBER

At last, I am alone.

And though before I might have felt this to be the end of the story, I realise now it must be the beginning. I left everything behind—bedclothes shrugged back against the wall, the naked wardrobe open, a river of torn photographs leading to the door, the single lily in the crystal vase by the window—everything still warm and in its place. I left no note behind. No explanation.

And now I stand at the window of my new room as night falls. The City looks black and jagged. This night marks my new beginning without Lilah. A cigarette dangles between my lips, but I haven't the energy to inhale. It's cold and I feel numb. Behind me there are only shadows, the broken outline of my paint-box and my unopened suitcase on the bed.

I can see my reflection in the dull rectangle of the windowpane. My face is almost invisible though my eyes shine in the light of the cigarette. It's a face without a name in this place. I could call myself Henry, if I liked. Or Gabriel. In better times I might've laughed at this bizarre anonymity, though I'd never claim my face was unique. Thousands have my face. In fact there's a picture of my great-great-

great-great-great grandfather in the *Encyclopaedia Britannica.* He has the same three worry-lines across the forehead, the same blackish blue eyes. But here, mine is a stranger's face without a definite jawline or history.

Perhaps I should burn my name on the wall with my cigarette, claim my piece of earth as it were. Or maybe I should just shut up and sleep. But then I can never sleep while this ache is spinning through my guts. Always this ache, this ache. This ache I know well, so well I'd almost call it a friend.

I breathe out and blow a circle of mist onto the glass. It's cold outside and my breath is warm. Then I begin to draw the outline of a face with my thumb.

I see it is Lilah's face.

Her face like it is in the only photograph that I was too afraid to destroy but left behind on our hall table: pale grin of thin lips caught unawares, small nose, high forehead, blue eyes without lines glancing left, red hair scattered and turned behind right ear, head tilted and resting on a shoulder of an unseen male. This outline is just an image, flat, without the shades of feeling or the insight of a true portrait like I used to be able to do: a stolen moment in time whose laughter and breath are long gone.

Lilah.

Dear Departed Delilah. Lilah of the Lilies. Delilah No More.

Now I rub in the background to let the shadows through the glass. I'll imagine the silhouette of the house opposite will dance itself into a frenzy of white, white light as the morning comes. But where before I was only a shoulder—she, shadows, not me—now, drawn out across the glass and the night, the emerging portrait dusted with time and cigarette smoke and other thoughts which press against the texture of its surface, I will paint myself in full.

There's just enough room on the window.

I sketch the outline of a man my own height. The man, just as I was myself that time, her head against my shoulder while the camera flashed and flattened her smile. All that is missing is the line on the face that this ache has since created. In this ghostly face the skin is clear and without guilt.

Lost In Lilah's Light.

No, I rub in the lines tight into his cheek—like the tattoo of a dead lover—it almost scrubs out his chest. I'll breathe again and let it lurk beneath the fog. Perhaps, instead, I'll draw in a smile.

His face is now my face. He has my smile. Yes. There.

From here I can see the edge of the City and the profane glow of the clouds as they spin northwards. My cigarette has almost burnt itself out. I heard the Guard at the train-station call it 'the City,' so that's what I'll call it. The night is black and moonless and I can barely make out its features; the constellation of streetlamps is alien to me, illuminating nothing but the jagged outline of the forest in the distance. Eyeless faces appear to dance in the shadows and thin grains of rain splatter the glass. The portrait on the window has vanished. The only thing I can make out clearly is the outline of the ruined cathedral, lit from below, that looks like a diseased angel against the skyline. Its silent clock reads a quarter to eight.

Here there is no history.

Here there are no faces with condolences congealing on their lips. I've got no name and no one knows my face. And I will be known as Bill. Or Geoffrey.

Here I'm almost invisible.

Here I might be able to forget that I was ever happy, that the person who made me happy is no longer with me, and is dead. I will forget. I will forget.

In this new city, in this new street, in this new room, in these new clothes, in this new night, I'm one of the shadows.

The cigarette's gone out and I can't see my face anymore.

At last, I am alone.

10th SEPTEMBER

I haven't spoken in over a week. Not a word. My tongue is getting flaccid and yellow and I often wake to find huge pools of saliva nestling in the palm of my upturned hand. This solitude has forced a search for some kind of interaction. I've hummed in the mirror. I've tried writing questions (small talk, weather, etc.) on the face of a plate to find later when I'm eating. Nothing quite works. At these times I examine myself in the hope of some unknown personal development.

Age: 28

Height:	6'2"
Hair:	black with flecks of white above the ears
Eyes:	blackish blue
Ears:	2
Nose:	1 (ample)
Mouth:	wide
Shoulders:	feminine and sloping
Arms:	spindly
Chest:	36'
Gender:	male
Posterior:	inferior
Legs:	longish
Feet:	size 11

Yesterday I discovered to my disgust that my toenails are growing faster than is usual. In fact, my toenails now measure an entire inch from the skin. They've the appearance of monkey-toes or the claws of feral dogs, hooked and rusty at the end. I can barely put on my shoes. Also, my beard is thickening, but apparently only beneath the jaw, not on the face itself.

Often I find myself borne along on streams of daydreaming in different colours—blues flowing into reds bursting through yellows and back into blues again—which arc in wide circles round and round and on top of one another until I feel pain and I stop and I look down and I notice that my thumb has burned a hole in my palm the shape of a pear. And I've discovered two types of daydreaming: the first, when I've got my eyes open and an object shivers into life (table into bridge, cigarette into fog across the headlights, etc.); the second, when my eyes are closed and faces visit. As I break free from these reveries, I have to go over to the sink and bathe my hand in cold water.

Mildly amusing is the crack above my bed in the shape of a breast but I sleep on my front and most of the time I forget its existence.

14th SEPTEMBER

There are two other people who live in this building, both ancients. I discovered them a few days ago. They're called Mrs Spinks and Mr Ridell.

Of Mrs Spinks (same floor, front apartment) I know almost nothing, except that she must be a widow and that she appears to have no breasts. Yet, I think, despite this deformity she somehow manages to be beautiful. Beautiful in the way an oak tree broken by lightening is beautiful: her cheeks are rivered with thousands of thin lines which give her a look of pretty wisdom. Sometimes I catch her standing in the corridor with the light off, as I make my way to the toilet, fingering the old and tarnished pendant that hangs upon her chest. She smells of soap. She has her eyes closed and her elderly body sways, her knuckles white from the strain of the repetitive motion of her hand. When I turn the light on, she opens her eyes and looks at me with surprise:

—Hello, my love, she says quietly in her sing-song voice, before turning away and disappearing behind her door. Every time: Hello, my love.

Mr Ridell (upstairs beyond the bathroom) on the other hand is more obviously curious. He leaves his door open all day and makes tea whenever I want. Sometimes, I think he listens out for me because whenever I go into his room there is always a cup of tea waiting for me. He is a gruff, avuncular sort with hands the size of dock leaves. The walls of his room are covered with prints of Eighteenth Century dandies (coffee-house cartoons where the wench's jugs are as big as the poet's head), and though seemingly incongruous to his character, Mr Ridell delights in sitting with his legs crossed—just as the figures in the prints do—with his big left hand bent and limp in the air before him. He has his armchair pulled to the window from where he is able to watch passers-by, and scoff at their follies. For some reason, he seems to have a particular anger against the female of the species. But in spite of his obvious pessimism he is perfectly talkative.

Today, for example, he told me he could read palms. I nodded and showed mild surprise, which I felt would cover up the feelings of dread that began instantly to boil inside me. He said he would read mine, if I liked. I said he was very kind but that he really shouldn't bother. He said that he would like to. I said perhaps it would be better another time. He said, no, the present is the hardest thing to predict and that now would be the perfect time. So I pulled my seat to his armchair and held out my left hand. He shook his head. He said that the left was the inherited hand—the hand of my ancestors—and that it would tell me nothing I did not already know. He said it must be the right hand. So I lifted my right hand for him to examine. Then he went silent for a while, spending a considerable time running his fingers across my palm and occasionally lifting it up to the light for, what I imagined, must have been a clearer view of my destiny. After a while he began to speak.

—You have a spade hand.

—Right, I said, and what does that mean?

—A worker's hand.

—All right.

He lifted my hand to my face and pointed to a line that ran horizontally across the top of the palm: —This is your lifeline and it shows that you have a long life ahead of you.

For a moment I contemplated the misery that this news implied.

—And this, he continued by pointing to another line, is a broken marriage line.

—And what does that mean?

—It means that you will not find love particularly easy.

I nodded.

—But then . . ., he began.

—What?

—Odd. Very odd.

Mr Ridell dropped my hand and moved over to the bookcase in the corner by his bed, pulling out a book and quickly flipping through its pages.

—What are you looking for?

—Amo Amas Amat.

—What is it? What have you found?

He turned to face me with a little grin across his twig-thin lips, his eyebrows raised in mild bemusement above the pages of the book.

—You've no heart, he said. No heart. Nothing. No heart line at all. I've looked all over. It's not usual. I've never seen anything like it. Sometimes there are breaks. Other times there are rings missing, things like that. But you . . . you've no heart. Fascinating.

Mr Ridell turned back to his book, muttering the names of the planets under his breath. He was away with the angels. Then, just for a second, he glanced up and let his eyes fix upon an invisible point on the wall, before quickly returning to the page and the riddle that flicked through his mind. I let myself out. The man was quite obviously mad. Mrs Spinks was in the corridor again as I descended the stairs, but I decided to leave the light off, and for once she didn't seem to notice as I passed her and went into my room.

They're both a mystery to me.

17th SEPTEMBER

Somehow, it is the little details that make me think of Lilah. In a walk, in a wave of the hand. In a shake of the head of a schoolgirl as she pretends to smoke at the corner of the playground. Such small things. And there are my own habits, habits I'd taken, but forgotten belonged to her. Take washing, for example. When I first met her I hardly ever took a bath—I was a lazyeyed twenty—and I remember that at the time I was vaguely proud of the fact. My smell was a man's smell, I thought. Lilah used to laugh and called it 'my biological egoism.' But in minutes of our first meeting (on the steps of the library with a huge art book under my arm—me leaving, she entering, a now-forgotten mutual friend in the middle—the sky burning red as the autumn dusk set in), she was grandly asserting:

—I can't be friends with anyone that does not take a bath at least once a day.

And so everyday from that time I've taken a bath or shower and brushed my teeth in the morning and before sleep at night. She made me clean. And then there was the buying of politically correct fruit, the setting of the alarm clock to wake me exactly at the hour of my birth (8 o'clock, I was told), and the picking of pennies from the street to bring me luck with my painting. I suppose I thought that by moving away and starting in a new city I could rid myself of her habits, of her.

But this morning, as I was pulling hair from between the metal teeth of my hairbrush, I almost expected her to reach round the mirror and hold out her hand and inspect it to make sure I hadn't bent the ends. I could almost hear her voice:

—Careful. Careful.

19th SEPTEMBER

To understand chance is to comprehend your place in the world. To believe in fate is to overestimate the power of the tides.

But then why do I dream only of seagulls?

And why do I wake feeling seasick?

20th SEPTEMBER

Dawn.

I stand on the walkway that arcs over the houses like a black scar across the horizon, and leads into the City. The vehicles are beginning to collect and move along the roads like tired insects, wasps and hatch-backed beetles, like flies—round the roundabout then straight then quickly back then half left and then gone behind the cathedral—their millioneyes blind to everything. It's cold and I blow on my hands to keep them from turning blue.

A middle-aged man with a cravat and a walking stick climbs the steps to my right. I follow the line of yellowing oak trees rooted in black concrete with my eye. The sun is white and low above the forest beyond the tower blocks, and the wind races along the walkway and through my legs and up my shirt. It's cold but the sun is beginning to warm my face. The middle-aged man pauses for breath beside me, resting his hands on his corduroys. He looks up at me and then out towards the scene below.

—Not like it used to be, he says, pointing to the road with his stick.

—No?

—Used to be the railway. To the capital.

—I didn't know.

—My mother used to take me there. To the station. She used to take me for tea in the buffet.

We both look left as a fish truck, stinking of the rotten sea, slowly wends and rumbles its way across the junction and turns off in the direction of the coast. I see a woman with high breasts and a towel round her waist swaying to unheard music behind a first floor window of an apartment block.

—And before that, of course, it was a bridle path.

—I see.

—Bit of a local historian, myself, he says with a smile. Like to know where I come from.

—It's very interesting, I say, as I light a cigarette and turn my head away.

The light is crystalline, white, and I can see the heavy city dew as it runs down the twisting gutters and over the feet of the gradually increasing number of men and women who disappear underground to catch the early train. I lift the cigarette to my mouth and take a long drag. My hands appear blue in the emerging light.

—And before, all this was bog.

—All of it? I ask.

—As far as you can see. Henry VII built the City upon that very bog.

—Interesting.

—To defend against the Dutch, you see?

—Yes, I say.

A fat black pigeon, as fat as a rat, strolls along the rail near the middle-aged man's left hand and he shoos it away with his stick. The effort sends him into a fit of coughing, and the pigeon flaps down to the pavement below to peck upon a spider, or a dead cigarette. I blow a cloud of smoke into the air and watch it feather out into the wind. I turn to the man as his coughing subsides.

—And was it always bog?

—No, no. Before the station, the bridle path, and before the bog, it was all forest.

—Oh. Yes.

—As far as you can see. Some of the trees in the forest are over a thousand years old.

—Incredible, I say, and mean it.

The middle-aged man straightens his cravat and points his stick at my cigarette. The sun breaks above the trees and shafts of white light cut across his face. He shakes his head with a grin and clicks his tongue, before turning away and making his way past me towards the City. I hear the church bell—that is really a recording in a supermarket—strike far off. The man turns just before he reaches the steps and rests the head of his stick on his temple. The City lights up all around us.

—Of course when it was forest we were monkeys, he says. We were just monkeys. So we couldn't appreciate the beauty of it, I suppose.

Guy Essex

Guy Essex was born in Yorkshire in 1970. He has taught English in the UK and in the United States and currently lives in Cornwall.

Spoons

Letting the smoke glide out of her mouth and over her top lip, she inhales through her nostrils, holds, and releases. The window is open and the smoke sways where it meets the breeze. She watches the cloud gather, waver then wreathe to disappear behind the half-drawn curtains of her room. Her room is in twilight but outside the day lingers. Smoking, now, feels good to her, as if it is the only thing left to do. In two hours her mother will return, but until then she lies unconcerned. The cigarette tastes good. She enjoys the feel of the butt between her fingers and on her lips, the smoke rolling over her top lip to her nose and down to the pinch in her lungs, the pause, and exhalation over her tongue. She knows she has years to go before even thinking of quitting. The smell will have gone before her mother's return. After she taps then squeezes the tip into the ashtray, she leans over his sleeping form to place the ashtray on the bedside table, next to the spent condom. She slides back down her bed and into his warmth.

He lies on his side in the place she had lain forever, with his back towards her and his knees raised. She matches her body to his and drapes an arm around his waist. Her other arm stretches up under the pillow and she rests her head upon it and the pillow. It is not comfortable but she does not know what else she can do. The muscles and coarse hair of his thighs feels good against the top of hers. Her body feels warm and strong next to his and it is good to have made him sleep; he is satisfied. No more doubt. She remains a little sensitive, as if bruised, but knows it is normal and that she will grow used to it. She still feels him there by his absence. She feels his breathing; his back rising and falling against her breasts; and she loves the slowness of it. She kisses his neck and feels the measured intake, slight pause, the deflation; and over again; automatic, thoughtless, and she loves him for it. He does not snore, she is glad of that, only a barely audible intake and exhalation from his nose. His lullaby. She wonders if she snores. How can she know? The thought makes her smile and want to ask him.

'You asleep?' she whispers, and kisses the back of his neck again. He does not answer and she thinks it is a stupid question.

'You awake?' She is uncomfortable at the sound of her own voice. Spoken, the words seemed to be an intrusion; it is a time for whispers. Spoken or whispered, he does not respond but continues to breathe in the measured rhythm she loves. She touches, with her fingers and the flat of her palm, the hair above and below the bevelled surround of his navel, and feels his backside against her stomach and caresses his neck with her lips. He does not stir. In the greyness she makes out the curve of his shoulder blade, and kisses it. She examines the freckles and moles on the nape of his neck and how his hair tapers to a fine down. With her eyes closed, she runs her free hand over his upper arm, feeling the contours of it, across the round of his shoulder and back to the flat of the blade. She feels the oil of his skin, the smoothness of it and smells his odour. She likes his smell. It is a surprise to her, but one she knew when she first smelt him naked and close. She had smelt something like it before on her father when he came in from the garden or when, as a child, she had shared her parents' bed. She thinks of something else. She wants to sleep, but her other arm deadens beneath the pillow.

The bickering of a blackbird shatters the stillness of the fading day. From the open window the cold breeze chills her naked back. She lifts herself from him, first taking her weight on her deadened arm then, as she feels the tingle of pins and needles, quickly uses her other arm to grasp the sill and hold herself up. She reaches over, pulls the window to, softens the blackbirds' squabble and brings a near silence to the room with a drop of the latch. With her right arm still tingling, she lies on her back next to him, pulls the duvet over both their bodies, and up to her chin. When she turns once more to match his sleeping form, she keeps her right arm out from under the pillow. With the warmth of their bodies comes the smell of their sex. In the darkness under the cover she smells him and herself as one, musty and saline and fresh; it reminds her of the ocean, but a synthetic odour mingles with theirs, cloying it. Her own odour is new to her, and unsettling. She sometimes wonders if others or even her mother can smell it on her. Now she carries a deodorant in her bag for this. Lifting her head out from the darkness she smells her duvet; its scent is that of a life she feels is past. It is the scent of her newly washed clothes, of towels in the airing cupboard, of fresh sheets stretched tight over her single mattress. Her mother's choice of powder and conditioner is the most familiar thing in the world to her and it too is tainted now, not by her odour or his odour, or even by the trace of tobacco, but by the latex smell of the condom on the bedside table.

She decides to go on the pill as soon as possible and smiles because he will love her for it. Then she won't have to smell them or worry about them splitting or coming off or leaking. She will make an appointment.

It is impossible for her to lie pressed against him with her right arm dangling out or deadened under the pillow for any time without becoming uncomfortable. She wants to slide her right arm under his arm, then she might match his shape and wrap both arms around him, but she cannot. Not without waking him. What she really wants is for her to be sleeping where he is and for him to be where she is and to engulf her in his warm body, and then she would press into him and feel him against her in her sleep. She gives up trying to match their shapes, turns, props herself up on her pillow and sits up, listening to him.

As he breathes beside her, she sees the shapes in the blue-grey half-light of her room. Opposite her, a desk with the lamp and the jar full of pens, needs organising. Papers, scribbled, doodled and creased, lie strewn across it and on them, a mug of cold tea. On the shelf above it her files with their sticker-covered spines, stand in a row. She sighs at the thought of the hours she must sit there before Monday's classes. Above the shelf a large cork pinboard displays the images she has gathered from half a lifetime's reading of magazines, alongside photographs of herself and friends on foreign holidays, two old rosettes she refused to discard, postcards, used concert tickets, discount vouchers for conditioner and mascara, and a strip of five laughing, gurning faces squeezed into a photo-booth in the shopping centre.

In return for being allowed to paint her room in the colours of her choice, her father insisted on the pinboard to keep the blu-tak off the walls. This thought makes her uncomfortable. She hadn't minded; she was too old for posters of pop-idols anyway, but maybe she gives in too easily. She no longer loves images; she loves the real thing. He is no male model, no chisel chinned, bright, grinning, glossy toothed, genuine leather clotheshorse. He is real and smells and breathes his steady rhythm beside her. He listens to her and she can tell him how she feels. After they finished she nestled into his body, his arm wrapped around her and they talked, slowly, softly, and she had asked him about his first time. It pleased her that he had been nervous.

'I wasn't very good.' he confessed, and she smiled.

'I'm sure you were.' he squeezed her and ran her hair through his fingers. She fingered a gentle line down his chest. She was glad she didn't know her. But she wanted to know of his life.

'Why did you finish?'

'I didn't like her.' he said, then grunted and shifted his trapped arm. 'My arm's gone dead.' She lifted herself off him, and as he turned on to his side she said, 'But you slept with her.'

'I liked her then.' His voice, muffled by his back being toward her, sounded drowsy. She cupped herself around him. 'I stopped liking her.' he said.

'And will you stop liking me?'

'No.' She felt his chest rise and fall in a slow, steady rhythm. His arm reached out behind him and he stoked her thigh, adding, 'I like you very much.' She held him tight as his hand left her backside and he whispered. 'Maybe too much.'

'What does that mean?' she had asked, but by then he was asleep. She had lain there until the fear of being asleep when her mother returned, and the discomfort of her arm beneath his body, had made her sit up.

She makes a note to herself that she needs a photo of him for the board. He is conspicuous by his absence. Across the top of the pinboard she'd draped a silk scarf. A dressing screen stands concertinaed, dividing her wardrobe area and the rest of the room. She sees the collage of cutouts she'd spent hours sticking on each panel to make it her own. She'd got the idea from a magazine and then the magazine became part of the collage, along with photographs of friends, flyers and stickers all underneath a clear coat of varnish. It screens her wardrobe, allows her to pile up her dirty washing without making the room look untidy, and stops her mother having something to moan about. Besides, she thinks it looks classy, sophisticated, and in the greying light in which she sees it, like it might have once belonged to a goddess from the silver screen. Along one wall, next to her dresser with its art class pottery bowl brimming with lotion bottles and cotton wipes, and backed by her large oval mirror, is the sofa, which folds out to make a bed where her friends sleep when they stay over. It is covered in bright cushions and throws, now dulled but textured with shadow in the dimness. She sees the stuffed bear he bought for her propped up on it. Between its paws it holds a stuffed love heart. On the heart is written 'Forever Friends.' It is such a soppy thing for him to have bought her she loves him all the more.

He shifts position next to her; his legs straighten then curl again, his backside pushes into her. She edges over, her hip touches the cold wall beneath the window. She wants to light another cigarette but knows there is no time. Outside it is nearly dark and her mother can only be an hour away. He would have to be gone before then, or at least up. But she knows if they were up and drinking tea or watching television together on the sofa, her mother would know what they had been doing. Her mother would say nothing, but she would know. Had she changed since? She has wondered if there is a look about her now. Perhaps she is more flushed in the cheek or her lips are redder since him. Her mother knows. She knows she knows. Probably knew that night or at least the day after. It is not something that she can place, just a feeling. She thinks that if she feels different, and she does, older, more womanly, then her mother must know, must have seen the change. Since it happened, she perceived a difference in their relationship. First she seemed distant but then always irritated with her, and the rowing became more frequent. It is no longer over staying out late; he has a car and always brings her home on time. She can no longer do anything right. As if her mother thinks she doesn't know her own mind. She thinks they like him. But he should be gone when she gets home. She wonders whether it will matter, she will probably know anyway, as if she can smell it on her. She will shower when he leaves and smell of talcum powder and conditioner like she did before, as a child. Even if she knows, she doesn't want to parade it in front of her. What if it was her daughter, how would she feel? She hopes she will understand when her turn comes. She looks forward to reading the signs, to knowing the signs. She only wishes she could have him curled around her and not have to think of her mother returning in an hour. Or think of her mother at all. She has not yet woken with him and wants to very much. Propped up against the padding of the headboard she views her breasts and the fold of her stomach and feels happy. He had told her she was beautiful and had kissed her there. Pulling the duvet over herself she knows how good he makes her feel and how it is never enough. She knows she made him wait for her to be ready and that he had been patient. Then she was afraid but he made her feel safe and never cheap. She was happy to have him. She is happy to have him sleeping and satisfied, curled under the warmth of her duvet. The pillow will smell of him. The sheets will smell of them. When, later, she is alone and lying where he lay, reading by the light of the bedside lamp, his smell will be there.

She slides down the bed and lies against him. She rubs her feet together feeling the dead skin on the sole of one on the arch of the other. Their time is running out. He will leave and she will wait for his call, fearful it may never come. When the telephone rings and the three of them are sat around the table after dinner, they will look at each other and she will know that it is his call, but not rush to answer it. They will know. Her mother and father will exchange looks and one will say, 'Well, answer it then, it's bound to be for you.' She will get up, desperate to run for it in case he rings off, but hold herself back, conscious of their eyes on her and the looks they pass between them. She will hear her father's voice behind her, 'Don't be on that phone all night' as she shuts the door on them, and she will feel guilt and excitement over being so secretive. When she returns he will goad her: 'And how's Prince Charming tonight, has he got himself a job yet?' It isn't meant to hurt, but she always feels hurt and embarrassed and knows she is blushing. So she will help her mother with the dishes in silence and try not to face him. Her mother will tell her father off for teasing her and then peel off her pink rubber gloves and hold her and look her in the eyes and ask her with so much care and love in her voice, 'Is he alright? Are you seeing him this weekend?' which will be worse and it will be all she can do to stop herself screaming at them or bursting into tears and she will only just manage, 'Yes, he's fine.'

'Hey, wake up.' She leans over him, whispers into his ear and strokes his hair. 'Wake up, sleepy head.' she says louder. The words with which her mother used to wake her are now hers. She is not sure how to wake him but decides to shake his shoulder gently, then stronger, and he groans. 'Come on, sleepy head, it's time to get up.' He turns onto his back and opens his eyes. She is leaning over him and watches the darkness of his irises as, between blinks, he recognises her and smiles. He reaches out and strokes her hair away to hold it from her face before saying, 'What time is it?' His voice is quiet and coarse from his throat. 'It's dark. Have I been asleep long?' he asks. She thinks he looks confused. She wants him to tell her he loves her; it is the right time and he has yet to say those words. She waits for him but his eyes close again and she covers their absence by kissing him on his lips. She feels his stubble as his mouth opens hers and delivers his tongue. He makes a groan as if he is enjoying a morsel of food and his arm pulls her on top of him. She does not resist. On his mouth she tastes the cigarette he smoked straight after, and his tongue on hers feels good in her body. His hands cup her backside and one runs up her back to her neck underneath her hair and she feels him harden beneath her and knows she must stop, but wishes not to. She wants him now more than before. She wants him because she knows she cannot, because there is no more time. She hates that her life does not belong to her but pushes off him with her arms. He lifts his head to hold her lips as long as he can, until his neck strains and she pulls her head away. He does not use any pressure with his hand to keep her head there. His eyes open and he smiles at her.

'She'll be home soon.' She tells him. 'You have to go.' He turns to look at the alarm clock on the bedside table, then sits up throwing her from him and swings his legs off the bed.

'I've got to go,' he says. He stands up, 'I'm going to be late.'

'What for?' she asks. She watches his nakedness as he searches amongst the clothes they discarded across her floor when they laughed in the tangle of jumpers and arms and legs and hair. She stifles a giggle. He switches on the bedside light.

'My pants?' he asks, rooting through the pile. Rushing, he searches about the floor, then turns and lifts the duvet cover she has pulled up to cover her nakedness. He finds them under the cover at the bottom of the bed. Hers are there too. He bends to slip on each leg in turn. She watches his penis, sees it shrunken and comic. It seems to want to retreat into its nest of hair. She feels more confident and cannot help but giggle.

'What?' He straightens, pulling his pants up, then bends again to find his jeans.

'Nothing.' she says, smiling.

'What?' he insists. She watches him button his fly, and fasten his belt.

'Nothing.' She alters her emphasis, feels bad she might have insulted him, and changes the subject. 'Come here.' Her eyes widen at him.

'What?' He smiles and moves to her. She reaches out one hand and draws his head to her. As he kisses her, with her free hand she grabs his groin through the denim of his jeans. She kisses him until she feels him begin to harden under the pressure of her cupped hand. Then she stops.

'You'll be late.' she says.

'I'm already late.'

'Sorry.' She does not know what it is he has to rush for. She thinks he's probably late for his dinner or a mate. Another girl crosses her mind. She's surprised that she doesn't need to know. She points to the condom on her bedside table. 'Take that with you, will you?' He looks at it and is about to plead when she says: 'I'd hate for my mum to find it at the bottom of the bin.'

'Fair enough,' he says. He pulls a tissue from the box on her dresser, wraps the condom in it and stuffs the package in his jeans pocket.

'Better safe than sorry.' She uses the same phrase he used when he took out the packet that first time and she was afraid. She is glad he will dispose of the evidence and even more so when the smell leaves the room with him. He has his shoes on and has tied the laces. 'I've got to go,' he says, 'I'll call.' He slips on his jacket before kissing her forehead.

'Yes, do.'

As he opens the door of her bedroom to leave, he turns to her.

'Thank you,' he says.

'No, thank *you, mister,*' she says, and blows a kiss at him. The tone in her voice surprises her. She sees him catch the kiss, and widens her eyes at him, flashing a look. She watches the door shut, hears him thump down the stairs and smiles. 'He'll call,' she thinks. Of that much she is certain. From behind the curtain she watches his figure walk away through the darkness until he is lit by the streetlamp, then disappears into the dark again. Later, as she sits on the side of the tub waiting for the shower to come to temperature, she looks forward to hearing her mother's key turning in the door.

Patrick Evans

Patrick Evans was the Director of Staging of the multi-award winning Edinburgh venue, Café Graffiti. *When it closed he went home to Glasgow to live with his cat. He has worked extensively in the low wage economy ever since.*

Equalizer

Darkness. Radio commentary from a football match. But not just any football match. An historical event etched in the memory of millions of Glaswegians for two competing reasons.
It is from the Old Firm game.
'The Demolition Derby.'
Celtic's 6-2 destruction of Rangers in October 2000.

COMMENTATOR: . . . Petrov to Sutton, just inside the Celtic half. Sutton releases Larsson. Larsson. Larsson on his own. Oh, he just sailed past Ferguson and Albertz as if they simply weren't there, Ricksen comes to meet him . . . Oh! Larsson's made a complete fool of the Rangers' international! Henrik Larsson has run half the park and just has the keeper to beat . . . He chips . . . It's a demolition! The heart's been ripped out of the Ibrox men. The balance of power has shifted east. Paradise is in rapture!

The sound of two men, TC *and* MICK, *singing—in the darkness and through discovery. The tune is 'You Are My Sunshine.'*

TC & MICK: You are my Larsson, my Henrik Larsson,
You make me happy when skies are grey,
You never know dear, how much I love you,
Don't take our Larsson away.

And then they chant:

> There's only one Henrik Larsson!
> One Henrik Larsson!
> There's only one Henrik Larsson.

As they sing an electric light bulb flickers and fizzes dangerously before deciding to stay on. What is revealed is a Glasgow public toilet. The English tongue is lucky not to contain enough words to describe the utter filth of the place. Scots, tragically, has plenty. Minging. Drooglet. Keich. Mank. At discovery, the place is infested by two Celtic Football Club supporters. TC *and* MICK. *They are bedecked in unmistakeable tribal icons: green and white hoops.*

Our first view of them is immediately sexually ambiguous. TC *stands awkwardly in front of a urinal, his legs unsteadily parted. His hands firmly grasping a water feed pipe above the urinal. It is obvious he is using this grip to support himself in this unnatural position.* MICK *stands directly behind him holding* TC*'s penis, guiding it towards the urinal. His other arm is snaked around* TC*'s chest, that hand awkwardly juggling an imported lager bottle.* TC*'s backside is pushed firmly backwards into* MICK*'s midriff.*

In the background is the only piece of stage furniture that does not fit the setting. It alone offers the only clue to the reality of what is taking place: a disabled person's wheelchair.

They sing:

MICK: Hail!

TC: Hail!

TOGETHER: The Celts are here!

MICK: (*To the audience*) What the fuck is youse staring at? Jus' gieing the guy a wee hond. Awright. No' the smartest thing to say. But it's what came out when the wee wank came in. And awright, straight up, if the guy wasnae wearing what the guy was fucking wearing none of this shite would've happened. It's no' what ye wear on your chest, it's what it says about your heid. Full stop.

End of sentence, paragraph, page and fucking story. (*to* TC) Is ye gonnae piss or whit?

TC: (*sings*) It's a grand old team tae play for!
It's a grand old team tae see!
And if ye know yer history . . .

MICK: Well is ye or isn' ye?

TC: 'Ssake man! Some things in life ye cannae rush, but. (*To the audience*) Yer mind's in the gutter. Yer filth! Fuck, the tube shouldnae've e'en been there. He should've known. They's rules. Territories, but. Shit ye grow up wi'. Shit ye learn as a wean. It's a pairt o' the patter. In ye 'fore ye get yer firs' jersey. Learning they rules is pairt and paircel o' learning the beautiful game. Break they rules and yer a lemming. Glesca mebbe a toilet but it's a well governed toilet and it gaes tae the winners. Tra-fucking-dition. As it is fae us, so it is fae they cunts. (*to* MICK) Wo-ho-ho! Here comes Niagra!

And finally TC *manages to piss.*

MICK: (*To the audience*) This is no' how it comes across. There's weird and weird, right. And this wis up there. I can think o' a million ways o' celebratin' the fuck-off result of the decade and standing in a pisser with another guy's tadger in ma hond isnae wan o' them. But whit else wis I gonnae fucking dae? TC's like family. We got history. Used tae gae tae the game as weans. Straight, man, we met in The Jungle. Six years each. Hiked on our faither's shouldies. Watchin' The 'Tic. Then aifter. Eating pieces ootside the Sarrie Heid as our Da's got fu' inside. Skiving roun' the Barras. Chasing through they staws. That wis afore. Everywan round our bit knows what went doun wi' TC. Everywan's still pure biling. Sae I wis nae-fucking-choice-man ... Fucking local hero wants a fucking wizz, but. 'Gonnae help us?' he says. Then o'er and o'er like some fucking-aye-fucking-shite action fucking replay. Bad fuck-off music or whit . . .

TC: I need a piss.

MICK: Aye?

TC: No. You're no' getting me.

MICK: Whit?

TC: Mick . . .

MICK: Whit?

TC: I need tae fucking piss.

MICK: And?

TC: Steps, man.

MICK: Whit?

TC: I dinnae dae steps. I'm a dalek.

MICK: And still I dinnae get him. Am I that fucking thick or whit? Whit?

TC: Daleks dinnae dae steps . . .

MICK: That's when it dawns. Chinks in ma heid. Fucking dunderheid man, me. The pub had steps. Ye piss doun stairs. Shite that's no' wi' ye if ye got legs. Y' need a push tae the pisser in the street? Why d'ye no' jus' fucking say so?

TC: Shite, man. Fucking-insight-insect. See you on Mastermind, but. Jeez-peeps.

MICK: Hawf ways 'cross the street TC reads the headlines . . . Zetecs wan way, Cosworth's the other, pure-zipping-traffic, I hear this . . . Pushing a fucking wheelchair 'cross the M-fucking-4 is nae a scene frae 'The Wizard O' Oz,' but. 'Specially when yer oldest pal tells ye he needs ye tae hold his riddler in yer hond—

Suddenly out of address. A minor accident has occurred.

TC: Shit man!

MICK: Whit?

TC: Hae ye' go' nae fucking aim?

MICK: Sorry.

TC: Hate tae live round yer bit, but. When youse goes d'ye hit the taps or the fucking cat? Ye seen the state o' ma chinos? Pish everywhere. Jeez, man, I wis up fae a bag-off wi' Julie and aw . . .

MICK: Sorry.

TC: Fucking toast wi' a map o' Orange Lodges on ma trews! Let's hae some precision-fucking-targetting here.

MICK: Radar on the noo, big yin. You is that cruise missile.

TC: And that's when the blue-nose walked in . . .

Enter CHARLIE. *Big, powerful and athletic. Booming bass voice. He is dressed in Glasgow's other tribal colours. The equally powerful blue and white symbols of Rangers Football Club.*

CHARLIE: Fuck's sake. Queer bhoys!

MICK: What the fuck is youse staring at? Jus' gieing the guy a wee hond.

CHARLIE: I'm no' blind, but, but if ye carry on wi' that he will be!

TC: 'Yer mind's in the gutter. Yer filth!

CHARLIE: 'Scuse me, darling.

MICK: This is no' how it comes across.

CHARLIE: Is it no'. How no'? Exactly?

And he walks to the urinal and begins to piss.

(*To the audience*) Aye, I could see whit wis going doun. I'm nae vacant, but. (*Taps his head*) There's no' sign here whit reads, 'lodgers required—nae Irish.' Jus' tell it as I see it. Fenian scum's off any decent cunt's Richter scale. I dinnae expect a pile o' liberal wanks to side wi' me. You people have grown saft. Surrendered. Look at whit they cunts wear on their fucking chests. Taking the piss oot o' ye. Warrington. Omagh. Brighton. Worn like medals on they green and white hoops. D'ye no' fucking get it? Is you cunts that fucking blind? They got wan response: they murder. They send bombs doun on ye. When I'se square up tae them this isnae aboot a game. Awright, six-two leaves ye real fucking sair. 'Specially when ye've dominated. Ruled fae sae fucking long. But we's'll be back . . . There will be nae surrender.

TC *finishes up and* MICK *helps him back into his wheelchair. He returns his bottle of lager to him.*

MICK: (*To the audience*) Fuck you! That's no' the way I mind it. Ways I see it he jus' picked it. Nae banter, nae provocation. Battle jus' recommenced. Ye need nae excuses when there's history. And we's got plenty o' it. It wis jus' a few months back they bastards wan the title at Parkheid. That's when it started, or mebbe before, aifter the las' meeting. We'd been defeated, right. Lost everything. Title and pride. Twa walking hame. Heids low. Back frae the war. Refugees on the Ally Parade. Then we's took the turn pas' the burned oot picky—hoose . . . That's when theys cam' a' us. This Shogun, stereo blazing 'Simply the Best,' swings up the pavey and five piles oot. Huns. Marauding bastards. We stood nae fucking chance. Rather he didnae. TC. I ran. I let him walk alone. I cannae forgie that. Willnae. I'll no' nae stond ma grund nae mair. No fucking mair. I get backs tae him and he's this mess. Jus' mess.

Face mashed. Blood seepin'. He wis lyin'. Ye could jus' see. Tell. It wisnae right. The way he lay. Tell he wis snapped.

CHARLIE *finishes and turns to go.* MICK *stands watching him angrily as he does so. Tension.* CHARLIE *reaches the door then suddenly turns:*

CHARLIE: Fuck's sake. Queer bhoys.

MICK: What the fuck is youse staring at? I'm jus' gieing the guy a wee hond.

CHARLIE: I'm no' blind, but, but if ye carry on wi' that he will be!

TC: 'Yer mind's in the gutter. Yer filth!

CHARLIE: 'Scuse me, darling.

MICK: This is no' how it comes across.

MICK *and* CHARLIE *square up to each other.*

CHARLIE: Is it no'. How no'? Exactly? Fenian shite.

MICK: Fuck you.

CHARLIE *and* MICK *go at each other. Neither initiates. They attack each other simultaneously. The violence is dirty and untidy. Scuffling.* CHARLIE *has the better of it. Throws* MICK *to the floor and then kicks him on the ground.*

CHARLIE: (*Chants*) Hello! Hello! We are the Billy boys!

MICK: See whit I think o' 1690 . . .

And MICK *sticks 'the finger' up at him.*

CHARLIE: Ye cunts ne'er fucking learn.

CHARLIE *goes to kick* MICK *again.* MICK *is ready for him and grabs his foot as he does so.* CHARLIE *falls. His head falls onto* TC*'s wheelchair.*

TC: Nah . . . We's remember.

And he whacks CHARLIE's *head with the lager bottle. The bottle splinters.* CHARLIE *falls back onto* TC*'s chair. Two handed, in a manner mocking a ritual sacrifice,* TC *brings the broken bottle down into* CHARLIE's *midriff.* CHARLIE *slides to the ground motionless in front of* TC*'s chair.*

TC: Wan fucking nil.

Silence.

MICK: Nae way, man. Nae way. That wis an equalizer.

Black Out.

Susan Fletcher

Susan Fletcher was born in the West Midlands in 1979. She graduated in English and Related Literature from the University of York, and in 2001 was the recipient of a David Higham bursary.

Eve Green

(extract from a novel)

Three things happened when I was seven years old.

In the spring I learnt how to spell my full name. Having mastered all fifteen letters I wrote them wherever I could—in books, on newspaper, in spit on windowpanes. Once I etched my name carefully above the skirting board in the downstairs loo. My mother never found it, but I knew it was there. I'd sit, swing my legs, and eye my handiwork under the sink. It shone out in blue wax crayon.

Then in the summer I burned for the first time. I spent the hottest day of the year digging for worms in the back garden. I don't know where my mother was, but I remember that the paving slabs were too hot to walk on and the shed roof softened. That evening I was scarlet. She put me in a cool bath and dabbed on calamine lotion, but I still wailed. For four days I couldn't sleep. I was feverish, sore, and the sheets stuck to my blisters. Two weeks later my freckles appeared.

And ten days before Christmas, she died.

It was a Friday full of heavy rain. I woke to no heating and a silent house, and when I crept downstairs the mail was still on the doormat, the milk in the fridge was yellow, and I found my mother curled up on the sofa under the patchwork rug. I watched her for a while. She murmured to herself with her eyes closed, and when I tugged her sleeve, she smiled at no-one and turned onto her side. She smelt warm. The wet creeper outside tapped against the glass. I made her some toast, just in case.

There was a little orange juice in the fridge, so I poured that into a beaker and drank it in the bay window. The Christmas tree opposite had twinkling lights. I watched a car swoosh past, listened to the clock ticking in the hall, and I thought it was strange that the dustmen hadn't come yet. They always came on Friday. I liked the hustle and roar they brought with them, how they shouted to each other as they slung our rubbish with one hand. For a while, I'd wanted to be a dustman. They would whistle and wave when they saw me. The street always seemed too quiet when they'd gone.

I pressed my face against the glass. Our binbags sagged in the street and grew glossy. A dog scuttled past, sniffed the bags, and lifted its leg against our wall. When I banged on the window my mother groaned. The dustmen never came. I waited for them all day.

She stirred at lunchtime. She raked her fingers through her hair, felt her way out of the sitting room, and when I heard the front door close I stood up on the windowsill. I could see all the way to the shop. She wandered down the street in the rain, wrapping her coat around her. The wind was picking up. The sky over the city looked steely and low.

When she came back she carried a clinking plastic bag, and for a while our house seemed lived in again. There were noises in the kitchen. I heard the loo flush and the sound of her slippers on the hall floor. I felt better. I went back up to my room and scratched my name into the windowsill. The trains creaked in the rain past the end of our garden. Pigeons hunched on the cables. I could hear the gas fire popping downstairs.

At four o clock the banister creaked and as she padded past my bedroom door, twisting a strand of her hair between her thumb and first finger, she said, 'Are you alright in there?'

Then, finally, she ran the bath. I used to love the sound. Running water would soften me, and if I was ill or unhappy, she left the taps on for five minutes, and I'd sleep right though the night. She always took long baths. She loved thick body creams and scented talc. She loved washing the city out of her hair, and combing it as she drifted through the house, and she loved white laundered towels, church candles, and that afternoon I smelt her lavender oil and cigarettes, heard her clothes drop to the floor, and my mother shut the bathroom door at four-sixteen, as the Snow Hill to Marylebone train rolled past the house, sounding its horn into the damp air.

She wasn't even thirty.

Mrs Willis next door made the phone call. I remember standing on the back step in my dressing gown and slippers watching the frost, not wanting to go back inside. The shed roof glimmered. I listened to the noises of the city after dark, and I gazed at the stars, tried to count them. There was an aeroplane up there, winking at me, and I watched it. Wind moved litter. The black cat from two doors down slunk over our back fence and dropped down the embankment. It had scratched me once when I'd tried to pick it up, so I knew better than to go near it again.

Mrs Willis wore a dark red knitted cardigan that night, and her skin smelt of roses and wintergreen. She came out to me with the patchwork rug, knelt down and arranged it over my shoulders. I kept looking at the aeroplane. She rubbed warmth into my hands and tried to smooth back my hair. She covered my ears as the sirens came, but I still heard them.

When she went to let them in, I pattered down to the shed, tugged at the lock and crept in. My tricycle was kept in there. There were old plant pots, bricks and a rusted barbecue. The place smelt of petrol, soil, damp wood, and I wedged myself between the wall and an old deckchair, nestled into the rug, stared at the darkness and stayed there until they'd gone.

I left Birmingham two days later. I couldn't stay. I had no relatives left there, and Mrs Willis was too old to take me in for good. She was nearly sixty, and Mr Willis was older still. He wasn't well, and needed rest. I'd see him whenever I went round to get my ball back—a waxy, thin man with half moon glasses and big jowls that trembled when he spoke. He watched the world with sad, watery eyes and coughed into a wad of cotton wool. They were the only people who might have had me. I think everyone else was afraid.

So one morning in December I was put into a car. The gritting lorries had made the pavements crunchy, little coloured Christmas lights were strung up between lampposts and I felt like a parcel in my duffle coat and scarf, clutching Dog by the ears. Mrs Willis helped me in. I watched as she pulled the seatbelt over my tummy, and I scratched my thighs and wiped my nose on my sleeve. She slipped a tissue under my cuff. Before shutting the car door she gave me a satsuma and a slice of soggy fruit cake for the journey. 'God be with you,' she said, 'and try to be good.'

Our house was at the top of the street. The paint on the porch door had been flaking my whole lifetime. The black gutter above her bedroom window was broken, and icicles had gathered there. Through the frosted glass of the bathroom window I could see the pot plant she'd bought from the market, the half-raised blind and a bottle of something dark blue. When I looked at that house for the last time, at the dead hanging basket and the heavy net curtains, I thought of a week before when she'd stood in the sitting room window, smoking, smiling, fingering her necklace, watching me ride my tricycle in the road. She'd waved back at me. That evening we'd had pink iced buns for tea.

I held Dog. The window looked empty without her. A piece of newspaper skittered past our gate, and blew up against our wall.

As the car slowly pulled away, Mrs Willis tried to keep up, blowing kisses, mouthing something at me that I couldn't make out. She was a soft, fleshy woman with thick ankles and a weak heart, and as the car picked up speed, I put my hand against the glass. She became smaller and smaller. Through the rear window I saw her standing by the letterbox at the bottom of our street, her left arm raised with a balled-up hanky in her hand. That was the last I ever saw of her. When the car turned the corner, her white apron shone out through the gloom.

Birmingham was all I knew. My early childhood was spent crawling under market stalls in the Bull Ring, sitting on the bus as it inched down Smallbrook Queensway, being pushed on the rickety swings in the park. I picked up the accent at school. I learnt football chants from the playground and sang them in the bath. When I was six I remember sitting at the edge of Gas Street Basin, dipping my feet in the water, and my mother tugging me out because of the greenish scum and the floating things. She made me scrub my feet till they tingled. I wasn't allowed there again.

My earliest memory is of the IRA bombings in '74. I found my mother sobbing on the stairs, and I didn't know what to do. She made me wear a hat tugged low over my hair for weeks.

And the Indian takeaway from three streets away made our house smell spicy when the wind was right. And we could hear the noise from St Andrew's when there was a home game. If I stood on my tiptoes, I could see the BT tower and the spire of St Martin's from our bathroom window.

They took me away from there. In the next street I saw our postman on his bicycle. Outside the chemist old Mr Soames stooped with his gnarly hands and fat labrador. Then my red brick school flashed by. The mosque with the turquoise roof slid past, and the bingo hall, and the indoor market that smelt stuffy, and I pressed my face against the glass when I saw signs for Moor Street station. She'd taken me on a train once, just so that we could see what our house looked like from the tracks. I'd left Dog in my window, and we'd seen him as we rolled by. That was two summers ago, when she was having a good spell. The clematis on the shed roof had been in flower.

Then I grew fretful. I grappled with my seatbelt, tugged at the door handle, and I banged my tiny fists against the glass so that people on the pavement looked up. The woman next to me took hold of my wrists. I saw the rotunda, and New Street, and I struggled, wrenched myself away from her. The car was hot. I felt flushed, weak, and I didn't want to look out of the window anymore, so I clutched Dog, breathed him in, and found home there—the scent of lavender, laundry, Embassy Lights. His button eyes looked up at me, and I quietened. I stroked them with the pad of my thumb.

The rain came with the motorway, and Birmingham was gone.

It was a long journey to my new life. I spent most of it with my head against the glass, listening to the weather hammer on the roof. The woman next to me wore brown. From time to time she unclipped her handbag, popped a mint into her mouth and cracked it slowly with her teeth. I couldn't see out of the window because our breath had steamed it, so I drew on it with my finger. A face with no mouth. My name. A hand with painted nails. She turned to me, pushed her glasses up her shiny nose and said, 'Don't do that, Evie.'

The windscreen wipers clicked on, clicked off.

I slept for a while, because there was nothing else to do. When I awoke, my scarf was damp, my head hurt and the light in the car was strange, sharper. I twisted in my seat. The woman beside me was reading. I looked from her to the driver, and back. I knew something was different, but wasn't sure what. The wheels crunched on gravel.

Of course I'd seen the countryside before. There had been a school trip to the Lickey Hills once, and I'd eaten my packed lunch under an oak tree. My birthday present when I was six had been a blue and yellow kite, and we'd flown it on Cannock Chase amongst the bracken and badger sets. Mrs Willis used to promise to take me to Stratford. She said we would go boating on the river and have cream teas. She never took me there, but I could picture it. I knew there would be willow trees and ducks to feed, and in my head it never rained in Stratford. My River Avon was always sparkly blue.

What Dog and I saw when I cleared the window with my sleeve was not like anything we knew. We looked without blinking at a brand new world. The houses and streets weren't there. The park with the slide and the ice-cream van were four hours behind us. Mrs Willis's washing line with its big white knickers, the railway with its rubbish and sweet oily smell, my school with the hopscotch chalked out in the playground—all of it had gone. I gripped Dog and stared.

Wales was empty and wet, with stiff grasses and a huge dark sky. The rain was like flung grit and it came in handfuls, smattering against the glass so that I flinched from it, startled. It raced up the windscreen like a hand. The car lurched up the mountain, throwing me from side to side, and my hands found nothing to hold onto. I knocked my head against the window and called out. I reached for the handle, and grasped it.

Outside the land was sodden. I knew sheep, but these were ragged and thin. They scrambled up rock to escape us, glared as we passed with iron-grey eyes. The ground they clambered through looked black and gluey and it seemed to stick to their legs, and their bellies were splattered and hard. The gorse shivered. Above, the clouds were gathering, and they grew thicker as we drove. I think I tried to say something. Dog was clenched in my hand. As we crested the hill, a blast of wind slammed against the car.

There were no other houses. I searched for one. We passed a stone wall, and there were a few stunted black trees that the sheep used as shelter, but that was it. No homes. No lights in the distance. I touched the glass with my fingers. The car plunged into a pothole and the engine roared.

All my life I'd known people living so close that we could hear their noises. Mr Willis was a heavy smoker and his lungs would bubble at night. When he went out to the pub before he fell ill, Mrs Willis played Elvis on repeat, and we could hear their egg timer through the kitchen wall. I thought people lived near people, because it's what I'd always known, and now all I could see was spiky grass and bony sheep, leaden skies, muddy ruts, and one stone farmhouse all on its own, wedged under the hillside with a grey slate roof and a thin, black wisp of smoke, rising into the rain.

'That's home for you, now,' she said. I looked at her, and saw the crumbs of Mrs Willis's fruitcake scattered on her lap.

In the city, nightfall is a gradual thing. Streetlights mean that even at midnight, the darkness can be walked through and life carries on. Cities settle down at night but they don't stop. There is still music, traffic, laughter. Sometimes it's like trying to sleep in the day.

In the summer months, Birmingham nights were pinkish. Birds never seemed to rest, and I would lie awake after bedtime and hear them through my open window. All year round, the city glow meant the stars were so faint that only a few could be seen. I was never afraid of the dark there, because it wasn't ever dark.

In Wales the evening rolled down the valley like a fog. It unfurled itself over the car, and brought with it worse weather. As we pulled into the yard a security light flicked on, and I saw the rain in it, slanting with the wind. The headlights snapped off. The hills were now hidden, and I thought of the sheep there, nipping their jaws in the dark. I kept Dog close by. I bound him to me with his loose stitching.

Next to me, the woman in brown powdered her nose, gathered her things and the door sucked shut behind her. I sat for a moment on my own, swinging my legs, swinging my black patent shoes with holes punched out of the toes in the shape of flowers. I waited. I could feel the wind buffet the car.

I'd never met my grandparents before—at least, not that I remembered. I know they came to visit me not long after my birth, that they bought me an elephant mobile that hung in my room for years, and I think when I was eighteen months old they came to Birmingham for the weekend, when my mother first weakened. But I didn't really know them. They'd send me pop-up birthday cards and pressed flowers, and my mother would send them photographs back. I know she sent them my first school photo—their granddaughter, aged five, with unbrushable hair and no order to her freckles. I remember not wanting to smile for the camera. The teachers had coaxed me, pulled faces, and at the last minute, when everyone had grown tired of my pouting, I had flashed my very best smile. My mother liked the picture. It made her laugh, and she used to keep it on the mantelpiece, next to the well-thumbed postcard of Dublin Bay.

My mother's mother opened the car door. She looked down at me with the dark brown, thick-lashed family eyes, and lifted her hand to her mouth. I must have looked terrible—swollen, wretched, flushed and struggling in my car seat. The eczema on my legs was starting to burn. I remember the farmyard smell—straw, dung, petrol, the stench of dead water, the tang of wood smoke. I think I whimpered. I think I held out my hands and flexed my fingers at her, because she knelt down to unfasten me then. She worked quickly, with thin pink hands. I could see the down on the lobes of her ears, and her scalp was as shiny as an eggshell under her white hair. I felt her hands on my waist, and she lifted me and Dog and my duffle coat up, out of the car and into her arms. The skin on her neck was soft and warm. 'Hello Evangeline,' she said, kissing my hair. 'Hello.' She wore a cream flowery blouse underneath a pale blue jumper, and I grasped the collar with my fist, would not let it go. I breathed in the smell of her, and she said, 'it's OK, my love, it's OK.'

She held me tightly, and I could feel her shaking.

Over her shoulder, I saw the wind in the trees, heard the trees creaking, and I thought they whispered my name.

YONA F. FRIEDMAN

Yona F. Friedman was born in Rome, Italy. She studied political science, anthropology, and worked in journalism. Winged *is her first novel.*

WINGED

The following piece is an extract from a novel in progress. The story has two main strands: the first is set in Rome and Manhattan and takes place during the Eighties and Nineties, the second begins in Fascist Italy, then continues in Eritrea.

The weeping willow stood on the curve, halfway up the hill. I walked by it every day on my way home from school. The branches drooped, caressing the cement; the leaves swayed, on tiptoe.

My book bag dug into my shoulder. When I caught a glimpse of that trembling green, I knew I was close. Once I timed myself, it took me thirty-five minutes to get home from the main road. I could have taken two buses, but the second, which was supposed to come by every half an hour and stop at the bottom of the hill, often skipped full hours and by the time it did appear, too many people wanted to get on. Some were left behind.

Sometimes I'd rest when I reached the willow. The asphalt surrounding it was bumpy and uneven—deformed over the years by the tree's roots. They looked like veins. I couldn't sit underneath the weeping willow because it was on the edge of a road with no sidewalk: cars would have hit me and mopeds zooming past would have sent me flying. So I'd lean against its trunk—a shower of green fell around me and a slice of blue sky forced its way through the foliage. No one could see me; I didn't move.

I gazed up at the last stretch, the steepest but shortest. It seemed endless—and with my every step, it was as if the road grew, becoming longer and steeper and longer.

Someone was always home: not Mother, not Father, not Grandma, not Great-Grandma, not my sister, but Birikti. She worked for my family in Asmara. My great-grandparents left Italy for Africa in the late 30s and when war broke out in Eritrea they shipped the coffins of their dead relatives back to Italy, packed the belongings they had collected in forty years and returned to Rome with Birikti.

The ground shook beneath my sister's and my feet each time a family member arrived in Rome. Father's relatives, who lived in the United States, told us we were Italian; Mother's that we were American. Friends considered us weird.

I wondered what it was like to have one language, one country, one song to sing; perhaps I wouldn't feel as if I were hanging off a weeping willow branch—so delicate, too thin. A tree can't be asked: *How did you get here? Who planted you?*

But families are a different story. I've asked my family questions, trying to follow their footsteps, but they've walked too close to the shore. The sea always rushes in, erasing traces, leaving behind a longing.

So, throughout my teens and twenties, I've sifted through the sand, searching. I've read the love letters sent to Mother by her first boyfriend, unfolded Father's prayer shawl, touched his three skull caps and sat mesmerised for hours, holding in my hands a letter by Mother's great-great-uncle, filled with indecipherable handwriting. Mother and I have eavesdropped on Father when he spoke on the phone with one of his brothers in Long Island. We'd stand behind the door, trying not laugh, as I'd translate what he was saying to Mother since she didn't understand English.

The years went by and I no longer looked up at the tree. Friends gave me rides on mopeds or in cars or if I went on foot I stared at the ground ahead of me, concentrating on my anger. *Why did you buy this house on a hill so far away from everything?* I screamed at Mother. *Don't be ridiculous,* she answered, her voice hoarse. *It's not a hill.* For me, that road was more like a mountain.

More than a decade passed before I held my head high again. I had finished college and was back home. The weeping willow was gone. No one in my family had mentioned its disappearance.

Do you remember that weeping willow on the curve? I asked Mother.

Mmm.

★

Great-Grandma, Grandma, Acu and I ride in a car. We're going to Lido dei Pini, a seaside town south of Rome. Grandma smokes as she drives, cheap state cigarettes. The car is hers—a red Fiesta she uses twice a year, during the Christmas and summer holidays when she comes to Rome. She teaches in Italian middle schools abroad and this past year she lived in Katmandu.

Grandma's mother, Great-Grandma, is next to her and I wish I was on her lap. I'm too big now. Sometimes I still sit on her, though I'm afraid of crushing her with my weight. Instead of holding me, her hands rest on half an apple cake and the black python bag she's asked me to open many times. I know what she keeps inside: her hearing aid wrapped in a napkin tucked in the small pocket, a figurine of St Rita, and a mother-of-pearl rosary entangled with her Chiaccherino—the golden spool she uses to do Chiaccherino, tatting.

I'm in the back seat next to a Singer sewing machine and Acu, whose cage is covered with a light blue blanket. Between my feet lies a thermos bag containing Parma ham and mozzarella sandwiches, sliced watermelon and a frozen bottle of water which, Grandma says, *will melt along the way.* Great-Grandma wears her false teeth for the journey so she'll be able to eat too.

Nancy Drew mystery books and beads of all colours are in a bag I put between me and Acu's cage. I wouldn't want it to fall on me and get bitten by that sharp black beak. I bring my beads because every summer I make necklaces, bracelets, and headbands with my sister and friends; then we set up a stand on the street and have a vendita—a sale.

Father, Mother, Leigh and Birikti are following us in a grey BMW. Mother can't smoke, it's Father's car. He drives. Leigh, my sister, is one year older than me and sits in the back with Birikti—just the two of them, nothing else, while I'm all scrunched. Birikti brought up Mother and her brother in Asmara and takes care of me and Leigh. She says she's waiting for the war to end in Eritrea to go back home.

As much as I want her family to be safe and her country at peace I can't conceive of her leaving us. Birikti takes up space but it doesn't count since she's so soft. Leigh has all the room in the world to move around in, but I feel lucky not having to listen to the classical tapes Father plays the whole way.

The thermos bag in their car doesn't contain the same things as ours. Father doesn't eat ham, he's Jewish—this morning, Grandma prepared a sandwich for him with scrambled eggs, tomatoes and mayonnaise. And Birikti only eats her food, she's Coptic. Last night she baked a pizza-esque bread for the trip. Everything is neatly secured in cellophane—under no circumstances are Mother and Leigh's ham sandwiches allowed to touch the other food. But everyone can feast on the other half of the apple cake, lying on Mother's lap.

Both car trunks are packed, there's no room left, not even for a pin. Brown leather suitcases, filled with clothes and shoes, fight for space with flour, salt, sugar, spaghetti, rice and coffee; food is more expensive at the seaside, so we stock up. Birikti's food, scirò and berberè, is also in the trunk—she must bring it along since it isn't sold anywhere in Italy; relatives and friends send it to her from Eritrea.

Empty glass bottles stand in wooden crates in the trunk because Great-Grandma, Grandma and Birikti spend two weeks each summer preparing tomato sauce for the winter. They tape an invisible 'Danger' sign on the kitchen door while they work, sweating, boiling San Marsano tomatoes in huge pots and the sauce splutters about—last year it burned Leigh's cheek. Then, the tomatoes are sieved and boiled again before the juice is poured in bottles which sometimes explode. Once the bottles have cooled off, they are laid outside, in rows, protected by wool blankets. My sister and I are given strict orders to steer clear of that area; those bottles are bound to burst, especially if we play ball nearby.

I stare in front of me at Grandma's pitch-black head and Great-Grandma's silver hair. Once in a while, I turn around checking on Leigh. I almost prefer it if she sticks out her tongue at me—then I'm sure she isn't lying on Birikti's fleshy legs. Staring out the window at other cars isn't very interesting but this time I see one carrying a couch on its roof. *Quick! Look at that car*, I tell Grandma, *those people are worse than us.*

After all these years of going to the same place, I recognise the road. When I see pine trees on both sides of the street and people on bikes in bathing suits, I know we are almost there. Pine trees, pini, grow everywhere.

Lido dei Pini is only a forty-minute drive from Rome yet *we look like a family of immigrants,* Grandma says with half a laugh as we unload the car. Mother scolds me for having stuck my tongue out at Leigh and won't let me explain.

On Sunday, tomorrow, my parents are returning to Rome. Every June, they leave us with Grandma, Great-Grandma and Birikti. They stay in Rome to work and visit us on weekends. Father is a dentist and Mother has a job at the Foreign Ministry.

This summer, my parents are moving from our apartment into a house with a garden. The new house is close to school, so I can wake up later in the mornings. Before we left for Lido dei Pini, our parents took me and Leigh to see the new place and choose the bedrooms. I'm starting middle school in September and I won't be sleeping beneath my sister on a bunk bed anymore, afraid of her falling on me. Leigh got the bedroom with the sliding door. That's the first time I saw one and I opened and closed it, opened and closed it, opened and closed it until she slapped my hand: *stop it, it's mine!* The following winter I had my revenge. I locked her in the bathroom and turned the stereo on full blast so no one could hear her banging against the door.

I wanted the room with the shutterless window stretching across the entire wall. It overlooks a field, three caves, trees and a castle—in the distance. Someone drew a sign, a Swastika, I know, above the caves. *There's a bad draft in that room, it's too cold and there's no closet either.* Mother had already decided: the two bedrooms at the end of the hall are perfect, *for two sisters.*

★

It's a dream come true. Mother owns a villa in Rome: walls, ceilings, floors and a garden. She'll never tire of transforming and changing this space every weekend or when she arrives home early from work. Her hobby is shifting stuff round, plants too, because she says, *I have to make some order*—as if she has just moved in and is forever settling down.

Mother kneels amidst boxes. A cigarette dangles from her lips: a Rothmans. The ash is an inch long. Brown eyes survey what is soon to become the living room. She's been wearing the same yellow tee shirt for the past three days and can't find another. Everything is packed. She must work, work hard to make this house a home.

She was weeding and planting roses, then thought better of it so came upstairs to unpack a box: plates and cutlery sit inside. The ash falls on a bowl. Everything Mother has reminds her of Asmara—she ate her wedding meal out of that bowl.

The kitchen is bare. She's still waiting for the wooden kitchen furniture to arrive, but it's August—that's like saying Rome has gone on a collective strike. Even flies move to the seaside. She was lucky the movers agreed to do this job, at least the piano, glass table, TV, antique cabinet, stereo, chairs, desks, coffee tables, clothes, books, and bathroom things are in the house.

Father didn't take any time off, though he's forced not to work for a few weeks in August. No one would dream of booking an appointment with the dentist. If his patients get a toothache, they call from their holiday destinations demanding an immediate solution. Father gives away his miracle cure over the phone, time and again: *boil water with coarse salt.*

Mother pushes, with her feet, the box with plates and cutlery into the empty kitchen, then goes back to the living room and tears the masking tape off another box, full of sheets. Old sheets, new sheets, linen sheets, cotton sheets, flannel sheets—for double and single beds.

Sitting cross-legged on the floor, she holds white sheets and matching pillowcases and towels she embroidered in her twenties with Great-Grandma, her grandma, in Asmara for her trousseau. They were sitting in the garden, under the shade of the fig tree, and Great-Grandma was telling her about the journey, by sea, to Africa.

I still remember the name of the ship. 'Tripolitana,' Great-Grandma said, a sparkle in her blue eyes. She didn't mix with the other passengers because most were wives of fascist soldiers joining their husbands. The trip took ten days and they had to stop overnight outside the Suez Canal waiting for a warship to exit. *Your mother,* Great-Grandma exclaimed, *was only eight and all she did was cry and throw up until we crossed the Canal.* Those golden dunes soothed her.

Great-Grandpa had left for Asmara a year before Great-

Grandma to find a house and prepare for her arrival with their children. He wrote her, describing the horse-drawn carriages, the Italian Cathedral on Viale Mussolini, the spice market with mounds of rusty coloured powders, the Coptic church, and the women wearing white cotton netzelas, shawls. But Great-Grandma couldn't imagine a place inhabited by a constant breeze, hot in the sun and cool in the shade, nor Massawa on the Red Sea.

Mother inhales and exhales the last cigarette of the pack as she puts the sheets back in the box. Leaning against the door, she wonders if the sofas should go on the left or right side of the room. It depends on where she's going to put the painting of the Dahlak Islands which used to hang above her grandfather's desk in her childhood house in Asmara.

But Mother can't think without smoking. The Tabacchaio in the area, which works the August shift, is closed for lunch. She must go to the centre of Rome, all the way to Piazza Venezia. The streets are traffic free, only tourists roam the roads, and it takes her a mere twenty-five minutes compared to the forty or fifty when Rome is in full swing.

Rome is quiet. The layers of the past glisten, sumptuous, under the setting sun. Mother doesn't notice. Smoking, she drives home, realising she has less than a month to organise the house before we return from Lido dei Pini and buy Acu a new cage.

⋆

My sister and I cycle to the beach every morning around ten. *Ciao*, Acu says as we shut the garden gate. Grandma and Birikti don't come with us and Great-Grandma is too old. No one watches over us and we return home no later than one, for lunch, and Great-Grandma asks us, *how many times did you go in the sea, today?* I don't go in the water more than twice. It's cold. The sea goes in my mouth, out my nose, and I'm afraid of choking. *Five*, I scream into Great-Grandma's ear, then wiggle five fingers. Her blue eyes twinkle, enlarged by glasses.

Great-Grandma does Chiaccherino all morning—sitting with her legs in the sun, dress pulled up above her knees, and the rest of her in the shade. We compare tans. I'm darker than her and Leigh. *Little chocolate*, my family calls me, *Birikti's daughter.*

In the afternoon, if the Pope isn't on TV, Great-Grandma teaches me Chiaccherino. Acu is with us on the terrace, caged, saying, in English, *Acu is a very good boy!* and whistling to birds on the branches of pine trees. I have my own golden spool this year which Father made me. Trying to get the movements right, I concentrate on the way Great-Grandma uses her hands. Her thumb is flat, her fingertips point sideways. Her hands are shaped for the Chiaccherino, but how will I ever turn my knots into lace, like her?

Great-Grandma decides I must use thicker thread to learn. I make so many knots that my roll of thread finishes quickly—buying more is an excuse to take Great-Grandma out for a walk. She changes from her slippers into her shoes and combs her silver hair. The hair behind her head is flat since she often falls asleep, her head resting against the couch. Great-Grandma's back is bent and she rests her weight on me as we walk, our arms linked, extra slowly. I don't dare let go; it would be a tragedy if she fell.

Here at the seaside, I spend a lot of time with Birikti, especially when friends and cousins visit her. Birikti has her own house in the garden and before I go in, I peer through the window to make sure they aren't crying, reading letters, or listening to the Vatican radio news—the only station which has a daily program on Africa. Eritrea and Ethiopia are fighting but the Italian news says almost nothing about the war. *Even though*, I heard Mother say once, *Eritrea used to belong to Italy.*

If Birikti, her friends and relatives are playing music and eating, I call out, *Birikti, can I come?* I like the food they cook more than ours because it's eaten with your hands—no one can scold me, that's the way it's done. If I'm lucky, one of her relatives or friends has arrived from Eritrea with real angera, a spongy sour crepe-like bread. Real angera is brown not yellow like the one Birikti makes by mixing polenta flour and other things in the bucket, covering it with a towel so the concoction rises almost to the brim.

I sit next to or on Birikti as she feeds me from her hand. *Shikorei, she's your daughter*, her friends say, surprised at how greedily I swallow their spicy chicken. When I leave, I wash my hands well before Grandma asks if I've been eating Birikti's food again. Lying is out of the question: she'd notice my red stained hands. I just have to be patient, my face serious, as I listen to her telling me that: I must not eat Birikti's food because she does not have much of it and the spices are impossible to find in Rome. And: I really should not eat her meat because she cannot touch ours and by eating it, I'm taking it away from her.

The summer days blend into each other until that afternoon when my sister and I watch Birikti walk towards us to open the garden gate. *Where is Acu?* I ask. Maybe Grandma's cutting his wings again. *Uwaii!* Birikti exclaims, covering her mouth with her hand, as she turns around to stare at the cage.

The little door sways gently. The cage stands empty. Acu spread out those wings, flapped them. Took off. I wasn't born when my uncle, Mother's brother, brought Acu to Rome. He lives in Kano, Nigeria, and he carried the baby grey parrot in a shoebox on the plane.

Grandma pokes her head out on the terrace, *how could it have happened?*

MATT FULLERTY

Matt Fullerty was born in Warrington. He studied English at Oxford University and worked as a schoolbook editor in London before starting to write. He is working on a novel.

FOR KICKS

I light a cigarette and throw stones up at the window of the nearest house. Phil appears.

'Try and make a bit more noise, would you.'

'Sorry.'

I'm not the least sorry and take a slow drag. He'll be down in seconds. Phil's window shuts and I stub the cigarette underfoot and check the packet—three to go. Then I get out the gin and tip, and it's cruelly sweet and takes your breath away like the TV advertisement says: *like the sweetest mint*. The house comes softly to life. Should I chuck another stone? I don't know. I'm still waiting. Lights flick on in the hall, then off, and finally the outside light comes on. He appears with a bag slung over his shoulder and we slip off in the dark.

Now I should explain really that this is where all the trouble started. We had something to celebrate, namely my new fortune, and since the early days, Phil was not the sharpest card to have around. I blame it all on him of course, and have this feeling I would have done better if I'd never met him. A bit cruel perhaps, and probably untrue. Let's just say I don't warm to everything that happened that evening, in terms of consequences at least. Some nights don't consider the future, and we were keen to stress my new invincibility with some of the bad habits that got Phil suspended from school in the very last week. *I got more time to practice being dangerous*, he says about it now, remembering the early summer as though it were a lifetime ago.

So out he comes and we drift down to the dingle, and speak little until we meet the common and its secluded trees. A few houses in the blackness; the streetlights have gone.

'Here, I reckon.'

'Nice.'

Phil tips up his bag on the grass. We line them up, ten or so gaudy fireworks, and stake them in the earth. I offer Phil a cigarette and he starts to chatter because we're repeating an old folly; an understanding left over from childhood, catching each other's eye.

'Light them.'

It was strange to be there, a week after an old man with his dog caught us and threatened to call the law. Phil was already suspended. The game was up after he set some off at school, and magnificently, he was expelled with only hours left before leaving. At home I got a clip for my trouble and was banned from having *those kinds of friends*.

I pass the gin, and Phil takes a swig and spits it out.

'That's for the women. Any whisky?'

'Sorry.'

'I thought you were a walking pub. Got any fags then?'

I hand over the packet.

'So you're rich,' he carries on, and looks over. All around, the common is just a sinking line of rooftops with a thin grey horizon over the trees. A few stars are out.

'I'm more loaded than you'll ever be.'

He takes a step towards me, half humorous and half aggressive. We're a similar height, but he's got the shoulders on me.

'True,' he says, and sounds like he's not thinking. Then he lights up with a nod, the glow orange in the dark.

'So how much?'

'I don't know really. The jackpot.'

'Oh, the jackpot, the jackpot. You should be all right,' he grins. Then he grabs me by the collar. 'That's a crazy amount!' But he's calm enough, just as quickly, to take another drag. 'And you don't even know how much?'

'A million.'

'*Millions* more like.'

His forehead creases in surprise.

'I'm going down to London to get it,' I say. 'Tomorrow.'

He flicks his cigarette on the grass. Phil is the kid who never grew up. At least, maybe he grew up fast and stopped. He's not yet twenty-one, and I forget he's the same age as me. The future seems never to bother him: working the BP garage at nights and weekends, fixing the scooters for Pizza Magic. He won't leave town. Then it will all be over for Phil. Born astride of the grave, thinking he's Dean Moriarty but that's the same glint I knew when I was sixteen years old.

'Can't they send you a bloody cheque?'

'I might lose a cheque.'

'So?'

'Look, it's bound to be a million. Why rush it?'

'If you've won a million, though, I reckon,' and he looks around and gestures over the grass. 'If you're a millionaire, then I'll stuff all the fireworks down my throat!'

'Right, you're on. Light them first.'

There's nothing else for it now, and he takes his stare away.

'I've not brought a lighter,' he quips, looking down, and I try not to laugh. His mind has gone somewhere anyway, and he scratches his head. Phil is with the fashion so to speak, as far as skinheads can be, and it suits him. He used to wear an earring but someone pulled it off. He takes a dramatic breath.

'Go on then.'

'You do it. You can pretend you're lighting all that money. You've really won. I can't believe it. Show me the ticket.'

'As if!' I say sarcastically. 'Maybe tomorrow.'

He points at the fireworks. I use a match on both cigarettes, inhaling and I'm off down the line of stacked fireworks. I feel like the crazy last scene of *The Dirty Dozen* when he's tearing off the pins and dropping fire in the hole at the German fortress. I can see myself. There's smoke in my face and I'm stumbling through a wave of phosphorous. But somewhat unglamorously the cigarette drops from my mouth.

'This was a stupid idea,' I complain, stuck unpeeling a fuse on the ground.

Then the first rocket cries into the air and sings with that peculiar and pained sound. It shudders, explodes, and quickly I rush to light the others. Of course the cigarette dies, so I stick it right inside the last one and roll away thinking about Lee Marvin. Then I'm on my feet as they tear in the sky.

A few sparks fall on us, and we gawp, making daft noises with the flashes. Some are duds and fall back on the common in their empty casings. Some dogs can sniff them out later.

The moon is horrified; the streaks burn her face a strange mushroom white and colours stain the blackness all around in fluorescent paint. Speeded-up traffic, and fireworks called *Killer Carnival.* They start to fade and crush themselves in a green snake, wheeze and vanish to nothing, and we're laughing like disappointed kids. A mischievous spinner implodes and showers some drops of fire. I twitch as they fall on my hands; Phil brushes them off his head.

'Thirty quid for as many seconds,' he says. 'Come on, let's get out of here. There's a fella hanging around one of those windows.' He points, but we're already scampering over the grass.

'What's he gonna do, shoot us with an airgun?'

Phil shines a torch from his hip and its light is enough to avoid the mud, and we're under the trees. He starts a little speech of reminiscence, as though the fireworks were still affecting him, and we slow and take a short cut through the children's playground.

'I wish we were somewhere else, don't you? With more going on, and better weather.'

'Like Spain?' I offer.

He looks at me. 'That'll do.'

'In the cafés at night,' I say, 'and music and revolution in the air.' I lift the gin and take a swig. It's very sweet and stings this time like it's overheated. 'I wish I had an ice cube, you know, for the bottle.'

'You sure you got no whisky?'

I swig more down near the seesaw. Then, with a spasm, up it comes in my throat, and out all over the tarmac. The seesaw rocks and goes down at one end, and I lose my balance and start staggering round. Phil's face has changed but he's not laughing too much. The puke is kind of dribbling by now, but I can feel the relief, and I wipe my mouth with my sleeve.

'Went down the wrong way.'

'Spain or Portugal,' Phil replies, and we separate among the ghostly shapes. There's a silence and he must be brooding on the future. He pulls his hood up like he's enjoying the moment in a half-private, strangely wistful way, like it might never happen.

'Maybe Spain.'

We meet up at the climbing frame, with its metal chipped paint, and kick some stones at the grass.

'Everything is drained,' I say, indulging some nonsense.

Phil sits on a swing and rocks aimlessly. Walking past it, I spin the merry-go-round.

'I'm not getting on,' I say. 'I'll be sick.'

'Anyway, I'm heading for the Costa del Sunshine. But how're you gonna live? Sitting on your mountain of cash?' I'm smiling. 'You are donating some to *me*?'

'A thousand. I said already. At least.'

'At least?'

'And this holiday.'

He says nothing. As quickly as it came, the moment goes, and talk of the hard cash is gone too, smoothed over.

'I don't know yet,' I say. 'There's the world to see and oceans to sail, that sort of thing. Maybe tomorrow, I'll let you know.' He looks at me with a straight expression:

'I knew there was five grand in it for me.'

For a moment it seems the night is over. We chat for half an hour, just nonsense. The spying moon creeps overhead, and shadows move in the playground. Now the night peacefulness is here. The moonlight glow is like from an insect, strange and ephemeral. There's nothing to touch or feel, no way instinctively to know it's late or early. The gin seeps further into my brain. Half asleep, we're gradually walking back home.

'Your life's over, and starting, at the same time,' Phil slowly says.

I say nothing, and the quiet grows. We turn a corner. A small pond borders the path and I can see over to the roundabout.

'Down the road,' Phil says and points. 'That's where I'll be.'

'Like the Littlest Hobo.'

But at this start of another nonsense conversation and regret for the summer, there it is, all on its own. What the evening has kept secret until now: a wreck of metal, twisted in a hedge. The driver's side is still smooth and I try the door but it's jammed. We walk around opposite ends.

'What a mess.'

It's an Escort with a battered side and bald tyres, and looks half-dumped, half-crashed. A tree leans precariously, painfully, from the passenger door and is buried in a tangle of branches. Not caring we pass on. Then Phil explains our duty, to our youth.

'It's too good to miss,' he says. 'It's a goner anyway. No one will miss a smashed-in tin box.' More words follow, something about the need for *carpe diem* and go reckless. 'Better to be a lion for a day than a sheep for a thousand years!' His soft face of dreams is gone, and now the muscles in his ears are twitching and his shoulders are restless. He raises both arms, paints the scene in the sky. 'This is a message. Not to end here, let us embrace what has begun!'

I remember him sounding unconvincing even then, and feeling this was a moment to let slide, but we're circling the vehicle anyway and Phil starts to talk about other times he's discovered wrecked cars.

'You know,' he concludes. 'You get few opportunities like this.'

'Well,' I'm replying. 'You should see this road near me. Crap bangers are dumped there every week.'

'Where's that?'

'Right outside my flat.'

'Well then, you said it. This can be a first for you, and the first of many.' We're standing in front of the headlights. Both are intact. I half expect Phil to kick one, just to see the glass fall. 'Just like those fireworks ripped the sky,' he says poetically, raising his chin, and looking at me sideways. 'So what would happen to *this* baby?'

The moon has slunk away. The next moment he's on the roof with a piece of metal I can't identify in his hand. I glance around. Not a soul. The sunroof comes off, the plastic cover, his fingers on the foam binding and the whole thing is torn out and over his shoulder.

On the opposite pavement a streetlight continues to whirr. It blinks on and off, a warning and an approval. For that moment I feel a rush of elation. Here we are! The commonplace forces of daylight mean nothing, and *this* is alive, living by the heel. Ruling the street. But, just as quickly, I feel my gums and a nervous rush of fear and adrenalin.

Phil is furious, and going wild. Feet spread to look more impressive. Now he uses his cigarette on the gin bottle and twists it overhead, a sly smile widening in the streetlight.

I look around, now really worried someone is watching. Two houses curve behind the hedge and there's nothing more to see. *Here we are!* I feel again, but without the same rush.

This is average suburbia, a miniature toy town fixed last century according to some bright young geographer's plan. There is no life, no randomness here, just ordinary days and nights of soulless nothing. No powers struggle for supremacy in these streets, they are quiet beyond hell, and the greatest distraction must be the trickle of graffiti or a milk float breaking the speed limit.

The houses are identical semis. Monoliths of plain paint, symmetrical between their garage doors, and white stone cladding of shared social aspiration. Space is important, but more important is the hunger for bland regularity, the desire to be enclosed safe behind floral curtains and simply disappear, blinds that hide the half-lives inside. But there is still something, a part of me that I cannot give up on, a comfort, however comfortably numb, behind those walls. Anyway, we all need *those kinds of friends* and fortunately no one is looking. Most important for our purpose, no lights are on, not that Phil is waiting for any signal from me.

He lights it anyway, and releases the bottle.

My heart drops and I shuffle away but there's nowhere really to go. I want to leave, but a breathless indecision has made everything clear at once.

'That's torn it,' I whisper. *What am I doing?*

Phil is shouting: 'For good or bad, for better or worse, things happen because you *will* them!'

I look for a reflection, a flame in his eyes, but his face is covered. Silhouetted with only dark trees behind, I feel like he's in a photograph or I see him through an imaginary lens with a sinking afterthought, as though from the slowness of a future moment. There is something sharp inside me as well. Something selfish telling me to get away: to run for it, that Phil is somewhere else now, in another space and spiralling down. I do not know him.

I am not involved, a witness to vandalism I tell myself, but it's true there are few words to describe the thrill, the driving feeling of setting something alight. Watching something burn, knowing you caused it, and then seeing it burn freely. It has a life of its own, and you gave it that life and can follow it. As we all watch TV wars and natural disasters. Horrified and fascinated. It's all voyeuristic viewing; in some room of your mind a seamy eye will be watching.

'It's because you *will* them,' Phil cries.

But looking back, I remember his persistence, the lengthening out of time. Standing there unmoving and waiting and in no real hurry, he lit it. *He* dropped the bottle. The match was an enemy in his palm but the damage he was causing was internal. And there were no innocents there that night.

'Get on with it, if you're doing it,' I call out.

So he teases the match under his chin, faces the imaginary crowd and makes the sound of a cornered snake. The fallen tree, lying demolished on the car, is still, and the branches straggle from the roof in all directions. Phil cries out he *feels like a kid!*

An ash-coloured darkness is suspended all down the street, the houses, the streetlight and the hedge.

Everything is waiting for the unreal glow of fire. Again he twists the newspaper in the bottle, but the flame goes falling and spins uselessly down the bonnet. He lights another and drops to his knees. Quickly the bottle is gone through the open sunroof, and immediately coughs up. A flash panics red between his ankles, and this local Dean Moriarty, a new kid god just looking for kicks, yelps as the car bursts into flame, front and back.

For a second, he's motionless. Wondering, perhaps, if to jump in the driver's seat, and drive to town slowly dissolving, as he threatened to do before, in a blaze of glorious bones. Then the fear kicks in and he leaps so high to avoid the temperature from the misting windows, the now shattering glass, that he catches his heel. He rolls and is sliding down the windscreen.

'Let's get the . . !'

Then we're on our feet and away, surrounded by cataclysms of light and sparks and waiting for unlikely explosions.

'Go for cover,' he calls.

At a good distance we watch the flames. They dip from the broken windows. The heat rises over the bashed-in car, going nowhere. We realise the fireworks were our real celebration. Tomorrow I am in London, and I can live in London how I like. Tomorrow Phil is back at his job; naturally I won't be going back to mine.

Looking back, like schoolboys we were only brief followers of this pyromania hobby, namely, setting things on fire. But walking away I still remember those flecks of soot and the smoke billowing over the trees. From a faint trickle of blue in the west, to the moon looking on, unpleased and smirking, as the smoke rose, and at those moments I am back there.

The car bonnet is open, and with the grumble of a burning oven, it startles itself, a low moan to a roar. It lets out a heartbroken sound and a kind of splutter. Death filling the engine and squeezing out the water and oils. Then that Escort, pride of our night, was ablaze at last.

I turn to Phil and see something like a strange hunger. Black marks all across his shoulders. For a second he is a dazed chimney sweep, and one with a skinhead, and a fixed expression with white flecks of ash.

He was the real nutcase in the end. On a night of bad tricks and some immoral living. And I never forgot. But that was the last night I saw him. The last image of that time was his teeth, spread out and happy, a smear of blood bitten from his lip caused by the firework stupidity, or the outright vandalism, I do not know.

'Give me a call,' he says, as though I am there now, and waves as he wanders the curb and back down the street. Something made me think even then of the insecurity and distractions of being young. How Phil would get into worse trouble, and more than likely by the end of that week.

Shaking hands and grinning at a night well done, that last moment was shared with the car creaking behind us. As the flames died, the hot metal started to sizzle and contract and cool. We looked back, and for a moment it seemed the hedge could give way, and the car slip backwards down to the pond. But it didn't: it just stuck there like either one of us, not really reaching for anything or going anywhere. Just fizzing in the darkness, waiting for the day before the night. For me to collect winnings that were probably only a grand, and for Phil to pretend why fireworks were missing from the BP garage. All in all, it was just a night that didn't seem meaningful, except I was leaving. It wasn't important, any of it really. My memory is unclear, though sometimes I'm sure Phil is calling the next day, still, to find out how much I won.

Jo Gallagher

Jo Gallagher was born in Yorkshire in 1970 to Irish & Indian/Jamaican parents. She now lives and works in London.

THE BOOKHOLDER

(extract from a novel)

ACT 1. SCENE 1.

THE PERSONS

SPENCER—26—*husband to Comfort*
COMFORT—17—*wife to Spencer*
VIRTUE—25—*sister to Comfort*
ALEXANDER—5 & JUSTYN—2—*sons to Virtue*
GRACE—60—*a midwife*

THE PROPS

a groaning-chair, a newborn baby

THE SCENE

Spencer's house. The Shire of Middle-Sex. January 1585

Comfort behaved as if her pregnancy would last for years. This morning, after a New-year's Eve spent dancing, drinking and fooling about with friends, she woke in grown-up agony. Locking one elbow around the cherry knob of the bedpost she eased herself up into a squat and wedged the vertebrae of her neck in a gouge in the headrest.

To balance her see-sawing body Comfort focused on the furniture, straining her head to see over the high footboard of her husband's bed, or rather her husband's father's bed, with not one fashionable feather in sight to soften the first year of their ruttish marriage. Apart from her linen trunk, which she could not see, what little there was in the narrow oak-framed room had belonged to her husband's ancestors. Outworn and cumbersome. Comfort looked back down at her stomach; she was burning up, sweating but at the same time shivering in the icy January morning. She stared at the empty grate, then at the scorched wall around the fireplace that needed whitewashing. The low-ceilinged bedroom, its bowed segments of grimy plaster bulging between the skeleton of joists and beams, appeared as close and gloomy as the inside of her trunk.

Comfort struggled out of bed away from her snoring husband; he had rolled over and his yesterday's-ale breath was making her more nauseous. In their inebriated state, both had neglected to put up a curtain as they had to prepare the fire. She gravitated towards the square of bleached-out sky but was diverted by a pile of their clothes—their church clothes—now smelling of pig fat, dumped on the floor with their dung-thickened shoes. Like a child confronted by a heap of neatly swept leaves she impulsively kicked everything about the floor, then abruptly stopped to pick up her best stocking with her toes. Underfoot, the month-old rushes, brittle and frayed, disintegrated between her scraping, scratching nails. She continued until, balancing on one leg trying to snatch up the netted hose, she began to sway, and stumbled towards the sky.

Holding onto the sides of the window-ledge as if it were a laden platter, Comfort glanced back at her soiled wet imprint in the thin flock-mattress—a curled-up girl with a swollen potbelly and immature bladder could have slept there. She caught sight of herself in the looking-glass-sized window, face all creased with frowning, and although her insides were being battered out of shape by the disgruntled creature within, it was her own ugly expression that distracted. Tilting her face vainly she examined her pained reflection in the honeycombed glass.

Carefully she raised a knee. Then, grabbing the hem of her nightdress, she tucked it under her engorged bosom and looked down on her rigid but throbbing stomach. She smiled. The snail shell, which her best friend Marion had drunkenly drawn the night before, was still there. While laughing and belching and flashing her elderberry-stained teeth, Marion had dragged a soft piece of burnt-out kindling round and round the enormous, seventeen-year-old belly. Comfort rubbed her spiralled body as if the last hours before motherhood could be savoured like a just finished banquet.

Sweaty palms turned the stomach into a solid grey boulder; despondently she pulled the nightdress down and wiped her ash-smudged hands across it.

Comfort's shoulders suddenly buckled. Steadying herself with a matronly stance—parting her legs to counteract the convulsing muscles—she heard herself calling out, 'Our son is coming,' in a strange deep voice.

Spencer wakes in an instant but has yet to gain control of his limbs. His arm flails over to the depressed space beside him and begins caressing the soggy mattress. When his fingers cannot find his little girl he propels himself out of the bed. From the floor he looks quizzically at the double-chinned with grimacing woman, leaning, hands on hips, against the sill. It has been snowing; the sky behind her is so intense it makes him squint till she looks like a coal-heaver, with her blackened straw-tufted feet and drawn out handprints across her front.

Comfort turns her back on him, grips the window-frame with two outstretched arms and leans forward to rest her pounding head on the sill. Waiting for the pins and needles to subside, Spencer stares at his grunting wife as she bends her legs and pushes her buttocks against the sodden nightdress. He goes to get help, blood throbbing in his groin as he crawls on hands and knees to the door, partly because his feet are still numb and partly to shield his erection.

*

Comfort often said she could never remember being in labour.

An hour or so later, petrified and still clinging to the window-ledge, she watches her sister Virtue, Spencer and an elderly midwife wading through the snow as if it were waist height. Through the warped hexagons of glass the three are in glaring contrast against the white of the fields, crude figures stitched onto canvas. The old woman's gory apron over a duckweed coloured smock; her willowy sister, cloaked and hooded, dragging a large folded chair which leaves a brushstroke of green grass in its trail; and her underdressed husband in his oversized boots, staggering behind with Virtue's two sleeping sons slumped like sacks over each shoulder. Comfort lets go of the ledge and rushes downstairs.

Even though they near the cottage it does not make a sound, the thatch above weighted by a foot of snow.

Once inside, the feet-stamping outsiders blow hot air into their hands which are shaped into cups around their lips. Mouths preoccupied, each surveys the damaged parlour and the ransacked kitchen. The chair, stools and benches lay with their legs upended; handles cracked off all the earthen crocks; bottles with shattered necks, their contents spattered across the walls where they have been beheaded; a thick carpet of trodden-in foodstuffs leading to the bedroom.

'Was it in such state when you left?' asks Virtue.

'Yes,' lies Spencer, and hastens up the stairs.

Comfort now cowers in a corner of the bedroom as though she had been flung about a ship; one cut and bleeding hand pressed against cold plaster, the other down between her legs pawing at the searing flesh. The meats and drink she has just hastily consumed, flows back over her chin with each lurch of her insides.

The narrow room, as if it had been dragged ashore and its lid swung back, fills with noise and warmth and light: Virtue fussing as she tucks her boys into the wet bed; the midwife Grace crouching by the fireplace like a green and red toad exhaling flames; Spencer apologetically explaining that he could not provoke any women from their drunken slumbers, but that he is a good man so will stay and help. Comfort's last childless picture is of her husband trying to open out the groaning-chair and it collapsing on the floor.

Now there are just voices, underwater sounding voices in her eyes' closed darkness, shadows moving in front of her crimson-lidded light.

Despite the vast consuming pain, Comfort's gripping fingertips can make out each hole in the woodwormed sides of the groaning-chair and every strand of the threadbare hollow seat which no longer boasts its padded rim. The grain of the wood will encircle her buttocks for days and, with a needle, Spencer will remove blackening splinters as he recoils from his wife's now spoilt behind.

'In the name of the Father and of the Son and of the Holy Ghost, come safe and go safe what we have here,' over and over and over.

Comfort's eyes are still closed, her sister's chanting silhouette receding and approaching, blinking back the light as she paces around with a broom. 'In the name of the Father and of the Son and of the Holy Ghost, come safe and go safe what we have here.'

Comfort grinds her teeth.

'Hold her upright, man,' the midwife starts to compete, croaking out instructions as she kneels beside the chair.

Spencer snaps at his sister-in-law: 'Cease thy religious incantations,' as he stands behind the seated, swaying Comfort and, as ordered, hooks his hands under her armpits to stop her sliding to the floor. Biting his bottom lip he looks down the heaving body of his squatting wife—at the miraculous nine-month breasts against her nightgown which is taut like a tent around the frame of the chair. He watches Grace's hands as they disappear under it to rub a foul-smelling grease into his wife's thighs. Even when they emerge, sticky with egg-white discharge and traces of excrement, he frowns enviously.

*

'Rouse her!' Grace says impatiently. 'She hath drunk herself to a stupor.'

Spencer shakes Comfort upright but her eyelids and head remain lowered like a corpse looking in on itself.

The foetus is turning damson; bruised by its mother's guttural moaning it starts coming up for air, assisted by her palpitating lungs pressing against the soles of its feet. Its features are mangled by her straining insides; its open mouth gagging on the syrupy lining; its hearing muffled by her reverberating wailing and their pounding hearts.

Then, as the top of its head emerges, the blur of noise, as when waking from sleep, becomes deafening as it rips into the different parts: the high-pitched hovering chant; the amphibious croaking; the overhead, distant rumbling of a man trying to pacify them all. Comfort opens her eyes to dazzling winter white daylight, pupils fully dilated and blinded.

Grace grips the viscous crown and it gives way like a soft-shelled crab to inquisitive fingers. Then, as if indignant to this prodding, the constricted foetus slips out into her grasp; the surrounding rushes flush pink as they absorb escaping fluids. Comfort slumps over and before Spencer has had time to see his son, the midwife has concealed him in her terracotta-crusted lap as her arms have gone back inside the tent to tug out the meaty plug. Grace yanks the cord, pulling it out like intestine until it goes taut, then pushes her hand into the gaping orifice to dislodge the bloody pouch.

Once she has uncoupled it from Comfort she slaps the veiny placenta down onto the baby's front. Looking up to see Spencer blanching, she cackles: 'Fancy some womb-cake?' and begins gathering the slimy cord around her knuckles as though winding seaweed covered rope.

With a russet blade she severs the pipe. The baby fills with air as she ties a crude knot and jams it with her nail into the navel; as if she has pierced through its belly with the force the baby deflates, exhaling with an almighty wail.

Grace gets to her feet awkwardly, holding the screaming baby like Spencer is holding Comfort, under the armpits. She cushions its back against her bosom and the afterbirth sac rolls off its front and splits open across the boards. The still plum-hued infant dangles in front of its family.

Spencer's and Virtue's eyebrows, which have been pushed far up into their hairlines with expectation, slide back down onto their foreheads.

Spencer raises his wife's head and whispers, 'He is girl,' into her ear.

The hush congeals as Comfort starts to imitate the crying baby, which wakes her two nephews, Alexander and Justyn. Scowling and blinking the boys pull at each other to stand up on the mattress. Seeing the jellied creature, the leaking placenta and the tarry mouth of the yawning midwife, they start howling for their mother. Spencer shouts at Virtue to get her sons from the room. Now everyone is yelling and sobbing and staring accusingly at the newborn baby, it finally falls silent.

and before I knew if I were girl or boy I knew I were a murderer

Ryan Gattis

Ryan Gattis is from Colorado Springs, Colorado, USA. He has currently completed his first novel, In Helios, *and is now laying plans for his second, entitled* White Boy *or* Boku wa hakujin desu.

In Helios

(extract from a novel)

Mightily, Demetrius Addison began to recite 'man very early made jars stand upright nearly perfect,' through wind-labored breathing; as coolly as possible whilst falling, he thought of the time that he overheard a too-cheery German tourist from his toilet stall at the visitor's center of some national monument, telling an unidentified other that singing 'happy birthday to me / happy birthday to me / happy birthday dear me-e-e / happy birthday to me,' while washing his hands, gave him the prerequisite fifteen seconds necessary to kill all bathroom germs, and finished by simply stating, with a vocalized umlaut or two where there should be none, that 'sometimes, the möst useful things in life are cräzy.'

Indeed, Demetrius considered this true, as he had recalled the solar system mnemonic learned in childhood that evinced the correct placement of the nine planets: 'man = Mercury, very = Venus, early = Earth, made = Mars, jars = Jupiter, stand = Saturn, upright = Uranus, nearly = Neptune, perfect = Pluto,' that, when said with a proper full-breath pause in-between each word, gave him the prerequisite nine seconds needed before he pulled the 'rip cord,' the open signal to his parachute, as he plummeted from a low-flying plane, on this, the final day of his vacation. Facing personal fears, like that of heights for example,

surely, is highly useful, and quite, quite, crazy. Particularly when partaking in such acts in countries that may, or may not, have the most stringent standards in regards to the personal safety of its participants. As he was out of any earshot at the time, Mister Addison could not be heard to curse the planets, or anything else for that matter, when his 'chute failed to open.

Below the falling body, she waited, leaning against a fence that ran the length of the rocky cliffs on a subtropical island, an unfrequented tourist point. In necessity's dread path, Aleina had no clear idea of what had gone wrong above her. She simply sat, hair in the wind, waiting. Her brief sunglass-shaded glimpses toward the sunny sky yielded nothing; when she thought, almost for sure, that the puff of a multicolored parachute would be visible any moment. Yes. She could see the plane. Yes. Its engines were audible. No. No parachute in sight. A glance at her watch, a coarse rub of her right hip, in the sore spot just . . . there, she awaited the arrival of her uncle, who had had 'just one more thing to do before we go.'

In a moment, Aleina would look up in time to see the descending body of her uncle rapidly disappear into the small coastal canyon stretched out before her. Not yet though. Feeling the wind pushing hard from the west, she still had a few seconds to check the sharpness of her nails against her scalp. Maybe time enough to move her tongue against her bottom lip, 'more habit than helpful,' as her mother had sometimes said. Maybe not enough time to get up and stretch as she had been meaning to for some time.

Oh no, most certainly not now: hand curled outward above her eyebrows, Aleina gaped at the blackened shape, obscured by the sun, that tumbled down the sky right on time. It could have been anything, a struck bird, garbage discarded from the airplane by careless operators, certainly not a man, unless . . . it *was* a helpless man, with disheveled hair and limbs distorted, sinking haplessly in the emaciated island air.

Experiencing the calamitous machinations of slowed motion time, Aleina heard her grandfather's voice after the body of her late uncle had disappeared from view. Measured, enunciated words from some time ago that seemed to drop from his mouth, dry and unfolded, into her presently ringing ears: 'few things more disconcerting than viewing a falling being.' Agreeing now, having seen it, her stomach made a noise it had never made before, like a crushed basso cricket flapping only one wing. Her grandfather had once been in some sort of air corps; he parachuted for his country. He saw some of his 'best friends, comrades,' the same age, falling out of the sky, too quickly being the first ones to the ground below. Wet old eyes, she remembered because it was the first time she had ever seen him cry.

'Helpless to stop, helpl . . .' curiously, the image of her grandfather's face held its place in her mind, long after her uncle's body had ceased to fall. She did not bother to look over the edge of the canyon, still hearing her grandfather's words inside her head, 'some things in life hold a heavy certainty.'

It is difficult to explain that Aleina was not exactly close with her uncle, or that side of the family, for that matter. Many words go unsaid now. It is best to skip that part about precisely how, exactly why, for the time being. Distance exists despite numerous efforts to the contrary and hard feelings still survive. If these words could be expressed at this moment, it must be noted that there may be no way to relate them impartially. 'If you don't have any*thing* nice to say, well, don't say any*thing* at all,' as Aleina's mother has said more than once, never casually emphasizing 'thing,' often while stifling herself with those yellow gloves she used to wash dishes with after family get-togethers, or the lapel of her least favorite business suit, worn thin from careful bite marks.

Consciously standing now, Aleina became a messenger, the bearer of bad news. The worst kind of news that needed to be delivered by means other than a telephone call, or a wired telegram, or a letter with one stamp too many. There was nothing else to do, not by caring people anyway. Not to tell her hard grandfather that his only son was dead from the worst kind of fall. After having made separate arrangements for the safe shipment of her uncle's body, she hopped a flight that afternoon, alone. Unfortunately for Aleina and many of the passengers aboard, that plane landed before its scheduled destination.

⋆

At roughly 30,000 feet, in a commercial airbus on its way back to the mainland that would have been deemed full if it had eleven more seats occupied, a Mister Maurice Gerald Finnigan, or 'Mo' to his friends, experienced a rather untimely heart attack. Just prior to the moment of myocardial infarction, Mr MGF had been musing proudly about this very flight as it allowed him to attend his only grandson's wedding in two days time. And so, as life-threatening accidents are wont to do, it happened without warning.

Spitting up twice-warmed and too-hot black coffee in the process of arrest, Mr MGF had pitched forward into the seat in front of him, then off into the aisle while listening to channel eight on the in-flight radio as it spilled out a faucet-like orchestration that had only moments earlier forced his wife to wad tissue up and plug it in her right ear to block out the itinerant treble. Two of the three passengers in row twenty-seven, the row directly behind Mr MGF, later swore that 'sudden turbulence,' or a 'drop in cabin pressure' brought it on. The fact that the headphones were still intact—at least in Mr MGF's ears, as the man screaming, 'I'm a paramedic,' saw to it that Mr MGF's chest got a good pounding and that his air passage had a good clearing—did nothing to confirm either eye witness account.

In point of fact, if not for the paramedic, Aleina would never have gathered the name of the man responsible for her delay. Mr MGF's abnormally quiet wife, now quite horrified, had husked a one-ear whisper out of her truly tiny vocal cornfield for the paramedic. Wasting no time, the paramedic screamed it at the unconscious man, now lying flat and apparently not moving, discounting the three-hundred-some-odd-miles-per-hour airspeed of their floor.

'Misterr Moreese Jerrald Finnigannn! Fight! Breathe! Fight! Fight! Pump some of that life-giving blood to your brain sir!' More than a few passengers will not now own up to internally repeating, 'Poor Old Michael Finnigan, Begin Again.' Although Aleina certainly would, for her mind had taken it one step further, and she wove a mantra out of it, like she used to do when she was younger, laying it over her breath as one might nest a quilt around a chilled child, 'poor old mister finnigan won't-your-heart-please begin again.' She was a kind young woman, still is.

Mr MGF had become the center of a ninety-eight person universe—minus the pilot and co-pilot; it would have been more if the plane had been full to capacity. Nothing else immediately available, his head rested upon a pair of old sandals as it was a day flight and all pillows had been stowed in the aft compartment. Said sandals happened to belong to Ms Summer Joy Maugham in twenty-six D. Her feet had recently walked them through a sunny country in Europe; they certainly would not tell of her excesses on a tiny island off the coast: a moment of which she actually recalled during the cardiopulmonary resuscitation being performed in front of her, with, it could be noted, a bit of paleness. Pumping frantically on the seemingly inert chest of Mr MGF, the paramedic did not notice that such a motion forced his patient's head back onto the sandals in a way that the light brown leathers became a bit truer to their name: almost as if they were completely made of sand, all, puffing up extra grains of borrowed beach onto the slanted pate of Mr MGF's surprisingly square-shaped head. For several minutes, not a soul aboard felt as if they were moving.

Behind the cockpit door, the pilot secured a quick emergency landing at a nearby airport just up the mainland shore. The plane was met with no less than six fire trucks: four red, two yellow; four ambulances: each with varying alternations of red and white across their broad backs; two police cars: one from the neighboring township, and one from the highway patrol; and one airport emergency vehicle: equipped better to hose down a burning plane than to transport a man in his mid-seventies to the nearest help center.

Some of the passengers would later describe the incident to the local constabulary as having happened 'in slow motion.' Still others, such as those in the back rows, or in the very front, as Mr MGF's unfortunate incident had happened somewhere near the middle, would describe it as, 'a bit confusing . . . it was more than a bit hard to breathe,' though with different accents and word choices, of course. Even more described heart pains of their own to the battery of leftover medical technicians who had arrived on the scene and suddenly had nothing better to do than to look after the stunned passengers because one ambulance had been enough to carry Mr MGF and his wife.

An unidentified passenger can recall hearing Ms S. J. Maugham mutter, 'mama says too many hands spoil the soup,' as she collected her sandals from the expectorating paramedic who had been told that he had no place in the third ambulance—the one with a red-white-red pattern; the one chosen to carry Mr MGF the distance. It had turned out that the 'paramedic' had confessed; he still had two weeks left on his training and was not yet a licensed medical technician.

One philosophy student, a former occupant of the C seat in the nineteenth row went so far as to describe it as, 'a collective, social, heart attack,' with appropriate pauses for punctuation. The local police did not record his comment. As for Mr MGF, he was rushed to the nearest hospital, where his condition was not discussed with people outside of the immediate family. He might have been transported to a bigger hospital later, via helicopter. Though to this day, many of those who shared in his dramatic interlude, are not sure of whether he lived or died, 'up there,' as some are fond of saying.

Stuart Glass

Stuart Glass was born in 1969. He lives and works in Norwich.

Minceman

(extract from a novel)

On Saturdays Mikey used to go with his Mum when she went shopping at the Co-op. She liked it at the Co-op, she said, because you knew what's what and where's where. Mikey would hold her hand while she pushed her trolley round the aisles. When she stopped to pick something up, he'd hold her coat.

It's a Superstore now, where the Co-op used to be. Things are constantly being moved around for the convenience of the customer, so finding what's where isn't as easy as it was. Nonetheless Mikey still goes there on a Saturday to buy his bits and bobs.

This Saturday, the first things people are faced with when they walk in are cucumbers. Mikey doesn't bother with them. He's never had much of an interest in cucumbers but, because they're right at the front, he can't help but notice them. He notes how uniform they all are. Straight as a rod, packed in tight transparent film. Very tidy in appearance, the cucumbers are. Mikey would have thought cucumbers had different shapes, like all things that grow under the sun. He doesn't know what happens to the others, but it seems it's only the straight ones that make it to the Superstore.

It's much busier now it's a Superstore. It's especially full this Saturday because of the holidays. Even with the weather being what it is, people are still being lured out. He has to wait in line for the butcher, who's taking his time serving each customer, telling funny stories about tongue, sharing butchery wisdoms, brandishing his cleaver with a flourish. The queue is moving slowly along, past the trays of sausages, then the pork, then the mutton, and finally to the beef where they get served. The people in the queue seem to like it, that the butcher is making them wait. Behind the counter it says he's as seen on TV. He's dressed up like a cowboy today, with his knives in holsters. At other times, when it's quieter, he just wears the cowboy hat with his white smock. They're laughing at him twirling his knives, calling them Ma'am and Partner.

The butcher's theatrics aren't for Mikey anyway. By the time he reaches the beef, it's a different story. The butcher smiles to show a peg-shaped maxillary lateral incisor and a newly fitted crown. He wants to get rid of Mikey as quickly as he can. 'Back again,' he says. He always says that. And then to the young lad there, 'Here you are, it's the Minceman. He's back again.' And then to Mikey, 'Two pounds of the usual, is it?'

The queue turns to look at who the Minceman might be, and their staring starts them swimming in Mikey's head. He's the only person there who can't see his teeth. Sweat prickles under his hat and his coat hangs off him like a great dead weight. Mikey would have thought he'd become accustomed to scrutiny. He's had that his whole life. Over the years he's managed to discern many types of look which, for the most part, fall into two distinct categories.

There's the look the butcher gives him, where the forehead wrinkles, the brow contracts into the middle of the face and the eyes roll quickly away. This is the one where those looking catch themselves looking so they have to pretend they're looking at something else. It's the ones with the sensitive natures that are prone to this. They're ashamed at what they're thinking, suffering from his suffering. At one time Mikey would look up and catch them doing it. Then he would be ashamed too. Their shame would weigh down on his own shame, and then weigh down on itself. Under its own combined weight the shame would sink even lower, all caught up in a choking, pitying backwash. A shame about shame.

Then there's the one the people in the queue are giving him. This is more of an open goggle. It tends to be the case that when people see evidence of a withdrawn blessing, it bothers them. Mikey was not blessed with good teeth and people don't know what to do with that.

His teeth are rotting away, piecemeal, and the sight of that, for some people, can be quite alarming. All that's left in his mouth are the sort of teeth people goggle at; a few crusted pegs, some of them fused together, the rest randomly set into receding gums, teetering at forks, hued in various browns.

With either of these looks Mikey can be no more than a passive recipient. The best way to deal with it all, he's found, is simply not to catch the eye. Of the whole face it's only the eyes that terrify. If there's candour in anything, it's in the eyes. Looks can kill things—it's not possible to do it with an ear or a nose. He nods an affirmative at the butcher, keeps his eyes fixed on the mince, ignores the people looking at him. Since his Mum passed on he can't remember the last time that someone gave him a genuine smile. He might smile back to thank them and then it would all start again, reminding him what he is. Perhaps the mouth can terrify too.

Course, he doesn't do so much smiling these days. With the exception of breathing, he keeps his mouth function to a minimum. With a periodontum like his, keeping his mouth shut was something he learnt quickly. He never really was much of a smiler. Talking too; that was always something of an ordeal. It comes from being born under Saturn. It's a quiet business, Mikey's life. He keeps himself to himself and lives day to day as best he can. The ups and downs of the world don't trouble him anymore. He doesn't bother anyone and they don't bother him, apart from Fetter and the butcher and the others whose mothers put no manners on them.

★

Mikey has always suffered with his teeth. As soon as they started coming through, everyone knew there was going to be trouble. Putting salt in his crib didn't help. Hanging a nutmeg round his neck didn't help. No one knew it at the time, but the fate of his teeth had been sealed well before that. Teeth start growing even before birth. There's a signal sent to where the tooth will form and a bud starts to grow in the embryonic jaw at that point. The position of the toothbud determines what type of tooth it will be, an incisor or a bicuspid, for instance. It just happened to be the case that when Mikey's teeth were budding, a terrible fixed foot was being planted and it wasn't going to be rooted up without trouble.

Right from the off he cried and cried. Nothing would settle him, not his rattle, not his blankey, not his Mum's right, nor his Mum's left. She was glad of it really, that he didn't like to feed that way. She was never too taken with that whole situation, taking down her necessaries, exposing herself like that. As soon as she could she stopped, saying he had left her red-raw. After that she just gave him formula and he cried at that too.

All that crying was inevitably going to have an effect on his periodontal development. His breathing was troubled; his nose was full of snotters all the time. Mikey learnt not to use it. His mouth was how he took in his air, all the time unwittingly drying out his mucal membrane. The upshot of that, of course, was that his salivary flow was almost entirely lacking and when it did flow it was of the type that is thick and viscous, the same texture and consistency as the stuff in his nose. Even now he's a chronic mouth breather. It's a terrible habit to have.

They thought it would clear up when his adult teeth started coming through, but that was when the problems really started. In the beginning it was just a bit of local irritation, a marginal gingivitis. When it got bad, his Mum would magic it better. She was a chime child, born on a Friday between midnight and cock-crow. She had the loveliest teeth. It's to be expected in a chime child. Healing lore is native to the soil with them. 'It's the worms,' she would say and always made sure there was plenty of hazel around for him to suck on.

It did happen at times though, that the magic was unavailing. Sometimes his gums were bright red, sometimes even reddish-blue. They would bleed at the slightest thing and with such frequency that, after a bit, it wasn't worth making a fuss. She soothed the inflammation with her wedding band, rubbing his gums with it. She always had the shiniest hands. It's common with chime children, that. At the end, when the blood stopped, she would say, 'There. We got all the badness out.'

But she never did get all the badness out, and what badness remained never stayed dormant for long. Calculus formed, cementing in a film on his teeth. There were ulcers, just at the gum line which she'd treat with cloves. The interdental tissues began to deteriorate. His mouth itched and hurt. The calculus caused irritation, and bacteria in the calculus caused more irritation. Between them they irritated from the position of the soft and the hard. It made no difference what they tried, how much hazel he chewed, how many poppies he ate, the deposits built up and up. They tried everything, even tried the old way, of sticking a lock of his hair to an oak, but not even this could stop the oral flora proliferating. His mouth was rife with it; all the usual types were in there, with long filamentous microorganisms and cocci predominating.

One time it got so bad that his Mum took him to see a dentist, to see what he had to say. It was against her better judgement. She'd seen what these specialists had done to Mikey's dad when he'd had his trouble. This one was called Mr Caries. He had a post on the Executive Council of the British Dental Association. When Mikey thinks of him now he thinks of a lovely delicate stippled gingiva, a cool coral pink. Mr Caries asked them how they had been treating the problem so far and leant into Mikey's mouth to have a proper look. He frowned while he looked around in there and he frowned some more after Mikey's Mum told him her methods. Mr Caries was a man who liked to take things on reason. 'You can't treat a child's teeth like that,' he told her, and said that the best way to go about it was with proper and regular dental care, the avoidance of sweets and chocolate and the maintenance of a good standard of oral hygiene. In spite of what Mikey's Mum told him, he seemed convinced that his way was best.

His examination revealed that Mikey was suffering from periodontitis. According to Mr Caries it's responsible for more tooth loss than anything else. Not only his teeth and gums were affected now, but also the maxillary and mandibular alveolar arches, the cementum and the periodontal ligaments—more or less everything in his mouth. He was very young to have it at such an advanced stage too. Normally it doesn't occur at all in boys his age.

Mr Caries took some photographs and then set about Mikey's mouth. He pressed his curette into one of the boggy swellings on Mikey's gums and suppurated it. It bled right there in front of Mr Caries when he did that. Mikey can remember that *Fine Swedish Steel* was stamped on the side of the blade. He fixed his eyes over Mr Caries' head and onto the halogen lamp shining into his mouth. The brightness of it warmed his face and spotted on his eyes. After a few moments without blinking, the spots obliterated his perception and all other forms around him started to decompose, the space in front of his eyes expanding to enormous blue size. Even when he shut them, the light persisted in his vision: a residual impression, thick and blue on his retina. The only things Mikey had in his head were the burning blue light and Mr Caries' knife. He became agitated. His grasp on the situation began to flutter. It seemed like the event was taking place outside him. He had the slight sensation of ants crawling about under his skin. His joints started doing things. Mr Caries pressed down on Mikey's chest with his elbows. He was undaunted by a bit of palsy in his patients and carried on slicing away, collecting all the matter and dead tissue into a kidney shaped bowl which he held under Mikey's chin.

It was only when Mikey's legs joined in that Mr Caries decided enough was enough. He left Mikey to rinse and went next door to empty his bowl down the sink. When he came back he handed Mikey a toothbrush and told him to make another appointment in a week. Mikey nodded his head, muzzily accepted the toothbrush. It was all he could do to respond at all.

He lay in Mr Caries' chair, dimly aware of his Mum and Mr Caries arguing behind him. She said that she didn't know what she was thinking of bringing her son to a place like this, that there was nothing either he or his executive council had to offer that she couldn't manage. Mr Caries told her that Mikey should have been brought in a lot sooner, that irreparable damage might already have been done to his teeth. Mikey's Mum didn't take at all well to that, to Mr Caries saying that she'd not been looking after him properly. She always felt herself to have quite a scrupulous regard to matters of health and hygiene, on account of having a natural aptitude in that area. 'Homemade cakes and homemade cures are always best, Mr Caries,' she said, and then came over to get Mikey off the chair. He showed her the toothbrush. It was an Oral-B, a yellow one. Mikey's still got it. 'That's a bobbydazzler,' she said, 'now get your coat on.'

Mikey hadn't really taken to Mr Caries either. There were bruises on his chest that Mr Caries had made with his elbows. They spread out in purple wings from his sternum up to his shoulders. That sort of treatment leaves a mark. They never kept the next appointment. After that his Mum treated it with Milk of Magnesia which she wiped across his teeth and gums with a rag. When it got bad she burnt henbane and fed him spoonwart.

Gemma Green

Gemma Green has been writing poetry since the age of nine. Twenty years later, a student on the poetry course, she feels there is still a long way to go.

Shell

You have the look of an angel, asleep on her hands,
or a Buddha folded in the lowest lotus.
Lonely but complete, without your maker
whose briny body is lost to the sea,
you have a span wide enough to cover my entire nipple.

Many times drowned, here you are resurrected,
warming to mimic the heat of my hand,
marked with the grooves of a half-opened fan,
as if the sea retched and threw out a question.
Perhaps like me it wants to persuade you
to speak and reveal the secrets you hear.

[βακτερια - translated literally means 'little sticks', as microbes appear to be when seen through a microscope. Latin 'Bacilli'.]

βακτερια *('LITTLE STICKS')*

He is not afraid to get his hands dirty.
Bacteria are like little sticks.
Love, like little sticks, rests under his fingernails.
He is not afraid to put them into me.
Little sticks, like love, growing into a tree.

Skimming

You make it look easy, skimming stones,
but nothing else moves that way
except the bouncing bomb.

For you the sea tightens its skin
and the stones jostle, vying for selection.
Now, you hand one to me.

I coax emulation of feet, hips, elbows, arms,
the confident dip of your cowboy wrist.
It feels cold, wet as a dog's nose.

My tongue moves absently to the roof of my mouth
as I level the stone and cast it to sea
willing a volley of watery sound.

Together we track its defiant descent
and final resonant solo splash.
I turn before it sinks to the floor.

Bending with laughter, you urge 'one more go,'
pinging a couple more over the horizon.
Still smiling later when we reached the bar.

THE BLUEBELL TUTORIAL

You took a picture of me walking off,
caught the back of me climbing,
preserving in chemicals those last days of May.

Not a great shot by any standards;
the blur of your finger a foggy intrusion,
betraying your location, giving you away.

Look closely, see the bluebell caught in my hair,
accidental crowning from the forest lair.
Wish I'd kept it, pressed as the perfect memorial,
lasting reminder of my bluebell tutorial.

Anticipation

The best times can be had
waiting for someone, anticipating
a kiss, a greeting or a non-touching of hands.

The glorious rehearsal,
the potential of arrival,
or the lusty recollection of last parting.

Today it's a book and the sun's rays;
caught through the window, quarter-lighting my hair;
the soft music of borrowed conversation,
voices lifting with the scraping of chairs.

Waitresses weave with aqua movements.
I imagine your face in the street drawing near,
cheeks flushed with the tinge of arrival.
I rise from the seat, open arms. You are here.

After Thought

I am thinking about it in lifts;
doors snap shut and you hove into view.
We tear at each other like dogs,
like we need to eat through each other.
But by the time we get there, you're gone.

I get into my car and you're there;
the briefest of thoughts and we're on again.
It's a cat-fight in the smallest of bins;
the need to pursue each other in a dead end.
But by the time we get there, you're gone.

Then evening comes and you slink inside,
infecting my dreams with a venomous spray.
It's a sweaty exchange, the venting of limbs.
The sun rises to bless our sneaky mingling,
but while she fattens to greet us, you're gone.

Kate Grunstein

Kate Grunstein grew up in Hampshire and now lives in London. She read English at Oxford University before qualifying as a lawyer in 1996. She is writing her first novel.

Lead and Sunlight

(extract from a novel)

When she worked it out, it was almost a year since she had last been back. It didn't feel that long because she talked to them on the telephone all the time. It was difficult to say anything much on the phone; their voices down the wires were like rays, passing through soft matter but stopping at the hard stuff: bone, metal, plastic. The receiver was a piece of lead, blocking everything out. Almost everything. She was only going now because Laura was having another baby. She asked Simon about names, but he said they hadn't really thought about it. They'd run out of family, he said laughing, a little sheepish (Harry was named after Laura's father, Leah had been Simon and Rosie's mother). Rosie could feel their father's name struggling up from inside her, strangling to be spoken. *Rufus.* Always in her head it was a rough whisper, foggy like breath on a cold morning. The word felt thick in her throat like phlegm across her epiglottis. If Simon were here with her it could have floated out into the air: hung there for their casual contemplation, a mote of dust caught in sunlight. But the receiver, a block of lead against her ear, was too clunky to bear it.

⋆

After all there had been no need to worry they would sell it before she arrived. Rosie left her bags in the office with Mr Cleto. She explained she was on her way down to see her brother. 'He's having a baby,' she said. 'Well, his wife.' Mr Cleto nodded politely and Rosie, feeling the information hang unnecessary and out of place among the stacked cards advertising specialist insurers, the water cooler, the yukka on the windowsill with dust thickening its ribbed leaves, was embarrassed. She went to wait in the doorway for them to drive it round.

The interior of the car was leather the colour of clotted cream, the stitching on the seats so well preserved it was hardly even discoloured. She ran one finger along the groove between the seat edge and its piped trim. It smelt of damp and oil.

'Should it smell of oil?' she asked, holding the door open by the window strap.

'Oh that's old cars for you love. She's been around that one. Besides she's probably picking up a bit from the workshop.' Dan the mechanic smiled at her and the white creases around his eyes disappeared into the tan of his face. His eyes were sailor-blue; he had a smudge of grease across his right cheek. The sky beyond the curve of his head was overcast, white; its brightness made her look away blinking. She was struck for a moment with a sense of unreality: what was she doing here? Perhaps buying the car was a piece of insanity. She had always known it was unrealistic; for one thing she couldn't afford it without using part of her inheritance. For another (as Simon had pointed out), it was impractical, environmentally unsound, vulnerable to theft and difficult to maintain. Simon had told her you needed to know about cars to own a car like that. In the background Rosie could hear one of his children screaming, Laura's voice raised in anger or placation.

'Well—*you* know about cars,' she said.

'Yeah, well I'm two hundred miles away, aren't I? Can't just take the time off to run up to London and fix your motor whenever it breaks down.'

She shook the thought away and pulled herself out of the car. It was true, Simon almost never left the farm these days.

Rosie put her hand carefully on the wheel arch; the metal felt cold and smooth, soft almost. This would be the first thing she had bought with the money. She couldn't tell Simon, but Greg knew about cars as well. She asked him one Sunday morning when they were having breakfast together. Or at least they were having breakfast at the same time.

'So will you check it over for me if anything goes wrong?' she said.

'Sure, yes.'

'Will you?'

Greg smiled at her over the top of his glasses; he leant back in his chair to hold the paper at arm's length and shake a crease out of it.

'Absolutely,' he said.

Now on the fuel-dripped forecourt she inspected the car, walking around it slowly. Since she came to view it two weeks ago she had revisited the image in her mind so often, stumping herself with questions of detail (how many dials were there on the dashboard and were they to the left or the right of the steering column? When the hood was up, were there any side windows?) that she found the reality of the car a relief. Rivers of light flowed silently along the chrome curve of the bumper. With the hood down the windscreen was a short slope of glass, rounded at both ends. She stood on the far side and contemplated the dense blackness of its new tyres with her arms folded; if she opened them something might fly out of her, something which would brush the polished metal with its large craggy wings before spinning through the dealership in the weak sunlight, hooting with joy.

'Alright for you is she?' Mr Cleto, the owner, had emerged from the office, making her jump.

'Great,' she said. Sincerity made her voice tremble as if she were forcing the emotion. 'Fantastic.'

'Come on in then.' He turned to go back inside.

The warranty, log book and service record were kept in a frayed leather folder, the sort with pockets inside the covers and a loop in the centre for a pen. It had that creased and flattened look of something which has been kept for years and years in a drawer. There was an old ring of a coffee stain on the front and the decorative running stitch around the bottom hem had pulled loose. Rosie laid it on top of some stacked papers on the desk and began to read through the documents. The contract was printed on the back with tiny paragraphs in newspaper-style columns. She scanned them too rapidly: for show more than anything else. Out of the corner of her eye she could still see the car through the office window.

'Beautiful car you got there,' said Mr Cleto, as if he had somehow divined her inattentive thoughts.

'Yes,' she said, without looking up.

'Kept her in the garage the last twenty-five years. Belonged to her father before, you see.'

'Right.'

'Kept up with her services though. Only time she ever took her out: drive her down to Dan and me for a tinker-up. And she kept her polished up lovely.'

'Yes.'

'Had my eye on that one for years! Such a waste I thought: beautiful thing like that, kept locked away. Criminal really.'

'I'm surprised you're selling her then.' Out loud the words sounded too bold, insulting even. To deflect this she smiled, but Mr Cleto still had his back to her. As she turned her head, he pulled out the drawer of a filing cabinet with a noise like the distilled echo of a train.

He sighed, 'Oh well. We all have to pay the rent, don't we?'

She had found the car through a collectors' magazine. As soon as she saw the picture of it she could see herself as the figure in the old-style advertisement: colours blocked in, the shine above the wheel arches in curved panels of light blue, teeth white, lips Russian Red, hair hidden under scarf, driving goggles, a camel coat. The car would be somewhere like Switzerland, advancing silently out of grassy hills, down a thin, snaking road the palest colour of dust, tall firs in a darker shade of green on either side. The drivers in the pictures were all men, of course. She had put the magazine away from her, but the wordless image came back. The painted girl of her imagination remained in her mind's eye: fearless, unbounded, driving towards the edge of the frame without waving anybody goodbye or turning her head, even to look at the artist.

So here she was now in Mr Cleto's office buying the car. She took out the envelope with the banker's draft in it. The draft was on thick creamy paper; it was much larger than an ordinary cheque. Ever since she ordered it on Tuesday lunchtime, a thrill of adrenaline had been twisting through her stomach.

Greg didn't think there was anything wrong with spending her money on the car. 'That kind of car's not even a wasting asset, provided you look after it,' he had said. For her birthday he had given her a first edition of an old children's book, now out of print. Seeing the hard cover (pounded a little as if kept beneath immense weights, frayed at the corners), she remembered it completely. She sat with the gold crepe paper unfolded across her lap, holding it upright with both hands. It was a thin book; when she opened it the spine creaked; its pages, shiny with illustration, smelt warm with age. 'It's the one you were trying to remember the title of,' Greg said. 'I looked it up on the Internet and had to order it from the States: you can't even get it over here. You should look after it, it's a collector's item.' In her mind she could see the two steps down into the bathroom, the Swedish chest with cork inlaid in its top, dusted with talcum powder. A knothole left a gap between the dark-stained floorboards, air came up from it which she could feel cold against the curve of her eye, but there was no light. She nodded seriously, 'Of course I will. Thanks, Greg.'

Mr Cleto passed her a pen. It was a heavy ballpoint spray-painted silver, with the words Mather & Cleto embossed along its side in an elaborately swirled font. When she clicked it on it made a loud twanging noise as though the spring inside were bent out of shape. The upstroke of the first letter of her name remained opaque and then the ink blotted as she turned the nib to make the loop, the rest of her signature spilling out, small and spiky: R M Hanway. She clicked the pen off again, and handed the page back across the desk. The ink, deep Prussian blue, glistened like the top skin of water in a covered well. She unfolded the banker's draft and held it with her finger along the crease, waiting for Mr Cleto to look up again. The desk between them was strewn with papers: invoices, receipts, typewritten letters on pale green copy paper. Papers rustled under her elbow when she shifted it along the edge of the desk. A packet of licence disk holders fell onto the floor with a hollow flopping sound. Mr Cleto was frowning down at the contract, making small grunting noises under his breath. Behind him on the back wall of the office a calendar hung crookedly. Rosie felt tension in a vein down her arm; the hand holding the draft trembled slightly. She resisted the urge to turn back to the window to see the car again.

Mr Cleto looked up at last and beamed at her. His cheeks were shiny as if he had painted them with a thin layer of transparent latex. 'All done then,' he said. 'Just need something off you I think.' His coyness was deliberate, but there was an edge of anticipation to his voice. Rosie passed him the draft; he looked at it and then put it down carefully on the desk in front of him. Anchoring one corner with two fingers, he smoothed his other hand across its surface. 'Topper,' he said, 'topper.'

As she drove off the forecourt, Dan and Mr Cleto both stood against the office wall and watched her. Mr Cleto, still beaming, had his hands behind his back; Dan's thumbs were tucked in the top corners of his overall pockets, his big hands spread across his belly. Rosie liked the idea that they were seeing the car off: honouring its maiden voyage somehow.

Seams of black tar striated the buff road surface making the car jump every few seconds. The steering wheel, shiny black and completely smooth, jarred at each bump in the road, preparing to fly out of her hands. She had to tense her arms and shoulders to hold it steady. The wheel was so large she had to strain her neck to see over it completely. Infinitesimal movements of her legs, on and off the pedals, brought contact between her thighs and the bottom edge of the wheel. To reach the gear stick she was conscious of having to lean to her left. The car seemed altogether much larger than she was.

She stopped at the traffic lights and then ground the gears trying to find first. Dan had explained the gearbox to her while she nodded impatiently. She learnt to drive on the farm sitting on two cushions and a telephone directory; passed her test two days after her seventeenth birthday. She should know about driving.

She drove along the slow lane of the motorway. There was only a single wing mirror, which stuck out from the side of the windscreen like a chrome-backed ear. Knowing this, the absent rear-view mirror seemed to haunt the car, forcing her eyes to flick up every few seconds in search of it until the jar of the movement, like a tic in her brain, made her head ache. The car had a top speed of 105 and would go over 80, Dan said. Its charge shuddered in her shoulder muscles. She drove at 45. Modern cars passed her in a stream, their passengers pressed against the windows to stare. When she tried to change gear, the stick jammed; the sound of the engine became hollow, wide-open. She took her foot off the clutch and then rammed it down again, pushing the stick hard out and up. The car behind flashed its lights twice and overtook, revving angrily as it sped away. Her hands were shaking, she felt slightly sick. At the next services she pulled in and stopped.

The day outside was sinking; brightness had almost gone from the sky above the flat roof of the services, leaving a cloud-screen of dull grey. She would be much later than she had said getting to the farm tonight. She took her mobile phone out of her bag. The experience of driving had made her feel flattened and appalled. She could feel the ghost of her earlier happiness sliding away from her, leaving her wraith-like, soulless, transparent here in the car park. As the light faded she could see highlights of her reflection in the windscreen, tilted inwards. Yesterday, Greg presented her with a steering wheel lock. He had stuck a rosette made out of shiny paper onto its yellow flank and apologised again that he couldn't come with her to pick the car up. He put his hand lightly against her waist. 'Sorry, Rose.'

'It's okay.' She shifted away from him.

'You know I want to see the car.' He was angling to look in her eyes.

'You'll see it. When I get back.'

'Rosie—' He brushed her breast with the side of his hand, as if by accident. She swayed back towards him for a moment and then walked away.

'Watch out, Mr Locke.' She paused in the doorway, waggling the lock in the air like a tomahawk. 'I have weapon.'

Remembering, Rosie smiled down at her hand lying inside the lower curve of the wheel. The lock was in the boot with her bags. Dan shook his head when he saw it. 'That won't do it,' he said. 'Never get that on. You need to get an ignition immobiliser put in. Cost a bit.'

'How much?' she asked, but he shrugged his shoulders, said he would have to look it up and do her an estimate. 'Might take a while,' he added, 'to get the parts.'

It didn't matter, the car would be safe at the farm. In her mind she caught a glimpse of the imaginary girl's tail-lights. It was night in the picture now and the girl was waving her hand in the air, still not looking back. Rosie switched on the phone to call Simon, but after all, the battery was flat. She would have to go in and call from a payphone instead.

Lucy Hannah

Lucy Hannah has worked as a journalist, a flower seller, and a radio producer.

Hoovering Up the Sand

An extract from Hoovering Up The Sand, *a novel in progress. Alice remembers her childhood when she used to help her dad, William, with his deckchair business.*

William was the deckchair magnate of Lyston-on-Sea. He was saving up to send me to St Braithwaite's School a long way away. Three good summers and he'd have enough money. I felt like a parcel waiting to be stamped and handed into strange hands. William worked too hard.

'He's out there all day,' Gillian would say as she picked garden earth out from under her nails. 'Then they ring him about the Save The Old Pier Campaign, all night.'

Often he'd sit very still when he came home looking pale and drinking a glass of hot milk for his ulcer.

'I don't know why they have to ring you at home,' she said to him. 'Can't you arrange it so that you have time off without these constant interruptions?' She liked it really. She valued us being vital in the local community. Nowhere else in the county had such a committed deckchair king.

Every morning we'd leave Gillian hoovering up the sand which had blown into the upstairs of the house during the night. She was often still tidying up when we came back but we never asked what she might have been doing in-between. I folded the chairs and William talked to clients. I folded and he talked. I never talked and he never folded. William had strategies.

'You need a plan, Alice, always have a plan.'

Take August 1965. The strategy was: how to avoid over large women ripping the seat of the deckchairs.

'They're just not built for it.'

It was simple, you sew two pieces of deckchair canvas together to make it extra strong and then you use the nails, the same large ones that are used to keep the shed upright, to secure the canvas to the chair.

'Always try to avoid embarrassment,' William said, 'it's not good for business.'

He enjoyed it when the Aunts came for their summer break. Edward Turner (no relation to Mrs Turner at the fish shop), MBE, publicity officer for Lyston, was the Aunts' nephew. St James' Park in London was their natural habitat where they could find deckchairs, sunshine, ducks, the smell of cut grass, all limping distance from Fortnum and Mason. They were very old. It was the same every year. William would say loudly, 'Have you met my daughter Alice? . . . of course . . . last year . . . of course. I know, she's growing up fast.'

I lined up the Aunt's chairs with extra precision. Of course I knew who they were, I'd been waiting for them. The Aunts were the highlight of summer in Lyston. Aunt Joyce especially. It was the way she just sat still and listened. She was interested in how I folded, which no one except William had shown any interest in. It wasn't that straightforward.

'It's an art, Alice, a real art. If you can master that you can give yourself a pat on the back,' William said.

I did master it and spent a couple of mornings trying to pat myself on the back. This made William laugh.

The Aunts arrived on July 14th—Joyce's birthday. She always had a crossword under her arm. William admired people who could do newspaper crosswords. He would try but there never seemed enough time to work out the clues. He liked Joyce's choice of words.

'It's the way she selects them, Alice. She uses carefully chosen words.'

He'd spent weeks trying to find a suitable name for the deckchair company. Aunt Joyce suggested that a slightly more imaginative title than *'Sit'n View'* might help business. She came up with *Diamonds Are Forever.*

'It's ingenious, William,' she explained as we looked up at the

Sit'n View banner which hung crooked above the front of the shop.

'A bicycle designer decided to leave out the rigid tube that supports the seat in favour of a loop of steel tubing, linking seat, back wheel, pedals and front fork. The bike 'diamond' is strong for the same reason that a deckchair is—the geometry distributes the forces in such a way that the frame stays rigid. All the efforts to redesign the bike frame have failed because the diamond is simply unbeatable. Triangulation is the strength of hundreds of structures. People often don't understand it at first, but you can see how it works in a deckchair.' Joyce loved solving problems.

'Quite,' said William.

'Quite,' I said. Joyce always sounded convincing.

Diamonds Are Forever made a big difference to business. No one quite understood why it was called that, but they liked the sound of it. It went with their holiday mood of hopefulness even though the sea never came in.

'How old are you?' I asked Joyce.

'Very old, dear.' She patted me on the head. William said that old people shrink.

'You haven't shrunk,' I pointed out. 'You can't be that old.'

'No, I haven't shrunk, dear, not yet.'

Joyce pressed boiled sweets into my hand when I positioned her chair. William asked me why I kept repositioning it when she got up to potter down the sand but I didn't let on that Joyce and I had a sweet thing going.

The Aunts sat in their row: Una read poetry, Jessie studied the racing form, and Joyce did the crossword. About halfway through the crossword—the difficult one, not the quick one—Joyce pottered to the shed to ask how we were getting on. William twinkled when she came in.

' "You can't do without it by a chalk stream in June." Two words, 4 and 13,' said Joyce. William looked up from stacking a pile of All Blues—new stock on approval from Holland. Gillian had spotted them in her 'Homes and Design' magazine.

'What do you think of these, Joyce?' William proudly presented his latest batch of chair covers.

'Very smart. I approve.' She read the paper with a large magnifying glass. She didn't wear glasses though she obviously needed them.

'Gottit! Tups Indispensible,' she said and scribbled on the newspaper. 'It's a fly for fishing in a chalk stream, Alice.'

'Like shrimp fishing?' I said. William and I went shrimping in the pools in Cornwall. Lyston didn't have pools. It had sludge.

'Trout fishing,' said Joyce.

'Brambles,' said William from underneath an All Blue.

'What's that, dear?' Joyce winked at me.

'Brambles is all I can remember about trout fishing. Getting stuck in them.' William wasn't a sportsman.

When the Aunts were staying, I folded as fast as I could to leave time to listen to Joyce's fishing stories. She'd fished all over the world.

'In Tanganyika we trekked to a deserted mission house at Tukuyu, a small post in the southern highlands. That's more than a thousand miles from Nairobi and Livingstone. You can imagine how it felt, so remote. We slept in grass huts and sat on packing cases. We saw crocodiles over the River Sabaki. They were lurking under flimsy wooden bridges. We had to drive over them, "straight on for a hundred miles and then turn right," the guide said. That's where the lake was.'

She used technical words to describe the state of the river. 'In spate,' she said, pronouncing the 'ate' very loudly. I repeated this to Harvey, the rabbit, as I refilled his water every morning.

'The river is in spate, Harvey,' I said.

He just munched and stared at me like he always did.

'I could tell you that I'd seen two dozen salmon parr and you'd still just sit there, wouldn't you?' Harvey sat and munched.

Joyce had seen two dozen salmon parr on a river in Devon.

'Well done, Joyce,' said William.

I'd have to look up 'parr' in the dictionary later, but I wanted to keep in with Joyce.

'Well done,' I said.

Joyce and William laughed and Joyce patted me on the head again. One year she brought her fly box to show me. I picked out the flies and matched them to a chart that she carried in her pocket. She knew all the names and all about them. Like a child hearing a bedtime story, I didn't mind how often I heard the story behind the Olive Dun or the Tup's Indispensable. Each time, Joyce told it with huge excitement.

'A Mr Austin, a tobacconist and fly dresser who lived in Devon, tied a fly in the 1890s which was probably an imitation of the spinner of the pale watery.' I didn't dare interrupt Aunt Joyce when she was telling fly tales. She often used long words, but I didn't want her to think I was slow. She continued, 'A famous fisherman tried it out, and Austin and his daughter were overwhelmed with orders. It was given the name "Tup" because part of the wool used in the dressing came from the genitals of a tup, and "Indispensable" because he couldn't be without it when trout were rising to pale watery spinners on the Itchen.' She'd wander off along the beach towards the end of each story.

'What's a tup?' I asked William.

'A ram,' he said, and threw me a pile of canvas to sort. I hoped that one day William and me would be like Austin and his daughter and be 'overwhelmed with orders.'

Gillian kept a tally on any new items which appeared in my bedroom.

'What are those coloured things on your wall, Alice?' Gillian asked.

'Flies,' I said.

'Are they for your hair?' Gillian inquired. 'They're pretty colours.'

'They're for catching fish.'

'Oh,' said Gillian, accidentally squirting the washing-up liquid across the floor. 'Where did you get them?'

'A friend,' I said. Gillian didn't understand our world on the beach. She didn't ever want to come and sort out the chairs or see in the new stock.

'I'll try and pop down later,' she'd say, but she never did pop. We didn't need anyone else, particularly when the Aunts were there. We were busy and so was Gillian. Very busy with chores.

'Remember we have the chairs like soldiers, dear. . .' said the Aunts. Sometimes their words came out together. They'd sit there in a neat row each day for the whole of July. There was the Venus Bathing Beauty contest every Thursday, and there was always Edward Turner's latest publicity scam. This time it was rain insurance.

'For every day of rain you get a refund of £1 whenever the rainfall measures one tenth of an inch between 10am and 6pm. Saturdays are not included. The trippers just say with their booking form that they'd like a 17/6d rain insurance. Brilliant.'

Edward Turner thought all his plans were Brilliant. He'd recently sent a bag of sand to Senor Philipo Salinas Croche of Havanna who'd asked for several ounces of Lyston sand for his collection which contains one hundred and ninety specimens.

'It's all about putting us on the map,' Edward Turner would say. He wore the Lyston coat of arms as a badge on his lapel. The motto, Ever Forward, seemed inappropriate for Lyston. Its heraldry, a seagull, a lighthouse, three swimming herrings and a thigh booted fisherman wasn't a great selling point, but Edward Turner was a natural at public relations. He slapped William on the back at the end of each of his sentences.

'Do you mind him doing that?' I'd say.

'There are some things you have to put up with living in a small town,' William answered. I knew he put up with a lot.

The Aunts and William listened patiently to Mr. Turner's plans for Lyston. William knew it could never offer the luxuries of Piccadilly to the Aunts, but it was a change.

'A change is always good, Alice.' He made sure the Aunts had the best chairs in the prime spot.

'The longest tidal reach in Europe,' he'd tell them as they sat in the middle of the muddy wasteland. Children shrieked at the one-armed bandits doing their thing on the Pier, and Don Trapnell, the donkey man, shouted, 'best ride in the south-west,' over the sound of the warped jingle of the ice-cream van which trundled up and down the sand under the grey slab of sky.

'Lovely, dear,' the Aunts would say, together.

If they had the money, and they did, why did they come here rather than going to a place where the sea is in rather than out and where you didn't have to take shelter from the wind. Aunt Una and Aunt Jessie wore their small-faced silver watches on the beach. Aunt Joyce took off her watch when she was on holiday.

'What's the time, dear?' she asked me as I folded. The other Aunts ignored her, irritated. Aunt Una was more concerned to hold onto her hairpiece which had a habit of being blown off. The wind invariably grabbed it when she stepped out of the Aunts metallic blue Morris Minor and dumped it in the middle of the road. William would dispatch me to fetch it and hand it back to Aunt Una. She would press it back down on her head, and sigh, 'thank you, dear.'

Gillian used the word tragedy when Harvey dug up her prize hosta, or when the hoover bag ejected itself and emptied sand all over the floor, a few minutes before the Gardening club were due to come round for soup and a roll.

'Oh no,' she'd shout, scrubbing the floor with a damp cloth which only made it worse. 'What a tragedy.'

'Tragedies happen in the newspapers,' I said, holding the limp hoover bag.

'They can happen here too, Alice. I'll never live it down.' Gillian often said she'd eat her hat. She never did eat it and she did seem to live it down.

William didn't use the word, Tragedy. If he was cross he would go out into the garden and give Harvey some more water.

The sign: DO NOT GO BEYOND THIS POINT, made no impression on Aunt Joyce. She didn't have her watch on, and she didn't have her glasses either. I watched her tiptoe towards the sea with her parasol that was more suited for Venice than Lyston. She must know that she shouldn't go BEYOND that POINT. William was absorbed in sewing up the side of an All Blue. The next time I looked up, Aunt Joyce was up to her knees in mud. Her heavy beige tights were disappearing fast under the quicksand. She flailed like a puppet who'd lost the strings to its legs.

'Keep still. For God's sake, keep still,' shouted William. He didn't have collapsible snow shovels and red triangles and pieces of rope in the back of his car, like some of the men in Lyston. Una and Jessie shouted out to Joyce, 'Come back, dear, it's half past four.'

'Deckchairs, William, get the chairs.' We laid a line of deckchairs out towards Joyce as she began to sink more quickly.

'It's known for this round here, they pull cars out regularly apparently.' Una had been reading the papers.

'She's smaller than a car,' Jessie said hopefully. 'Smaller and lighter.'

'I can't help thinking she shouldn't be moving,' Una observed.

'We don't want her to stop moving, do we?' Jessie gasped.

William and I inched our way across the sinking area on deckchairs laid out on top of the mud.

'We need a rope. Run, Alice, run and get a rope.' I ran back to our house and found a rope underneath Harvey's cage, alongside Gillian's stash of hoover bags. By the time I got back to the beach, Jessie, Una and her hairpiece, stood very still with William. They gazed out to the non-existent sea and the non-existent Joyce as if they were on the bridge of a ship.

'You did your best, dear,' said Una, adjusting her hairpiece. She placed her hand on my shoulder. I shook her hand free. I didn't want Una, I wanted Joyce. I let the rope drop in a coiled heap at my feet and stood to attention with the others.

'Could we have a drink, William?' Jessie asked. 'It's all been a bit sudden.'

They drank whiskey and thermos tea by the deckchair sheds, under the shelter of the seafront wall.

'I hope I go quickly.' Jessie stared out to sea.

'Yes, dear, it's not going to be much fun for the one who's left.' Una's hairpiece blew off again and landed, perched, on the DO NOT GO BEYOND THIS POINT signpost. I couldn't reach it and it seemed inappropriate for William to handle the toupee.

'Leave it with Joyce,' said Una.

William didn't mention it to Gillian. A few nights later they went up to bed as usual, chased the sand out of the bath, separate baths but the same water. They read in bed lying side by side as they would in their joint plot of cemetery land, which Gillian has been awarded after ten years of being a local churchwarden. Gillian spotted an entry in the Births, Marriages and Deaths: Joyce Singleton, from Piccadilly, aged 82, in a sudden accident.

'Isn't she one of those Aunts?' said Gillian.

'Oh, yes.' William made a note to himself to buy a long piece of rope and keep it in the deckchair shed. The windows whooshed open and another pile of sand was deposited in the corner of the room.

'Blast.' Gillian looked aghast as if she'd completed a jigsaw puzzle and discovered that there was a key piece missing.

William continued to read. Gillian glanced at the hoover which stood at the ready for the morning's challenge.

Nick Harrop

Nick Harrop graduated from Pembroke College, Cambridge, in 2000. Previous plays have been performed in London and Edinburgh.

The Bomb

(extract from a one-act play)

A London tube station in the early evening. JANE, *early twenties and dressed in a suit, is sitting on a bench.* TRENT, *about thirty and returning home from a city job, stands nearby.*

TRENT: When's it coming? Has there been an announcement?

JANE: Are you talking to me?

TRENT: Yes.

JANE: I've only just arrived.

Beat

TRENT: That 'train approaching' sign's been up there over five minutes now. It's a disgrace.

Beat

TRENT: Where are you heading?

JANE: Sorry. Are you still talking to me?

TRENT: Yes actually.

JANE: What did you want to know?

TRENT: Where you're heading.

JANE: Does it matter?

TRENT: Not really, no. I'm just making conversation.

Beat.

JANE: Heathrow.

TRENT: The end of the line. Wow.

He sits down next to her.

TRENT: You normally get off at Hammersmith.

There is an announcement: 'Will you please stand behind the yellow line. Thank you.'

JANE: That's correct. Yes.

Beat.

TRENT: Sorry. I've noticed you before. We often get on the same train.

JANE: Do we?

TRENT: Yes. Am I being weird?

JANE: A little.

TRENT: Sorry about that.

Beat.

TRENT: My name's Trent, by the way. Trent Roberts.

Beat.

A lot of people ask me why I'm called Trent.

Beat.

I was conceived in a hotel by the river.

He grins. She doesn't.

An announcement: 'We apologise for the delay to the Westbound Piccadilly Line service. The next train will be approaching shortly.'

JANE *stands up, moves away.* TRENT *gets up too.*

TRENT: What's your name, if you don't mind me asking?

JANE: Matilda.

TRENT: Right. Nice to meet you.

Beat.

TRENT: When is this fucking train going to arrive?

Beat

TRENT: And what d'you do for a living, Matilda?

JANE: My name's not Matilda, I lied.

Beat.

TRENT: Would you prefer it if I stood somewhere else?

JANE: I don't mind.

TRENT: Right.

Beat.

TRENT: Your name's Jane, isn't it? I've heard you talking on your mobile.

Beat.

TRENT: What I hate about London is the anonymity. You're not allowed to talk to anyone. You get crammed onto a tube, rammed into someone's armpit, so you can hardly breathe for the stench of their sweat, but you're not allowed to speak. You're not allowed to say, 'Hello, I'm here too.' It's not a good way to be. It's not a good way for humanity to operate.

Beat.

TRENT: Have you been crying? You look like you've been crying.

JANE: Yes. I've been crying.

TRENT: Why did he leave you?

She stares at him.

TRENT: No. Wrong guess. Why did you leave him? What did he do to make you leave him?

JANE: You're asking the wrong questions.

TRENT: Am I?

Beat.

TRENT: You can tell me, you know. I'm a stranger. What you say to me means nothing in the grand scheme of things.

JANE: I hate that phrase. There's no grand scheme.

TRENT: Maybe not.

Beat.

JANE: Why should you care anyway? It's nothing to do with you.

TRENT: I'm nosy. I like knowing things.

JANE: You're not nosy. You're just weird.

TRENT: Come on. Give me a chance. I'm a red-blooded male confronted by a damsel in distress. Of course I want to know.

JANE: Alright then. I'm upset because I've just committed a crime. I've just murdered my husband.

Pause.

TRENT: Nice weather we've been having.

JANE: Yes. Very mild.

Beat.

TRENT: I wouldn't let you murder me if I was your husband.

JANE: Would you not.

TRENT: Then again, I've never been your husband.

JANE: I think I'd remember.

Beat.

TRENT: So. You've murdered your husband and now you're off to Heathrow to flee the country.

Pause. JANE *ignores him.* TRENT *makes some kind of decision.*

TRENT: I'm upset too, you know. I'm upset because I've had a really bad day at work. My boss, a fat man called Neil with an enormous stomach and smelly hands, criticised me about something I did last week. If I can be more specific, it's not his hands that are smelly but his wrists. I don't know why, but they smell of cat food—I think it's the smell of his drying sweat. Perhaps it comes from his watchstrap. Anyway, all this is by way of painting a picture. This foul specimen of humanity, this image of corpulence on a pair of legs, asked me into his office not merely to criticise me, but to humiliate me as well. I currently earn thirty-four grand a year. He asked me to move down to thirty-two. Obviously I informed him that his conduct was unacceptable, and threatened to resign. And Neil, this ugly, enormous man, this rancid, stinking brute . . . decided to snort. Not an involuntary snort or a nasal chuckle, but the full, five second, I-hate-your-guts snort that only comes with lots of practice, and a large reservoir of phlegm. And I could see him swallowing what he'd summoned from his nose, gulping as the bogey and the spit and the shit from his cavities slopped down through his gullet . . . He did that, he made me watch that . . . and then he smiled . . . Not the sort of smile that you or I would smile—even to an enemy—but a disgusting parody of a normal expression. Not a wince, and not a sneer, but an expression of all that is wrong with the world and ever has been . . . And it was at that moment that I had my realisation. My moment of truth.

Beat. JANE *is captivated by this rant.*

I decided to punch him in the face. Not hard—I don't know how to punch properly and I didn't want to break my knuckles—but hard enough for him to remember for the rest of his life. And then I walked out of the office, down the road and eventually along to St. James' Park. I decided to change the way I live my life, to do all the things I've always wanted to do. To swear at my dad . . . laugh in church . . . spit at children, strangle my cat, piss in the streets, ask out that girl I fancy on the tube (that's you, by the way), drink when I want, sleep when I want, do nothing at all when I want . . . It was quite a refreshing decision . . . For about five minutes. But then I realised that I was still bored. Still going nowhere. So I apologised to my boss, cleaned up his nose, and accepted the pay cut with good grace. And then I came here.

Pause.

I wonder why that train's late.

Announcement: 'Due to a bomb near Holborn, all westbound Piccadilly Line Services have been suspended. Please travel by an alternative route.'

JANE: A bomb.

TRENT: It's alright. You can take the Northern line to Waterloo and change there. If you do ever want to go out for that drink, well … you'll see me around.

She stares at him.

Blackout.

Sara Heitlinger

Sara Heitlinger was born in Melbourne in 1973. She has lived in Jerusalem for nine years, where she studied computer and cognitive sciences. This is the first chapter of her novel.

Goodbye!

Goodbye the Misses Collins! Goodbye Fanny! Goodbye Marianne! May you have happy travels and find a worthy new home. Farewell! I'm so sorry that you're leaving, but I can't keep lovely ladies here when they think the time has come to move on. Oh, the Misses Collins! What emptiness without you!

Such a heart-wrenching morning it was in the autumn of 1920 when Fanny and Marianne packed up the last of their possessions and went back to live in Aberdeen. They had climbed rather inelegantly into the horse-drawn cart, and were now being carried away to the station in Wymondham, where they would board the train for Norwich. What lovely ladies they were: gentle, caring, and quiet. Just the sort I like to have around—keeping to themselves, never banging the walls and trying to change things. The village had not yet awakened, but there the two ladies were, already traveling down the muddy road, holding their hats with one hand, their skirts with the other (the hem of Fanny's white petticoat flapping in the wind), until they disappeared behind the Buck public house, and once again I thought how hard it was for a house like me to be left alone when lovely ladies feel they must move on.

How long would it be this time? I wondered with dread, as the autumn sun began to rise behind the stables. It could be days. It could be weeks or even years. Inside the other houses along Deopham Road people were waking, getting dressed, and making breakfast; but there was no human to rise inside me. Sun rays hit my terracotta chimney pots, slowly spreading down the two crumbling chimneys, warming the mossy thatch, hitting the pale yellow walls, and then slamming through the windows into the dusty emptiness within. I was choked with fear.

In the afternoon, when the sun moved around and up my back, I pretended to wait expectantly for the Misses Collins to return from work in Wymondham, where they had secretarial jobs in the banking company—rather respectable work in those days of underpaid ladies—even though I knew very well they had resigned a whole seven days earlier. Their mother had died of flu in Aberdeen, and that was that. The father needed looking after. They packed up and left.

They never came back, and I never saw them again.

It was hardest, I thought, when the lovely ladies left. I got very attached to them you see, and it always hurt less when the gentlemen moved on. But that was before I knew the pain of Oscar Winther leaving.

It was on that day, eighty years ago, when the Misses Collins moved house, that this story begins: exactly three months before the Winthers arrived, and with them the seeds of the present unhappiness.

In a way, time compresses as one gets older, and heaven knows I'm no spring chicken. I'm over four hundred years old. When exactly I was built, has recently been an issue of contention amongst the scholars of East Anglian cottages. After neglecting us for centuries, everyone is suddenly terribly interested in old timbre-framed houses. I suppose we're considered a curio. The entry on myself in the 'statutory list of buildings of architectural or historic interest,' states: 'Fir Grove cottage, grade II, plastered and thatched, two storeys and attics, Seventeenth Century'—with a question mark next to the date. (Grade II—what an outrage!)

And then, in 1989, some chaps from the University of East Anglia came around to work out my history. How they amused me! I watched them clumsily measuring the beams and peering into the roof, making obvious mistakes and complete fools of themselves. I wanted to help them but I had no way of informing them that the joists in the dining room they thought were three hundred years old were in fact excellent reproductions that clever man Sutton made in 1825. These 'experts' confidently announced that I had been built in

1630. Why they chose that particular date is beyond me, but I think it had something to do with the width of the bricks in my chimney stack.

I was born in 1592, which makes me 407 years old this year (not that there's much to celebrate). Yes, I am an old house, older than all the others in the village, and, of course, infinitely wiser. Four hundred years might sound like a long time to you, but if you take into account that I could, under different circumstances, survive another four centuries, then that means I'm about fifty in human terms. In the prime of life. Healthy as a horse. Four hundred years of experience, of learning from people and books, newspapers and, latterly, the television, which is more than any of you lot can claim, so don't go asking me how I know so much. I wasn't built like those flimsy modern houses, you know, such as the ones that have sprouted across the road like a disease. They'll be lucky to survive the century.

I apologise. Forgive me. I'm being arrogant. And rude too. It's just that things are somewhat difficult at the moment, to say the least. Humour me if I present myself in a flattering light. Pretty old houses like myself are prone to pride, and there's no one to stop me if I exaggerate. I can't rely on others to give me praise: I go into fashion, and then out of fashion. You wouldn't believe the sorts of houses people choose to live in. It isn't good for one's self-esteem.

I admit: I lied about being the oldest house in the village. It's true, only if you don't count Sedley Old Hall ('grade I, projecting wings, moated'), which was built in the Fifteenth Century, so they say. But it was restored, of course. I can't actually see it from here, for although it's only a mile away it's hidden discreetly behind a thick line of trees. (One can't have the commoners looking on now, can one.) But I've seen plenty of pictures in Oscar's books, and believe me, the Old Hall has had a little touching up, if you know what I mean, whereas I've been left virtually intact since the day I was born, when they assembled my prefabricated timber frame on this exact spot, in the gentle valley of Deopham Road, Sedley St. Peter, South Norfolk. Four hundred years old. And proud of it.

Back then, of course, it wasn't called Deopham Road. I wasn't even called Fir Grove; I only got my name in 1889 when the lovely Mrs. Haughton christened me. (Oh I do love the lovely ladies. There's something less intrusive about them.) Before that I was just 'Henry

Eldred's house,' which isn't the highest compliment a house can be paid. And Deopham Road used to be called Goodwyn's Lane in the Nineteenth Century, and before that it was just Dirty Lane. Yes, I was built on the dirtiest lane in the village, but it was the only proper lane, and it was the only place for a squire to build a dower house.

In constructing me I can assure you no expense was spared. I was (and I still am) a handsome house, built from the hardiest oak beams, clay lump walls, and Norfolk reed roof. I am six bays wide, and presently—after the floors were added in the late Seventeenth Century (a minor alteration)—I have two stories and an attic. My two front entrances are pure mahogany, with brass knockers and ornate doorknobs. I may not be one of those polite gentleman's houses that I used to gaze at jealously in Miriam Winther's London magazines, but I do have carved floor joists, and stained glass windows which let pretty green and red and yellow light into the dark stairwells.

It's not easy to look after an old house like myself, and I didn't blame the Misses Collins for not taking care of the dry rot, or for letting the thatch slide. I had pain in the beams of the north gable where the kitchen was slowly sinking, and there was damp in my cellar, but they chose to turn a blind eye. By the time they left, the ridge on my roof was a mess; the horrible dirty doves had removed most of it for their nests. I must say it wasn't entirely pleasant to have people walk by on the road below, looking up at what was once my crowning glory. It wasn't respectable. But Fanny and Marianne had their concerns, and it wasn't the easiest thing to get a thatcher, even in those days. It wasn't until 1977—a dot of happiness in a half-century of despair!—that I was finally given a new thatch roof, and a beautiful one at that. But I'm getting ahead of myself.

The westerly wind pushed at my back throughout that awful day when the Misses Collins left, and continued into the evening, when it came in gusts that made silver snakes in the grass, and the trees in the paddock sway like underwater plants. The crows, flying in the other direction, seemed as though they were tied by some invisible anchor, until they gave up and dove down to wait under the bushes. I felt the wind pushing me in the direction I wanted to go, after the Misses Collins, and I wished it would push harder so that I could follow them.

Naturally, it is futile to want a thing like that. It is my lot to be stationary, and I have come to terms with it. That doesn't mean, however, that I don't move. On the contrary: the tension of my beams, rafters, plaster and brick, causes an incessant vibration of all my parts. The wood is constantly bending, the windows changing, the plaster crumbling, and the ground eroding. (I have no foundations; my constituent parts were built separately and then assembled on site, directly onto the ground.) A structure as large and as intertwined as myself must be in a state of constant readjustment in order to remain standing. Although one might perceive me as inanimate, I am moving as much as, if not more than, any of you. And, of course, I have been known, when pressed, to release a subsidiary beam at a particular angle. An act of self-defence. But I run ahead of myself once more, so to speak.

The wind let up when darkness fell. Yellow orbs from gas lamps were glowing in the windows of the village houses, giving them the appearance of sneering, grinning faces. Farmers, labourers, tradesmen and women, schoolteachers, and shop owners were all eating supper with their families, sheltered from the cold night. In 1920 there were two hundred and fifty-six people in the village, and now there were two less. I was used to hearing the hiss and sputter of the lamps outside my front doors, but tonight they were not lit; whoever looked up at my windows was welcomed by darkness.

Being empty, I believed, was worse than having the rowdiest, most violent occupiers of space as lodgers. Worse than being renovated, or squatted in, or being split into apartments (as I had been, temporarily, in the 1700s). I am a house that needs to be lived in. How does a house justify its existence if it is not being lived in? I am not just a collection of walls, ceilings and floors: I am the space between all these. A room, I reasoned, is not vacuum: it is habitable space, and it gets its character as much from its container as from the way it is filled, the way it is disturbed. A room is defined by its function. If it is not a bed-room, or a dining-room, or a bath-room, then what is it? And the function of each of my rooms depends entirely on the people who use them. In a way, I thought bitterly, I am nothing but the sum of all my inhabitants.

As the village lamps were extinguished, I grew more and more distressed. Paranoia descended like the darkness. It was evident that I would remain empty forever; no one wanted to live in me. It was better to be broken and mercifully disassembled. Indeed, at this very moment, I convinced myself, the official letters from South Norfolk Council Planning were being typed up, with the phrases, Fir Grove, although of architectural and historic interest, is in a decrepit condition, and, is not viable to maintain, and, set for demolition, together with a date, giving me a few days to say my last words to the horrid pigeons, and have my final thoughts.

I thought about the time I had to wait sixteen years, only to have the Cockrelles move in. That was in 1722. I was still a young house—my rafters strong, my chimneys intact, my earthen floors ready to be smoothed down again by drunken feet. I wanted good country people to come and live in me. So imagine what it was like to go for sixteen years without having anyone step inside. And then imagine what it was like to have the Cockrelles move in. Twenty-seven of them, including twenty screaming brats, all illegal. Squatters. Oh, the violence of those years. Not just to me, you understand, but to each other. There was no peace at all. The Cockrelles arrived in 1738, and in 1739 the Lord of the Manor's strongmen entered me with their shining swords and their uniforms, and kicked twenty-seven filthy, undernourished, and now homeless, Cockrelles out of the village.

It's not that I had anything against the poor. Nor did I have anything against squatters, as long as they didn't stay too long and didn't do too much damage. Squatters don't have money you see, and there's no two ways about it, I am an expensive house to maintain. Not that money guarantees I will be looked after. One 'owner' of mine, Shadwell (may he burn in hell), had money, or at least he had before he squandered it. A gentleman. A real gentleman. As the rain dripped slowly into my clay walls, Mr. Shadwell poured alcohol down his throat. That was in the mid-early 1800s. I can see him clearly, his wispy red hair smoothed down from one side of the pink dome of his head to the other, as he huddled in the corner of the middle attic room, the sloping roof pushing him down to his knees. A rat would scuttle unnoticed across the grimy floor by his feet, while he thought of his enemies in King's Lynn who wanted him dead. He shivered with cold; liquor gleamed in the corner of his mouth. They got him in the end.

Good riddance to Shadwell! Give me the Misses Collins any day.

The sense of emptiness was worse at night, but by morning I was feeling better. It was a sunny clear day, and in the calm of the moment I took a good look around me. As far as the eye could see there were flat fields, the teams already ploughing the brown soil, each one twenty yards apart. There was the old flint church to the north, with its broken clock in the tower—below it, the well-kept churchyard where Oscar Winther's bones now lie. In the fields, solitary trees stood like ancient tribesmen, and before them sat squat cottages all up Deopham and the Attleborough roads. There was the village school, with jars of tadpoles in the window, and the post office-cum-shop with the doorbell that tinkled whenever somebody entered. Outside, men with crutches and children on bicycles, had gathered in front of the water pump, while others, I knew, were inside buying sweets and stamps from Mrs. Peacock. A horse-drawn cart was making its way through the village, and in the distance I could hear the rumble of a motorcar on its way to Wymondham.

My gaze turned closer, and I looked over the three acres of Fir Grove land. At the south end, the growing grass was busy blurring the edges of my tennis court. To the east of this was the unattended orchard, where hundreds of Bramley Seedlings and Dr. Harvey apples hung from overloaded trees. On the front lawn, near the road in the north, a glorious male pheasant and his harem of hens were pecking half-heartedly in the sun.

There's nothing like being suddenly left alone to heighten one's powers of perception.

It was Sunday the 23rd of September 1920, the afternoon of my second day without Fanny and Marianne, when the other squatters came out. They were quiet, but not silent. Twenty-nine people have died under my roof, and when there is none of the living to appear suddenly from around a door or a corner, they tend to be less shy, and emerge at first hesitantly, then gleefully, from their resting place.

Look, look, there is Cook (1703, gambler), hopping out of the cupboard. He died when he swung his axe at his wife, and ended up cutting off his foot and bleeding to death. Served him right. Mrs. Cook treated me well after she was left to live in peace without her husband.

And here's the baby Tina McIntyre, died in 1851 from consumption, still coughing blood as she crawls from the dining room fireplace.

Mr. Mercer, the lawyer, swallowed arsenic, in 1886. Blue as a pickled egg, emerging from the larder.

There were the others too. Sawlittle (1835, apothecary), who died in his sleep, aged ninety, in the very same room he'd been born in and never moved out of; Mary McIntyre (1872, housekeeper and mother of baby Tina), died from dysentery, after the well was contaminated.

There were illnesses, old age, and accidents (William, in 1905, and Quiney, in 1715, both crashed down the stairs, the former tripped, the latter pushed).

Lively dead people came from the cellar, the wattle and daub walls, under the floorboards, from beneath the rafters in the roof, out of the cupboards, the unused rooms, and the dark corners. They now had the whole place in which to roam. The Misses Collins had left two days ago, and now, as the sun went down, I felt a little less lonely.

The days became nights, the nights became days, for exactly three months. The trees in the paddock and the orchard had shed their fruit and leaves, and one could see straight through the acres to the other side of the property, to the pond where the ducks bickered like jealous women. The church on the hillside never changed; a house was being built across the road.

It was the winter solstice. A vehicle with wheels and an engine, an unusual sight in those days, drove through the gate. A family dropped out onto the lawn. A man and a woman, and four sons, the tallest being taller than his father.

He was almost sixteen.

He had his mother's lips. They were shaped like an obscene love heart. These lips were the beginning of my end.

Andrew Knight

Andrew Knight was born in 1979 and grew up in Brewood (pronounced 'Brood'), a village near Wolverhampton in the West Midlands.

Something Shorter

Beatrice Lather / 2 Short Stories; 1 Start of a Novel

Hey gang,

I'm a cover letter. No, not really. I'm a writer *writing* a cover letter (ooh, how clever!), and here *is* that letter in all its beauty. And I've written it 'cos our lovely tutor told us we should attach a cover letter to explain, or summarise (or something), any writing that we hand in.

Well, I've been experiencing great difficulties writing one coherent piece for this first week, so here are a number of incoherent ones instead. First though, me:

I'm Beatrice Lather (no jokes about lathering *you* up, *me* up, or *anybody else* up, please). I write anything that takes my fancy: short stories, children's fiction, poetry (I dabble). Ok, down to business.

Story 1, called *Jimmy Two-Bells*, is about a Morris dancer who starts a protection racket in the Cotswolds. Implausible? I'll write anything, I'm so dizzy! Story 2 called simply, *You Stay, I Walk Away*, is about bodily movements.

Beneath these two, at the very bottom of this pile, you have the beginning of something longer: my Wild West extravaganza, *Flute McGovern.* If any of you are from the U.S. of A. then you might get to thinking that *Flute McGovern* is heavily based on the life of James McGovern, the mid-19th century artist and photographer regarded as one of the first to have captured the locations and people of 'Wild West' America on film. Well, howdy! Say you darn Yanks sure would be right! I assure you, however, I merely intend to use the real life of ol' Jimbo McG as an inspirational device to bounce off, if need be.

Anyhoo, hope you like them all (oh, how I hope); they are, as I said, a mixed bunch. To quote a great comedian: 'Some of them are funny and none of them is.' (It was not one of his best jokes.) Thank you for your patience,
Beatrice.

Hugo Farrelly-Fortescue / *It's Grim Up North*

I am Hugo Farrelly-Fortescue, son of Lord and Lady Farrelly-Fortescue, both of whom, as you know, also wrote novels, all of which were very successful.

This is the first chapter of my novel entitled, *It's Grim Up North.* The novel is concerned with the lives of the Northern people during the 1980s; in particular their experiences in connection with the failing coal, steel and shipbuilding industries. I believe that as I am not a Northern person myself, I therefore have the advantage of an objective perspective upon my chosen subject, and while some amongst you might disagree with my views and opinions, I feel that rather than exhibiting prejudice I am in actual fact doing nothing more outrageous than writing the truth as I see it.

Zacharie Briar / *Sweeter Love* (a novel in progress)

Tout d'abord, I must introduce myself. Hello everyone, I am Zacharie and I write about feelings. I am to say a little about this submission, am I not? Well, this is the first chapter of my very personal project, and do you think it is working?

Josie Giant / 3 Poems

Christ, it's like bloody Blind Date this! Hiya, Cilla. My name's Josie, I'm a student, and I'm from SHEFFIELD! WOO-HOO!

In my poetry I'm trying to capture what it must be like to have to grow up down South. To begin with this week I'm submitting my triptych of poems, individually called: *Daddy, Won't You Buy Me a Pony; A Fondness for Their Privates;* and *Posh Bottomed Boy.*

Ta very much.

Vaughan / *Recurrence: Self* (a meditation in progress)

I am Vaughan, *just* Vaughan (not *V*, not *Van*, not *Vag*, as some have called me in the past), and Tetia, my bitch-model girlfriend/muse, has just left me; and this is my life, so this is my art. But since Tetia has left I have no one to draw, to paint, to inspire me, and so, for the purposes of this writing class, I shall be expressing my art specifically through the *written word*; the spoken word holds no interest for me. When you speak you can make errors and it is not my desire to make errors. In writing too, of course, mistakes can be made, but in rewriting you can make those mistakes disappear. You cannot *re*-speak. When words escape your mouth they cannot be *re*-captured. So, to *re*-peat, I deal only with inked words on blank white paper: the erasable.

And now our *illustrious* tutor informs me that I must write cover letters such as this: I submit Chapter Two, and so for the sake of context must summarise Chapter One; I ask specific questions that I would like the group to address in reference to my work. . . . In my opinion, these cover letters amount to nothing more than excuses, preambles, glorified forewords, prologues, acknowledgements, etcetera, etcetera. But this is Week One, and therefore no explanations are necessary: merely introductions.

I am writing about writers. This, of course, will become obvious when you come to read what I have written.

★

Beatrice Lather / *Andy's Andes* (short story)

Ola amigos,

Just to keep you up to date, I've put *Flute McGovern* to one side for the mo, and ok, I'm just gonna let you read this new one.

It's influenced by a line from handsome Zacharie's novel, from the bit about how the empowered Eros felt he could fly Psyche to the furthest hills. Well, I went from hills to mountains, to mountain ranges, and then I threw in a Mountie called Andy (big and strong, broad shoulders, unshaven), and plonked him down in South America. Anyway, on with the show!

Beatrice xx

p.s. I've just noticed there's a spelling mistake on page 5, and rather than printing the whole story out again I thought I might just tell you

about it here and you could perhaps change it yourselves? Anyway, if you could, when reading the 16th sentence on page 5, replace all the letters in the word 'Kazoo,' with all the letters in the word 'Panama Canal,' it should be a lot less confusing for you later on, when Andy's woman, Pattygonia, wakes up next to an anxious lama.
p.p.s. Thank you, Zachie, for the inspiration, and for everything else. x

Hugo Farrelly-Fortescue / *It's Really Grim Up North*
Some of you commenting on my first chapter stated that my depiction of the Northern people as simian degenerates lacking the ability to spell their own names—or indeed to spell any word of more than one letter—expressed nothing more than an explicit bigotry I commonly direct towards anyone living north of Epping. I certainly hope you will be a little more open minded with regard to this latest submission: Chapter Two.

By way of a small postscript for Josie: You submit your work under the pretence that it is poetry and then all you give us are words heaped randomly atop each other, much the same way as one might see manure being piled atop more manure.

Zacharie Briar / *Impassioned Love* (a novel in progress)
I bumped into Vaughany in the bar yesterday and we had a talk about errors. He said he did not like them at all, but I said that errors were très important. I remember my French mama used to say to me when I was a boy: 'Zacharie,' she would say, 'Zacharie, humans are fallible, and this is fine. *C'est une bonne chose*. It gives them character. Remember, Zacharie,' my mama would continue, 'human error is the most human of errors and as such should be embraced as we would embrace a loved one.'

Here is Chapter 2, and I have thought to change the title of my novel. I have also made a change that I should let you know about, *maintenant*.

In the Chapter 1 that you read last week, my hero, Eros, went away with Psyche, who was a dancer. As a few of you complained that 'Psyche' was an unlikely name for a dancer, I have since revised Chapter 1 to make her a *mécanicien auto*. She is still very flexible though, because this is imperative.

If I could just add a personal message to Beatrice: I so enjoyed your story, *You Stay, I Walk Away*. You told us it was about bodily movements, and can I say to you that it *moved* my heart? You are a writer after my emotions, I think. When Mitzy took Bobby's false hand and polished it as if it were her own, and then told him that the other mannequins had all decided to let him wear the very expensive sweater in the shop window . . . oh, I am crying many tears thinking about it now. If you have any more stories about similar heartbreaks I would love to read them. x

Josie Giant / *Southern Buggers*
As you'll see here, I've now collected my triptych and some other poems under the single title, *Southern Buggers*. And while I'd appreciate your input on my writing in general, I'd mostly be interested to know if my themes ring any bells for certain lanky titheads in our group from Tunbridge Hells who wouldn't know a steel girder if they were hit in the face with one—and that can be arranged. It's *me* that's writing the truth! You might learn something about yourself!

Vaughan / *Recurrence: Myself*
Error has been eradicated from the episode of my novel that I submitted last time (just as Tetia, the heathen slut, *eradicated* herself from my life). To prove this claim I am resubmitting that episode as it exists in its current form. I defy you to locate even a typo.

⋆

Beatrice Lather / *The Hapless and the Disaffected*
Hey there,

To kick off . . . Thanks for your comments on my previous submitted work! They were all useful and fantastic (the comments, not the work)! You are all brilliant critics!

Now, I don't really know what to say about this next thing. (I 'hmm' to myself.) It's a little ditty about a small group of revolutionaries who are continually beset by calamity. But I think you might have trouble following it. I guess what I'd mostly like to know are the following:

1) Is my principle protagonist, Vim, believable as a person? If not, what is he believable as, and how many legs does that have?
2) Should Vim's girlfriend, Katia, be prone to fits of quacking, or are her webbed feet and propensity to upend for duckweed in park lakes across Moscow, enough to get my point across?
3) Do animals feature too prominently, just prominently enough, or not at all prominently?

I suppose these may seem like silly little points but they've been bothering me till the cows come home (and they're still not home, and I'm running short of milk). Help!

Once again, your thoughts would be appreciated. Thank you kindly. You are all attractive individuals.
Beatrice xx

Hugo Farrelly-Fortescue / *Devolution*
In many ways my submission this week is less a story, and more a scientific theory. Within it I contest Darwin's position that humans evolved from apes, instead claiming (far more realistically) that, in actual fact, both humans *and* apes evolved from Geordies.

Zacharie Briar / *Obsessive Love* (a novel in progress)
I worry that my hero, Eros, comes across as being too much in love, as if such a thing could be possible. *Je n'ai rien à ajouter.* I hope you enjoy it, but if you do not then that is ok too. xx
p.s. I have been learning so much from all of you. I feel so good about being part of this group. x

Josie Giant / *Home on the Range Rover*
Before we get onto my work and that, I've a brief verse here, dedicated to my good mate Hugo Spottily-Arsey-Face:

My Old Man's a nobleman,
Because my Grandpa's dead,
For centuries inbreeding,
Two eyes, two ears, two heads.

I hope it was to *one's* liking, you snotty, monocle-wearing twat.

Vaughan / *Recurrence: Me*
Still you are not satisfied. You cannot see the luminous brilliance in my work that *I* see as self-evident. I must assume that your perceptions have been systematically dulled through the constant exposure to your own inferior products—exposure governed by nothing more than your own narcissistic selves.

Why must I be subjected to this idle game? Questions? Questions? Well, apart from minimal stylistic queries I might have about the way I have written about writers in general, perhaps my only concern—the concern that I insist you address in review—is whether or not my writing comes across as being too self-reverential.

⋆

Beatrice Lather / *Flute McGovern*
Hello,

Powered by the power of the secret power of love, I've been powering ahead with my longer piece, *Flute McGovern*, without telling anybody (aren't I naughty!). To keep you up to date with some stuff I've done: mostly I've just been moving things around a bit—'faire l'imbécile,' as Zachie might put it (I 'ain't too good at me Français).

So: Chapter 5 is now Chapter 1, and the original Chapter 1 is now Chapter 3. Chapter 3 has been substituted with plucky Chapter 9, coming off the bench for the first time since pulling a hamstring in early May. Chapter 6's place will be taken by the ever-reliable Chapter 4. There is no Chapter 12 (the book is simply not that long), but there is a Chapter 13! I'll move it closer to the Contents Page, post haste.

Oh, you don't need to know all that though, 'cos you've only ever seen Chapter 1 (Chapter 3). Hope you like it (kissy, kissy).

Hugo Farrelly-Fortescue / *Home County Hero of the 22nd Century*
Overcome by your short-sighted and contentious remarks regarding *It's Grim Up North*, I have, therefore, put that book to one side in order to concentrate on my science-fiction novel, *Home County Hero of the 22nd Century*.

In summary, my novel is about one man's journey into the heart of an impenetrable grimness. It takes place in the year 2101, fifty years after the Big Divide of 2051. The Big Divide, to explain, began with an anomalous tectonic rupture and culminated in Britannia being physically broken in half. Prior to this rare geographical occurrence, all humanity's technological advances had been created and housed in the South of England. Therefore, in the post-Big Divide years, the population of what became known as North Island found life to be extremely arduous.

At the beginning of my novel, the North Islanders find themselves close to extinction. There is no running water, people have to defecate in holes in the ground that they have to dig themselves, and their only means of entertainment is to throw needles, primitively decorated with feathers, into a circular-shaped target in places they commonly refer to as 'The Local.'

Fortunately, a lone stranger from East Grinstead takes it upon himself to help those less privileged than he. Selflessly swimming across the treacherous Class Channel, our hero transports with him both the knowledge and the equipment needed to educate those Northern vagrant pillocks in modern day methods of sanitation.

Zacharie Briar / *Withered Love* (a novel in progress)
Bonjour, mes amis. To explain . . . my heroine, Psyche, if you remember, had red hair. Now her hair is brown (like Beatrice's was before she decided to make changes and be difficult). Eros, *aussi*, has not gone unchanged as I have made him seven centimetres taller than he was before. This is because at this new height he will be able to reach the front door keys that are on the top shelf in his kitchen, without needing to get a chair from another room. I thought this would help speed up the action in that scene, and in any scene when Eros might need to leave his house.

To warn you . . . at the end of the first chapter I have added a short paragraph (suggested to me by Beatrice), in which all my characters have narcoleptic fits and wake up in Chippewa Falls, Wisconsin. This is not done simply to appeal to the U.S. market, but again because I think it is going to be necessary for a later scene in my book that I have yet to imagine up. Continuity is always my first concern. Thank you, Beatrice. I hope we can always be friends.

Josie Giant / *The Southern Shandy Drinker*
This week I'll be submitting my magnum opus, *The Southern Shandy Drinker*. It's a longer narrative poem about a *distinguished* Southern gentleman called Rupert. In it's first part my poem tells about how Rupert can't drink more than two ginger ales before fainting and then, a few days later, waking up married to one or more of: his aunt, his nephew, his butler, his second cousin (who's also both his brother and his gamekeeper). The second half of the poem's about how Rupert struggles to admit these affairs to, and rekindle his love for, his wife (who barks in her sleep—and when she's awake—'cos she's a corgi). The idea for this poem came from me considering the truth universally acknowledged, that a single man in possession of a good fortune must be in want of an obedient pet.

Vaughan / *Recurrence: Inner Me*
I have nothing to say about my work. Rather, I use this coversheet—this superfluous space—to describe a recurring dream I have that will be of significant interest to you all.

I see myself, the artist, hanging upside down in the darkness. The shackles, above me, that bind my ankles to the stone wall of a dungeon, afford me only a limited range of expression.

Before me, beneath me, upon the worn-away ground, rests a sizeable pile of blank paper sheets; above it, attached by a single thread to the dungeon ceiling, hangs an elegantly crafted fountain pen. Again, as with the paper, the pen is just out of my reach though, nonetheless, I strain for it. And fresh black ink begins to drip deliciously from its nib: *plip . . . plop, plip . . . plop, plipping* and *plopping* on the bright shining white below. And I look at the picture that the ink makes on the paper and it is a portrait of Tetia, my absent muse. And then I see myself again, the artist, still shackled to that wall, growing hungry and tearful; stomach, eyes, mind and left hand; all of them aching to write. It is then that I awake screaming. Only geniuses dream as I do, I tell myself.

★

Beatrice Lather / 2 little, 2 late
Hello friends (lame attempt at my usual cheery self),

In this, our last week, I find myself saddened by the cruelties of life. Secrets out, loves dead. . . . Oh, I've been having great difficulty writing anything this week. What I *do* have, however, is here:

> *This is the beginning of something shorter. If you could, for my benefit, edit it down to only four or five words max, then at least I'll have a title.*

Barely worth the paper it's. . . . Is that a phrase or a cliché? I don't even know that anymore. I think I just need some more time. Bye bye. Adieu.
Beatrice xx
p.s. Wishing a big dollop of luck to those among us who *do* find happiness.

Zacharie Briar / *Love* (a novel complete)
My story of feelings . . . It was in the beginning, I think, tentative and exciting; in its middle it was passionate and tender; and at its crescendo, when Eros, my hero, turns away from his love, Psyche, and flaps into the sunset, my story was sad, it was bitter, *et c'était tragique.* These are the feelings *d'amour*, I think. *Fin. Au revoir*, x

Josie Giant & Hugo Farrelly-Fortescue / *Moving to the Midlands*
Hi, Josie here.
And Hugo.
Yes, me and Hugo, we're—
Hugo and I—
Don't start with me, ponce, or I'll kick your arse (pampered) over your tits (puny). And get your stinkin' hands off my keyboard! Hugo and I have decided that we're going to collaborate on a book that's loosely about how him and me got together despite him being a tossin' knob-shiner—
And you a barely female, barely human, ignoramus.
You still find me threatening, don't you, aye?
One is often afraid of a thing that one does not understand.
Oh, one is, is one?
I am sorry, dear, I didn't understand a word of what you just said.
Boo!
Wah! . . . You know, my dear, some women now think it fashionable to shave under their arms. Just something for you to think about. Also you might try walking upright every now and then. With practice you

will improve, I assure you.
Shut it, you buggerin', horse pokin', wanker! Somehow ME and Hugo found that opposites attract. I'm chuffin' fantastic in every way, and Hugo's my opposite.

Vaughan / *Reinvention*
I failed. Mistakes existed; anomalies thrived; they bred; error begot error beget eror, etcetera, exit-error . . . I must begin again, and maybe Tetia will come back to me, but. . . .

I shall continue to write, I think, until I stop. Until the words simply cease to flow, until they run dry. I shall begin, then middle, then climax, then be able, once and for all, to *re*-lax at the end, finally? Finally . . . The End.

DAVID LAMBERT

David Lambert was born and grew up in Trinidad and Tobago. He is of Irish/Trinidadian parentage. He has completed one other novel, Mulatto Moon, *also set in the Caribbean.*

PROVIDENCE

This extract is from the opening of the novel. Luther Gordon has come to his parents' island in the West Indies to scatter their ashes.

1

It was down there somewhere. On one of those green hillsides dotted with coconut palms, snaked with the red earth of rutted traces. Providence. I'd heard them talk about it all my life. Providence. Three hallowed syllables. With the last one stressed. Pro-vi-*dence.* A promised land. Now it lay somewhere beneath me.

They hadn't made it; they'd put it off too long. It had taken their deaths, first one and then the other so soon after, to bring me here for the first time. I hugged the heavy package to me, a tightness in my throat. A flight attendant was making her way down the aisle, practised eyes scanning laps on either side.

'Seatbelts fastened for landing, please,' she said to a passenger a few seats ahead. When she got to me, she looked at my legs cramped in the window seat and the empty seat beside me. Her pale blue professional glance fell on the cardboard box, tied with string, that I held.

'Pop that back in the overhead compartment for you, sir.' It was a statement not a question and she was holding out her hands.

'It's . . . fragile. I'll put it here beside me.' I hadn't spoken for the eight hours of the flight and my voice came out gruff and uncertain.

'I'm sorry, sir, landing regulations don't allow that. It'll be safer stowed in the overhead compartment.' Her smooth arms were already reaching up to unclip the plastic door.

'I really prefer to keep it with me . . .' I said.

'In that case, would you please stow it under the seat in front of you so it isn't a danger to other passengers.' She smiled tersely and moved on to the next row of laps.

I hesitated. Then I opened my legs, reached down and placed the package on the floor, where I hugged it with my trainers. They'd put it off too long. They hadn't made it. So this was how they were returning. Stowed between my feet under an economy class seat, in a heavy granite urn.

The large plane banked steeply over the sea, its shadow rushing up from the hammered blue surface. The landing gear went down with a weary whine and the aircraft righted itself as it began the final approach. The plastic overhead compartments creaked and whinnied under their burden like excited horses. The aircraft lurched down towards rusty corrugated roofs until it seemed it would clip the tops of the coconut palms flying past the window. Its speed became suddenly apparent. I imagined the heavy machine bursting into flames as it hit the runway, the raging conflagration too much for the stunned black firemen hanging off the toy fire truck I'd seen parked ready outside a flimsy hangar.

The body glowed white hot, carbonised in the blue gas flames. I had watched the coffin glide off on the conveyor belt into the incinerator. Blue velvet curtains had flared the length of the shiny maplewood sliding by, riding over its turned brass handles and flopping down in its wake. You see nothing of what lies behind. When the incinerator doors are later opened, all that is left, apparently, is a granular grey ash which staff spoon into the receptacle of choice for relatives to take away. Any receptacle will do. Sometimes a small hammer is used to gently break up the larger pieces of bone, the pelvis and the skull, still black and charred and not ash at all. Like those velvet curtains admitting the coffin, rubber flaps had flopped over the cardboard box now stowed under the seat so it wasn't a danger to other passengers. It too had been trundled away from me on another, faster conveyor belt, this time into the maws of the baggage scanner at Heathrow. The small Asian security man had seen my concern when asked to put it through and he assured me, 'Film-safe, sir. No harm will come.'

2

Emerging from Arrivals, I felt the heat press for attention against my skin and the first trickle of sweat in the small of my back. 'Well, we're here.' My low mutter reverberated on the box held against my chest. But for all the talk about 'going back', for me at least, I could already see this would be no homecoming; I was of the island, but had never set foot on it. I was only aware of differences: the slowed-down quality of the people, moving as if through some thick almost tangible medium; the glaring tropical light bouncing off the hasty, temporary structures around me; the currency exchange; the taxi rank; a sagging lottery station. My suitcase in one hand, precious package in the other, I made my way across the road to the rental office, only the speed of my gait singling me out from my people.

I stood the package on the counter as the girl came over to serve me. She was what my parents would have called fair, her skin a dusty cinnamon, her short braids spiky around a wide, vivacious face. I noticed her eyes, an unusual green, and wondered if she wore lenses.

'Yuh sure yuh want a Micra?' she asked in the island sing-song, and motioned me away from the counter with a small hand. I obeyed, stepping back beside my suitcase. At some leisure, she took me in, my scuffed trainers, jeans, cotton T-shirt. Standing awkward as she appraised me, I ran the side of my palm along my jaw and heard it bristle.

'Eh-eh,' she said. 'You too tall for a Micra.' She pushed back her short braids though there was no need to. 'Hear what, I could let yuh have a Sunny at the Micra price. But I'm not tellin' my boss eh, 'cos he will vex.' She flashed her eyes and laughed at the prospect. Her familiarity was disarming. It was taking me away from my sombre preoccupation. She read off the table of rates and I followed her finger, the clear-lacquer almond nail.

'How long yuh all wantin' it for?'

'I'm here by myself. Say . . . a week?'

'Yeah, the average tourist only stays a week, two max. We're a small lil' island. Licence, please.'

'Well, I'm not your average tourist.' I smiled and got out my licence. 'I'm not here for that.'

'You . . . comin' home?'

'Kind of. . . . First time here, in fact.'

'British,' she confirmed, glancing at the pink licence and handing me a form. 'Fill this in, name, where yuh stayin', all particulars.' She held me for a moment in a jade gaze. 'I'll have the car brought round, Mr Gordon.'

She went to a back door which led into the yard. She was slight of build, quick and leggy in a short skirt and halter-top.

'Les-ter!' she shouted, hand on hip, studying sandalled feet, awaiting the response.

After some time a drawled 'Ye-ah' came from the back.

'Get de white Sunny rong here fuh me, nuh! It have luggage to load so move yuh arse, ah ent got all day!'

I placed one hand on my package on the counter and tried to give my attention to form filling.

3

Aunt Ernestina's was a small ramshackle wooden bungalow with a verandah of potted plants. Dusty fowl pecking in the yard scurried away, cackling, as the Nissan squeaked to a halt in the shade of a mango tree. Approaching the steps, I saw a stout man sitting on the verandah, white stubble against dark skin. Clouded eyes watched me mount the steps, alarm or hostility on the stiff, lined features.

I put my suitcase down gently. 'Uncle Clyde?' I said. Then a little louder. 'It's Luther . . . from England.'

'Doh worry, he wouldn't un'erstand yuh.'

The voice, which came from behind the curtain covering the doorway, startled me. It was my mother's voice, the same reedy alto, the same intonation. The curtain was drawn back and a woman in a cotton shift came out.

'He had a stroke a while back, yuh didn't hear?'

'Aunt Ernestina . . .' I put down the package on a small table, bent to embrace the plump body of my mother's younger sister, and felt my eyes prick. I'd never met her before and hadn't had a chance even now to get a proper look at her.

'Luther! But eh eh, look at you!' she said as I released her. I searched the round face for some resemblance. Aunt Ernestina was plumper and shorter. And she was alive.

'Come in an' bring yuh suitcase,' she said, moving into the deeper shade of the house. I glanced at the old man we were leaving on the verandah; he was gazing into the black depths of the mango tree or the hillside beyond. I pressed my lips and giving a respectful nod, picked up my suitcase. I followed Aunt Ernestina's swaying form across the boarded floor of a dark parlour set with stiff chairs and too many occasional tables. She led me into a side bedroom dominated by a massive, bow-fronted wardrobe, its polished wood inset with designs in paler marquetry. The thin veneer had swollen and lifted at its edges, like the pages of a book left out in the rain, revealing the local wood beneath. Above the hard double bed a wooden cross was all that adorned the wall.

'Yuh goin' be comfortable here,' she said, turning to me. Perhaps there was something of Mum in the drooping eyelids, the fall of the upper lip.

We sat out on the verandah.

'I see yuh carry it dong, eh.' Aunt Ernestina nodded at the cardboard box on the low table between us.

'Yeah . . . It's granite. I'm sorry you couldn't make it . . .

'Well, I cyan't get away.' She glanced at her husband, still lost in the mango tree. 'But she was suppose' to come back. The both o'them! Since Ninety-Two when yuh went to college. Up to now the lan' sittin' waitin' . . .'

'They left it too late.' It was a phrase I'd heard repeated ever since Dad had taken sick and died. They'd always talked about one day building a board house up in Providence where the island breezes blew, hanging up the uniforms they had worn for forty years. Dad used to tell me how the land would give plantains 'big like so' (the distance from his upper wrist to the tip of his shiny brown index finger). I imagined a land of milk and honey. But as I grew older, I was no longer sharing their nostalgia, unable to miss what I'd never known. The island became obscured in the mists of other childhood landscapes. The Caribbean seemed as remote as Narnia.

And suddenly it was there, Crayola green, intensely real, looming up under the cowl of a jet engine. Earlier in the journey, the captain had announced there was a party of three West Indian couples on board, after forty years finally returning to their island. I think everyone but me clapped. Later, as the Azores drifted by like specks in the frosty expanse under the wing, the captain had come on again to thank, on the returnees' behalf, the passenger in Club Class who had sent back champagne. There was another ripple of applause and a warm feeling united the passengers sitting thirty thousand feet above the Middle Passage. They had made it back.

'So yuh didn't want to be lawyer?'

'Lawyer?' I laughed. '. . . I studied English.'

'Or a doctor? Yuh Mammy worked hard up there in that hospital. Yuh Daddy too. I hope yuh would do 'em proud . . .'

'Actually, I have got quite a good job lined up.' I attempted to stem the disapproval immobilising her face. She looked more like Mum than I'd first thought. 'After I get back. In publishing. It's quite . . . well paid.'

'Oh ho,' she said softly. She knew nothing of publishing. 'My eldest, Bertrand, is in Canada, y'know. He workin' for the telephone company. An' I have Marlena an' my youngest, Charisse, in Brooklyn. Yuh don't know 'em, Marlena has her own salon . . .'

We sat for some time in silence.

'I have to think about . . . doing something with Mum and Dad's ashes,' I said eventually. 'On the land up in Providence.'

'Is what Eugenia an' Selwyn wanted.'

'Can you take me there?'

'Yuh know how long it is I haven't been up Providence! I wouldn't know where to look. . . . Is five acres it have up there, y'know, boy? Good lan' jus' waitin' to plant an' cultivate. Yuh don't have no ward sheet?'

I'd never heard of one.

'Well, yuh must go dong an' apply for it at Land Registry. An' put the lan' in yuh name.'

'Yeah? I'll see to it first thing tomorrow.'

'Well, tomorrow yuh could start,' said Ernestina. 'I don't know what yuh could do in two lil' weeks. This ent England. Tings dong here slow! Meanwhile, I goin' an' organise a nice ceremony up on the lan'. The preacher from my church doin' the blessin' an' the choir could sing . . .'

'. . . A choir?'

'It what yuh mother an' father woulda wanted.'

Alone in my room at ten o'clock, when Aunt Ernestina and Uncle Clyde had already gone to bed, I could feel my spirits sinking. A naked bulb hanging from the ceiling cast a murky light on the bed and the bow-fronted wardrobe. A breeze lifted the thin voile curtains, while outside the night was as black as if the earth had spun out of the sun's orbit. I wished Rachel there, wished I could speak to her, hold her. It would be after three a.m. in her Frankfurt hotel room. I don't know what I expected to find here, relatives probably, people who knew my parents stopping by. Everyone seemed to have died or emigrated. I told myself it was just jet lag, that I was recently bereaved. As I got under the sheet on the hard bed, I wondered how I would get through the two weeks, locate the land, register it in my name, do what I'd come to do with Mum and Dad's ashes. Aunt Ernestina said Providence was 'waiting to cultivate.' As if I could return and grow plantain. And there was the other business Rach and I had discussed. What good was five acres on the other side of the world?

4

Rachel called the next evening. Aunt Ernestina picked up, handed me the receiver and left the kitchen. Rachel's voice sounded disarmingly close. She might almost have been in the next room; desire tugged crudely at me.

When Aunt Ernestina heard the receiver go down she heaved herself out of her chair and returned, creaking across the parlour floorboards. A faint tang of bergamot wafted in through the open louvres. Dusk was thickening on the citrus trees in the steeply sloping garden.

'Yuh spoke to yuh young lady?' she said, turning the kitchen light on. 'I'm goin' an' make a nice brot' with that fish head it have there.'

'Sounds good. Yeah, I did. She says you sound just like Mum . . .'

'She think so?' Her head was in the fridge. 'Yuh Mammy had a different voice than mine. I was in the church choir, y'know. I sang soprano. Eugenia couldn't keep a tune an' her voice deep, y'know, kinda low. They wouldn't take her . . .' She stood up from the fridge. 'What the girl name again?'

'Rachel.'

'She didn't sound small islan'.'

'That's because she's not, Aunty.'

'Where her people from, Jamaica? I know it have a whole set of Jamaicans up there in Englan'. They not like us small islan' people, eh . . .' 'Her folks aren't from the West Indies.'

'No?'

'No. They're English. Well, Jewish, actually. Her grandparents were Lithuanian Jews.'

Aunt Ernestina stood with half a kingfish head, grey and bloody, in one hand, a knife in the other. She widened her eyes minimally and pursed full lips.

'Rachel's a commissioning editor,' I said. 'She's lovely. You'll see for yourself if she comes.'

Aunt Ernestina was intently cutting up the kingfish head, her breathing heavy with the effort.

'Anything I can do to help?' I asked.

'I am queen in my kitchen,' she gave her habitual reply. 'Just hand dong that pot for me, nuh.' She pointed at an aluminium tureen on a high shelf. 'Yuh gettin' through wit' those lan' registry people?'

'Well, I've applied for the ward sheet . . . to locate it. It's slow, five working days they say . . .'

'Yuh Mammy get the best parcel. Five acres bound by the river! Yuh know how long that lan' cryin' out to cultivate! Well, it still there, *land don't rot*. It good yuh come dong.'

The red granite amphora had been removed from its cardboard box and placed on a low cabinet between two armchairs, so that when you sat down it was oddly like being there with them in the stiff little parlour. As if they had made it back after all. As the days went by, I found that my aunt shared several quirks with Mum, so that I was constantly reminded of her. There was the similarity of voice, of course, which Aunt Ernestina curiously denied, some sisterly jealousy preserved intact to old age and now beyond. There were echoes of Mum too, in the way Ernestina held her hands in her lap, or touched her wiry grey hair as she spoke, as if to check it were still there. Some of these, I suspected, were simply ways of behaving common to most elderly West Indian women; it's hard to tell what is specific to the individual from what might be general to a people.

Not all similarities were benign; Aunt Ernestina's attitude to Rachel, my 'young lady', was Mum's exactly. It was as if Ernestina had taken up the baton of petty prejudice my mother had passed to her in dying, neither sister evincing the least solidarity with a race which, like their own, history had scattered over the face of the earth.

Zoe Lambert

Zoe Lambert was born in Manchester and graduated in English Studies there. She has taught English in Italy for one year. Carol's Cross *is an extract from her first novel.*

Carol's Cross

Carol thinks Julie's become a bit of a paranoid android as they walk through the Arndale Centre between Argos and a café that smells like they have fried fags with the sausages, past Sports One and a fake designer perfumery. Carol watches Julie glaring from beneath her blonde fringe at the other shoppers as if they are really spies: as if the groups of teenage girls looking in shop windows are wearing wigs and are carrying bombs in their Benetton bags, or the crotchety mums with uncontrollable prams and sticky brats have cameras hidden under the handlebars, and old blokes sitting on benches peer through eyeholes in their newspapers.

God, Carol hates this place; the harsh light that gives your skin a yolky tinge, and Christmas music blaring from the speakers, even though it's only October. Why did they agree to meet in this boxy arc of shops? It's already making her feel queasy and her head's starting to pound after an hour's pilgrimage with Julie; the stuffy heat and the millions of little kids running round the fountain that's never switched on. Though it's less busy than it was five years ago when they were thirteen and trying on dresses in Miss Selfridges. But Julie preferred shell suits to dresses when they hung around together. She must still do now. Carol inspects Julie in her red and white shell suit; she doesn't seem to have changed, except that she's bigger, taller, wider hipped. Rudely so, like she's decided to take up more space than she was allotted.

'So what about Mandy and Joanna? What happened to them?' Julie asks, stopping next to the fountain and sitting down on the marble edge.

'Pregnant. Both of them,' Carol says, perching next to her, trying not to let her white jeans actually touch the splashed surface. But it's hard because the ledge is high and her feet don't quite touch the floor despite her three-inch stackers.

'No shit.'

'Joanna's got two kids now.'

'Must be catchin'.'

'I hope not.' Carol looks away.

'Must be lots of Immaculate Collections,' says Julie. 'You ok?'

'Yeah.' Then Carol laughs. 'Conception. Immaculate Conception.'

'What did I say?'

'Collection.' Immaculate conception. Yeah right.

'Oh God, my fave album that one,' says Julie, laughing. 'What about you? Did y' go to college then?'

'Yeah, Pendleton. I finished in June. I'm working at Morrisons now.'

'Do y' like it?'

'Nah, it's rubbish.'

'At least you've got a job.' Julie smoothes her blonde fringe, pulling it between her fingers. Carol notices that under Julie's hair there aren't any eyebrows, just two black lines. She must have shaded her eyes with the same kohl pencil. It gives her an odd gothic look, like a blonde witch. Carol really wants to take her in hand, give her a makeover and sort out her scrambled eggs skin. But more than that she's dying to know why Julie left in fourth year. There was so much gossip about her after she vanished, whispers about drugs and gangs while they crowded in the loos, slapping on layers of lipstick. 'Can you believe it's been like four years now?' Carol asks. 'But where did you get to? You just disappeared.'

'You know, moved away.'

Carol waits, twirling her hair around her fingers.

Julie looks straight at her. 'I was put in care,' she says, kind of spitting it out like a piece of chewing gum, splat on the blackboard. 'Supposed to start at this new school, but I just wagged it. Fuckin' waste of time it was and then I got caught up in stuff . . . you know . . . ended up in prison.'

Carol shouldn't have asked. She doesn't know what to say, so she bites her nails and shifts uncomfortably on the ledge.

Julie spits out some more. 'My mam kicked me out. Said she couldn't cope with me. Told them I was violent, that she was scared of me. Not that she would have noticed, she never came out of her gin bottle.'

Carol has a genie-like image of Julie's mother living inside a gin bottle, banging on the glass. 'I'm sorry,' she says, as if Julie's mother has died.

'Don't matter.' Julie shakes her head as she stands up, as if to get it all out of her ears. 'I've just been to visit me mam. Not seen her for a year. And I found your number with a load of old schoolbooks she'd kept. Come on. Want to look at the CDs in Woolies?'

'Sure,' Carol says. 'I'm glad you rang.' Julie links Carol's arm as they walk along. Perhaps Julie wants to be mates again after all this time. But she was always so changeable at school; friends one minute, rivals the next, usually for some lad's attention. She probably expects a trade of info, a titbit to even things out.

They stop outside the window of Woolworths, which is full of Halloween gear; vampire teeth and witches' hats, Frankenstein's bolts and werewolf masks.

'Have you ever gone trick or treatin'?' Julie asks.

'Nah. It was always too dangerous down our end.'

'Me neither. Shall we have a look?' Julie looks mischievously gleeful or excited, like a nine year old with a poopy cushion and an aunt about to sit down. 'Go on. Try on a mask. You'd suit the Frankenstein look.'

They enter Woolworths, past the CDs to the Halloween section. Carol picks up a monster mask. It's green and covered in boils. Might as well try it, why not, no one's looking. She puts it on, then sticks her tongue through the hole for the mouth and waggles it at Julie who laughs, putting on a purple witch's wig and black pointy hat.

'Suits you,' says Carol from behind the mask, picking up a bottle of fake luminous slime.

'I vaunt you!' Julie murmurs through a pair of fangs. Then she gets out a mirror from her bag and peers at herself. 'I really should go purple.'

Maybe Carol could tell her here . . . from behind the safety of green boils. She has to tell someone and maybe Julie would know what to do: she should know about this kind of thing. She was always in the know at school. Julie's picked up some face crayons. She takes out the fangs and applies blue to her lips.

'Julie.'

'What? Do y' like me in blue?' Julie asks, as she draws a mole on her chin.

'I think I'm pregnant.'

'What? Take the bloody mask off, I can't hear you.'

Carol shakes her head. 'I think I'm pregnant.'

'Shit! Are you stupid? Are you fucking stupid or what?'

The monster mask folds into Carol.

'I mean, I get pregnant, bloody Joanna gets pregnant, but not you. You work for Morrisons . . . well . . . anyway . . . are you sure?'

'No.'

'Have you done a test?'

'No.'

Carol starts to cry. She tries not to, holding her breath and screwing up her eyes, but it's no use. Before she put it into words, it lurked at the back of her mind, a growing blackhead that she could cover with concealer. Now its angry head glares at her, about to burst.

'Why not?' Julie gives Carol a tissue, which she dabs at her nose through the hole in the mask.

'I don't know. I didn't want to know . . .'

'How long since . . ?'

'Two months.'

'Shit, you should do one . . .'

'I'll go to the doctors on Monday or something.'

'Yeah, you do that!' Julie takes off the hat and wig, wiping the blue off with the back of her hand.

It wasn't supposed to be like this, Julie was meant to comfort her in a bad-girls-together way, not point an accusing finger or shout at her like a mum. Carol wants to take off the mask, but she can't; everyone will see she's crying. A mask is better than runny mascara and blotchy skin.

'Come on,' says Julie, and touches her shoulder. 'Want to go for a fag?'

'Yeah,' she mutters, sniffing. That's more like it. Bad girls together

now. 'I'll just pay for the mask.'
Outside, Julie asks, 'So what you gonna do? Are you gonna keep it?'

'I dunno. I'm trying not to think about it.'

'Who was it . . ?'

Carol looks away.

'Have you told him?'

'No.'

They walk along in silence. The Arndale is swimming away from Carol, receding behind the mask, becoming murky through the tears; the fake plants, the lighted shop signs, and the voices seem far away as if she's underwater and can hear echoes of children's shouts and see flashes of kicking legs. She can see her future in a murky swimming pool, drowning her, like water pouring through the holes in her mask.

She can see herself alone in a council flat, drinking PG Tips. There's a baby crying from a cot, another in the kitchen, 'cause once you have one, they pop up all over the place. She looks old and haggard, with a wrinkly forehead as she takes a drag from a cigarette. Oh God, she's going to be sick . . . her stomach's all scrambled . . . where's a potted plant when you need one . . ?

'You ok?' asks Julie.

Carol pulls off her mask and is violently sick in a bin full of Burger King wrappers and leftover chips. All the straws seem to point out of the cups and stare at her.

Some little kids run up and clap.

'Fuck off, the lot of yers. Come on, Carol, the loos are over here.' She pulls Carol over to the public toilets.

Carol sinks to the floor in a cubicle and leans against the wall. No, her future, or their future, has swept up behind her and tapped her on the shoulder. Excuse me, it says.

'You all right, Carol?' Julie calls from behind the toilet door. 'What you doing?'

'Yere, yere. Just a minute.' She sits very still to see if she'll be sick again, so her future will mistake her for someone else and slink off through the Arndale, so her future won't dump her cross on her shoulders.

No, she won't be sick again, her stomach has settled. She looks at the walls. They seem strange; too bare and too white, there's no graffiti. Must have been repainted recently. She traces the grain of a brushstroke with her finger. If only she were that white, not sickly white, but washed in Persil, whiter than white. She can nearly make out the signatures and scribbles under the sheen of paint.

'Are you ok, Carol?' Julie asks from behind the door.

'Yeah. I'm just coming.' She gets out a pen from her bag to write *Carol was here 26/10/1999*. But the pen's a biro, it won't write on the wall. She scribbles hard, but only leaves a vague scratch of circles.

'Listen, Carol . . . I've got to tell you summut.' Julie knocks lightly on the door.

'What?'

'I had a baby.'

'What? You did?' Carol jumps up and yanks open the door. She's face to face with Julie, who pulls back a bit to take a hard drag on her cigarette. 'Yere, they took her off me.'

'When was it?'

'I was 15 . . . I'm trying to get her back, you know . . .'

Two other girls come in chatting and go into other cubicles. Carol goes to fix her face in the mirror. She's a bit of a state; mascara all over the place. God knows what on her chin, hair all frizzy. She rinses her mouth and rubs at the black with soap on a paper towel; it's hard and rough against her skin. She watches Julie in the mirror, finishing her fag. Her face looks tired and pinched as she inhales; she seems a hundred years old.

She has a kid.

They took her away.

'Do y' feel any better?' Julie asks again, grinding the stub end in the sink. 'Do y' want to go home?'

'Nah. I'll be ok.' Carol smoothes her hair and turns to Julie. 'Will you get her back?'

'Dunno. When my parole officer's happy, probably.'

'I'm sorry . . .'

'Want to see a picture?'

'Ok.'

Julie opens her bag and brings out a photo of two little blonde haired girls in a bath, splashing each other with water. 'The one on the right,' she says. 'She's called Katy.'

'She's lovely. And who's the other girl?'

'She's one of the other foster kids.'

Walking out of the loos, they feel awkward in their newfound intimacy. They don't know what to say; they can't go back to reminiscing about school and there's no competing with Julie's revelations. Carol realises Julie is watching her from the corners of her eyes, as they make their way through the shopping centre. Carol smiles to keep this frail intimacy that floats between them like a bubble of Fairy Liquid bobbing in the air. 'So,' she says, but no words come to her; perhaps they're not able to help each other; they're just swimming in their own bubbles with the ghost of a baby reflected in the soapsuds. 'There's Top Shop,' she points out instead.

In Top Shop they split up to look at different things. Julie goes over to the accessory section and Carol wanders round the stands of jeans, her hand trailing over denim and buttons. She looks at a pair of indigo bootleg jeans. She's wanted a pair like this for ages, but what's the point of buying jeans? It's good old Mothercare from now on—that's if she's definitely pregnant, there's still a hope and then . . . she might not have it . . . but the baby girls in the bath . . .

Carol picks up a pair of jeans and makes her way over to Julie, who is looking at the jewellery. Julie's hand is hovering above some long amber beads. She fingers them. Her eyes lighten up as she holds the beads against her neck, staring at her reflection in the freestanding mirror. She looks at the price ticket, and then throws them back on the stand. But they must be calling to her because her hand finds its way back to the stand where they are dangling. Her hand starts to gather them, bunching the beads in its palm.

'Hey, Julie,' Carol says. 'Found anything nice?'

'Nah,' she says, letting go of the beads. 'Not much. I'll just look at the sale stuff.'

Carol leans against a stand, she isn't in the mood for shopping now. Though perhaps she'll just buy the jeans and try them on at home; she won't turn into a frump in leggings with baggy knees just yet. Perhaps if she buys them and they fit, it'll mean she's not pregnant. She listlessly watches Julie rifling through a basket of sale items; bikinis and flip-flops left over from the summer. Something's not right. She looks round the shop, at young girls searching through the stands, at a man alone leaning against the pillar. He seems to be watching Julie.

Oh God. Perhaps Julie's stolen something.

He must be a security man in plain clothes. It's easy to recognise one after doing security training at Morrisons. He looks like a normal bloke in a black cap and bomber jacket. He could just be someone waiting for his girlfriend, slightly impatient with telling her how great she looks in this or that outfit, glancing at his watch. But he doesn't seem quite right; he's not bored enough, he's too alert, watching people, glancing furtively around as he leans against the pillar. And odder still, his mouth is moving; he must be talking on an intercom system, with a little speaker in his ear and a microphone in the button of his shirt. Maybe the bloke near the cash desk who is talking to an assistant and looking towards Julie is one as well.

Perhaps Julie is a known shoplifter. She could be on file. Security firms have files. Carol flicked through one on the training day and looked at the pictures of shoplifters taken by security cameras; images of blurred, grainy people. But Carol's not sure if Julie has actually taken anything. It's hard to say. She heads over to Julie. 'Julie,' she murmurs, leaning over the basket of underwear on sale. 'I think we're being watched. There, that bloke behind you.'

'I'm being watched, you mean.' She glances around; the one by the pillar pulls the cap lower over his eyes. 'We should go.'

'Ok.' Carol starts to feel really nervous and guilty; as if she's stolen things without realising it, so she puts the jeans quickly back on a stand. She doesn't want to open her bag, there might be a top crammed in there with a pair of sunglasses. All her blood is rushing to her brain: adrenalin isn't exciting for her; it scrambles her wires, makes her head scream.

They walk quickly round the accessory section, between the stands of vintage clothes. They go around the mannequins dressed in grey pinstripe trouser suits—the single-breasted jackets open to reveal purple corsets—and they're nearly there. Carol can see the harsh light of the exit looming up and an assistant in a white mini dress stood by the barrier, watching them go. Then they're out of the shop and into the light, but the alarm barrier is beeping shrilly; its tentacles of noise reaching out to grasp them and suck them back in. Carol looks round again and her stomach turns to a hard-boiled egg; one of the security men has swept up behind them and taps Julie on the shoulder. She turns and frowns, as if she knows him.

'Excuse me,' he says. 'Can you show us your bag, please?'

'What? I haven't done anything.' She tries to push past him, but the man in a cap from the shop is on her other side. 'Can you come with us, please?' He places his hand on Julie's arm.

'Let me go. You have no right to do this . . . I haven't taken anything.'

'Yes we do. We'd like you to come this way.'

'Julie!' Carol wants to take her handbag and hit one of them on the ear.

'I haven't done anything.' Julie's voice is rising in hysteria. 'You can't take me in now . . . it's not fair!'

'Julie!' Carol reaches up to clobber the one in the cap, but Julie's free arm is also raised.

Julie's eyes are hard and accusing, as if it were Carol that betrayed her, kissed her on the cheek. She points at Carol. 'It's her,' she says, suddenly calm. 'She's taken things. Check her bag.'

Why's she saying this? Is she mad? They were supposed to be mates again. 'Julie . . . why . . ? I haven't . . . what's wrong with you?'

The security men turn to Carol. Her lip quivers.

'Are you with her?' the capped one asks.

'Erm, yes . . . Julie . . ?'

'Can I check your bag, please?'

But they turn, a little surprised, as Julie backs away and tries to make a dash for it. If Julie could just get to the other side of the fountain, hide behind a potted bush, mix in with the crowds. Carol finds herself urging Julie on silently, waving a flag at the sidelines. But it's a silly trick; Julie's wearing the wrong sort of shoes, they are too high and clumpy, so her ankle goes over and she staggers. She might as well try and cast a spell on the security men or pull out a few miracles from her sleeve, because they have already caught up with her and are grabbing her arms and she starts going mental. 'You can't do this!' Julie's shouting, as they move her back to the shop, while she thrashes her arms as if she's possessed by squealing pigs.

Best thing though, for other shoppers, is to pretend it's not happening.

Andrew Loudon

Andrew Loudon is a professional actor and theatre director. He was recently commissioned by Snap Theatre Company, under an Arts Council bursary scheme, to write a new play provisionally entitled, She Moves Through The Fair.

Road Rage

Extract from the middle of Road Rage. *The protestors have been told there is a murderer in their ranks, and Footie has appointed himself as chief investigator.*

Cast

FOOTIE (a.k.a. The Chief, Swollen Foot)—Eco warrior, traveller
LEE—Protestor
CORRIE—Young protestor
RUSS—Travelling poet, Corrie's boyfriend
IAN—Jo's brother, local solicitor
JO—Footie's girlfriend, Ian's sister, pregnant
RAT—Older protestor
E—Very young protestor
SECURITY GUARDS (played by members of the cast)

⋆

A clearing in woodland. An anti-road protest. Late morning. CORRIE *sits by a firepit, making a dreamcatcher.* RUSS *enters with firewood and dumps it by the fire. He pulls out a grubby notebook and starts writing.*

RUSS: Look at the state of this place.

CORRIE: You all right then? What happened? Night in the cells, was it?

RUSS *nods. He finds a dog-end of a spliff, inspects and brushes it clean.*

RUSS: Ooh. Forgotten about that. Nice one.

CORRIE: (*groans*) Too early for me.

RUSS: Didn't offer you any.

CORRIE: Is that all you've got?

RUSS: Yeah, but don't worry, Ian's sorting me out later.

CORRIE: I am so pissed off. I just can't face going down the tunnels again. My fucking feet are agony.

RUSS: Corrie, you've done enough time down there. Get a chain and lock-on up here if it comes to it. Come on. We should be celebrating last night. We saw them off, didn't we? Bastards. Well, at least the old weather came to our rescue. I'm telling you—Sphinx Security—they're worse than the pigs.

CORRIE: I've got fucking trench foot. Our fucking beds are waterlogged and I'm the first reported case of trench foot since the First World War for fuck's sake. (*Russ passes her the now-lit spliff. She accepts.*) Yeah, we should be celebrating. It's so good to see the Sun again, but it feels so open out here. It feels empty. So many people arrested now and the trees are going too.

CORRIE *takes her boots off and rubs her feet.* RUSS *reads a poem from his book.*

RUSS: Life after life goes down
Watch the trees go down.
So much death,
No end to the death—
Generations strewn on the ground

Unburied,
And nobody left to mourn them.
Oh Mother Earth be kind to us
Help us fight the bulldozers.

CORRIE: (*furious*) Fight the bulldozer-uss. For fuck's sake, Russ. That's so bad. And you can't rhyme 'down' with 'down' . . .

RUSS: What?

CORRIE: And you can't rhyme 'death' with 'death' . . .

RUSS: Why not?

CORRIE: And . . . And you know you promised not to read your poems at people.

FOOTIE *and* LEE *enter.*

RUSS: Corrie!

LEE: What is it, Russ?

CORRIE: Don't encourage him, it's his poetry.

LEE: I thought we'd agreed about your poetry at the last meeting.

SFX of helicopter overhead.

CORRIE: Oh oh! Here they come again.

LEE: What is the point? What are they trying to prove?

RUSS: (*waving about stupidly*) Woo hoo. Hello.

CORRIE *and* RUSS *'moon' at the helicopter.* FOOTIE *looks skywards, worried.*

CORRIE: Woo-oo. Hello-oh. Fuck o-off.

FOOTIE: They're checking how many people there are on the ground.

LEE: They're just trying to wind us up.

RUSS: We should have a bit of a party, eh, Chief? Lift the old spirits a bit.

RUSS *takes out a percussion instrument and begins to play.*

FOOTIE: Yeah, all right. Bit later on though, yeah?

RUSS: No, now. I'm bored.

FOOTIE: I wish I could be bored. I'm too restless, I can't stop thinking about stuff. I can't be bored any more. I long to be bored.

Others drum and play along. FOOTIE *makes some tea. The music ends.*

RUSS: I've got 'shrooms. You fancy mushroom tea?

FOOTIE: Not for me thanks. I don't touch them. I took acid once, and I swear . . . (*shakes his head*) Never again. I still get flashbacks.

RUSS: It's not like acid. It's a natural thing. It's more fluid, just like more slidey and dreamy . . .

FOOTIE: You're all right, Russ, thanks.

RUSS: It's not flashy. You get the highs and lows, but you don't get the flashes.

CORRIE: Christ, Russ, they could have you on telly as some sort of drugs connoisseur. Mmm, I get vanilla. I get strawberry, I get flashy, slidey, oakey notes.

LEE: Just be careful, will you? That's the perfect excuse to kick us out of here, as if they needed any more. Can't you see you're playing into their hands? It's like when they brought in all that legislation, forcing all travellers onto designated sites. Suddenly all these dealers start appearing. And everybody's accusing us of being druggies. Can't you see there are forces at work here?

CORRIE: God put magic mushrooms here on this Earth for us to have. They're a natural thing.

RUSS: (*to* FOOTIE) You just haven't taken them with the right people! Corrie'll keep an eye on you.

FOOTIE: No. Really, honestly. I don't wanna know.

RUSS: Has Ian been flashing the cash around? We could do with a bit of a lift. See if he can get us some more Tequila.

FOOTIE: All right. Listen everybody. (*Pause*) The way I see it is this: either the murderer is on this protest or they're not.

CORRIE: My God, it's Hercule Poirot as I live and breathe.

FOOTIE: No, but it is though, isn't it? It's that simple. Now if they are here, it's either (a): One of us did it. Anybody want to confess? Or (b): Somebody knows something. Does anybody know who killed Layton? Come on. (*Pause*) If you're shielding a mate and not talking, it's your last chance. Right. (c): We've gotta start doing some detective work.

CORRIE: Or (d): None of the above.

LEE: We got nothing to go on but old rumours.

FOOTIE: What rumours?

LEE: People say he was killed by travellers, but then they would, wouldn't they?

FOOTIE: I just don't understand how you let this thing go. Just handed it over to the enemy, as if you didn't know what the police are like around here. You should have investigated it.

LEE: Don't tell us what to do. I'll do what I want, and you're not gonna stop me. And no, I didn't, incidentally.

FOOTIE: Well, whoever did, it is fucking this protest. This cunt doesn't know what passive resistance is all about. We don't fucking deal in aggression and violence, and anybody that does just fires a fucking missile straight back at his own camp.

LEE: Just listen to yourself.

FOOTIE: What?

LEE: You're full of anger and aggression and 'fucking' this, and 'cunt' that. Just sit down and shut up.

FOOTIE: It's just words, I'm not hitting anyone. Sticks and stones . . .

RUSS: Yeah, but we do believe in the power of words, I mean you've got to. That's how we're gonna win this thing. That's how we beat their violence.

FOOTIE: Spot the poet, eh? I'm talking about swearing, that's all. All right. Without swearing, here's my little message for the murderer. If you're in this forest, I'm gonna make you suffer. Wherever you are, I hope you suffer.

*

Tunnel beneath an eco-protest.

E: When did all this happen?

RAT: Oh, months ago. Last summer. Biscuit?

E: No thanks. I'm all right at the moment.

RAT: Oh, well, don't mind me if I do.

E: Who's that philosopher who came up with that thing about the tree falling?

RAT: What thing?

E: You know, if a tree falls in the forest and nobody is there to hear it, does it make any sound?

RAT: Oh yeah. Oh . . . um . . . God! Pretty fucking apt for us, eh? I guess we're here to hear the trees fall and make a noise about it.

E: Quite a philosopher on the quiet, aren't you?

RAT: Well, you know. There comes a point when you have to . . . delve into yourself.

E: Is that why you came here? What are you looking for, Ratty?

RAT: What? Oh, I lost a contact lens six months ago, and this tunnel's the result.

E: No, come on. What are you tunnelling after?

Silence.

E: I came here to . . . I'm trying to find . . . meaning . . . justice, truth, love.

RAT: Not much then?

E: (*laughs*) Hmm. Do you ever wonder if it'll all be up there still, when you get out?

RAT: No. They'll let us know if any trouble starts. That's really what these things are for (*he waves a walky-talky in the air*).

E: No, I don't just mean the trees. I mean the whole lot. The sun, the sky, the people, the air.

RAT: No. I do get a bit paranoid down here sometimes. It makes you think, that's for sure.

E: I sometimes think I'll wake up and find I'm just a brain in a tank, with these electrodes all over it, and some mad professor's just been downloading this virtual reality life. Hotwiring sights and sounds straight into my mind.

RAT: That's that movie with Arnold Schwarzenegger.

E: Which one?

RAT: Can't remember. (*Pause. Laughs.*) Nah, only kidding. 'Total Recall.'

E: Oh, yeah. But I get it in here. I think I'll stick my head out the tunnel, and the mad professor will just turn the switch off.

RAT: Well, why don't you go and stick your head out?

E: No, honestly, I'm happier here.

RAT: You ever done mushrooms?

E: No.

RAT: Yeah, perhaps you shouldn't bother. Russ used to find wicked magic mushrooms round here.

*

The Firepit. Night. FOOTIE, JO, RUSS, LEE *and* CORRIE *around a dying fire.* JO *is asleep.* RUSS *is pouring out the Tequilas. He hands them round.*

RUSS: (*Waving Tarot cards.*) I think maybe we should ask them who the killer is.

CORRIE: Ooh, Tequila. Very nice. Where did this come from?

LEE: Ian, I think.

FOOTIE: Russ, maybe we're making a bit too much of the spiritual stuff, eh?

CORRIE: Fucking hell. Speak again, man. I can see your words.

JO: Just a tiny taste for me.

FOOTIE: Don't wake her up, Corrie.

CORRIE: I didn't.

RUSS: Come on, shuffle.

FOOTIE: I don't wanna do it, Russ.

RUSS: I know I'm right, Chief. I know we've gotta do this. Shuffle the cards.

JO: (*to* RUSS) Where did you come from?

RUSS: I not here really.

CORRIE: Oh fuck. Oh fuck.

LEE: (*to* RUSS) Have they charged you then?

RUSS: I'm not saying. That's my own personal business.

LEE: Oh, don't start all that shit again.

FOOTIE *shuffles. Looks puzzled.*

FOOTIE: You sure you're in a fit state for this?

RUSS: Concentrate! Cut the pack.

RUSS *takes the cards from* FOOTIE *and lays out a classic 10 card Tarot spread.*

FOOTIE: (*smiles*) So what is your surname, Russ?

JO: Don't, Footie.

RUSS: That's my own personal business. I don't know who I'm telling that to, do I?

LEE: Here we go. We're all spies for the D.O.T.

RUSS: Maybe.

LEE: Surely you trust somebody by now. Can't you even tell us if you've been charged?

RUSS: I might have been. That's my own personal business.

LEE *laughs.* RUSS *starts to do the reading. Tension. At card 4—distant past—he starts.*

LEE: What's that then? The ten of penguins?

CORRIE: Don't, man. Don't. You'll send me on a bad trip.

RUSS *takes a great effort to concentrate.*

RUSS: Oh shit.

LEE: Sounds good.

RUSS: (*snaps*) Look, maybe this wasn't such a good idea. Believe me, Chief, it's not good.

FOOTIE *shares a grimace with the group.*

LEE: This is a bit unhelpful, Russ.

RUSS: You don't know. None of you know. And I'm not telling you.

JO: Come on, Russ.

LEE: Do you know something?

RUSS: I'm telling you nothing.

FOOTIE: (*snaps*) Russ, you are really pissing me off. Come on, just spit it out!

RUSS: You're here but . . . and I know that you're really Footie, but you're not really Footie 'cos you're not acting like Footie. You don't know who you're living with.

FOOTIE: Are you trying to say Jo did it? You had to get wasted to say that?

RUSS: Don't, man.

RUSS *turns card 5—recent past. It is the Death card. He waves it in* FOOTIE's *face.*

RUSS: I hope you suffer. I'm gonna make you suffer. D'you remember? You've cursed yourself.

LEE: What?

FOOTIE: You are unbelievable. Do you think you're gonna get away with this?

RUSS: I have the power of truth.

FOOTIE: Who put you up to this?

RUSS *points at* FOOTIE.

FOOTIE: What? Okay. Say what you mean. Let me get this straight.

RUSS: You're the murderer.

FOOTIE: What?

RUSS: *You* are the murderer.

FOOTIE: That's twice.

RUSS: Shall I say it again?

FOOTIE: As much as you want. You're talking shit.

RUSS: You're guilty. You and Jo are living together. Guilty.

FOOTIE: Are you going to keep this bollocks up all night?

RUSS: I have the power of truth.

FOOTIE: Russ, shut up with your power of truth. You have the power of being off your fucking tree. You're faceless. You're not here, mate. You've lost it, man. You've lost contact with the real world.

RUSS *has picked up card 6—broad future—and is waving it.*

RUSS: They'll say the same for you soon.

FOOTIE *shakes his head as* RUSS *turns over 7, 8, 9, 10—final destiny—it is the House of God.*

FOOTIE: Was this Ian's idea or yours?

LEE: Russ, stop now.

RUSS *picks up card 8—environment—it is the Sun. He waves it in* FOOTIE's *face, so the audience can see it.*

RUSS: Ian's not your problem. You are, Chief.

FOOTIE: You and Ian, eh? What's he given you for this, eh? (*Pointing to a bottle of Tequila*) Is that all I'm worth, Russ? A bottle of

Tequila? Eh, matey? I've a good mind to smack you one, you bastard.

RUSS: Bastard? You're the bastard. (*laughs*) Who are your parents? Do you know?

FOOTIE: Hang on a minute, Russ.

LEE: Leave it, Russ.

RUSS: Today's a big day for you. Birth and destruction.

FOOTIE: You're just playing mind games. I've had enough. Just fuck off, Russ.

CORRIE: I wanna go, come on, Russ.

FOOTIE: Fucking crazy. How can you attempt to do a reading in your state? You're crazy.

RUSS *goes to leave.*

FOOTIE: Yeah, just go.

FOOTIE *turns his back and moves to exit.*

RUSS: Listen. The murderer is here. I know it. He comes from here. He comes from where his father came. He's got his father's blood on his hands.

RUSS *exits.* LEE *gathers up his cards, throws them in the firepit and exits.* JO *and* FOOTIE *stare at each other.*

James Manlow

James Manlow was born in Hertfordshire in 1978. His poems have appeared in magazines such as Orbis, The Rialto, Staple, *and* Dream Catcher.

Documentary

We stare through the window
of the TV screen:
fresh footage of snow,

a single tree drowning.
We haven't been to Switzerland.
We haven't done much

but sit here, inching apart.
Tonight, when you switch off
the TV and go upstairs,

I watch the avalanche lily
blowing in the still path
cut through the mountain rock.

THAT AFTERNOON

That afternoon we saw the lamb.
Its head was near all bone;
the carcass swarmed with efficiency
as we stood, stripping
apples with our teeth. Looking
down at the body, it wasn't mortality
we were aware of when
we threw our cores inside.

We continued on through the heat,
our new world a dull
head cropped close with bracken
in a perfect blue-purple
picture. We took our photos
of tumuli, where the land stretched
like the flat edge of a blade
we found buried in heather.

We were children—thirteen, fourteen,
departing on a thirty mile
New Forest expedition. Your mother
had given us those apples.
Neither of us could foresee
that by the time we returned
she'd have received her diagnosis.
We walked in the sun. Oblivious.

Smuggled Treasures

Unable to sleep you contemplate how
you were conceived and born,
lifted free from your mother's womb,
then down again, to feel
your weight on cotton sheets.

At school you watch a film
that shows a woman giving birth.
You look away.
Yet there's a stirring too:
the woman's thighs, her open mouth.

Slowly you begin to long for darkness.
In the half-light, shadows lick
and curl across the carpet.
You lie wide awake on the fixed
mattress, floating and adrift.

A Question of Love

Did we honestly know from the first moment,
or was it because we were both away,
the night unexpectedly hot and part
of another hemisphere?

What we meant is no doubt different
from what we say together now,
exercising the art of language.
At first, each time I heard myself say 'love,'

it was like a blind shot into the dark.
In a way, nothing's changed: a single word
has never been able to describe what
you do to me

when you enter a room, or leave.
Don't worry about what love is,
the importance of when and where and why,
or about what our future might contain.

I'm the idiot standing with roses,
a brave scaler of garden walls.
When I say I'll move the mountain,
I'll move the mountain.

Loneliness Is the Wolf

A portrait of Ezra Pound

Loneliness is the wolf in the late afternoon,
eyes stood at horizons.
He has a way with muscles
that keeps his expression fixed against the Cosmos,
and when he howls it's his whole self,
opposites pulling like tides.

As the day yawns he sharpens his gaze on the floor,
a deliberate concentration when the dark sinks in.
Now an eclipse works steadily across the hatches of his skin.
He continues to avoid my lens.
Old man in the sun, propped up by pillows,
between nurses administering their bright needles.

When We were Slugs

We spent our afternoons
beneath the brick's shade, speaking
about life, vague memories
of shells, how our ancestors
were Land-Snails and Sea-Snails.
It turned out we had both
shared the summer once sealed
to the underside of the water-meter,
the way we have secured ourselves
to bedroom, kitchen, living-room,
as if we miss carrying
a house on our backs.
It was a small world then.
I think of those nights, our
glistening trails across the lawn,
how reaching the middle of the garden
we'd suck hard on the flesh
of the fallen fruit, then lean
into the sweetness and mate.

ROBERT MCGILL

Robert McGill was born in Wiarton, Ontario and lived in Canada before moving to England in 1999. His short fiction has appeared in the Canadian magazines Descant *and* The Fiddlehead, *as well as in the UK's* May Anthologies. *He is currently trying his hand at something longer.*

THE TREATY OF URSA MAJOR

Lappinger was a mean one, all right. He never forgot that O'Hare and I were the newest cadets at Thornford, and on the days he trained our platoon we were the first ones selected for anything rotten. When the graffiti started appearing on the wall in the obstacle course every morning, we knew who was going to be cleaning it off.

'What's he got against us?' I asked as we scrubbed at six feet of brick for the third day in a row.

'We're fresh meat, Foxworthy,' O'Hare replied from the other side of the wall. 'He can smell us. An old Tom like him, it stands his fur on end.' She took Lappinger as further proof of her family's knack for bad luck.

O'Hare was a local girl who grew up in a subdivision adjacent to the base. Nothing ever happened at Thornford except training, so most of the time there was public access to the scrubland that dominated the place, and O'Hare told me that as a girl she thought of it as her back yard. She and her brothers had played hide-and-seek in the tangles of stunted trees, and occasionally they taunted cadets who wallowed through the obstacle course. Now her brothers were coming to mock her in turn. O'Hare said it was another sign of the family curse.

'What about your great-great-grandpa?' I protested. I wasn't sure whether or not to add a few more greats. 'You said he escaped slavery on the underground railroad. That's not bad luck.'

'He left his family in Virginia for nothing but snow and white people,' she replied. 'You call that good luck, Fox?'

I shrugged, suspicious that O'Hare was exaggerating. I was local too, although we'd never met before coming to the base, and I knew her subdivision was full of African-Canadians, so her grandfather couldn't have been alone. But I was too embarrassed by my ignorance to challenge her and I returned to scouring graffiti. My family had been growing apples south of town for close to ninety years, and there were always men from the Caribbean working for us as harvesters in the fall. I wondered if that was the reason O'Hare and I got on so well. Some of the other cadets had probably never talked with a black person before. I doubted that a few had ever talked to a woman, either. They seemed in awe of everything about her, even her eyesight. It was O'Hare who first noticed the graffiti.

'Sir, look,' she said to Lappinger, with as little fanfare as when she first showed up at Thornford. I'd arrived the day before her and was hoping for someone to replace me as the platoon's whipping boy, but none of the cadets knew what to make of O'Hare. They kept expecting a major-general to turn up and proclaim her a symbol of the nation's diverse and egalitarian armed forces, so they left her pretty much alone. All except for Lappinger, who had a rigid sense of hierarchy and knew how a novice was supposed to be treated.

'You and Foxworthy report to maintenance and get something to clean up that mess,' he told her when she pointed out the wall. There was no mention of what was written there, not even when it reappeared the next morning and we were ordered to remove it again. After a week it became an expected ritual. No one could stop talking about it, except when Lappinger was around and we weren't allowed to speak at all.

Brereton was the other officer responsible for training us, a phlegmatic career sergeant close to retirement who acted like a kindly uncle. At lunch we gathered around him in the mess hall, full of theories.

'Sarge, it's got to be those little rats who were watching us last week,' said Lacroix. 'There's six of them that live east of the base and walk their German Shepherd through the tank range every morning. Their *German* Shepherd,' he repeated. 'And they're all blond.' Lacroix was the only one to put any weight on hair-colour or breed of dog, but most of the platoon agreed that it was probably the Van Overbeek boys—not that they knew the family by name. Only O'Hare and I did, and we kept it to ourselves, because we had other suspects in mind.

When I told O'Hare my theory she scoffed.

'Lappinger's not a racist, Fox,' she said. 'He's one of those old-fashioned military types who despise everyone equally.' I had to admit that she was probably right. But O'Hare's own theory was even more outlandish.

'I think it's my brother Warren,' she whispered to me as we dug out a latrine at Lappinger's behest.

'What?' I hissed. Warren was seventeen and the family's oldest child after O'Hare. 'How could he possibly write those things?'

'He didn't want me to join the forces. He hasn't even talked to me since I signed up. He might be trying to intimidate me into quitting.' I shook my head.

'O'Hare, he'd have to be one self-hating man to write stuff like that. Let's face it, you don't need to be very creative to come up with better suspects. There are plenty of bigots around here.' She frowned at me, and I realized she probably didn't need me to tell her that.

The next morning was the first in two weeks that no graffiti appeared on the wall, and speculation ran high until Brereton informed us that Lappinger himself had taken up the case. He'd patrolled the obstacle course through the early hours and was going to continue to do so until the vandals were apprehended. We were all impressed. Lappinger had a reputation for knowing every square foot of Thornford, for seeing perfectly in the night and moving as stealthily as a panther. According to cadet lore, there was even a complex network of tunnels running through the scrub which Lappinger had cut himself and used to his own advantage during war games.

'It's true about the tunnels,' O'Hare told me, her voice wavering. 'We used to play in them when we were kids.' I could tell she was afraid for her brother. The next day the graffiti returned and she approached me with a plan: we would go out and catch Warren ourselves, before Lappinger could get his hands on him. I grimaced and said it was stupid, but O'Hare wouldn't let go of the idea. In my mind it seemed like Lappinger and Warren were in a battle for her soul, and the best I could do was to keep the peace. Finally I agreed on the condition that we get permission from Brereton first. When we asked him the old coot passed the buck like a spineless father.

'Go ask Lappinger,' he said. 'It's his investigation, he'll let you know if he wants any help.' But we knew what Lappinger would say. New cadets were for erasing words, not for catching the people who wrote them. So that night, an hour after lights-out, we crept out of barracks. There was no moon.

'Foxworthy, what are you doing?' O'Hare whispered. I'd bent down and was rubbing mud into my face. 'Don't be an idiot. Let's go.' We crouched and ran towards the obstacle course, keeping to the grass beside the gravel track so as not to make a sound. I was dressed only in long underwear, the darkest clothing I had, and as I followed O'Hare through the cool midsummer night I felt more free than I had since joining the forces, exhilarated by the recklessness of our disobedience and by my eager deference to her knowledge of the land. After a few hundred yards she slipped towards the edge of the scrub and motioned for me to follow before she disappeared. The foliage was dense and twisted together, but when I got down on my hands and knees there was a low opening, and I wriggled through.

The tunnel was just high enough for us to move smoothly on all fours, and I had to trot vigorously to keep up. Every few yards there was a fork presenting an alternative route, but seldom did O'Hare pause. I peered intently down the other tunnels, each time more certain that I would see Lappinger tigering towards us. Somewhere not so distant he was hunting, and we might be his prey as easily as anyone else. If O'Hare was right, Warren was out here too, and for some reason the prospect of stumbling across him was just as terrifying as Lappinger. I prayed for some Van Overbeeks to turn up quickly. We seemed to travel miles, and finally I reached out to tug on O'Hare's leg.

'Are you sure you know where we're going?' I demanded. She pointed upwards silently, and for the first time I realized that there were patches of open sky above us, ribboned with stars.

'We're following Ursa Major,' she whispered. 'The obstacle course is due north. We're almost there.'

A few minutes later the tunnel widened and she stopped moving. I crept up to her side and peered ahead at a gap in the undergrowth. It was half-filled by the silhouette of a kneeling figure. We had agreed on what we would do, and wordlessly she handed me a rectangle of duct tape. My heart beat so loudly that I was sure it would be heard, and I almost didn't move with O'Hare after her fingers counted three.

Then we were on him, O'Hare taking the legs and my hands reaching for his arms and mouth. I slapped the tape over his lips and we dragged him back into the tunnel. He put up a fight, straining to yell the whole time, and by the time we'd bound him I was covered in scratches from the surrounding bushes.

'Shut up, it's me,' O'Hare was whispering. 'It's Angela. Shut up, shut up.'

We held him down until he relaxed, and then I leaned over to look at the face.

'It's Warren,' O'Hare confirmed. 'We'd better get out of here. If Lappinger's anywhere close he'll have heard us.' Warren was trying to speak through the tape.

'Listen,' I whispered into his ear. 'She belongs to us now, you got that? She chose us. No matter how many times you write it, she isn't going home.' O'Hare pushed me away from him.

'Warren, we're not going to get you in trouble,' she said. 'We have to get you out of here before they catch you. You understand?' He nodded, and she reached for his mouth. He gave a low cry of pain as the strip came off, then whispered angrily.

'It's not me. I swear it's not. I've been out here watching the guy. It's that commander of yours.'

'Brereton?' I said hopefully. 'The fat one?'

'No, the mean one. Lappinger.'

'You're not just making it up, are you?' I asked. I was just as eager to believe him as I was to think him a liar.

'Save it for later,' said O'Hare out of the darkness. 'We have to get going.'

'But O'Hare, did you hear what he said?' She ignored me and turned to scramble down the tunnel once more. Warren followed, and as I took up the rear I felt a cold chill replace the exotic intimacy of night. I didn't bother to look down the other passageways anymore, and I wasn't even aware that we'd left the tunnels until I crawled right into Lappinger's legs. He already had a hold of O'Hare and Warren, one in each hand.

'Both of you back to barracks,' he said. It was the first time in hours a voice had spoken at full volume.

'We know what you've been doing, sir,' said O'Hare, equally loudly. 'My brother saw you.'

'Don't you dare speak back to me,' Lappinger said. 'Get going.'

'We're not leaving without him, sir,' said O'Hare.

'Do you know what will happen when I report you two?' Lappinger said. 'Alone at night? Two cadets, breaking curfew? In a relationship?'

'What are you talking about?' cried O'Hare. She looked at her brother. 'Don't listen to him, Warren. Foxworthy is just an accomplice.' But Warren was looking at me head to toe, surprised and sceptical.

'Are your parents going to be pleased about this, Foxworthy?' Lappinger asked. The question was so shocking that I couldn't manage a response.

'It's not going to work, sir,' O'Hare said. 'We'll fight you on this. You'll lose. It's not the fifties anymore.'

'You can't threaten me,' Lappinger replied. 'I've got nothing to fear from you. Two cadets trying to cover up being caught in a compromising position.'

'The graffiti—' O'Hare began. Lappinger cut her short.

'Your brother will have to answer for that.'

'But he saw you doing it,' she declared. Lappinger wheeled on Warren.

'Is that what you told them?' he asked. 'That you watched me?' Warren took a step back.

'I didn't actually see him doing it, Ang,' he whispered. Lappinger pounced.

'Of course he didn't. Because I saw him. Don't bother denying it,' he said to Warren.

'I told you, it wasn't me,' protested Warren. O'Hare was shaking her head very slowly.

In the end they made a bargain. Warren was allowed to go, but O'Hare and I would have to answer for ourselves. Through all the threats and bluffs along the way there were no admissions made, so that by the time the negotiations finished it felt like everyone was guilty of everything. For all I knew, it was me who had been spray-painting the wall.

Warren left, flashing me a look of contempt as he went, and then Lappinger marched us along the gravel track, following so closely that I was sure I could feel his breath on my neck. When he'd shut the barracks door behind us, I grabbed O'Hare's hand and pulled her close to me. If Lappinger had his way we wouldn't be long for the forces, but perhaps, I thought, heroic gestures could be made in other fashions.

'I won't deny anything,' I declared, and kissed her cheek. 'I don't care what my parents think, or yours. I like you. It doesn't matter what colour your skin is. As far as I'm concerned, you could be white as day.' But she stepped back, wrenching her hand out of mine, and her eyes swept over me, full of anger.

'How can you say something like that?' she cried. 'Haven't you been paying attention at all? Even Lappinger knows better than that. Foxworthy, where have you been?'

Sarah Emily Miano

Sarah Emily Miano is a native of Buffalo, N.Y. Former private eye, tour bus driver and pastry chef, her fiction has appeared in Pembroke Magazine. *Her first novel,* Encyclopaedia of Snow, *will be published by Picador in 2003.*

Don't Take the One I Want

When Mama was really messed up she carried around a doll all the time. On rare occasions she placed it in a wicker baby carriage—the flexible kind with the handles. Then she'd reach under the recliner for her knitting needles to make it a seaweed-colored sweater with matching cap. The doll had one lazy green eye, and one not-so-lazy brown eye, so when Mama thrust it in my face, I turned my head away. *Wahhhhh,* the baby cried with ewe-like resonance. I grimaced. Some day, I thought, the dolly will pull a Pinocchio and come after me ala razor-sharp instrument with the intention of gouging out my eyes. Maybe he would even use Mama's knitting needles to make the job easy-peasy. But I vowed to fight him the whole way. Pinocchio-like Doll = Familial Discomfort.

And you slept with him. You say you didn't, but you damn well did. Brian came to my rescue when I was sixteen, sexually unfrequented and tired—of Mama Josie's affairs, of Papa Noah's impotence, of Sister Martha's Motley Crue-style boyfriend, of Brother Jonah defecating in bank drive-thru vessels out of boredom. I couldn't control them any longer or will them to love me by clicking my heels and chanting, *There's no place like home*. Could I? God had rolled the dice and I got double ones. No wonder they called life a crap shoot.

When I first met Brian, Mama and I were visiting at his parents' house. Brian reclined in his family's rocking chair; I sank awkwardly into a huge divan; Mama a.k.a. Josie crouched next to Brian. Meanwhile, Brian's mother made us cappuccinos in the kitchen. The hissing of the milk steamer sounded like a weeping willow capturing the breeze in its swaying leaves.

'Brian, we're so glad you're back here from Indiana,' Mama cooed.

I nodded, token-like, and Brian beamed.

Mama's crouching made her rear look huge; it jutted out: 'Helloooo! Look at me!' as her billowing boobs rested on her thighs. Her black eyes were like a Siamese cat's when she looked at Brian.

We are Siamese if you please. We are Siamese if you don't please.

'I got laid off at my job in Indiana,' Brian said. 'So I moved back home for a while. No sweat! I'll get another job with my skill.'

'What do you do?'

'At Durez I did assembly line stuff.'

'Oh! How neat!" Mama exclaimed.

I looked around. The various flower and ivy patterns scattered about the room on wallpapers and fabrics dizzied me; and for a minute I was inside a greenhouse looking for the exit because the stench of old plants was making me sneeze and wheeze. *Ahhhchoooo!*

'But I sell too,' Brian said.

'Oh? What have you sold?' Mama asked.

'The usual. Rainbow vacuums an' stuff.'

Brian. Brain. Coincidence? Oh, definitely.

'Thank you,' I said as Brian's mom set our mugs of cappuccino on the coffee table.

'Fab!' Mama nestled into the plush chartreuse carpet, legs broadcast in front of her—and the boobs still billowed. *Josie and the Pussycats.*

I rolled my eyes, then carefully put my own mug to my lips and slowly sipped. The liquid hit my tongue, seared and scraped all the way down and left the roof of my mouth like sandpaper. My taste buds had temporarily gone to pot.

'Mmm . . .' Mama remarked as she embarked on her first sip—and as I watched the dark fluid pour into her mouth I was suddenly glad we had come to this place for sweet conversation and scalded coffee; and when Mama's panic-stricken face revealed her torment I relaxed. She bolted into the kitchen.

Brian turned toward me. 'So, Libby, what do you do?'

'High school.'

'She's an artist,' Mama piped in, as she returned from the kitchen with squirrel mouth.

'Cool!' Brian exclaimed.

I nodded. 'Figurative art.'

The art conversation ended there. The amount of cultural awareness invading the room was equal to the amount of love, which was in the negative digits according to my gauge. I looked at Mama and silently conveyed to her, with widened eyes, that I was ready to leave.

We stood near the doorway. 'Want to go to a movie sometime?' Brian asked.

When he spoke, his chin, so carefully cut, looked mechanical. When he laughed his eyes lit the room pale green; and when he stood next to me his full lips were just above mine. I never stood so close to a man before, and when I smelled his aftershave, I tingled.

'Do you like Jackie Chan?'

I did not. But there were two kinds of guys in Buffalo: those who digged cars and those who didn't. Those who didn't dig cars had a fetish for sports. Seldom did they go to the cinema.

So nearly prostrating myself in the hopes of having a movie-going companion, and a cute one at that, I said: 'Yes! Do you?'

He nodded. I smiled. And we said goodbye.

Mama and I drove toward home. She cranked up the radio, playing bad 70's disco, so we wouldn't have to speak. She jiggled in her seat to 'Hooked on a Feeling,' as I watched my breath make visible puffs in the bitter air of the car. Mama's two-door would take ten minutes to warm up, but by that time we'd be home. I wrote my name in the frost on the window then wiped it away, exposing a vista of falling snow outside. We passed our neighbors' houses lit up like primary-colored cupcakes for the holiday season. One house had an elaborate Nativity scene in the front yard. Joseph and Mary, Christ and the manger, the hay, the Three Wise Men, the Immaculate Conception, a lone star. I caught the Virgin's intense stare, thinking she might tell me something, but the light turned green and Mama drove on. The empty branches of the trees poked up at the sky, which boasted an ominous gray cloud—the one that stretched for miles and lingered for months over upstate New York, the gray cloud we all knew could be credited to factories and landfills. After this, I thought, the long winter departs—spring comes, then summer. As we pulled into our driveway several minutes later, Mama asked rhetorically, 'Isn't Brian the cutest?'

He took me cruising in his car, a royal blue, two-door, manual-speed Pontiac Sunbird; and with Def Leppard guiding us along the Scajaqueda highway, I heard the wind off the river providing background vocals. We talked sometimes, but mostly savored the silence or the music between us. I envied the Hawaiian hula girl plastered to the dashboard as she dipped and bobbed. She was 99 percent love and 1 percent magic. With long dark hair and a grass green skirt, her breasts as ripe as mangoes, she was so unlike me. I had fiery red hair, mosquito bite-sized tits, and baby fat everywhere else. I couldn't gyrate either, with hands that trembled whenever he touched me, and a tongue that either flipped around too much or didn't move at all because his face was so close. *Look at me now.*

Then, on a snowy day in January, on the corner of Delaware Ave and Sheridan, at a red light, Brian leaned in and kissed me. Bang! Lightening streaked up the sky and plowed my heart and I thought oh!

Oh!

'Pull over. I'm going to be sick!'

'What?' With an abrupt movement we were on the side of the road, hazard lights blinking.

'Ya okay?'

'Yes. Just don't look,' I said, then opened the door and eased out of the car. I threw up—there and then. Pulled over, door open, on the side of Sheridan Drive, on the pristine white lawn of the Talking Pages, on cue. The sausage links I'd snatched from the $1.99 breakfast platter were now chunked and green and nestled in the snow like worms. Five-hundred thirty-nine calories jettisoned. *Everything was too perfect for words.*

When I entered our two-story house in Buffalo, the smell of American cheese floated from the kitchen into the hallway. Papa was making late-night tuna melts. 'Hello, Papa,' I greeted.

'Oh hi, Lib. I was just trying a new edition of my famous—' He

answered with a low mumble, but before he could continue, I swam away from his voice, away from shore in a fight against the ocean current; and hands on my proverbial ears, into the bathroom.
With the door closed, I checked to see if lipstick had been smeared on my chin. I rinsed my rank tasting mouth with Listerine, but the aftertaste of vomit was all I had to remember of Brian's first kiss. And then my hearing returned and Papa's one sentence, three minute-mumble, so far, was like a bee's nest had exploded outside and would invade my privacy any minute now. *Stop! Just stop!*

Papa's métier was breadcrumbs. He made his calls in the morning from the kitchen bar, discussing consistency, as the serpentine coils of the cord would go *swish, swish* like broom whiskers on someone's backside.

He only liked me because I looked like you, bitch. Someone asked me at what age I realized I was beautiful and I replied, 'I don't know.' But I do know; I never realized it, especially not then. I still don't. Because I am a precise replica of Mama—a plastic blow-up doll—complete with her dark Jezebel eyes and childbearing hips. Mama's beauty is a façade, something intangible; the glance of a gypsy and the shake of a whore cause a reaction in any male, fooled into believing they see beauty like a bull is drawn to anything red, but it is only a trick, an illusion. I am an illusion.

Brian kissed me again. He stopped by on weekend nights and we hung out, talked about hockey or bowling, in the living room, alone for a brief moment until Mama came home, when I'd say with faux surprise, *Hey! There's Mama Jo! Hi Mama!*
'Want to play pinochle?' Brian asked me.
'Sure, I guess so.'
'Cool!'
Mama Josie was the pinochle queen. So there we were, the three of us at the walnut dining room table, cards sliding over the leaf edges back-n-forth with a *shwooo, shwooo.* The jack of hearts stared back at me, so I had to get up, dizzy. I made a batch of instant brownies. After letting them cool, I placed five on a plate and set it on the table between Mama and Brian. After Brian took his, I went for the one with the least nuts. As my hand wrapped around the moist edges of the

chocolate square, Mama belted out, 'That's the one I want! Don't take the one I want!'

The Alaskan wolf prints on the dining room walls shook with disbelief. I pulled away from the brownie and glanced at Brian who was intently scrutinizing his pinochle hand.

'Okay, Mama. Sorry.' Then I reached for the other one, which was equally as nice. They both had the same amount of calories, nearly a thousand, and mine would just get flushed eventually anyhow. *Life is all addiction and subtraction.*

I'd made it all the way to 11th grade without making more than two friends. But suddenly kids began to notice me. Guys who never spoke to me before leaned on my locker in their flannel shirts and ripped jeans and said, 'Lookin' good!' Cheerleaders said, 'Wow, you've lost some weight!' During lunch I picked at: 1 Celery Stick, 3 Saltine Crackers, ? Container of Non-fat, Non-flavored Yogurt. I watched the hoard of them eat way-too-much-cheese pizza, loaded-with-fat fried chicken and pack-on-the-pounds chocolate cake and I thought, *Look at them all. They're out of control!*

Brian wanted to have sex, of course. After everyone had gone to bed, we sat alone on the sofa. He slung his arm around my shoulders and slurped my ear. 'You're so sexy.'

I smiled in the dark and kissed his neck at his Adam's apple.

He moved his warm hands up my shirt. 'Can I come upstairs?' he asked.

'No, you'd better not,' I said.

'Honey! Why?'

Sweat trickled from his sideburns.

'My parents!'

'Don't you want it? I know you want it!'

'I want it, but we have to wait.'

I pushed his hands away, adjusted my T-shirt and ran upstairs. I heard the door shut too loudly for midnight and the engine of his Sunbird roar out of the driveway. I was angry at myself for being so prudishly callow and for caring too much; I was angry at Mama for being the kind of woman who wouldn't have pushed a man like Brian away.

Mama always told me Papa was impotent, she told me even before I knew what that word meant.

The following week Brian went away to visit friends in Cleveland. I missed the ten-minute rides home from the restaurant when I could be silent in the aftermath of rude customers and Brian wouldn't mind. So while he was away, I inhaled: 1 Carton of *Ben & Jerry's* Chubby Hubby ? Bag of Ridged Potato Chips 6 Chocolate Chip Cookies 1 Big Mac 1 Large Order of Fries Takeout Moo Goo Gai Pan 1 Bag of Licorice 2 *Almond Joy* Bars. Purging was an easy procedure—lifting up the toilet seat and gagging at the stench of dried up urine, kneeling one knee up, one knee down on the hard tiles, gripping the sink with my left hand and then sticking my right index finger as far down my throat as possible, leaning over the open bowl, jabbing sometimes once, sometimes thrice, whatever would make all that sick hilarity come up from my stomach and burn my esophagus . . . Exhilarating!

One afternoon, Brian and I stretched out on our backs in the front yard, fanning our limbs until our two bodies and our arc-like movements made celestial impressions in the pure snow; and for a moment the sun made a brief appearance from behind the gray cloud.

'You're too skinny, Lib. You could use some pounds,' Brian said several weeks later. 'I completely understand . . . Sometimes I'm not in the mood to eat either.'

I remained quiet in my seat with my hands acting as a cushion for my rear to ease the pain. Brian rose from the divan and pivoted on his heels. 'I'm ready for that pinochle match, Jo!' he shouted, dashing out the door, while I remained watching the pendulum rock of the grandfather clock; and the weeks that followed passed quickly, all those days when the only words I heard were: 'How are you feeling today? What did you do today? Did you eat?' Those questions from Brian, from Mama Jo, from Papa Noah comprised the trinity that my holy ones handed me, the three strands always in sequence and always clustered together. But I didn't reply, and thought of the Nativity. Everything rots away, little by little. I had enough brains to recognize it.

I slept in the attic-turned-bedroom on a futon underneath a skylight, where I gazed up at a backdrop of sky behind wooden telephone poles and their hundreds of connecting wires. I slept only on my stomach and when I awoke during the night, I remembered that statistically 96 percent of women who sleep on their stomachs are in love. For me, this was clearly not the case. I just liked the feeling of my belly squashed against the hard wood of a futon frame, which had an optimum emptiness effect with only a thin layer of mattress in between. Empty Cavern Facing Down = Feeling of Greater Emptiness.

Come springtime and after the first big melt I began to see the grass again. At the end of my work shift I wished I could punch the time clock, walk out and never return to that late-night, truck-stop diner.

Brian's car became a haven.

Tonight, without hello, he roared, 'What is this? You're not having any periods?'

I shrank. 'How do you know?'

'Josie told me.'

'It's none of your business,' I said.

He put his hand on my leg. 'Yes it is! I'm your boyfriend.'

'I can't be in a relationship right now.' I swiped his hand away.

'Don't avoid the subject. You've changed.'

I haven't changed, I thought, *you just never knew me*.

We rode the rest of the way in silence, and when we got to my house he followed me inside. 'Wait. We can work this out.'

'Just go away,' I said, lowering my head.

'Fine.'

I ran upstairs and listened for the door to slam. The house was quiet for five minutes and then I heard Brian downstairs in the kitchen talking in whispered tones to Mama. I sensed she was making him a strawberry daiquiri. Whispering + Daiquiris = Bliss. *Goddamn her.*

I walked two miles to school with my hands in my pockets, and felt my legs because of the holes in the liner. My toes, like frozen blocks of ice, hit up against the front of my boots when I walked, even though most of the snow had melted and the air felt warmer. I couldn't wait to get to art class, where I could emancipate myself in a self-portrait. I decided to become *The Girl with the Pearl Earring.* For weeks I stroked and stroked until my Old Holland oils captured her unpretentious virginal gaze. Alas, I was staring at myself in the form of a tiny Dutch girl. Then, one day, my trusty Isabey Special Hog-Hair Bristle #6 Filbert brush slipped out of my hand and clattered on the floor. Flesh Ochre rubbed across the tiles. 'Oops,' I said, looking up. Then to the onlookers, fellow painters, an explanation: 'How stupid of me. Don't know what happened. One minute I had it, and the next it just slipped out of my hand—'

The day after I finished final exams, right before summer vacation, Mama and Papa checked me in to the mental hospital so specialists could pump food into me through clear plastic tubes. 'Something must be done!' Mama exclaimed. The first week the nurses wheeled me in a pushchair up and down the dismal hallways, up-n-down, back-n-forth, in a bipolar motion that was somehow comforting. 'You're too fragile to walk,' the nurses said, but I was fine. The corridors of the hospital smelled like ammonia and hints of cigarette smoke and alcohol that dawdled on everyone's breath. At times the others spoke to me in mellow tones, with tics, telling me their histories. I listened politely, but it was all a crock. I returned to my room and forgot them all.

Everyday at 6 a.m., the nurses weighed me. They told me I was 80 pounds. Like the other girls, I drank loads of water before my weigh-in so I would appear to have gained.

I painted every day. My psychotherapist Dr. Wilinski called it *therapy*. I hung my paintings all over the walls: bewitching, Boticelliesque, bare women who drew me into their sadness—pursed lips, downcast eyes and tangled hair, sometimes pulled back to reveal the whiteness of their necks. One nude in particular, the darkest queen of them all—full breasts with round pink nipples, arching hips, rolling thighs and a fleshy paunch—resembled me. Frailty was in her eyes and stark white eyelids without lashes, setting off a muddy gaze.

The nurses continued feeding me; and finally I was ready for visitors. Papa came alone on family day and cradled my skin-n-bones hand. Mama Jo and Brian visited me together like two old chums. Brian brought me gifts and Mama looked on with smiles. Handsome Dr. Wilinski—forty-something, metal-rimmed glasses, a large round nose and intense blue eyes—told me I could leave the hospital if I reached

100 pounds. *Fat chance,* I thought. I wanted to tell him about Mama, Brian, Papa, my uncles and breadcrumbs. I wanted to divulge my great fear that every person whom I loved would walk out on me. I had a premonition: I *knew* they would leave. But I couldn't share.

Three months is too long to wait for someone to get healthy, especially if their sanity is in question, so I didn't blame Brian when he stopped coming to visit. And by the time I was discharged, 15 pounds heavier, Brian had moved away, and I had to commence my senior year at Kenmore High. Now that Mama had lost her job, she had nothing to do. Hence, her doll obsession sprang from loneliness—not the kind you feel when your daughter gets married or your dog passes away—the kind of loneliness you feel if your lover leaves you. Mama cradled the doll at every chance, amidst long hours lying on our country-rose carpet, legs up, head reeling under the power of Sony headphones—every day, without speech. Every day, in the same place as we stepped around her to get to the stairway, I practiced ignorance and whispered to myself, *Don't mind her.*

Eventually Mama took off, moved to Florida, without giving the rest of us notice. No note—suicide or otherwise. Just the constant ticking of the upright clock and a sizeable oil stain in the driveway where her Toyota used to sit. The first week we waited for her to return as hastily as she departed, but she didn't. The second week I cleaned the house, taking special care of the living room rug, in case she wanted to return to lying on the floor. I even set her headphones out. But by the third week, when we hadn't heard from her, I said to Papa, 'She's not coming back.' I painted, I healed, I recreated Libby. I touched the piano again, and refurnished the room with Chopin. I fell in love with love as I sang alone with Mimi in *La Bohème*. This way, I could not hear Papa mumble. 'She's coming back,' he said. 'Don't worry—'

Five months later and the first winter post-Brian, Mama rang from her cheap motel. The cockroaches scampered along the floorboards loud enough for me to hear.

'Hi,' I said. 'Are you okay?'

She smacked her lips. 'Yes, I've just needed some away-time. I've found the most wonderful doctor who says I have manic depression.

He wants me to go on Lithium!'

Lithium? Don't they make something stronger?

'So did you know why Brian and I kept talking after you broke up?'

'No.'

'It was because we were talking about *you*. We wanted to help *you*.' I heard the sound of a seagull. She must have stepped outside.

'Oh,' I said.

'Brian and I had a connection,' she explained through orange juice-stained teeth. 'I just don't want you to be mad. I really cared for him—'

Connection with Brian + Papa's Impotence =

'Did you sleep with him?'

'No, sweetie. Our relationship was emotional. Don't be upset. It didn't have anything to do with you.'

Of course it didn't. I am exempt from all dictionaries and encyclopedias. I am the absence of meaning.

'I'm not upset,' I said. 'But I don't believe you—'

So, for the first time I was honest with her—a short but candid moment as I imagined her in a pair of faded jeans and a sweatshirt that took the chill out of a winter Florida morning. The day would turn warm, I knew, when she'd toss off her clothes to reveal a bathing suit from which her flesh, dark like figs, would spill. Later she'd sip a strawberry daiquiri poolside while her ill-starred family was stuck north in some snow bank. Got to hand it to her, though. Buffalo winters, Florida was the place to go.

JoAnna Minshew

JoAnna Minshew has lived all over the world. She currently resides in Norwich.

Boundless Boobs

I'm in the dressing room at Macy's, putting a bra through its paces. Most chicks, I know, select their bras (or upper-decker-flopper-stoppers as Brenda calls them) on some elusive quality known as 'cuteness'. I can't say I quite understand this term. It seems to apply randomly and equally to pink lace and baby chickens. Yeah, well, lace itches, chickens peck your toes, and women who like cute bras probably don't take a size 38DD. I was talking to Michelle about bras the other day, and mentioned about how the underwires chafe your upper arms if they're too long. Michelle is a B-cup, and she gave me that long, blank look I'm getting really familiar with.

Nonetheless, each of my bras must pass a rigorous pre-purchase trial. In the dressing room, I jump up and down a couple of times, first looking in the mirror to see how much individual and in-tandem motion the bra allows, then looking down at the boobies directly, making sure that they are restrained enough to not give me black eyes. It may look like Baywatch from a distance, but up close, each boob takes on the appearance of a half-feral bulldog, doing its best to creep from its lair unnoticed so's it can attack without warning. Once again, this brassiere simply cannot stand up to the long, pounding ride my tits will give it on a daily basis. It's already looking tired and decrepit, as if it has run a marathon without water. I notice that it has slid down a solid two inches, so now I look like those braless women who wander around Berkeley in sacking with flowers woven into their hair. 'All well and good for them,' I mutter, 'they don't have to run for the fifty-eight bus at seven in the morning.'

I throw my boobs over my shoulder and retrieve my old bra from the floor. It's of the steel mesh, cantilevered variety, more like military gear than underclothing. This was once a good bra; it used to be an act of gymnastics to get in and out of it. But it's been washed and worn and stretched and ineptly unhooked so many times that it has lost much of its elasticity to say nothing of shape. There are sad, broken bras scattered around the dressing room, looking like veterans of foreign wars. I wonder if this is a day they'll tell their grandchildren about—the day they wrestled the giant boobs from hell.

Today was supposed to be such a simple expedition as well. I wasn't supposed to (gods forbid) actually have to try anything on. Two years ago, I discovered the bra to end all bras. Wide straps, non-floral design, and a back you could really sink into. A stern taskmaster, a bra that could really keep restless boobs in . . . err . . . hand. Every time I needed something new in the restraint department, I would take the tag from one of my old bras and bring it to one of the lovely, sprightly, B-cup salesladies who roam the lingerie floor like well-groomed pumas. They would take the tag from me with a sad, compassionate smile, and return a few minutes later with an armful of heavy artillery. They would avert their eyes kindly from the unruly bosom, and ring up my purchase speaking to me in the quiet, well-bred, sepulcher tones that one uses to discuss the deceased. It was hard on the wallet, but comparatively easy on the psyche.

So, today I sauntered into the mall feeling almost cocky. I'd just deposited my paycheck, so I had plenty of bra-money. I had a tag from my last bra, so I wouldn't have to describe it. I had a spring in my step and a smile on my face.

'I'm terribly sorry, but this style is no longer being manufactured. In fact, the company went out of business. Can I help you find something similar?' The sales-chick is smiling timorously, as if I may bite her. I haven't decided yet whether I'm going to or not. Anyone who says 'terribly sorry' (or, actually, 'teddibly sawy'), probably deserves a good beating . . . err . . . biting. She pulls her measuring tape from around her neck and advances on me, intent on manhandling my knockers.

'That's OK,' I reply, stepping backwards quickly. 'No need to measure, I know my size.' She looks incredibly relieved. So relieved that I decide not to inform her that, if I wanted to, I could pin her without using my hands. My friend Lorraine and I used to joke that if we ever had children, breast feeding was out of the question—the poor little tykes would either suffocate or have their necks broken by the poundage of boobage they would be forced to navigate. I am tempted to run, screaming, from this den of satin and lace, but instead find myself corralled in a dressing room and ultimately surrounded by lifeless bras to whom CPR would come too late.

'None of those are going to work, I'm afraid,' I say to the beleaguered saleswoman. She looks exhausted. I don't think she's used to carting around bras that weigh more than she does. 'Have you got anything a bit sturdier? Something in metal, for preference?' She titters a bit, icy reserve cracked. I don't know why, but I always revert to about fourteen years old when bra shopping.

In fact, the first time I ever went bra shopping I was fourteen. I had needed boob restraint for about four years, but my mother denied the evidence of her own eyes until I turned around too quickly one day and knocked her over. She was a bit surprised to find herself on the ground, and even more so that, when I loomed over her to help her up, she couldn't see my face.

I will just mention in passing, that there is nothing, not nuclear war nor random street violence nor enraged crabs, nothing more terrifying than a junior high girl's locker room when one has no bra. The tactics one employs to keep oneself covered are downright Machiavellian. Show me a chick who got through junior high school without a bra and I will show you a severely disturbed individual whose twisted mind should probably be their country's first line of defense.

Anyway, I was fourteen and had a strong antipathy towards tits. I walked with a perpetual slouch, and looked angry all the time. The last, I'm afraid, was more indicative of my adolescence than my aversion to breasts. Similarly, I was already incredibly embarrassed by the fact that I HAD a mother, let alone that she might want to take me shopping. In her defense, she didn't want to go anymore than I did, and had already tried to circumnavigate this expedition by purchasing me a couple of training bras and leaving them on my bed. They were about as useful as postage stamps, since I was already pushing D-cup, but at least she tried. Even the training bra debacle, however, did not force her to see the truth about my knockers—that they were unfettered continents who could create new mountain ranges when they banged together.

So, we walked into Macy's together, and I immediately gravitated towards the uber-useful, no-nonsense old lady bras. Even at that tender age, I new I had little patience for cute. My ma, however, had other ideas. She picked up a wispy scrap of satin and waved it at me.

'This looks like about the right cup size for you,' she muttered.

'I don't think so, Ma,' I replied, rolling my eyes. 'That's a garter belt.' She dropped the offending garment as if it were red-hot and threw it a disgusted glance. How dare it jump into her hands like that? After surreptitiously kicking the garter belt under a display rack, she wandered away to check out the A-cups. I stayed in C/D range, testing underwire flexibility, lining softness, hook sturdiness. I had no idea what I was doing, or what I was looking for, but felt that I'd rather make my own mistakes than suffer through my mother's. Still, I needed a hand. I glanced around and a kindly old lady who looked like everybody's grandma caught my eye. She detached herself from a group of her colleagues and approached me, reaching my side at the same time my mother returned.

'Can I help . . ?'

'I found a few . . .'

They spoke over each other, then the salesperson gestured for Ma to continue.

'I found a few, honey,' Ma said, holding out wispy, underwireless bits in my direction.

'Umm,' I said, 'Ahh, I don't . . . I don't think . . .' I wasn't a very articulate teenager.

'Ma'am, those aren't going to fit her,' the woman said firmly. I could've blessed her as a saint.

'I know, they'll probably be too big,' Ma said in an aside to the saleswoman. 'She wants to keep herself . . . covered . . . in gym class. You know how kids are.' Ma tittered uncomfortably and I seethed.

'Certainly, Ma'am. But your daughter—this is your daughter?' She continued as Ma nodded. 'She's a bit . . . large for a teenager—' Ma cut her off, not wanting to hear what she was about to say.

'Surely she can't need more than an A-Cup,' Ma said. 'For

Christ's sake, she's only twelve!'

'I AM NOT! I'm fourteen and I'm standing right here, so please stop acting like I'm deaf!'

'Well, if you're fourteen, stop acting like you're twelve!' she snapped. I reddened, mortified, but kept my peace as she turned back to the saleslady. 'Do you think she's big enough for a B-cup?' Ma asked.

'Well, that's a good question,' the woman replied brightly. 'Perhaps I could measure?' She steered us expertly towards the dressing room. It was late August, the week before public schools in the area started back after summer vacation. She was no doubt used to befuddled mothers and surly daughters. In fact, out of the corner of my eye, I saw an equally reassuring saleswoman giving what looked like the same schpeil to an equally disgruntled duo.

'Hold your arms out, please,' she instructed, as she whipped a measuring tape from around her shoulders. I stood, hot with humiliation, as she heaved and hoisted, hitched and handled. It wasn't like I'd never had my rack wrenched before, but this was the first time I'd ever had my mother actually watching instead of just worrying she was watching. 'OK, you're at a 36-C. We have a wide selection in your size. Why don't you just sit for a minute and I'll see what I can find. Do you have a color preference?'

'Black,' I said.

'White,' Ma contended.

'I'll bring you some of each, and maybe a couple in some brighter colors as well.'

'No red,' Ma said. For once I agreed, albeit silently. My boobs decked out in red would put one in the mind of carcasses awaiting the butcher.

'No red,' the lady agreed. 'But we have some burgundies and blues and I think a nice dark green in her size.'

'Just no beige,' I begged silently. 'That would be as bad as the white, cotton, high-waisted panties Grandma used to give me every Xmas.'

'Black!' Ma hissed, interrupting my revery. 'Black! You want the world to think you're some kind of brazen hussy?'

'Ma, the only people who are gonna see my bras are already gonna know I'm a brazen hussy,' I replied, trying to lighten the mood.

'What! WHAT!' she screeched. So much for that plan. 'What's

that trashy talk! You're TWELVE!'

'I'm fourteen,' I mumbled, and the saleslady returned, the brightly colored bras making her hand resemble a peacock.

'Here's a selection of what we have,' she said all chipper. 'If there's a style that you like, but you don't like the color, let me know and I can probably find something else.'

'Thanks,' I muttered, grabbing them and sweeping into the dressing room. I turned to shut the door, and almost shut it on Ma. 'Oh, no,' I continued. 'You are not coming in here with me.'

'Oh yes I am,' she countered. 'I'm paying for them, I make the decisions. And anyway, you don't know how they're supposed to fit.'

'I know enough to know they're not supposed to cover a mere sufficiency of nipple,' I replied, my voice arctic. 'I think I can figure it out. And you can decide if they're OK after I take them off.'

'Not a chance,' she said, voice just as cold. I looked her up and down, enraged, but she didn't budge. 'You can let me in graciously, or I can make a scene, whichever you prefer,' her eyes told me. I sighed and opened the door wider.

Ma settled herself as comfortably as possible on the ledge in the dressing room. Because of the three-fold mirrors, her gaze followed me, every way I turned. I settled on a sort of sideways twist—she could still see me, but at least I didn't have to look at her. I skinned off my shirt, hoping that the bruises Jeff left had faded to invisibility. That boy bit HARD. I was always a little surprised that both my nipples were still intact, after.

'Merciful heavens,' she said, gawping at my graspers. 'When did you grow those?'

'About two years ago,' I replied, turning, defiantly aiming them directly at her. Well, technically, they were pointing straight down, but in theory I aimed them directly at her.

'Why didn't you tell me?' she asked in a wounded tremolo. But I wasn't letting her off that easy.

'I did. You bought me training bras. Those might have helped if I coulda sewn two of them together, but . . .' I shrugged eloquently, watched her watch the ripple effect. This was kinda cool, actually. I'd never before considered using the boobs as weapons, except in relatively straightforward ways.

'Cut that out,' she snapped, as I shimmied and shook. But I

didn't. I rolled my shoulders. I jumped up and down. Then, still shirtless, I started on the tap routine they'd been teaching us in gym. With every two or three taps, a knocker flew up and knocked me in the jaw. Her eyes got wider and wider. Then, I started to laugh. I laughed and laughed. Her face went from angry, to incredulous, to blank, and then she finally saw the joke.

'Dear Lord,' she guffawed, her restraint failing. She laughed, then wiped her streaming eyes, then laughed some more. I pulled myself together, still giggling, and slid my arms into the straps of the bra at the top of the pile. 'You're as bad as your Aunt Susan!' she continued, still snickering.

'Aunt Susan?' I asked. 'Why? What did she do?'

'Oh hell, when we were in college, she got herself some pasties with tassels and taught herself how to get her boobs going in different directions so the tassels would swing in circles.'

'Aunt SUSAN did!?' I exclaimed, flabbergasted. 'No way!'

'Oh yes she did,' Ma continued. 'You should get her to teach you that trick one day. It got her invited to all of the frat parties.'

'But . . . Susan . . . she . . .' I paused, feeling like I was moving onto shaky ground.

'She didn't always have four kids, you know,' Ma said, correctly interpreting my stuttering.

'I guess not,' I replied, still shaken. 'But still, . . . Susan.'

'Oh, she was quite the wild child,' Ma finished, wiping her eyes again. 'Now get some restraint on that . . . bosom of yours, before you kill yourself,' she sighed, then added, 'or me,' under her breath. I grinned and complied.

When I turned back, I saw her eyeing a sickly yellow/green bruise that was still vaguely visible over the top of the bra. But she didn't say anything, so neither did I. We'd done enough bonding for one day.

I managed to pick out a few bras that passed my stringent examinations and adhered to the parental cuteness criterion, and we left in a much better mood than we had arrived in. But, despite the dancing, I retain a terror of bra shopping. It's just not entertaining. So when the high heeled automaton reappeared with another stack of underclothing, I asked her a question that made her drop her stock on the floor.

'Tell me,' I asked, 'have you got any pasties?' Her stock dropped.

'Maybe with tassels on?' Her eyes boggled a bit, and I felt momentarily bad for harassing her, even though she didn't really seem all that shocked. Still, she was looking at me oddly, so I apologized. 'Sorry,' I said. 'Inside joke.' She grinned at me as I scooped the bras up off the floor. 'I'm sure one of these will be fine,' I continued. 'Thank you so much for all your help.'

'No problem,' she replied, icy reserve cracked. She glanced around furtively, then surprised the hell out of me. She twitched her shirt aside, exposing pasties shaped like starfish gripping her nipples. 'Try Fredrick's,' she muttered.

Dave Paul

Dave Paul was born in Portsmouth in 1980. He has worked as a farm labourer, an industrial cleaner, a petrol station cashier, a shelf stacker, a barman, and as a disaster recovery specialist. King *is his first novel.*

King

(extract from a novel)

Having failed to get onto the History of Art course at St. Andrews, William has come to his second choice university in Norwich. It is here that he meets a thirty-one year old first generation raver called King.

'Trust me on this one. My Dad's lot have been keeping it in the family for over a thousand years and look where it's got us. Porhyria, William. Tints your pee port red. Got kicked in the nuts once and didn't sleep for three days. Could be infected for all I know. Have to pull a stool out the throne every couple of months just to check it ain't stained funny, and if you got it real bad your teeth go chocolate brown. Know the scary thing about it? Little bastard lies dormant. Hangs around for ages then one day—bam!—you're chatting up radiators, flashing that million pound Cadbury's smile of yours.'

Still dressed in his raving attire from the weekend before—black tracksuit bottoms, singlet and trainers—King reached across to turn down the volume on his car stereo. He'd stopped swaying and was looking serious. 'End up with this rash on your back, look like you've been scourged. Then before you know it your eyes gone yellow and you're pissing purple. Take Henry, dead relative of mine; skin eruptions, fits of hysteria, bilious attacks . . . Eventually loses all control over his body. Marries this sixteen year old French girl who gets washed ashore at Portchester during the middle of a thunderstorm. No tunnel in them days. Anyways, eight years later she's pregnant and Henry's claiming it had nothing to do with him; goes round telling everyone that the father's the Holy Ghost, giving it the old immaculate conception line.'

'Did he have—' Will tried to shape his mouth around the alien word. 'Porifia?'

'Riddled with it. Course then there's George—premature baby—tries to rape his niece and kill his son, then starts raving about some grandmother he thinks he's in love with. Comes up in all these big bulbous sores that you gotta drain the puss out of, and can't sleep 'cos he's got these pains in his face. One minute music's the greatest thing in the world, the next he can't bear to hear it. Talking to trees by the time he'd hit fifty. . .'

Will drifted off and tried to think back to the maddest person he knew. Five years in an all boy's boarding school had convinced him he was no stranger to peculiarity. If it were indeed the task of antiquated institutions to breed eccentric individuals, Eton College had proved itself the centre of excellence its welcoming brochures professed it to be. As Will's parents exchanged pleasantries with the housemaster and received assurances that their eldest son would be well looked after, a nervous looking Chinese boy from the year above had leaned across a table laden with sandwiches and whispered that it was better to get out now while the going was good. Ignoring Albert's counsel in a hopeless tide of optimism, Will soon found himself alone in a large dormitory with seven other thirteen year olds who'd taken exception to the old wooden trunk which contained his belongings. Steven Warren's was newer, James Pembrook's was bigger and Anthony Jenkins, already emerging as something of a leader, was wowing the others with a handcrafted mahogany chest he claimed had been used to smuggle munitions in the Second World War. Only blind luck had saved William from certain social exclusion. When the lights had been turned off and the low conversation began, a boy in the corner called Miles Gimblett had quietly asked if women had bottoms. At an age when most kids pride themselves on what limited information they've cobbled together about the opposite sex, the severity of Miles' mistake was immeasurable. The abuse persisted until pupils, even teachers, had forgotten his real name. His comment was the equivalent of turning up with a handbag.

So Gimplett became pals with a pigeon. Twice a day he would ascend a steep spiral staircase to the top of Lupton's tower with a piece of Betterbuy bread he'd taken from the kitchen, assume his regular seat beneath the window and scatter crumbs about the ledge. When Hushwing descended, fanning her wings as she fell from above, they would talk about how ghastly the other boys could be and all the wonderful creatures in the world that were labelled vermin. But it was not long before someone who knew had told somebody else who'd mentioned it to James Pembrook. And within a matter of minutes, Anthony Jenkins, whose father had rowed for Cambridge in the dramatic race of '54, was interrupting Gimplett's description of a conical flask he thought looked like a willy and demanding that Hushwing be handed over. Just to say hello, of course. Too feeble to refuse, Gimplett passed his new friend over to an old enemy on the condition that she came to no harm, keen to point out that whatever differences the boys had between them did not concern the bird. It came as something of a surprise when Anthony cradled the pigeon in both arms, ran the back of a free finger along its white neck and rocked her from side to side as if she were his own friend too. Perfectly still in the arms of a stranger, Hushwing had only a moment to register the sudden darkening of the world as Anthony closed his jaws about her neck, divided the bird unevenly in two, and spat the contents of his mouth back at Gimplett's forehead, beak and all.

King was still going. '. . . Alicante wine apparently. You'd have thought he'd keep himself to himself, but that's James for you. Marries this great big Norwegian lass who's into amateur dramatics. Didn't get off to a great start, illness or no illness—his Mum married her husband's murderer, then left the country when the Family realised it was her what put him up to it. Caught up with her in the end though—don't like anyone killing their own unless it's them what's doing it.'

'Do you really think you might have it?' Will asked.

'Difficult to say, William, but one thing's for sure, the Family don't help much with all them policies about diluting the blood. Proud bunch, Dad's lot; got it in their heads that they're better than the rest of us. Worse than that, they're surrounded by people who seem to agree. And even if I don't got it, thinking you're gonna go mad might just be enough to make you go mad anyways.'

Will faced front, enjoying the pause in conversation. His new friend was certainly high spirited. And then King was off again, rambling on past signs to Banham Zoo and the Butterfly Gardens, becoming more and more the lunatic historian, tracing wild paths through a family contaminate with thieves and adulterers, drunkards and gamblers, murderers and usurpers. Occasionally he would pinch Will's cheek between his fingers and pull him across the gearstick, their faces nearly touching, to whisper some treachery as if others might be listening, some relative's scheme to inherit the great fortune which swelled and diminished as it made its way through his dysfunctional lineage. 'Money don't buy you friends,' he would begin, 'but—just ask Richard, and he'll back me up on this one—you'll be well assured a better class of enemy.' Then, falling quieter, he'd return his thoughts to the road, his brow furrowing as he relived some hard confirmation of his erratic monologue, before turning wide-eyed to begin again where he had just left off. 'It's not so much them, the messed up ones, that I feel sorry for,' he'd say, taking a gulp from his bottle of water, 'it's the other half, desperately trying to keep the whole sorry circus together.'

'Is there a cure? Can't you do something?'

'Nah,' King continued, 'just got to sit around waiting for your brain to do a runner. Protein's supposed to help—minimum of seventy grams a day should do the trick but I reckon eighty-five is erring on the side of caution. Don't look at me like that, you'd have read up on this shit if you thought it might happen to you. Scares the hell out of me, anyways. Veal, eggs, tuna, salami, sardines, shrimp, crayfish—then you got your plant sources: wheat germ, lentils, cocoa powder . . .' King nodded towards Will's knees. 'Take a look in the glove box.'

Will did as he was told, pulling at a plastic lever in front of him. The small space was crammed with insurance details, a Toyota owner's manual, two anonymous brown packets and a can of de-icer. He pulled out one of the packets and looked it over in his palm.

'Almonds,' said King. 'Haven't had a fit yet.'

The dual carriageway narrowed into a single lane and they slowed behind a supermarket lorry. King cursed Waitrose and the A11. Every so often he steered the car into the centre of the road, looking for a break in the oncoming traffic, muttering a few unsavoury words about lines of communication in and out of the county. Distances on the workmen signs grew smaller and smaller until they were no more than two hundred yards away from the Roudham Heath to Attleborough Improvements, where a forty mile speed limit had been strictly imposed. *Those are the worst signs*, King grumbled, *the ones that warn you to speed up.* The workmen were obviously taking their caution to *slow down* seriously; there was little activity other than the odd mechanical arm stealing sand from banks flanking the beginnings of a road.

'You like sport, William?'

'I like cricket.'

'Cricket? Five days sitting around waiting for a draw or the whole damn thing to be rained off? That's not a sport, William, that's a waste of time. Boxing's a sport. Two blokes slugging the living crap out of each other till one of them falls half-dead on the floor. *Honesty*, William. You got Benny Lynch—the pride of all Scotland in his day—Freddie Mills, the milkman from Bournemouth. Then there's Bob Fitzsimmons—the Cornish blacksmith with the hammer punch—Cardiff's Jim Driscoll. Jesus, when Jim starts out boxing he can't afford gloves so he improvises using waste paper and string he finds on the floor at the print factory he works in. *Honesty*.'

'Chloe said you box.'

'Used to. Trying to keep my head down at the moment. Never that much cop anyways—wouldn't have made it past amateur level. Sparred with this older Trinidadian guy called Mickey Linton for a couple of years, he's pretty good, bantamweight like myself. His Dad's fight against Jackie Brown at the Belle Vue was one of the best of all time. Linton holds the British bantamweight title, Brown's the former flyweight champion; Brown puts on a few pounds, moves up to bantamweight and challenges Linton for the title in 1937. Everybody's scrabbling to get tickets for Manchester that night . . .' And on and on, the boxing enthusiast, punching the air with a succession of straight lefts, the Toyota veering occasionally from the road as Linton Senior's deadly right was illustrated in all its glory, every round, every exchange, every hook, jab and parry.

'. . . And the only reason Brown's probably still standing is 'cos of his weird flat-footed, legs wide apart stance. Then somehow or other he manages to land a suspiciously low left in the twelfth and gets in a right to the chin while Linton's doubled up. So the referee tears them apart and gives Brown a warning—well, that's it, Linton's decided he's had enough. Starts to really dish out some punishment. Brown goes down after hitting the ropes—somehow or other he beats the count, I mean, this guy just don't know when enough's enough—only to get one more final right to the side of his jaw—bam!—and one thing's for sure, Brown don't get up the next time.' King shook his head. 'Now that's a sport, William, not all that walking around and "after you" and bein' gentlemanly.'

'Cricket's cool too, you know,' said Will, already convinced he was going to mess this one up. 'It's not all gentlemanly and boring. There was one match between two local teams, Heresbury and Theresbury, who'd been rivals for as long as anyone could remember. The Heresbury captain won the toss and decided to bat, walked out to the crease and waited for the first ball of the innings. He got bowled this *amazing* ball, had a go, but missed the thing completely, shouting *"Well I declare!"* as it flew past. Hearing this, the Theresbury captain told the rest of his team that they should leave the field to get padded up, since their opposition had passed play over. So an argument began between the players while the umpires read through the rule book—'

'Was there a big punch up?' asked King, taking a slurp from his bottle.

'Well,' Will paused, 'no; but I think there was some fairly fruity language being thrown about. Eventually it was decided that the Heresbury captain had officially declared, so now two Theresbury players went into bat, needing only one run to win the game. But the Heresbury captain had a plan; he went over to this little guy on his team, Herbert, who'd never bowled in a match before, whispered something in his ear and gave him the ball for the first over. When the umpire called play, Herbert took a massive run up towards the bowling crease, took a sharp left at the wicket and began running in circles around the pitch, still holding on to the ball. *He was playing out time.*'

King looked less than impressed. 'Did Herbert get beaten up or was he just on the receiving end of a good talking to?'

'Well,' Will continued, 'this was the thing. There was nothing in the rule book which said he couldn't keep on running; the Theresbury batsmen refused to leave the crease in case they got bowled out and all the Heresbury fielders could do was lay themselves down on the grass. The spectators left for lunch, came back to see if anything had changed, then left again for tea. By the time the church clock was nearing seven, when it had been agreed to draw the stumps, a larger crowd had gathered. It seemed as if Heresbury had managed to keep the game level. But on the chiming of the bells the Theresbury captain rightly pointed out that it wasn't legal to draw the stumps in the middle of the ball—are you listening?'

'Yeah, yeah, get on with it.'

'So Herbert keeps on running until the moon has gone behind a cloud, when he swings back through the outfielders towards the wicket. The opening Theresbury batsman has to strain through the darkness as Herbert sends down a juicy full toss; the batsman swipes blindly at it, but the ball flies past and gets stopped by the mass of fielders who've gathered behind the stumps in case of a bye. *"Match drawn!"* shouts the Heresbury captain, but the batsman, who's had a lot of time to think, turns around and says that if you can't draw the stumps in the middle of a ball, then it follows you can't draw them in the middle of an over. But then the Heresbury captain appeals against the light and it's game over.'

'So it was a draw?' said King.

'Yes.'

King slowed the car as they approached a roundabout, looking towards the flow of traffic and signposts to Grimes Graves; Bury St Edmunds was a short distance down the A143, first exit on the left. Ignoring both, he steered the Toyota around the island and continued two hundred metres up the road, where he swerved the car into a lay-by and applied the brakes sharply, bringing them to a sudden halt beside a small mobile food stand. An English flag pulled gently at a makeshift mast mounted on the trailer's roof, while a motor whirred away beneath a sheet of canvas.

'My Dad told me that one,' Will added.

King undid his seat belt. 'Guess that Herbert guy was a bit messed up.'

Will breathed again. '*Complete lunatic*,' he giggled.

'No,' said King.

A. Pearmain

Born in Leeds 1954, spent 70s in Manchester, 80s in London, and 90s and 00s in Norwich. Variously: gardener, student/student politician, punk poet/comic, bookshop worker, teacher, now father, Social Services manager and City Councillor.

Picture Me (in Ten Years' Time Watching)

This is an extract from a novel, which begins in Manchester in 1974 and finishes in Bristol in 1994, spanning the years of the death of the British Left and the triumph of Thatcherism. It's a love story, a historicist romance, set amongst Euro-communist punks. Mills and Boon for New Order fans.

Ian, Bristol 1993

If I can't remember, or managed to forget, much of Florence's short life, then the following year, the rest of 1979 and into 1980, might have happened to someone else for all I knew. I nearly added 'or cared,' because really and truly all I wanted for myself was to die, like her, my dear sweet darling, baby daughter. And the only reason I didn't was that, for that whole long lost year, I didn't have enough life left in me to do it. Or, for that matter, to commit much to conscious memory. Or sequential order. All I have retained is fragments, in no particular order, like newspaper headlines cut up for hate-mail, or a pile of warped negatives of photos which were taken badly in the first place, out of focus, with a smudged lens or an intruding finger.

What follows is a string of incidents, put together more or less at random. This is what stands out from the daily struggle to survive a year I did not want to survive, a river of gloom with occasional falls, dams or diversions. Some were good, some were bad, but most were in some way scary, because I was never entirely sure that they were happening to me, or to someone else I just got stuck next to. And I am still not entirely sure that it wasn't all some awful, jerky, drug and sex and pain-induced, bad dream.

I boiled a kettle dry one day. I didn't just leave it. I knew I was doing it. I watched it whistle and steam till it stopped, and the bottom burnt right through. I turned the gas off then, but just so I could upend the kettle, and look in wonder at the twisted, charred, steel bottom, still glowing at its frayed edges. I remember thinking how thin it must have been in the first place, to burn through like that, and throwing it out of the open window into the backyard.

That's how I know where I was, at Terry's place in Castle Road, because I can clearly remember the jumble of bins and old bikes and piles of sandy earth and builders' rubble in the yard, otherwise visible only from Terry's window on the first floor above. They used to add to it whenever something needed chucking out. I always noticed anything new, and pointed it out to Terry, who never seemed quite so interested. 'Yard-fill,' Richard used to call it, and said at least they were taking responsibility for their own rubbish. I also remember looking at the palm of my right hand, where I'd held the kettle by the metal handle when I lifted it up, and where a great, blistered, angry, red weal was beginning to form, too deep for me to feel it.

I remember the chequered pattern on a tablecloth, sitting down to eat a cold, silent meal with Helen, while I was still in Manchester, or when I'd gone back for a few days; I don't know which. We'd never bothered with tablecloths before Flo died, not even when Helen's mother came, though she'd given us several, one Christmas. Helen had wrinkled up her sweet little button-nose when she unwrapped the parcel, as if she was disgusted by the smell of fresh, new haberdashery. She expressed the customary thanks, and couldn't bring herself to give them back or throw them away, but she regarded it as a matter of pride, and maybe a token gesture of defiance, to leave the tablecloths folded and unused at the back of a wardrobe.

I sat looking at the small blue and white squares, on crinkly dimpled material, with red and yellow roses in a kind of diamond pattern fussily superimposed, and asked Helen, 'Why are we using a tablecloth?' She didn't answer. 'Why are we using a tablecloth?' I asked again, louder, 'We never have before.'

She looked up, and said, 'Well, I've been using them while you've been away, wherever that may be.' I hadn't told her, just said I'd been away, and she hadn't pressed me any further.

I gripped the edge of the tablecloth with both hands under the table, where it lay across my thighs, and I tried to summon up enough strength and will to pull it away from the table. Somehow, I thought that if I pulled it fast and hard enough, I would be able to leave the plates and cups and cutlery intact. I'd seen it done somewhere, probably on the telly. I sat there like that for what seemed like an age, frozen in my anger, and then thought better of it. I stood up and walked out.

And earlier, still in Manchester, on the afternoon Flo was dying, lying in an incubator in the Intensive Care Unit of the children's ward, with tubes in her nose and attached to her scalp and her arm, and a mask over her mouth, surrounded by bleeping machines and monitors. I am on my own with her, sitting by the incubator in a hard, iron-framed hospital chair. Helen must have gone to the toilet, or to make phone calls or something. The doctors had said it was still too early to say how things were going, but I thought I could tell from their eyes that it wasn't looking too good. They would check again in half an hour, or if anything happened in the meantime. I wanted to ask what that 'anything' might be, and how long 'the meantime' was, but I could see they didn't want to be pushed.

I sat there with her, alone, just me and her, and willed her to live, come on baby, pull through for Daddy. I sang, 'Hush little baby don't say a word,' the mockingbird song, with my own improvised words, silly clumsy awkward lines that didn't rhyme, about how much I loved her and wanted her to get better, and if she did I'd be so proud of her, and I'd never let her go again, and she could love me and rely on me always. I shut up when Helen came back, and just hummed the tune, till Helen said it was getting on her nerves and could I stop? Please.

Going to see Patti Smith with Terry at the Hammersmith Odeon, though we thought it was at the Hammersmith Palais and got the wrong directions from the tube station. Something to do with the Clash song, I imagine. We found the Palais dark and shut, no sign of

'Dillinger and Leroy Smart', let alone any other white people besides us. We went off running around unknown West London, up alleys and down streets, turning onto bijou mews and coming out into desolate council estates, through a pub and into a park. Where the fuck are we? They seem to be rearranging the map as we dash across it.

Finally hail a cab, collapse into the plush black leather back seat, giggling and sniffing, and at the back of my throat, tasting the residues of the cocaine we'd snorted before we'd come out. Get there well into Patti Smith's set, she is howling and swaying, one of her ridiculous mystic-punk 'poems'. Her band look embarrassed, and more like women than she does; Lenny Kaye in big hair and glasses pouting and thrashing his guitar in twelve-chord sweeps, about nine more than most other guitarists could be bothered with at the time. Terry stands stock still, studies Patti's every move, occasionally mouths the words to the few songs we recognise, and then turns to me and says, 'Fucking hippie musos. Shall we go?'

Standing in a kitchen at a party smoking dope with hot knives and a broken milk bottle, trying between giggling fits to think of words that rhyme with milk and bottle—ilk, silk, mottle, glottal—and when we can't think of any more, just making them up—dilk, jilk, thilk, dottle, phottle, yottle. Ha, ha, ha. Hee, hee, hee. Later some guy with big frizzy hair used the broken milk bottle to threaten people, going from room to room, sending cups of drink skittering across the floor and bare light bulbs swinging round the ceiling, waving the bottle around and shouting, 'Back off!' as if everybody wasn't already, and then saying he 'was only joking, man,' when someone started screaming. I asked who he was, and nobody knew.

Waking up on my own the next day with my face on a hard dusty floorboard, and finding I'd shut myself in a tiny box-room at the top of the house, wherever it was. I looked through the dusty attic window at the London rooftops, thought of 101 Dalmatians and the midnight barking, and Rapunzel, Rapunzel, let down your hair. I might have let myself down, out of the window, across the rooftops, but I'd just had my hair cut, nearly shaved, because I was sick of it flopping around all over the place, and wanted to forget about it, and avoid myself in the mirror, for at least a few weeks. I started thinking of all the other fairy tales I could have read to Flo—Goldilocks, Rumpelstiltskin, The Ugly

Duckling—if she had lived just a few months more. I had to call out for someone to come break the door down and let me out.

One time when Terry was away with the band, I caught sight of myself in a butcher's shop window, with my face reflected back at me from within the carcass of a pig, so it looked like I was wearing its ribcage as some strange kind of helmet, or a glam rock-style meat-wig type of thing. I panicked, and formed a plan to walk the entire length of the Grand Union Canal towpath East to West, as some kind of penance or diversion or something. I traced the route on an A-Z I found in Richard's room, and it looked straightforward enough, with a few diversions through nearby streets, where the canal presumably went underground for a while.

I started one night at Hackney Wick, cutting my hand on glass embedded in concrete on top of a wall I had to clamber over to get down to the canal. I left a trail of blood behind me as I set off through Old Ford, Vicky Park and Haggerston, the intestines and digestive tract of old London town, past De Beauvoir and the Kingsland basin, up to the Angel and down to Pentonville, where the canal resurfaces and loops around Kings Cross/St.Pancras and up through Camden Town, through the Lock and down to Regents Park. Round the Outer Circle, talking to the animals in the zoo, singing as many zoo-related songs as I could remember, only one really—Daddy's taking us to the zoo tomorrow, we're gonna stay all day.

Past Lord's cricket ground, under Lisson Grove, and down along the Westway, nearly deserted at whatever a.m. it was by then, through Westbourne Grove and Kensal Town, pausing for breath and a drink of canal water at Meanwhile Gardens, (a real place, honest, but I imagined a literary allotment for the cultivation of plotlines). The railway and prison wasteland of Old Oak and Wormwood Scrubs, out to Harlesden and beyond, and there before me, a snarling dog behind a bale of barbed wire strung across the towpath of the Manchester Ship Canal, as the sun comes up behind the engineering block of Salford University. I had no idea how I got there, started in one city and ended in another, or how long I'd been away, or where in the world I'd been.

Listening to a scratched, crackling single of 'Stand by me' by Ben E. King, over and over again on headphones, swaying with the strings and twitching with the beat, strumming my soul and shuffling my feet, dimly aware of the glare of irate eyes on my averted back. Ben E. singing about, 'When the night has come and the land is dark, and the moon is the only light you'll see', until Terry (or was it Helen?) gave up on me and went to bed.

The normal, everyday sounds of a family, coming up at me from the flat below, which means it must be Hulme, and they've just moved in, or I've been away again. Doors closing, chairs scraping, things being dropped or thrown. Children laughing, adults arguing, water running, babies crying, driving me out of the living room, up the stairs, down the landing, through the bedroom, out of the window. I end up on the upstairs balcony in the greasy rain, crouching, a long way from the ground, shrinking into a corner, holding my head, hands clutching my eyes and ears. Two whole floors, twenty feet and two thick concrete ceilings away, I am still hearing it, only now it's my own voice I hear, and Helen's, and Flo's, as though my pain and tears are stored in the walls, growing in the mould and the moss, nurtured by the breath and secretions I continue, against all logic and desire, to emit.

Watching 'Apocalypse Now' on the biggest screen I'd ever seen, so big I had to turn my head to watch the helicopters float past, whomp-whomp-whomp, and the tracer bullets whistle, pheew-pheew-pheew, from one side of the cinema to the other. Seeing a helicopter detach itself from the others and from the screen, and head out over the audience, back through the smoke and dust-motes, over my cowering head, and back into the projector it had come from. I stagger out into a blue West End afternoon, with hours of accursed daylight to endure before I can turn out the light and be sure of proper velvet-soft darkness to snuggle up into.

One day, a good day, going with Terry to a Marxism Today study session on whether we could appropriate the Union Jack for the left. Somebody had even prepared sketches of how it could be done, which were propped up on flip chart stands around the room. The simplest and most fetching had a big red star in the middle, with a yellow edge round every other colour, to temper what was described as the 'stark, macho nationalism' of the red, white and blue, 'with its connotations of blood, race and reaction.'

Others were more complicated, and somehow missed the point, such as the traditional design done in Rastafarian colours, or one that deconstructed the traditional components—crosses of St. George and St. Andrew and so on—and rearranged them apparently at random, so it ended up looking more like a road sign meaning, 'Don't go there'. Terry and I sat at the back, and became increasingly incredulous, until someone suggested setting up an alternative England football supporters club, and we exploded in splutters and guffaws and fell out of our chairs, out of the room and, we swore, right out of the Communist Party.

Another day, not good but a little better, with Helen. She'd just come back from a Party women's aggregate, where they'd been discussing what positions to adopt at some forthcoming feminist conference. One motion in particular had caused much troubled discussion. It said simply, 'Penetration is rape, and all men are potential rapists.' The Party women knew it was divisive and utterly impractical, but they recognised its political and emotional force. They also knew they'd have difficulty if they just opposed it, and lose potential allies on other, more immediately practical issues to do with the economy and the law.

So they decided to put up an amendment saying that penetration was acceptable in certain circumstances, so long as it didn't involve any thrusting, since that was what represented the violence of patriarchy in heterosexual relationships. Helen was quite keen to try it out, penetration without thrusting, so later on we did. It didn't do much for me, as I recall. In fact I lost my erection after a while, but Helen claimed it felt more cosy and intimate than the way we usually did it. Not that we were doing it much by then. I stayed up after she went to bed, and wanked in the bathroom, imagining lots of faceless women all too enthusiastically thrusting.

Sitting down to a meal Jackie had made for us at Castle Road, in an attempt to lift the gloom, and get everybody back together again. We're all sitting round the big dining table that Richard had constructed from stuff he'd found in skips, and somehow turned into something people would have paid £500 for in Camden Lock, only that would have been against his principles. 'A thousand and I'd have to reconsider,' he said, as he passed round the roast potatoes and the lentil mush, all vaguely curried to a recipe from one of Jackie's cookbooks. Then she served up another dish, a great big earthenware bowl of some kind of dark greeny-brown gloop. 'It's Aubergine Bharti,' she said, 'traditional in Northern India, or so it says in the book.'

It reaches Richard, and he says, 'It looks more like that Henna stuff Caroline plasters on her hair.'

Caroline responds 'Oh ha ha, very droll. . . .'

Richard passes the dish on to me, and I say, 'more like babies' first poo. . . .'

Terry, next to me on the other side, and keeping up the jokey-dopey banter, says, 'How would you know?' and then as things go quiet, realises all too clearly from the look on my face how I would.

Richard, bless him, throws me a lifeline. 'That's right, it's called encomium, and it's completely sterile. Not many people know that.' The conversation resumes and moves on.

Some time later, or possibly before, watching Helen crying, after months of stony pallor, slowly and quietly at first, just small tears rolling singly down her cheek, a sad little snails' race down her face, where I think I see some colour returning. I'm thinking that this is good, about time, healthy, an emotional thaw. Maybe we can get through this together, instead of staying stuck in it apart, and I put my arms around her shoulders and draw her close. I can taste and smell the salt in her tears.

She gives out a quick, suppressed roar, more like a growl really. She shrugs my arm off, and her sobs deepen, till they're rolling up from her chest in heavy, crashing waves. She tries to prop her head in her hands, with her elbows on the table, but her upper body is rocking backwards and forwards so violently that she keeps missing. Her hands skid up her teary temples and the sides of her head, and her elbows keep sliding on the pool of snot and off the edge of the table. It looks like some strange, demented, unfunny mime.

She is angry now, and I can't work out why, or what with. Me? Herself? The table? The whole fucking wide world? She cries out like a tortured animal. I don't know what to do and back away in my chair.

I'm terrified. She starts throwing her arms around, and connects with me almost by accident, great swaying windmill swings, like a little kid fighting in the playground. I back off even further, her flailing subsides, I stand up, leave the room, put my coat on, leave the flat. It's unseasonably mild outside but I am freezing cold, shivering, and I'm never going back.

Siobhan Peiffer

Siobhan Peiffer grew up in Southampton, New York, and attended Yale and Oxford Universities.

The Architect

When his wife left for the last time, she moved
with the children to the suburbs. He moved
his bed next to the bathtub. He wanted
room. He stretched measures as far from corners
as he could, and yet on paper, corners
tightened sooner than his pencil wanted.
He drew through sleepless nights. If he must sketch
within what was already there, his sketch
would always be too small. He dreamed design.
From then on, for others, he never wrote
'Schläft im Bad' in faint pencil script; he wrote
inked capitals whose angles still design
sturdy purposes for squares they live in:
HALL, MUSIC SUITE, BUTLER'S PANTRY (doors IN
and OUT.) Then bearings thinned, the wide glass walls
of blueprints became rafts of cyclic light,
and floors floated above a stream, too light
to last, it seemed. They have. His final walls
no longer meet. Lines remain where they end.
To make no room, he found, might be the end
of making. He destroyed plans to save space.
When he looked again at what he had drawn
in his first finished house, his eyes were drawn
to a blank bedroom in what would be space.

TO A BIOGRAPHER

Admit it: self-righteousness isn't a phase.
I kept my doubts, which are still unwritten,
and watched you purchase a round-trip ticket,
consider dust-jacket picture and type.
You can't be too careful with someone's life.

Now, you cancel dates to search
letters and manuscripts, checking a list
of unpublished work by your famous subject
meant for the book that you haven't begun.
But I've seen another archive, your own:

Write every morning, treat people better.
Twelve months later: *This time I mean it.*
Meet my deadlines, try to be kind.
I trust that life: unaccomplished, right.

Oscar Wilde

Place betrayed him last. He wouldn't flee
his home, or his imprisonment; he knew
a nighttime flight to Paris would undo
the emigrating wit that kept him free.
No, he would serve his sentence. Even laws
had period and finish; he would earn
such artful flourish in his right return.
And yet the endlessly dependent clause
of judgment settled London with his sin:
the flat he once had decorated let
to someone else's taste, his greetings met
with stares, and friends he called on never in.
He waved a wrist, and left for Nice. Alone
and trapped all afternoon at a café,
his elbow on the bill he couldn't pay,
or walking miles one evening to postpone
a night in ugly rooms, he thought of how
his warden listened at the padlocked door
to lectures from his famous speaking tour.
'House Beautiful' would take him nowhere now.
No more addresses, ever. If the shamed
should be forever leaving, why not leave
forever? Grammar promised no reprieve.
He went to Naples, to the garden famed
for suicide. A proper spot, he thought,
an emptiness. But then he heard a whir
as clouds around his chair began to stir.
These must be souls. And would his, too, be caught
eternally in Italy? Absurd!
And hardly fitting . . . He resolved to die
in better exile. Outcast, he would try
to live beyond the reach of any word.

WINTER TERM

Leave when late afternoon
defines the window's neon.

Walk the waning beach
as the tide laps the last of the dock.

Then go higher, till the town
is one story of shadows,

the clock tower a cautious
finger against the sunset's mouth,

and pass the greenhouse, lit
and hollow in the growing dark.

Wait in a field until the moon
splits open a fattening cloud.

You are the height of empty trees
that refuse to show any more cold.

The Oratory

The only manmade landmark
on our maps, a weathered
rise in corbelled hills.
We pass our hands across
the rocks: rough, overlapping,
stacked foot-thick, compressed,
each weighing, bearing others
mortarless. From plinth
to pitch, the ancient vault
breathes in. The lintel squares
its shoulders, spiny corners
stretch, and gables pull
the climbing layers toward
a ridgeline, as the building
falls: the walls are sinking,
stone by separate stone.
Inside, whoever made
this shifting balance, monks
or masons, prayed. We tourists
duck to enter, straighten
near the center's space
and wait for our adjusting
sight. The room erodes
around us, watertight.

Eleanor Rees

Eleanor Rees was born in 1978 in Birkenhead,Merseyside. She has a BA in English Literature from the University of Sheffield. A collection of her poems, Feeding Fire *(Spout, Huddersfield) was published in 2001. Recently she won an Eric Gregory Award.*

Rooting

Crocuses rise in the spring-blown garden,
aware of the redbrick distance between
their earth-caught stems and shelter.
Over rain pocked soil they lean to the house,
leaves thumping like the wings of moths
summoned by the single lamp upstairs.
The lawn is puckered with grassy barrows
preserving remains of the conservatory.
Clematis clambers the barbed wire.
On the playing field beyond, dandelions
judder as east winds hit and run. Shaken,
they sit tight and track frequencies
—radio masts on the edge of classified ground
on Salisbury Plain passed once in a car.
Electric light from the window shines
over the black, wind-slammed gate. A siren.
Fire in a five-storey building across town?
The city-planned street is riddled with pipes.
A yellowed H marks the hydrant.

THE DANCE

In his jacket and neat tucked tie he is slender.
He holds my hand warmly as the child behind us dances a two-step.

Under the moon the heel of my court shoe sinks into sand
on the beach where I swirl to a whirligig tune

we all hear when the moon is full. It starts in our sleep
and then gets stealthier and the whole of town

discovers itself on the shore waltzing
to music that seeps out of cliffs beneath the house with two chimneys.

Helen has a yellow skirt tonight and hips
like a rocking horse. I watch his hand hold her

so close and smirking. We hear nothing but music,
a church organ in one of the caves, and feel no cold

or the wind that will give us all chills tomorrow when
we return home and wake fretting,

surrendering our bodies again to the sound,
sweating, staying in bed for days, almost remembering,

taking tablets and noticing in every house
our warm feet under duvets still dancing.

Fairies in the Guttering

Fairies in the guttering clamber over pigeons
as they decompose, polluting the cistern.
They are trashy these fairies;
hang out down town

in dirty rock clubs, wear bits of lace
they pretend are clothes,

and at full moon go naked,
couple in the park with elves

that live with the cider drinkers
in burrows under the community garden.

Gregorian Chants at Four in the Morning

Skulking downstairs so your parents
can't hear, we collect the cassette player
and take it to your garden where you run
an extension lead out of the garage
as I whirl over gravel

and roam with a candle among shrubs.
Recorded voices float
into the familiar night like flares
to lighten hundreds of heads
quiet on pillows. They inhale and breathe

across the city over rooftops,
chimneys, aerials, satellite dishes;
warm air carries them to docks,
past the main road where terraces
thin out as the river crawls like a bear
loping home from hunting in the hills.

At Kenwood House

The didgeridoo player says we should
go to a party at a squat in Hampstead.
A summer's day and we sunbathe
in front of the white façade at Kenwood.
There is a phantom bridge, a folly,
that leads to an island over the lake
and looks like a model with trees
made of polystyrene painted green.
A young woman with a pushchair,
and well-heeled ladies stroll by.
I blink my eyes. They wear empire line
dresses, bonnets to keep skin pale.
We lay our bodies out for the sun.
That weekend we may go to party
in a white painted mansion draped
with fairy lights, dance under chandeliers
to a quality sound system, punching fists
against a corniced ceiling.

WAITING FOR THE BLACKSMITH

Horse heat rises in the drizzle.
When it arrives the van is blue,

the blacksmith, blustery.
I stand silently by my horse

while his feet are sawn and cut.
He has foot rot,

the result of too much mud.
Molten metal fizzes sparks

when thrown suddenly
into a black bucket.

Local radio plays out of a van.
Then it is done. I ride home.

My horse lifts his feet higher
aware they are heavier.

Seventeen

I put you on the train though you woke
under a caravan in a pensioner's garden.
The police drove you home and next day
your mother made you take chocolates round.
You drank a handful of weed in a pint of water,
and misjudged distance so your head
swung low and clipped the rim
and a thin bruise creased
your forehead as we talked till last orders
and went home along the prom past
the life buoys that mark deep water.
It takes two of us to support your walk;
you cling to a lamppost, too close
to the dock and say out loud you want
the girl to help you. But I won't.

VISITATION

A land girl in the war she heard words among leaves.
When they retire to the sea she paints trees on walls
with emulsion. Pink buds in the woodchip hall
creep claw-like round the preformed plastic switch.
A shadow crawls the papered valley. Fairies,
Grandma says, walk the corridor, dour and desolate,
dragging torn satin wings along the floor.
They rub scabby backs against rough bark,
crouch and caw at visitors like ravens in the tower,
guard the door as light darkens the stained glass,
while sea at the end of the road licks its tongue
up the slipway, past a pebble-dashed hotel's neon,
to catch fishermen, tiny in green cagoules,
sat like gnomes on upturned buckets on the prom.

We close the brocade curtains to black out clouds
and sit by the three bar fire in hats and gloves,
drinking tea beneath a standard lamp's muted glow.
November and the illuminations are turned on.
As we wait for this to happen we play eye spy
and I say a word exactly as electricity brightens
bulbs hung along the front. Lit by magic?
'Living next to the power station is a good thing,'
—a family maxim—'If there's another war we'll
be the first to die.' A good thing. The red
guiding light on the station's roof flicks on and off.
The sea picks up its skirts and walks the street
to rap wet knuckles on the door. Leaves shudder.

Trunks ooze sap. The wallpaper peels in the dark.
I walk when I sleep and Grandma walks with me
telling the way. Stories are our guide through glades
of petrified wood, a forest turned to stone
under sediment, hard as steel, agate monuments
to centuries trees grew, rose and swayed into,
and lord over now; black crosses under stars.

We examine the rings in the rock that remains
realising slowly how long time took to push
back up through the earth, to reach us sheltered
under their monstrosity, the return of substance
out of nothing, after the fall out and white light.

Chris Regan

Chris Regan graduated from the University of East Anglia in 2001 after studying for a BA in Film and English Studies. During that time he was president of the Creative Writing Society. He has written three feature-length scripts as well as several shorts, some of which he has produced and directed himself.

Jenny Ringo

INT. SUPERMARKET, SHELVES—DAY

The supermarket is full of people dashing from shelf to shelf in a desperate attempt to fill up their trolleys.

Walking calmly between the shoppers is JENNY RINGO. *She is an attractive woman—twenty-three years old with long black hair. She is wearing a long, ragged black dress with huge black boots and a large tattoo running down one arm. Her eyes and mouth are painted with black make-up and she has several piercings.*

JENNY *occasionally stops to pick something from the shelves. The loud, nu-metal music she is listening to on her personal stereo provides the* OPENING THEME.

CUE OPENING TITLES:

'JENNY RINGO'

INT. SUPERMARKET, CHECKOUT—DAY

JENNY *is placing the contents of her basket onto the checkout. As she pays for them she takes out her earphones. The metal is replaced by the romantic pop song that is playing in the supermarket.* JENNY *shakes her head in disgust.*

END OPENING THEME AND TITLES

EXT. SUPERMARKET—DAY

A busy high street on a weekday afternoon. JENNY *is walking out of the supermarket carrying two full shopping bags.*

As JENNY *walks onto the street we see* ROGER *walking towards her—a tall young man in his early twenties.* ROGER *is extremely attractive, clean-shaven and floppy-haired.*

JENNY *bumps into* ROGER. *The collision sends* JENNY *to the floor, scattering the contents of her shopping bags.*

ROGER

I'm terribly sorry. Let me help you with that.

As she tries to stand, ROGER *bends down to help her and they bump heads.*

JENNY *climbs to her feet, allowing* ROGER *to pick up her shopping whilst mumbling apologies. She turns to us.*

JENNY

(*to us*)

Do you ever feel like you're stuck in a romantic comedy?

ROGER *hands* JENNY *her shopping.*

ROGER

Look, I have to make this up to you somehow. How about I buy you a drink?

JENNY *gives us an exasperated look and walks away, leaving a bemused* ROGER *behind.*

EXT. COURTYARD—DAY

The courtyard for a set of flats. JENNY *is walking across the courtyard.*

JENNY
(*to us*)
It's been like this for weeks. Every time I leave the flat I walk into a comic encounter with an attractive young bloke.

JENNY *retrieves her keys from her handbag and opens the door to her flat.*

INT. JENNY'S FLAT, STAIRS—DAY

JENNY *is climbing the stairs to her flat.*

JENNY
(*to us*)
I wouldn't mind if they weren't always so fucking boring.

JENNY *reaches the top floor and unlocks her door.*

INT. JENNY'S FLAT, KITCHEN—DAY

JENNY *steps into her kitchen. It is small and cluttered.*

JENNY
(*to us*)
I slept with a couple of them, of course.

JENNY *places one of her bags onto the kitchen table and begins to unpack it. She pulls out a packet of condoms and looks at us. She then pulls out a further five packets of condoms.*

INT. JENNY'S FLAT, LOUNGE—DAY

JENNY *steps into the lounge. It is small and full of designer furniture and tacky ornaments. Various bland paintings hang from the walls.*

JENNY *collapses onto the sofa. She lights a cigarette.*

JENNY

(*to us*)

Oh don't look at me like that. Don't tell me you wouldn't take advantage of a situation like this. And it's the principle of the thing. Some benevolent force obviously expects me to form a wacky relationship with one of these men. Cynical witch falls in love with floppy-haired English gentleman—hijinks ensue. Fuck that.

INT. JENNY'S FLAT, BEDROOM—DAY.

JENNY *walks into her bedroom. The room is a complete contrast to the rest of the flat. The walls are plastered with posters depicting various metal bands and cult movies. She has several shelves, all lined with books and CDs. There are also various candles and occult artefacts lying around—ornate daggers, pendants and figures.*

JENNY

(*to us*)

Do I look like your typical cooky rom-com heroine?

JENNY *pulls a huge, ancient-looking book off one of the shelves and begins flipping through the pages.*

JENNY

(*to us*)

Maybe I can make this clearer for you.

INT. JENNY'S FLAT, LOUNGE—DAY.

JENNY *pushes all of the furniture against the walls, clearing a space in the centre of the room.*

JENNY

(*to us*)

There was this one bloke—fuck, I can't remember his name . . . we'll call him Bastard.

INT. NIGHTCLUB—NIGHT.

A large commercial nightclub full of people. A loud dance tune infects the room. We focus on BASTARD. *He is an extremely attractive young man wearing expensive, trendy clothes.*

JENNY

(*Voice Over*)

Bastard was a bastard.

BASTARD *is watching the dance floor intently as the two attractive* WOMEN *sitting either side of him compete for his attention.*

JENNY

(*V.O.*)

I'm not going to go into the gory details of his past in an attempt to explain why.

We pull away from BASTARD *to find* JENNY *sitting on the floor of the club some distance away smoking a cigarette. She has her earphones in and we can hear the death-metal she is listening to before she takes them out to talk to us.*

JENNY

(*to us*)

Some of the stories have a kind of rock n' roll cool to them in their excess and I'm not about to make him look like a cool bastard.

INT. JENNY'S FLAT, LOUNGE—DAY

JENNY *has finished moving the furniture and has closed the curtains.*

JENNY
(*to us*)
As much as I hate to admit it, me and Bastard had quite a bit in common.

JENNY *lays the book out on the floor and pulls a large container of salt from one of the bags.*

JENNY
(*to us*)
He knew his Crowley from his Copperfield, his Ouija from his Game Of Life, his Voodoo doll from his Barbie.

INT. NIGHTCLUB, BAR—NIGHT

JENNY *pushes her way to the front of the queue.*

JENNY
(*V.O.*)
Bastard used his extensive knowledge of these most ancient and sacred arts to pull girls.

JENNY *turns and looks across the crowded room at* BASTARD *who now has a third* WOMAN *sitting opposite him.*

As JENNY *turns back to the bar* SAM *shuffles up next to her.* SAM *is slightly older than* JENNY *and wearing an excessively small red dress. She is clearly quite drunk.*

SAM
Jenny! I thought I'd lost you!

JENNY
(*to us*)
This is Sam, my flatmate.

INT. JENNY'S FLAT, LOUNGE—NIGHT.

JENNY *is sitting cross-legged on the sofa reading a comic.* SAM *is also in the room arguing with her boyfriend,* GAVIN*—twenty-six, short hair, clean-shaven. They are shouting at each other over* JENNY's *head.*

JENNY
(*to us*)
Earlier that night Sam had been arguing with her boyfriend, Gavin. I guess the best way to describe Sam and Gavin's relationship is 'loud.' When they weren't shouting death threats at each other they were fucking noisily in the bedroom next-door to mine.

INT. NIGHTCLUB, BAR—NIGHT

JENNY *pays for her drink.*

JENNY
(*to us*)
So Sam and Gavin argue and I get dragged to this shit-hole in Gavin's place.

INT. JENNY'S FLAT, LOUNGE—DAY

JENNY *is pouring the salt onto the carpet, copying the design on the open page of the book.*

JENNY
(*to us*)
Whilst I hid in a corner and tried to drink myself into a coma, Sam spent the night trying to convince herself that she could do better if she tried.

JENNY *forms a circle on the floor with the salt and proceeds to draw a pentacle inside it.*

INT. NIGHTCLUB—NIGHT
JENNY *leaves the bar and looks around for* SAM.

JENNY

(*V.O.*)

Actually, she could do a lot worse.

JENNY *looks towards* BASTARD. *The other women have gone and he is talking to* SAM *who has her arm around him.* JENNY *walks towards them.*

JENNY

(*V.O.*)

This was not a result of Bastard's overwhelming charm and good looks, this was not Love Potion Number Nine, this was nasty, evil magic at its worst.

INT. JENNY'S FLAT, LOUNGE—DAY

JENNY *has finished copying the design from the book onto the floor. She pulls five candles from one of the bags and proceeds to put them into the five candlesticks she has placed on each of the points of the pentacle.*

JENNY

(*to us*)

I know this because love spells do not work. I went through a whole string of them at high school—bad memories. However, there are spells to get people into bed with you. You can find them in old, dusty books written by mad, medieval conjurers with aching wrists and bad eyesight.

INT. NIGHTCLUB—NIGHT

JENNY *is sitting down opposite* SAM *and* BASTARD, *who are now kissing violently.* JENNY *lights a cigarette and blows smoke into them to catch their attention.* BASTARD *detaches himself from* SAM. SAM *remains frozen in the same position, her tongue still writhing around in midair.* BASTARD *calmly pushes* SAM's *tongue back into her mouth and tilts her head down to stare at the floor.*

BASTARD
(*to Jenny*)
Sorry, princess, you'll have to wait your turn.

JENNY
Leave her alone and I won't have to hurt you.

BASTARD *laughs.*

INT. JENNY'S FLAT, HALLWAY—DAY

There is a scratching at the door as JENNY *approaches. She opens it and a black cat strolls calmly into the hallway. This is* TED.

JENNY
(*to Ted*)
You're late.

INT. JENNY'S FLAT, LOUNGE—DAY

TED *sits on the sofa and washes himself.* JENNY *follows. She has finished setting out the candles and has lit them all.*

JENNY
Right, where was I?

TED *looks at her blankly.*

JENNY
(*to us*)
Oh, this is the exciting bit.

JENNY *takes a bottle of whiskey out of the bag. She opens it, drinks some and then offers the bottle to* TED. *He leaps off the sofa and sits in the corner.*

JENNY
(*to us*)
You see, I happen to know some particularly nasty magic myself. Don't try this at home, kids.

JENNY *places the open bottle in the centre of the circle.*

INT. NIGHTCLUB—NIGHT

JENNY *stands up and stubs out her cigarette in the ashtray on the table in front of her. She then tips up the ashtray and spreads the collected ash out onto the table's surface. Using her finger* JENNY *traces a symbol into the ash.*

BASTARD *watches this with an amused look on his face which changes to one of horror as* JENNY *whispers an incantation.*

JENNY
(*V.O.*)
I think he recognised a few of the words which scared him enough to let me take Sam away from him.

JENNY *pulls* SAM *to her feet and drags her out of the nightclub.*

INT. JENNY'S FLAT—DAY

JENNY *is sitting cross-legged in front of the circle with* TED *in her lap. She is reading from the book.*

JENNY
I conjure you, O unclean spirit, dragon, I adjure you by the six fiery furnaces, by the wings of the winds and by the light and the earth and all its creeping things.

JENNY *and* TED *look at the circle in expectation. After a moment* JENNY *turns to us.*

JENNY

(*to us*)

Anyway, that's it. That's the story of Bastard the bastard. Oh, you want to know what I did to him, don't you.

INT. NIGHTCLUB, TOILETS—NIGHT

BASTARD *enters the toilets and joins the line of* MEN *at the urinals. He unzips his trousers and urinates.*

JENNY

(*V.O.*)

Let's just say that the next time he went for a piss, something fell off.

There is a 'plopping' sound and BASTARD *stares into the trough at his feet in horror.*

INT. JENNY'S FLAT—DAY

JENNY *is still staring at the circle.* TED *is washing himself.*

JENNY

(*to us*)

So you see, I am not the kind of girl you want in your sweet little romantic comedy.

JENNY *looks at her watch.*

JENNY

Come on, Suzi, where the fuck are you?

The candles suddenly flare up into huge flames as the room rapidly becomes darker. A grotesque figure appears in the centre of the circle, obscured by the flames. This is SUCAX.

SUCAX

Who dares summon Sucax, Marquis of the Mad,

Duke of the Damned, Lord of the . . . oh, it's you.

JENNY

Hello, Suzi. I thought you might fancy going for a drink.

Sarah Ridgard

Sarah Ridgard studied history at the London School of Economics. After graduating, she worked for voluntary agencies in London and Oxford, and taught English in Spain and Japan. She now lives in Norwich.

Suffolk Lace

(extract from a novel)

I should never have started doing it. You see things you shouldn't when you crawl around in ditches. I used to be afraid that if I fell off my bike, or tripped and fell, that I'd crack my head open and they'd spill out everywhere. The stuff I knew, the secrets. That they'd lie on the road in shock for a moment, trying to get their bearings, until some got caught up in a gust of wind, others crawling off under hedges, into ditches, to wash up in people's back gardens, or in the gutter outside the village shop for all to see.

'Norman, you'll never guess what I've just heard.' Mrs G would step back indoors from the garden where a secret has just landed on her purple sprouting broccoli like a Red Admiral. 'Pam has been carrying on with Bernie from the garage. For years apparently. They were seen in the back of a Ford van brought in for repairs from out Bedfield way. And there was me feeling sorry for her, all that trouble she was having with her electrics.' Or further up the road by the council houses a gang of kids would be skipping and chanting, 'Hubert Ling wears girls clothes, Hubert Ling's a girlie.'

I knew about Pam and Bernie long before anyone else. I'd seen them a couple of miles out of Worlingworth, parked up in a lay-by one evening. You couldn't see them from the road. The ford van was on the concrete next to the ditch, hidden behind a twenty foot high pile of sugar beet. I was walking the ditches in Starvelark field on my way back home, stepping over the cooker that somebody had tipped down there months ago, now invisible in the dark. I was on a level with the van's tyres, the suspension. The near right looked a bit soft as the van rocked around, its chassis creaking, the springs pinging up and down like it was a dog flea with its feet stuck down. I wanted a thumb to come out of the sky and squish it or drown it, burn it with a match. He didn't do that to me, Bernie Spink. He didn't make the car rock and roll for me. He'd given me a lift straight home after pushing into me against rubbish bins out the back of the village hall.

There's a stack of them in my head, secrets and stuff, solid up to the roof like hundreds of straw bales wedged-in tight. Take one or two out from the bottom and they'll all come tumbling down, bales exploding all over the place like when you cut the bailer twine if they've been bailed too tight and the straw busts out of the middle, becomes twice, three times the size, dust flying up everywhere.

I set the sack of spuds down in the back porch. A sack of Saxons. She won't have Maris Pipers in the house any more.

'It's me.' I shout to Mum through the kitchen door. It couldn't be anyone else, now it's just the two of us, but she likes me to shout out, just in case.

She's in the kitchen frying pork sausages, moving them around with a plastic spatula. She's not in a good way. The pads of her fingers are looking sore.

'What have I been saying? Look at that,' she says, pointing the spatula at the window frame. The blue bottles are spread thick on the flypaper that hangs at the kitchen window above the sink. They've been muck spreading around us this week, the flies worse than usual. 'There's a new one, look. Another blummen crack,' she says.

Big cracks already run down the outside of the house from the roof to the tops of the windows. 'Not built to last,' Mum says. Sometimes I wonder if me and Dad loosened it, the render, by using the back corner wall for all that bashing. Maybe it was us two that made the first crack appear. I want to pick at it sometimes, see if it'll come off in slabs like icing.

Our house sits on the side of this road, out here in the middle of nowhere. Three miles to Worlingworth one way, three miles to Framlingham the other. Sometimes it looks more like a brown concrete dolls' house in the middle of all these fields and sky. Big open Suffolk fields. A prairie desert, some people round here call it. You can see for miles now they've taken out all the hedges and trees. The fields are brown right now. Should be turning pale green in a month or two, winter barley out back, early wheat over the road. The best time is when Carver plants rape. Some people moan about it, say it stinks. But it's worth it, just for the few weeks it brightens the place up. The rooms all shine bright yellow. It's like sitting in the middle of a seabed, the tide all gone out as far as you can see. And beans. The bean flowers are something to look forward to, the way their smell fills the house, takes away the sour smell of jumble, as if we've put everything through the wash. I used to love peas, the smell of them in the air and the sound of the pea harvesters through the night. It was like town noise, their headlights flashing on my bedroom ceiling as if we were next to a busy road. They don't grow them round here anymore. You see them more on the other side of the A12 around Saxmundham, Leiston way. Anyway, Mum doesn't like having peas in the house. Peas or Maris Pipers.

She says one day the house will get ploughed in, ploughed under, taking us with it. I don't like the way she says 'us'.

The electricity pylons are the only other things out here besides the two of us. They march over the fields from Sizewell, thirteen miles of pylons, coming right past the end of our garden before disappearing out on the horizon. I listen to them humming at night, thinking of Nana being on the end of them. Or rather at the start of them. It's a comfort, lying in bed, thinking she's just up the line. When the wires go quiet, I get worried. Think I must go over and see how she is. Check she hasn't electrocuted herself, that she isn't lying in a zigzag shape on her front room carpet, her legs all busted up beneath her. Other times, foggy wet nights, the wires crack and spit, and I know she's fine. Back to her old ways, working on something new.

'Elmy Gobbit came in the shop today,' I tell Mum. 'He asked after you.'

'Oh?' She waits for me to go on.

'Black trousers and a grey shirt, collarless, with a waistcoat.'

He'd caught me up a stepladder this morning.

'Now there's a sight for sore eyes,' he said. 'You look as if you could pull a plough without breaking sweat from where I'm standing.

If I were only twenty years younger . . .'

Daphne pushed him away, telling him he was a dirty old goat and he only made things worse by teasing me.

'Anyone else?' Mum asks.

I don't tell her about Frieda. Frieda Creasey in a white tee shirt with blue and silver flowers on the front, a tight skirt all bellied out, and bare legs that look like a pair of cod fillets.

I had to get away, get into the stockroom when she came in at the far end of the shop, but not before I'd smelt the sour beer on her and she'd managed to shout, 'How's your mother, Desiree?', holding a bag of Birds Eye frozen peas out with one hand. She always swipes one out of the freezer when she sees it's me serving.

I want to shut her mouth, with the bag rammed in tight, shut her up for good. Instead I'm forced to ask after Tina, her daughter. It's the only way to make her set the peas down, to make her look away for a moment, so I can disappear into the stockroom.

'Daphne says her boy knows the London people who've just bought the barn over at Hubbard's place.' I have to shout over the noise of Mum's frying. 'He did some work with the bloke years ago up Sizewell. Some nuclear engineer brought in specially from London.' She turns round triumphant.

'What do I say?' Mum waves the spatula at me. 'I tell you, it's getting smaller every day.'

I tell her that to brighten her up. She gets hopeful when people say, 'it's a small world'. On the telly, the radio, up the shops in Fram.

'No, but it really is,' she says. 'It *is* getting smaller every day, don't you think?' And she'll go on and on about it, and if she's saying it to someone she hasn't met before, some of the new people in the village, or tourists in Fram, their faces start to change. They'll be all friendly at first, nodding and smiling, then they start to edge away when she talks about Holland sliding up the Orwell, Portugal coming up the Bristol Channel.

'The Japanese are getting closer,' she said last week, 'they've reached as far as Fram.' That was the last time she went out, when I dropped her off there for a jumble sale. She'd been in the Co-op afterwards when a couple of Japanese kids came in. They kept on after rice, 'white rice, white rice,' to the lad stacking the shelves, so Mum says. They must be from the College, there's a ton of them up there now. Sometimes I think Mum really believes they've stepped out of their front doors in Tokyo, taken a wrong turn and found themselves in Fram Co-op or stuck in a queue by the fish van in the market square.

Most evenings she kneels in front of the globe that sits in the front room next to the television. Dad got it for her from a car boot at Wickham Market. It's twice the size of a beach ball. She spends most evenings spinning it, slowly at first, braking, measuring, then spinning again. Recently she's taken to flashing it round and round so fast it looks about ready to fly off its axis.

She wants to wake up one day and see a new place out the back door. Paris, Lisbon, Reykjavik, the suburbs of Tehran. She'd probably settle for somewhere like Diss, just to see it out there instead of fields and pylons, somewhere she can walk to.

For a long time it was Iceland. This was about the time she started going on about driving lessons. The globe always stopped on Iceland, and she would tell us about geysers, and couldn't Dad teach her. Dad said he didn't have the time, they couldn't afford lessons or the risk of her wearing out the clutch on the Morris Marina. I heard her mutter then that she wished she'd gone to Iceland.

⋆

Mum used to love telling us the story, about the time she had to stay in Ipswich Hospital for a week. Being on the top floor of Heath Road, a view all over the town, the multistorey, Greyfriars and Portman Road. There were nurses and people everywhere, coming and going, everyone asking how she was, how the baby was doing. Then she and Dad came home from the hospital with their baby boy all bundled up in a pale yellow cot blanket against the November cold. They hadn't got a clue about names. He left the hospital as Baby White. Nana was already there, tidying the house for Mum, getting tea ready. Then as Dad opened the door to the back porch to let Mum go in first, she tripped against the sack of spuds that usually sat under the porch shelf. Mother and Baby White went flying and would have gone through the glass window of the back door if it hadn't been for Nana. She'd seen the car pull up and opened the door just in time for Mum and baby to fall into her arms. And as Dad was cursing and kicking the spuds out of the way, a sack of King Edwards, Mum said, 'Edward, that's a nice name. Why don't we call him Edward?' She only dropped the 'King' under protest from Dad, but there he was. Their baby potato. Edward White. But it started something. Because when I was born, the middle one, there was a sack of Desirees under the same shelf in the porch. And by the time Piper came along, they were halfway through a sack of Maris Pipers. So there we were, the spud family. 'Funny thing is,' Mum said, 'after naming Edward, he did look like a potato. He kind of grew into one. All pink and arms flailing like tubers.' He became his name. So did Piper in a way. I'm still waiting for it to happen to me.

Mum later tried to edit the story. She tried to get rid of Nana and her open arms, but left in the bit about how it had been Nana who had pulled the sack out in the first place, to get at the large bakers at the bottom, leaving it right there in the middle of the porch. It didn't work. We all remembered Nana's arms, how she used to come to our house, and that suddenly one day she stopped coming. There was no more tea and chessboard cake. Nana and Mum stopped phoning and speaking to each other. They both said it was nothing. But then nothing had obviously been something. For a start it was around that time when Mum refused to have any more Maris Pipers in the house. Anything which was something tended to be nothing after that.

That's how we all worked it out. Nothing ever happened to us, out here in this nothing place. Then I picked May blossom that spring. I wasn't thinking but I should have known better. May blossom, burning alder, killing robins. I'd heard it all often enough.

It was up by the Lings' place, about half a mile out of the village on the way out towards Horham. Some people think it's not healthy, when they hear about the Lings at World's End. Though it's usually only the people from the new estates who talk about them.

'What do they get up to in there? Three brothers and a sister living together like that. It's not right. It's not normal.' But they don't get up to much, keep themselves to themselves. Ivy keeps house for them, walks the half mile to the village shop, lugging a basket on wheels behind her. The brothers, Walter, Albert and Hubert look after the cows and hens. Elmy Gobbit says they used to keep pigs in the top field, that there used to be some rare old times hog riding in there. The place is a lot smaller than it used to be, but Hubert still runs away from women.

'Always been terrified of them,' says Elmy, 'every single woman, except for Ivy.'

There's a narrow ditch that runs away from the road alongside the hen field, overshadowed by a thick hedge of hazel and hawthorn. It was a good place to go down. Dark and deep, running past the barns and the house. The Ling brothers all looked the same from that level. Tall beaky men, with noses that dripped dewdrops in winter. They wore grey-green overcoats tied round the waist with bailer twine which only seemed to come off around June time and were always back on by the middle of September. Ivy was the colourful one, wearing summer frocks even in January. Her arms looked red raw as she walked round the hen huts collecting eggs, her legs covered with a red rash up one side. Fen leg. I recognised it even at forty yards. Nana said that's why we shouldn't sit so close to the fire, especially me if I was ever going to wear frocks like Ivy.

I watched them till the lights went on in the kitchen, could hear Walter calling out for Hubert.

'You out there Hubert? Come on in, it's time.'

The kitchen curtains were drawn, through which it was possible to see only the neon striplights. Leaning against the bank of the ditch, I thought about the ways to go in. Through the keyhole, maybe the crack under the back door, or riding in on the back of the farm cat, taking up a position next to the ticks on her ears.

'Come on in. It's time.'

Hubert was laying his collection of feathers back between two bottom bales in the barn. Susan and Frank were his birds. Arabian Peacocks. They shone out amongst the grey Marrans, flying onto the roof of the house every morning as they did, calling out and setting off the cockerels at farms for miles around.

Walter, being the eldest, was the one who put the records on every Saturday evening. He wore his best Sunday suit, his sister wore her dress and mother's stole. He would take her by the hand and they would begin to dance while Albert danced with Hubert.

Hubert wore a dress. He had to if he wanted to join in. But then he danced with Albert only on condition he could wear one of Frank's feathers in his cap.

He'd mucked up the patterning being the last born and a boy.

Mother would poke him in the chest sometimes.

'I wanted you to be a girl,' she would whisper. 'I used to watch you in the cradle and pray to God, please let him grow some little bubs, turn him into a girl.'

She wanted more women, more than just her and Ivy in a houseful of men. Her husband was pleased though. More help around the place. He didn't like the way she dressed Hubert up in girls' clothes but he let it pass. To keep the peace. To stay close in bed to her after their dancing on Saturday nights, when the rest of the house was asleep.

Silent squabbling about hen feed, the milk fats would stop as the brothers and sister danced under neon striplights, stiffly at first, their bones popping and cracking, before loosening up, sweet sherry on their breath.

KATHRYN SIMMONDS

Kathryn Simmonds was born in Hertfordshire in 1972. She worked in publishing then travelled for a year before coming to UEA. In 2002 she received an Eric Gregory Award.

RODIN'S LOVERS INTERRUPT THEIR KISS

I slid my hand from her marble thigh,
removed my tongue from her mouth
and opening my eyes found someone
leaning close enough to brush us
with his lips. Stepping down, I circled
him. My love drew back her hair
to press an ear against his heart.
We turned our heads, saw other scattered
strangers dotting space. Hand-in-hand
we crossed the polished floor to study them;

the grave-eyed loners, slope-armed lovers,
crocodiles of children charmed to statues
in school uniform. I touched a face in flower
beneath a canvas sun. Beyond the door
another world revolved through segments
made of glass. Traffic streaked and stopped
in front of watercolour lights which blurred
from red to green, then back again.
A ribbon of brown river wound away.
Her fingers fell from mine so gently
I could hardly feel their absence afterwards.

SOME DAY MY PRINCE WILL COME

This is my song, the guaranteed request.
Once upon a time I trilled it in a little-girl
falsetto—long before I knew that charm
wears thin and handsome men steal more
than just a kiss or two. The cigarettes
and Stolichnayas took their toll:
I dropped an octave, learned to scat,
let Miles Davis lead me to a kingdom
of his own. He rearranged the melody;
what's left is something short of melancholy
—not hope, and yet not quite regret.

Tonight I'm perched in spotlight on a stool.
My skin is white as powder will allow.
My hair is bottled ebony. The audience is full
of men who princes trample on. Their faces rise
from late-night smoke. The bashful ones
who catch your eye and blush. The balding,
lost and loveless ones. The dopes. All my life
I've heard them whistling home from work
to keep their spirits up. And when I sing
they nod in time, as if to reassure themselves
there might be someone waiting to be found.

Judas

I looked down on the city, small and picture-still.
My shirt clung damp against my back. No breeze.
No stars. The bitter scent of olive trees,

their callused branches old as Abraham.
I wanted to fall into them and weep. Instead
I sat considering the thing I'd done. My head

was full of Him. At supper, when He said to me
act quickly, I got up and left them sharing wine,
crossed silver streets, deciding on a sign

that would deliver Him. I put my cold lips
to his cheek and in that moment knew
I sealed a covenant that nothing could undo:

I was the chosen one and yet He still
proclaimed it better I had not been born.
I watched the night dissolve until a red dawn

split the sky. Without me, He'd be just another man
of minor miracles. At once I saw our destinies;
our bodies hanging from their separate trees.

TURNING JOHN

At three a.m. we trail silence through swing doors
to find him gurgling in a dream, breathing
like a snorkeller.

The night is flannel-hot. We wake him, whispering
his name until he flounders up to us,
hauled from sleep.

Our gloved hands feel beneath his bones
as we prepare to pass his weight
between us in the dark;

and it is agony, although we try to calm ourselves
by soothing him, the fact that he
is still a man is agony.

His ribs expand for air and when we lift he barks
across the night, a seal that we cannot
deliver to the sea.

News From Home

Are there new Lears outside the tube? Write down
their rage. Point out the market's latest tat,
give me a flash of gold-watched touts, a snatch
of chatter in a queue. Then lead me through

the Underground and let me rise to streets
where adolescents flirt and fight, jeans slung
from their skinny hips. Repeat their slang.
Record their songs. Remind me what I miss.

Send hubcaps from wet taxis, and the top
deck of a London bus. Send chimney-stacks,
bright plastic bags, but most of all send this:
an envelope of English sky, stamped with

a pale sun and franked with blackbird wings,
the seal on tightly folded winter days.

OCTOBER CLOCKS

The clocks have leapt towards the dark
and now the sad time comes too soon,
the daylight changes to a private sodium,
curtains screen the flickering of other lives.

The night my father died, they put his things
into a plastic bag, his wedding ring cut off
and given to my mother; two cold halves
of gold sealed in an envelope. His watch

I swallowed whole—it breaks apart inside me
as I walk from work, the cogs and springs
that measured out his life whir out of sync.
I pause beside the railway bridge to see
the little town mapped out with pins of light.
A train gasps from a tunnel and is gone.
The moon accompanies me home,
incomplete, whiter than a clock-face.

Natasha Soobramanien

Natasha Soobramanien was born in 1971. She lives in Norwich. The Gift *is an extract from her first novel.*

The Gift

That's London, Paul said, leaning across me with all his weight, pointing down to the sticky patches of light on the ground below. Looks like God's been gobbing.

Mam would normally have snapped at him for that malpropté, but she seemed not to be aware of anything around her. When the plane began to tremble and shudder in anticipation of its landing, Mam seemed equally apprehensive, leaning further back into her seat and gripping the armrests as though trying to resist the inevitable descent.

We had been flying for hours over an empty grey desert. When I pointed it out to Paul, he grabbed my head—still annoyed that I had been given the window seat—and pushed my face up to the glass. I realised then it wasn't glass at all, but plastic.

You idiot, he said, that's the wing of the plane.

I can't remember getting to the house. Perhaps we took a taxi from the airport. And then, when we finally swung into this wet, leafy street and stopped outside the front door, perhaps I was asleep; perhaps I was carried down the path, up the steps, into our new home in London, Paul following behind, rubbing his eyes and fighting his tiredness.

And now, twenty years later, I'm back, standing outside our old house in Tufnell Park, a narrow Victorian terraced house barely distinguishable from the others crowded around it. I'm standing here staring up at the blank windows because Paul has gone and I don't know where to find him.

*

We lived on the ground floor with Grandpère, Grandmère and our uncle Daniel. Sometimes, if Daniel was studying in the front room or Mam was having a lie-down with one of her books or her headaches, Paul and I would play in the corridor, which smelt of old newspapers and the cold air from outside. We would crunch in to dust the dead leaves which had drifted in by the door, or play post office with the pile of mail for ex-tenants who had left no forwarding address.

I was five and Paul was ten, a difference which Paul resented but was forced to overlook for the sake of company. We were in between schools then, and had no friends; only each other.

The front room where Paul and I spent most of our time had orange walls and a bay window looking out onto the gloomy front garden—a patch of long grass and a dustbin, closed in by an overgrown hedge. I remember looking out there once and seeing between the clumps of dark weeds a clutch of daffodils which had seemingly appeared overnight. I was shocked by their waxy brightness. I pointed them out to Paul and suggested we pick them but he said, no, it was a stupid idea. And then later, when Grandmère was kneeling at my feet with a mouthful of pins, taking up the hem of my dress, I heard the front door click and saw Paul go out into the garden and scavenge for the daffodils. I cried out and tried to run after him but Grandmère had me pinned in place.

Reste tranquil, ta.

I could do nothing while I watched Paul tug up the daffodils. I saw him carry an armful back into the house. He went into Mam's room. I heard her tell him off for picking them.

You should leave beautiful things where you find them, Mam said, they're all going to die now.

The front room where we played was also where we slept, along with Grandmère and Daniel. Paul and I slept in the sofa-bed with Grandmère, and each night she would patiently bear our squabbling over the squashy pillow until Daniel called out to us in the dark from his corner, Come on, pack it in you two. The sheets were a soft, brushed cotton, which always felt warm when I first got into bed, a grubby familiar warmth, as though someone else had just been there.

Every morning, when the sun rose and set the orange walls on fire, I would pad across the prickly carpet in my bare feet and climb into Daniel's bed. We would lie there staring up at the ceiling together as though contemplating the night sky and my heart would rise like a balloon. We had long aimless conversations: I would ask him how thunderstorms happened; for stories about my dad, and Paul's, or why a chair was called a chair. From the other side of the room Paul would say, Don't you talk about my dad.

I was sure for a long time that Daniel was Jesus with his long hair, his odd beauty (Chinese bones, Creole skin, Indian eyes—green eyes), and the righteous anger that was never directed at me. He was surely the Lord we had learnt of in the Bible classes Grandmère took us to, the Lord I would draw portraits of obsessively until Mam got angry and shouted at Grandmère and Grandmère stopped taking us to church.

As Daniel and I lay there in bed, I stroked his smooth brown skin, tweaked his chocolate button nipples and tugged lightly at the hairs in his armpits which were tough and silky like the fibres from the corncobs Grandmère would strip and boil for us. I asked, Why don't you come to church with us? He laughed and tightened the arm he had around me.

Christian in French is chrétien, he said, which sounds a bit like cretin to me.

I wasn't sure what he meant but whenever Daniel laughed, I laughed. And Paul, from across the room said, Why are you laughing? You don't even understand what he's saying.

I asked Daniel if he would ever get married.

Oh I don't think so, he said. Maybe when I'm ninety.

I would have preferred him to say no outright, but ninety seemed quite far away.

How old are you now? I asked.

Twenty-two.

It takes a long time to count from 22 to 90, I said.

And then I offered to marry him. Paul laughed nastily. He chucked aside the squashy pillow and ran across the room which was skewered with sunlight. He kicked Daniel's bed and told me I was stupid, that you couldn't marry your uncle. Daniel said, Relax, she's only little. Then Paul called Daniel a pervert. This is how it usually ended: with Paul getting angry and calling us names. And then Daniel would say something like, Shut up you little shit. And then Paul would go running to Mam's room next door saying, Mam! Daniel said shut up you little shit. Then we would hear Mam sigh and rise heavily out of bed and come into the room and tell me to go down and ask Grandmère to give me my wash.

On his days off from the Poly, Daniel would take us for walks around the neighbourhood.

Let's go popom, he said, and Paul would screw up his face at this babyish corruption of alle promner—to go for a walk. But still he raced to pull on his shoes and jiggle his piggy bank for leftover pocket money—supplemented by Daniel—to spend on flying saucers or comics or football stickers on the way to the park, where he and I would play on the slide (Paul throwing himself down headfirst), while Daniel read his paper.

We would walk under the trees along St George's Avenue, the pavement wet from recent rain but still crusted here and there with stubborn little lumps of dog shit. Swinging from Daniel's hand, I would point these out to him.

How helpful, he said, thank you, Genie. You have a special doo-dar.

What are you on about? asked Paul.

A dog-do radar: doo-dar.

And then Daniel began to make a sound like a police siren: doo-dar doo-dar, which I would repeat on pointing out further trouble spots. Paul pulled up the hood of his anorak, head down, hands deep in pockets and dropped back a few paces, even though he had no friends here to witness his shame.

It was at the park that I first saw blossom. It was a scruffy little park, its tough grass matted with dog shit, but by the playground area was a little hill crowded with apple trees. When Daniel took us there one Easter, I was shocked to see these trees in blossom: thick fistfuls of creamy, foamy blossom spilling from the branches. I thought I would explode, felt I had to do something because it was so beautiful. I ran up the hill and Paul followed me, clambering into one of the trees. From where I stood looking up at him, the sky was full of the stuff. Paul wrenched off handfuls of it and threw it at me, laughing as the crushed petals whirled about me like snowflakes. And then Paul, taking pity on me, seeing how badly I wanted to possess these blossoms, broke off what seemed like huge branches of it, which I dragged behind me back home, refusing Daniel's offer to carry them. And then later Mam had followed this trail of shredded petals to the branches under Daniel's bed and slapped me round the legs with one of them—for making a mess, for damaging the tree.

Some months after we had come to live here, Daniel came home from Poly and told us that he was getting married. He winked at me but I felt he had bitten through my heart. I noticed that my mother was hesitant with her congratulations.

Faire attention li pas envie gagne ene passeport anglais, ta.

Watch out that she's not just after a British passport.

This on hearing that he was marrying a Mauritian girl he had met at the Poly. Fanchette was only here for her studies. Daniel told us the moment when he had fallen for her: they had been kidding about in the lab, sharing their newly-discovered Mauritiusness, when he had asked her if she could do the Sega.

Qui to croire?

What do you think?

And there, in the lab, she had danced one for him.

I tugged at Mum's sleeves and asked her to show me how it was done.

You couldn't dance it, she said sharply, you need hips.

And then she softened and told me all about the Sega. How it was danced by the slaves on the beaches of Mauritius at night to cheer themselves up.

We have slave blood, she said.

Grandpère's skin was grey-brown and dusty, with a light white scurf like the bloom on old chocolate. Grandpère had psoriasis. He used special cream on it which made him smell unfriendly. He was on long-term sick leave from London Underground so he sat at home all day in his chair in the kitchen, watching TV and drinking rum. When I saw him sober, he seemed as foreign to me as he did when he spoke in English. When he stood up he had the grand proportions of a monument but when he walked he staggered like a man caught in a gale. Paul and I were scared of Grandpère.

Grandpère did not make it to the wedding ceremony, but was waiting for us at the hall when we arrived for the reception. He had appointed himself barman and was serving drinks at the trestle table in the hall. We took our seats at the top table without him. The tablecloths were decorated with marguerites and asparagus ferns. Mam fussed over them to make sure they were not wilting, and when I asked how the flowers had appeared there, Mam told me she had taken them from the garden and sewn them on herself. Paul tugged at Mam's sleeve.

Mam, Mam. You said you should leave beautiful things where they were, or they would die.

What are you talking about? Mam snapped.

Paul turned on his heels and ran into the crowds of guests who were milling about, looking for their place settings.

Later, at the buffet table, Grandmère nudged Mam and nodded at the biryani she was spooning onto my plate.

Li parait un peu lourd, non?

It looks a bit heavy, don't you think?

Mam asked who'd made it. Grandmère pursed her lips and tilted her head in the direction of a large Creole woman in a tiny pink pillbox hat: Fanchette's aunt. While Mam was sighing and reassuring Grandmère that, yes, her biryani was much lighter, we heard a commotion at the top table.

Aiyo!

I followed Mam who had gone up to see what the fuss was about. Fanchette was trying to calm her aunt who had lifted the pink veil away from her large damp face. She was shaking her head and asking what kind of person would do such a thing.

Pas tracasse, Tante Mireille, li pas grave.

Don't worry about it, Auntie Mireille, it's nothing.

Someone had bitten off the head of the bride figurine on the wedding cake. Mam took me roughly by the elbow and sat me back down. Was that you? she hissed in my ear. No, I squealed, shocked. I would never have done that. It seemed like such an act of violence to me. Then Mam looked up and narrowed her eyes,

Kot to frère?

Where's your brother?

I was sent to look for him. I looked all around the hall but I could not see him. Walking past the kitchen, at the back of the hall, I heard shouting. The door was ajar. I looked in to see Grandpère slumped in a chair, long legs splayed out, with Daniel astride him, shouting into his face and gripping Grandpère's wrists to restrain him. Daniel was crying. I couldn't hear what they were shouting about but I knew that I shouldn't be seen here. I went back to the table and sat down quietly next to Mam. I put my head into her lap and sobbed. She gently pushed me aside, anxious for her new silk dress.

From that night on, everything was different. Daniel and Fanchette were staying in a bedsit they had rented in Camden. That night, Grandpère slept in Daniel's bed. Paul and I were supposedly asleep when Daniel and Tonton Serge brought Grandpère in. They staggered under the dead weight of him, a limp crucifix, and lay him on the bed. There was a business-like tone in Daniel's voice that I had not heard before.

Met li lors so cote, tenshion li touffé si li malade a soir.

Put him on his side, so that he doesn't choke if he vomits in the night.

After they had left the room and switched the light off, I began to cry quietly.

You better get used to it, Paul said.

I had no idea he was still awake. Something in his voice crackled like static electricity,

Daniel's going back to Mauritius with her.

The next day, when Paul and I went with Grandmère to visit the newlyweds in Camden, we sat on the bed while Daniel sat in the only armchair with Fanchette on his lap.

A week later, after Daniel and Fanchette had left for Mauritius, Grandpère came into the front room.

Allez vini! Nous pou alle promner

Come on you lot, we're going out.

This was the first time Grandpère had ever taken us out, and we trailed silently behind him out of the house and down the road, apprehensive about where he could be taking us. We crossed Junction Road to Tufnell Park tube station and went down in the lift, from which we emerged into what seemed to me the belly of a giant vacuum cleaner.

We got out at Embankment and walked alongside the Thames, Paul leaning over every now and then to look down at the water, while Grandpère swaggered a way in front, his long legs incapable of taking smaller steps to accommodate us. Soon, we saw him stop and we caught up with him. I looked up and saw the flaky bark of the plane trees.

Look, he said, look at that.

He was pointing to a great concrete column. An obelisk.

Cleopatra's Needle.

He read the plaque aloud in his stiff, heavily accented English, and I understood little of what he was saying. I did not know who Cleopatra was. I did not know why she had given Britain a needle. I did not think it looked much like a needle. I looked at Paul but his face was turned in the opposite direction. I followed his gaze to a hotdog stand across the road. Paul stared at it meaningfully, willing Grandpère to notice, his nose lifted to the breeze, smelling the onions.

We might have been passing en route to some more exciting spectacle but the memory ends there, on the banks of the grey-brown Thames, the water churned up by the autumn wind, with Grandpère lurching around, his arms thrown wide, laughing,

Ki commeraz cadeau! Ene cadeau fesse!

What kind of a bloody stupid gift is that?

Later that night, through Grandpère's snores, I heard Paul cry. I slipped my hand into his. He did not push it away.

KIM UPTON

Kim Upton was born in Norfolk and now lives in Cambridgeshire. She writes comedy/drama for screen and is inspired by the cinematic works of Alan Bennett.

SHOPPING FOR ENGLAND

FADE IN

EXT. CITY CENTRE STREET—DAY (RACE DAY, PRESENT)

The screen has a date at the bottom left corner. A red spot and the abbreviation 'rec' are in the top right corner as though it was being recorded live. (This exists for all 'race day, present' scenes.)

The street is cordoned off with crowds of people behind barriers. In front of the barriers a TV INTERVIEWER *(40s, sheepskin coat) thrusts a microphone at the face of* NIKKI *(20s, short hair, competitor's bib on top of ordinary clothes). She gasps for breath.*

NIKKI
It's the taking part that counts.

TV INTERVIEWER
By my reckoning, that was a personal best.

NIKKI
That's great. I couldn't have hoped for anything more.

In the background another COMPETITOR *crosses a line carrying many bags and is swamped by people. The crowd cheer.*

TV INTERVIEWER

How did it come about? What got you started?

NIKKI *frowns as she recollects.*

INT. LOUNGE—DAY (PAST)

The lounge has Ikea based décor. ANDY *(20s, neat, unremarkable) sits on a sofa flicking TV channels with a remote control. He is fed up. He drinks the last of a can of beer, scrunches the tin and throws it at the TV.*

He hears the sound of the front door shutting and footsteps. He doesn't look up. NIKKI *(who has long hair in all 'past' scenes) staggers in through the lounge door, laden with shopping.*

ANDY

The football results are over.

NIKKI *drops the bags.*

We're supposed to be going out tonight.

He turns round and sees the mountain of bags.

Jesus Christ!

(*beat*)

You've shopped for bloody England!

NIKKI *picks out a small box from the large bags.*

NIKKI

I bought you this.

ANDY *raises his eyes to the heavens.*

EXT. CITY CENTRE STREET—DAY (RACE DAY, EARLIER)

The race finishing line is now a start line. People are behind the barriers shouting encouragement. Eight competitors stand behind the line, each with numbered bibs, envelope and a handbag, including JES *(20s, gay, wearing a gaudy belt).* NIKKI *is in the centre. She stands next to* JES. *They all flex their arms and legs nervously.*

JES
(*to* NIKKI)
New hair-do?

NIKKI
Short helps reduce wind resistance.

An OFFICIAL *walks along the line checking their feet are behind it. A* TV CAMERAMAN *(with camera) films them.*

OFFICIAL
You have your list of five items. Four are as prescribed. The fifth is of your own choice. You must spend exactly five hundred pounds. You are not allowed to buy more than one item from any one shop. No cheating.
(*beat*)
One new rule for the final. You cannot buy shoes.

One COMPETITOR *passes out. She is carried away by St John's Ambulance first-aiders.*

JES
There but for the grace of God.

He strokes his belt.

The OFFICIAL *stands at the side with a starting pistol in the air. Each competitor holds their envelope, poised ready to open it. The* OFFICIAL*'s finger twitches at the trigger. The competitor nearest him (*COMPETITOR 1*) begins to tear her envelope open just before the pistol goes off. The pistol goes off again and all the competitors stop and look at each other. The*

OFFICIAL *points at* COMPETITOR 1. *She screams and cries. She is removed.*

JES *looks at the remaining competitors.*

JES
(*to* NIKKI)
It's between you and me, babe.

The remaining competitors line up their envelopes again. The pistol goes off. JES *and* NIKKI *tear open their envelopes.* NIKKI *scans hers.*

NIKKI
Hmm. Not bad.

JES
Yes! Number four. Men's black leather belt with a square diamante buckle.

He dances round with a big hip wiggle.

NIKKI
Like there's millions of those.

JES
Nikki, my favourite shop? Duh?

The other competitors run past them.

I'm going to win. I'm going to be famous. I'm going to be on Parkinson.

JES *grabs* NIKKI *to dance with her in anticipated celebration. She pushes him away with a determined look.*

EXT. CITY CENTRE STREET—DAY (RACE DAY, PRESENT)
The INTERVIEWER *points the microphone at* NIKKI. *The shot drifts off and focuses on a* YOUNG WOMAN's *cleavage. There is a tapping*

sound and the shot whizzes back to NIKKI *and the* INTERVIEWER. *The* INTERVIEWER *pulls a 'grow up' face at the camera.*

TV INTERVIEWER

Was the training gruelling?

NIKKI

Oh, yeah. I've been on a strict diet.

INT. BEDROOM—NIGHT (PAST)

NIKKI *climbs into bed with* ANDY. *She is wearing a silk camisole and underwear. She turns out the light and turns on her side.* ANDY*'s hand reaches over to stroke her. She moves it back. He tries again. She turns the light on and gets out of bed. She disappears from view.*

NIKKI *returns wearing a full length brushed cotton passion-killer nightdress with a high collar. She climbs into bed and switches out the light.*

ANDY*'s hand creeps over again.*

NIKKI

Andy!

ANDY

What?

NIKKI

It's the semi-finals tomorrow.

ANDY *punches the pillow in frustration.*

EXT. SHOPPING CENTRE—DAY (RACE DAY, EARLIER)

NIKKI *is in the race. She comes out of a shop with two shopping bags. She checks her watch. She sees* COMPETITOR 2 *jogging past with no shopping bags and a worried expression.* NIKKI *gives a self-satisfied smile.*

INT. LOUNGE—DAY (PAST)

ANDY *puts a telephone down and drops onto the sofa. He stares at a blank TV screen.* NIKKI *bursts in.*

NIKKI

I did it! I did it! I made the final!

ANDY

Is that all you ever think about?

NIKKI

No.

She jumps on him straddling him.

I am so horny.

He pushes her away. She nibbles his ear.

ANDY

My mum's got cancer.

NIKKI

We can still have a shag, can't we?

EXT. CITY CENTRE STREET—DAY (RACE DAY, PRESENT)

JES *runs behind* NIKKI *happily waving at the camera.*

TV INTERVIEWER

There he is.

He signals for JES *to come over.*

JES

In a minute. I've got some magic to perform with a test tube.

He hastily hides a small packet in his pocket. The TV INTERVIEWER *looks confused.*

NIKKI

He means a urine sample.

TV INTERVIEWER

(*to camera*)

We'll edit that. Where were we?

He pulls NIKKI *back to the microphone.*

A couple of competitors haven't finished. Did you ever think that you wouldn't make it?

NIKKI

I hit the wall after I'd bought three of the items on my list.

EXT. SHOPPING CENTRE—DAY (RACE DAY, EARLIER)

NIKKI *walks into a women's clothes shop, very tired. She holds some shopping bags in one hand and the list in the other.*

NIKKI

(*to herself*)

Please let it be this one.

INT. CLOTHES SHOP—DAY

The shop has one young skinny ASSISTANT *in it.* NIKKI *looks round the shop. The* ASSISTANT *beadily watches her. A dress fills the screen. She checks her list.*

NIKKI

Yes!

The Assistant slinks over to her and looks her up and down.

ASSISTANT

Can I help you?

NIKKI *holds up the dress.*

NIKKI

Do you do this in a twelve?

ASSISTANT

(*patronising*)

I'm afraid we don't do double figures.

EXT. SHOPPING CENTRE—DAY

NIKKI *comes out of the women's clothes shop. She sits down against a wall and thumps it.*

NIKKI

Shit!

She stares into the street. Lots of people walk past. She sees a MAN *who looks like* ANDY. NIKKI *makes to speak to him then realises her mistake.*

EXT. NIKKI'S HOUSE—DAY (PAST)

NIKKI *runs down the street with several shopping bags. We only see the path and houses (not the road). She gets to the house. The front door opens and four* MEN *carry out a coffin.* ANDY *follows with* FAMILY. *They look disapprovingly at her.*

NIKKI

It's not what it looks like.

ANDY *ignores her. He gets in a hearse.* NIKKI *goes up to him.*

Andy. I won't be a minute.

ANDY

We're through.

NIKKI

It was my worst performance so far. I thought I'd be back in time.

ANDY *ignores her and the hearse moves off.*

EXT. SHOPPING CENTRE—DAY (RACE DAY, EARLIER)

NIKKI *gets up, picks up her bags and strides off with determination.*

EXT. SHOPPING CENTRE—DAY

NIKKI *stands outside a coffee shop looking at two* WOMEN *eating cake and gossiping.* JES *appears behind her.*

JES

I miss proper shopping.

NIKKI

How far have you got?

She looks at his bags.

JES

(*smugly*)

One more, then the belt. I've seen it in the window display. I'm saving it till last.

NIKKI *tries to conceal her bags.*

NIKKI

You know that diamante has the same class as cubic zirconium don't you?

JES

Bitch.

JES *walks away.*

NIKKI

Bastard.

She walks in the opposite direction.

EXT. SHOPPING CENTRE—DAY

NIKKI *walks briskly down the street. She stops at the window display of a small shop. There is a black belt with a square diamante buckle. She stares at it for a moment. She walks on for a few yards then stops.*

EXT. SHOPPING CENTRE—DAY

NIKKI *comes out of the small shop. She walks away and puts a bag in a bin.*

EXT. SHOPPING CENTRE—DAY

JES *chirpily approaches the same belt shop. He looks at the window display and sees that the belt is no longer there. He throws down his bags in a tantrum.*

JES

No! No!

He drapes himself on the window in tears.

My future. My life. Oh Parky.

He stops crying and realisation dawns on him.

The cow! That sly, devious whore.

He smooths himself down and instead of going in the belt shop he walks into a pharmacy.

EXT. CITY CENTRE STREET—DAY

Tape is across the finishing line. The crowd cheers. NIKKI *sprints down the street. She breaks the tape screaming in delight.*

EXT. CITY CENTRE STREET—DAY (RACE DAY, PRESENT)

NIKKI *wipes away sweat from her forehead.*

TV INTERVIEWER

Thank you, Nikki, and good luck in the World Cup.

NIKKI *beams as she holds up a gold medal to the camera.*

The TV INTERVIEWER *turns to the camera but he gets barged out of the way by* TWO OFFICIALS. *They grab* NIKKI.

NIKKI

Hey!

TV INTERVIEWER

What's going on?

OFFICIAL

Switch the camera off.

NIKKI

Get off me.

She tries to wriggle away.

OFFICIAL

Switch it off I said.

The TV INTERVIEWER *faces the camera and gestures for the cameraman to keep rolling.*

TV INTERVIEWER
(*to Official*)

If we must.

We see a black screen with 'PAUSE' in the middle. We still hear the people. We also hear the movements of the cameraman.

OFFICIAL

Positive drug test.

TV INTERVIEWER

Really?

NIKKI

No! I haven't taken anything. It's ridiculous.

OFFICIAL

Come with me.

NIKKI

I won. I won.

She sobs hysterically.

The picture is restored but we look up at people's faces from ground level (the cameraman is on the floor). We see the stern face of the OFFICIAL. *The camera shot moves to the excited face of the* TV INTERVIEWER *and then to* NIKKI*'s crumpled sobbing body. The shot moves back to the* TV INTERVIEWER *then stops and moves back a little. We see a blurred image, which is then brought into focus.* JES *smiles in triumph.*

FADE OUT

LUKE WILLIAMS

Luke Williams was born in 1977. He studied history at Edinburgh University and worked for several years before coming to UEA. Questions, 1 *is the first chapter of his novel.*

QUESTIONS, 1

Who are you?
My name is Evie Steppman.
Where were you born?
Children's Hospital, Lagos.
When?
1948.
In any special circumstance?
I was late.
How late?
Two months.
Go on.
Not all children grow by the clock. I, for one, was not ready to emerge after the allotted time. Happy in the womb, unaffected by the laws of substance, I felt no hurry to budge. I possessed the foetal license—indeed, the prerogative—to moot and gambol. Trembles met with, 'Do you feel him kick, dear?' or, 'Certainly a strong one.' Hands and ears and whispering lips were pressed to my mother's stomach. 'It's like a factory in there,' joked my father, 'I can hear clattering machinery, a baby-building works.' I delighted in my formlessness. Half fish, half girl. A mermaid! I tumbled free from gravity. I luxuriated in the confusion of it all. Such licensed disorder.
[Pause.]

How did your belated arrival affect your life?
It killed my mother.
Yes.
It caused my father to lose his faith in Progress.
Yes.
It gave me the power of listening.
How so?
In the evenings, when each day's duty as District Officer for Lagos was complete, my father crouched down beside my mother and chattered to her bulging belly. He was a second son, lesser both in age and strength than his brawny brother. He received neither inheritance nor family home. And so my father fought back with the only weapon he knew: Learning. Kneeling awkwardly on the hardwood veranda floor, his hands gripping the *chaise longue* upon which my mother lay, he read me Dickens and Darwin, *Typhoon* and *Treasure Island*. In sombre tones he recited Housman and the Lord's Prayer. I learned how the elephant got his trunk, the principles of Indirect Rule. I entered with Al-Idr?s? into the distant corridors of his geography. We accompanied Mungo Park east along the Niger and with Sir Frederic Lugard sojourned at Lokaja. He lectured me on zoos and craniology. He told of masks, of goblins, turning solemnly from myth to biology to Christmas. One evening as he attended to the names of the seven seas, in between the Indian and the Aegean, I punched him on the nose. Undeterred, he opened the Bible and related the seven sins. While I turned somersaults and figures-of-eight, Father worked through the volumes that informed his rigid mind.

And perhaps it was the monotony of this daily address (accompanied by the steady *tic-toc* of Father's pocket watch, which invariably slipped from its niche to rest—an inverse stethoscope—on mother's belly), that bred in me the will to listen. He spoke in the most formal and stilted manner, as if I were a schoolboy—but I was a girl!—his voice dull and always earnest. Each history, novel, treatise, sounded to my fragile ear as if rendered from stone. In this way I found it hard to distinguish H. Rider Haggard from Aunt Phoene's letters, the Great Chain of Being from the Nocturama at Edinburgh Zoo. Be it lecture or tall tale, each was delivered in Father's reading voice.

Week after week he persisted with this schooling. I felt the discomfort of one who hears a badly told joke. Setting out to read a story, which may have been a fine one, Father invariably failed. The world he brought me via my mother's stomach was a colourless place, devoid of nuance, a world in which every legend and report, every plot and character, appeared alike.

How strange it was, then, to find in the outside world contrast, division, *difference.* Inside my mother I had had the sense that out there a giant space existed, a territory far greater than our little home allowed. Already my ears had started to pick out certain sounds from the amorphous hum of '40s Lagos. I recognised, for instance, the whisper of the sea. This was easy, for I grew in moon cycles. I perceived the sharp salute of gunfire and the chimes of Lagos Clock. These sounds I feared. Yet these scattered tones were engulfed in the coursing hum of blood, soothing to my ear, and by my father's nightly readings. It was to be much later that I perfected my art of listening.

[Pause.]

You dallied in the womb because you were afraid of the outside?
I was comfy.
Did you enjoy your father's readings?
They wearied me. He gave me lessons and I wanted stories. But I listened. With frustration I listened. And as I did, a remarkable transformation took effect. My ears began to develop in size and acuity. The more I heard, the greater and more esoteric my infant knowledge became, the bigger my ears grew. And as they grew, so too did my powers of listening. There's no chance for other senses to refine themselves in the womb, for what can you see inside a silky space chamber? The amniotic fluid—salty, viscous and vile!—is the only smell and flavour. But my eardrums just wouldn't stop expanding.

[Pause.]

Tell me about your powers of listening?
I am losing them. Slowly at first, but with increasing alacrity, the sounds that I once so clearly perceived are starting to merge into clamour. No longer can I distinguish, sort and finally order each little noise. It is true, my hearing is still uncommonly acute. With effort I can pick out certain echoes from the hustle-bustle of my childhood in

Lagos. Seated uncomfortably in my wicker swinging-basket, suspended above our immaculate lawn which sloped toward the bay, I hear the unknown calls of Jankara market women, broadcasting the succulence of their commodities in myriad vernaculars so that amidst the commonality of staple foods—palm oil, tilapia, yams, groundnuts and spices—I hear entreaties to enter card games, river cruises, witch hunts. The elephant grass at the edge of our garden obscures my view of Ade—our servant-boy—but I can hear him; he is making telephones from empty cans and lengths of string. In the distance the thud of leather striking willow tells me that Captain Macaulty has scored another 4. I hear teacups, Father playing solitaire, clocks, footsteps, the bulb-horn of a goods lorry; listening harder, I hear the sound of the driver's forehead pressed against the windscreen, vibrating in time to the engine idling. In the harbour, below the mastheads, there is the clamour of men unloading soap, pots and pans, mail, saddles, an umbrella, tea, sugar, gin, boxes of cigars, rifles, tuxedoes, steel, fireworks, brine, chocolate, camp-chairs, and an elegant high-sprung dogcart made in Manchester. I hear the cries of merchant seamen and they commingle in my mind with older, less familiar voices; those of the first English explorers and their crews, those unfortunate men who not two hundred years ago sang that most sinister of sea shanties as they neared the Niger coast:

Beware and take care of the Bight of Benin,
There's one comes out for forty goes in;

and those of the slaving ships, their silent crewmen, and the barely audible dirge of their living cargo. All these sounds I can hear, as if before me.

Yet there are disturbing lapses in my audition. I find, for instance, that I can no longer play my favourite childhood game. During the long hot hours after lunch when father was taking his afternoon nap and Ben—our cook, Ade's father—was preparing dinner, I would slip from my bedroom and into the streets of Lagos. I recall the brightness. The smell of sweating bodies, of drying fish and open sewers. Concealed between the flagpoles at the intersection of Victoria I would close my eyes. Amid the strangely intelligible street-sounds—by my eighth year I had distinguished between the pitch of the

Governor's Austin 12 Tourer and the Chief's Mercedes—I detected other noises, new to my ears; noises that disturbed and delighted; noises that appeared to a maturing girl at once violent and inspired. Back home I would play out the drama of these stolen moments with my little dolls. I had Red Ridinghood kissing Paddington Bear, my Victorian china doll groping with the nigger minstrel from America. And if now I can only describe these sounds in insipid terms it simply proves the inadequacy of my failing ears.

Still worse: I find I can no longer listen to neighbourly chit-chat; as if, in my infirmity, I am turning into the vacant, fidgety child I never was. Where once I possessed the power to listen, I now squirm, empathise and feel compelled to interject. How different it was then! I grew, developed like any child. I began to see, to touch, to smell and taste. But before it all I learnt to listen. It was this still quality, this gift for rapt attention, that made me the darling of the African imperial. Admittedly, there were questions. Subtle inquiries that inspired prolixity in my subjects. Tranquillity and soft examination; a combination irresistible to the men and women of British Africa. You see, the architects of empire were a muddled bunch: second sons, bored wives, athletes, soldiers, clergy. They each had something to prove, to boast about . . . *to confess*. 'Why did you come to Africa?'—none knew precisely, but everyone had a story—'How I got here? Well . . .', 'Those pesky clerks!', 'I love to shoot monkeys.' Unlike my father's stern address these stories were alive, they changed and evolved, they gathered elements from disparate places, over and inter-lapping.

And it was I, Evie Steppman, who heard it all. I am the—until now silent—repository of the dreamers of empire.

Why did you put up with it?

Simple: I found in these confessions the stories that were bluntly absent from my father's lessons.

[Pause. A scurrying among the rafters.]

It is these same stories that I am now forgetting.

What are you going to do?

I must write. Set down on paper. Faithfully record my past before it merges into a tinnitus and recedes from memory. But how dreary.

How dim and unnatural words are! How distanced from the live thing, the unknown generous gentlemanly thing, the cutting and distorting yet strangely exact pitch of my child's hearing, are words. There are no words that can transcribe the vibrancy of my audition.

Reluctantly I write.

[Pause. Silence. From which opens quiet sea-sounds, dully, distantly, echoes of surf purl, rockwhirl, seawrecks, tin-can music. Silence. Through which rasps a shrill whistle, a dog's bark, softcrunching boots. Silence. And now whispers of civilisations, battles, seagulfs, sirens.]

What time is it now?

Early 2001.

Where are you?

Gullane, East Scotland.

From where, exactly, are you writing?

From the house that we—Ben, my father and I—lived in from October 1960, after Nigeria's independence from British imperial rule.

Tell me about this house.

It is a two-storey detached villa on the sea front designed with Victorian furore, fuelled by cash and images of Britain abroad. I have been all but confined to the ground floor, being unable without pain to climb stairs. Though of late I have made frequent trips to the attic, which I am attempting to clear out.

What, may I ask, is there to expunge?

A machete, a Lord's lamp, intricate carved ivory, a box marked Uncommon Things. There's a silver pocket watch with a missing hour hand. A railway sleeper. A Gun and Moore cricket bat. Hanging by a single hook is a map-of-the-world, with great gaps bitten from it. Books line the west-facing wall: histories, novels, treatises, a set of Encyclopaedia Britannica, 1911. But most of all, dominating the room, are my father's men's magazines, the entire *Playboy* catalogue from October 1960 to May 1977—being the month he could no longer turn pounds into pink ladies. He quit his glossed monthly and with it his last link to the wider world. It was also at this time his mind became riddled by 'Cat'.

'Cat'?

Back in Britain, Father sank deeper and impenetrably into his past.

Spending more and more hours in the attic, listless with memories of a glorious career, he receded into the incongruous corridors of History. Time was stalking him like a shadow cat. During his great top-floor retreat (he descended only to pass water, and, latterly, not at all, pissing in a metal pail) he bewailed the scratching noise—mice?—resounding about him. Even at this moment, writing these words from my own station in the attic, I can follow the sound of tiny feet up beyond the ceiling, and across, left, right, to the oak-wood walls; yes, the scratching is all about me; the mice are in the attic, making homes among the discarded items of Father's addled mind.

The thing about the attic is that you can hear every movement, any little noise a body might make. Just as now, after dark, I report the scurry of mice, I recognise other sounds. Sounds from an impending past. Sounds echoing loud in my head, so that sometimes I'm unable to distinguish between the mice and the hubbub of my recalling. Weeks, months, decades are ringing in my ears. Births and deaths, salt water and fixed cricket matches are crying for attention. I hear cooks, whole continents and stubborn stains. There are bats too, and sparrows. Small life my attic sustains.

Though, equally, my attic bears objects inanimate. Once-life. Like the old trunk full with Mother's clothes, unused and not useful, smelling of naphthalene.

But what of Cat?

Let me tell you a story. When Sagoe was eight years old he saw a sheep hanging in a butcher's window. Hungry for the flesh, for he hadn't eaten meat in months, Sagoe told his father about the sheep.

'Go, buy me the head of the sheep,' his father commanded.

Sagoe went to the butcher and bought the head. But on the way home he ate the meat and returned with a skull.

'What have you brought me?' his father cried.

'It's a sheep's head,' Sagoe said.

'Where are the eyes?'

'The sheep was blind.'

'And where is the tongue?'

'The sheep was dumb.'

'And where are the ears?'

'The sheep was deaf.'

'Cat,' cried his father. But Sagoe had already run to the forest, leaving scorch marks on the dirt road.

. . . But I tell too much.

Go on.

[Pause.]

Tell me more.

[Silence.]

You can't stop there.

[Pause. Silence. A cat's cry. A scratching of sharp clawing paws. A winged insect, possibly a crane-fly, or a moth, thunders against the skylight. Silence.]

Picture this: A woman, not young, sits at her makeshift desk; ponderously, with shaky hands—for it's cold—she searches the room; her eyes rest first on the keys of her computer, then rise to the skylight, taking in the darkening sky; she hears the noise of the traffic; slowly, eschewing the city-sounds below, she turns from the skylight, rubbing her palms together for warmth, and begins—where to begin?—to recount her life—which is really the lives of her and Ben and her father, the impossibility of a mother who died in childbirth and the lives of countless others—and what to tell?—what is true, what was once true, what has been, might be, is?—and how to go about it? She asks herself a question—*Who are you?*—and another—*Where were you born?*—because this is what she knows best—at the outset, in the middle, she always asked questions; and here come the words, bit-by-bit; bit-by-bit the words form upon the page . . . .

Anna Ziegler

Anna Ziegler grew up in Brooklyn, New York. In 2001, she received her BA in English from Yale University. Her poems have appeared in The Threepenny Review, The Saint Ann's Review, The Southeast Review *and* Poetry Ealing.

After the Opening, 1932

Why hadn't he thought of it before?
He turns to Jo, to the waiter handing out
buttered rolls, glasses of wine, caviar:
everyone must go! He realizes chairs
should remain in disarray, windows open,
gleaming ends of rump roast steaks and salmon
pâtés cooling in neglected browns and pinks.

At the Whitney, earlier, he was approached
by a small man with a quivering grin.
If you don't mind my saying so, he began,
but Hopper did, and turned to admire
his lost faces, lights flirting with darks,
the tip of a steeple just brushing the sky.
You've really got it, you know—
what it's like when no one's around.
Hopper took an inward bow, then noticed
the white tied bow in the *New York Restaurant*,
quiet blue back and perched beige vase towering
over a *Room in Brooklyn*, where light
and afternoon would have done.

It will not do! He can scarcely eat;
Jo chats with the Rockefellers,
the Pierpont Morgans, Guggenheims,
while Hopper's lost in an empty room.
From now on, he vows, all will be absence—
shadows the dreams of long gone men,
roads into the distance only roads, eyes
only eyes, with nothing behind them.

GAME OF CATCH

1.

You ask how much remembering
has to do with the acting
as opposed to the writing,
whether the set plays a part,
or the director. We are standing
out front waiting for a cab
and I remember your leg bouncing
during the play, the way your hand
fell into mine when we weren't sure
what could happen next.
While we wait, two actors
in long coats emerge and stand
with us, quiet in a way
we've never seen them before.

2.

I'm reminded of a photograph
you took before we were
married, in which I stand alone
in front of a ruined church
in the Welsh countryside.
To look at it, you'd scarcely know

I was twenty-two and about
to propose, that for months
I'd known what I'd say:
'It's been a long time,
and I love you, and . . .'
or that our rented Fiat was burning
in the sun behind where you stood,
that soon the seats would be too hot
to sit on and we'd park the car
beneath a tree and wait to move on,
an hour or so in which the birds sang,
your leg quivered, the countryside
grew hotter, and I said nothing
I'd intended.

3.

It's curious, you remark now,
how they're able to repeat
the same things every night.
Don't they get tired of it?
The two on the curb
certainly seem tired; one slumps
on the other's shoulder, eyes closed.
The real question, I say,
is how they remember to turn up at all;
God knows they have other things
on their minds. Then a cab comes
and whisks us home, where,
as on most nights, we get in bed,
drink a half-glass of wine,
pick up a book and talk a bit
before falling to sleep.

*

When I was a child, I knew quickly
how to throw a ball, then learned
other things gradually: my mother's

birthday, what to say when asked to
clear the table, how to treat my sister
when she was sulky and emerged
from her room only to eat.
But to this day, I remember best
evenings of tossing a ball back
and forth with my father, the power
and the comfort when I was twelve,
or maybe thirteen. Always autumn
and my father just home from work.
I could do no wrong, the energy in my arm
there long before I was born, the trees
settling into darkness around us
and my father in his lace-up shoes
yelling, *'that-a-boy, that-a-boy'*
across the yard.

The Whole of America

And another thing is how beautiful the morning was,
how the bricks of each house on my block were redder
than ever, trees filled with frost even in April; how my mother
stood at the door as though I were twelve again and off to camp,
duffle-bags sent ahead to choose my bed for the next two months,
the angle from which the crickets would sing at me
and I'd sense morning starting through the veil of the screens.
And how, once I arrived, I would never get quite right
the redness of the bricks, or the hazy feeling in my head,
the look on my mother's face as I walked down the steps,
whether she was nervous about something more than travel.
Or the weight of the bags on my back and in the trunk
like the load in my arms every other Sunday now when I drag
my basket of laundry through the morning and sit
for a couple of hours drinking coffee and reading the paper,
scanning each page for something about New York,
or Brooklyn, or really the whole of America as though
it were me and I were it, each scandal a breach of trust,
a photo of Iowa cows treated for disease a dream of home
even though Iowa looks nothing like Brooklyn or even Maine
where I went to camp those five summers, where I learned
about make-up from New Jersey girls who knew everything,
read books by flashlight under the covers: *Wuthering Heights*,
The Thornbirds, my mother's recommendations, and scarcely
wrote home.
I remember it all: the smell of pine in the showers, the bats
(two who landed one night in Dana Flechner's hair and wouldn't
leave),
my birthday in the middle of July and what it was to be thirteen,
suddenly,
and not at home; the lake in the early morning full of snakes and fish
and god-knows-what, biting eels and biting flies and those bugs that
swim
at you on the surface of the water, how they made us jump in
against our will,
and how it hurt.

Song For My Wife

My wife sings in a chamber music ensemble,
twice-weekly therapy that consists of two basses,
Bob J. and George, who, it's rumored,
go home together on Wednesdays; of Patrick
and Bob H., the tenors, though Patrick insists
he can sing much lower; of my wife and Ann,
the clear-voiced altos, one very beautiful;
of Lisa and Julie, sopranos, overweight
and warm, each with her own burgeoning clan
and bearded husband. The piano player is Yolanda,
sad divorcée, and the page-turner her only child, Kim,
also sad, also the product of divorce.

Tonight, they are performing at the very reputable
Bargemusic, where the floors rock and one or two
first timers inevitably fail to leave quietly,
just in the middle of my wife's solo. Tonight
they are performing an obscure Buxtehude cantata
for four voices; Ann and Lisa and the two Bobs
sit proudly in the front row, ballplayers happy
to be benched. Yolanda's hands settle on the keys,
graceful and arched like our cat Oliver on the sill
when he believes he's seen or dreamed something
scuttle across the floor. My wife is poised by the piano
and they are about to begin. The barge moves
beneath us; programs swim in our hands.
I am not a particularly creative soul. I see a therapist
for therapy; I work late and sleep late and for purposes
of relaxation attempt to finish the *Times* crossword
in fewer than fifteen minutes, a feat performed
successfully only twice. Once was before I met my wife
on a street corner, where she stood, rather swayed, above
a tattered *Mets* cap, nearly empty, playing the violin
with her eyes closed. I was entranced, not so much
by the music, but because her eyes were closed, because
why in the name of God would you do something

for money and then fail to keep an eye on your earnings?
The hypocrisy wouldn't release me. We were married
half a year later in a small ceremony in which my wife
sung her vows.

Yolanda has begun to play. My wife is singing.
She has a mind of her own but sometimes I wonder
what she would do without me. She hits a high note
and the audience holds back breath—will she do it,
can she hold it? She does. We are relieved, consumed,
grateful, for this simple metaphor, this song
in which one might not succeed. At home, I iron
her clothes; I pay the bills. It's not a job, I tell her—
it's a hobby. But you can't compare crosswords with
Buxtehude, she pleads. She says maybe you don't *want*
to understand. I wonder, when we start a family,
what the kids will make of it, their mother who escapes
to the chords of Bob and George and Patrick and Bob,
for whom pain is a sore throat, her husband a spectator,
and life is fullest with eyes closed.

AMAGANSETT SUMMER

In August 1977, on a rainy morning,
the beach parking lot is empty and my parents
are at the general store buying brown sugar
for oatmeal, two years before they're parents,
before the rain stops and they move to a city
to start their lives. While my father pays,
my mother watches, remembering how the room
looked when they left, white on white and untidy,
full of morning shadow and the dappled
reflections rain makes when it's early in the day,
when anything can happen and the light seems
to whisper: *get up, go now, before it's too late,*
to anyone, to my parents, to the empty room.

paper scissors stone

The Paper Scissors Stone team are:

Guy Essex
Sue Fletcher
Bettina Haydon
Andy Knight
James Manlow
Sarah Miano
Dave Paul